LIONS OF THE REACH

RAGE OF LIONS BOOK THREE

MATT BARRON

BLADE OF TRUTH PUBLISHING COMPANY

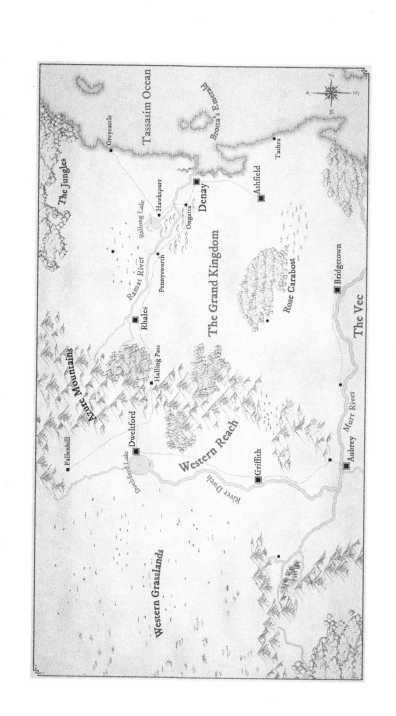

CHAPTER 1

"How can it be haunted? We just built it."

"Not the damned hut, the whole bloody thing."

The two convicts laboring to clear the rubble around their newly built hut paused and looked about them. In every direction was the wall, three times the height of a man and built of thick stone, with battlements on top. Once it had encircled a town, a thriving mining settlement where silver ore and iron ore were brought and smelted before being sent south to Dweltford, the capital of the Western Reach.

This was Fallenhill.

Once a town, now it was a ruin. During the summer, invaders had come out of the west and sacked it. Capturing the settlement with lightning swiftness, they had chained the entire populace together in the town square. Then, they had made a mound out of every piece of precious metal they could find—gold, silver, and copper. The town's leader, Baron Stopher, was chained to a cross on top of the mound, trapped in his ornate, ceremonial armor. When all that was done, the invaders set the town ablaze, letting it burn to the ground. All this they did as a message of terror. The invaders had not come to steal or to conquer, only to destroy. They would take no prisoners and no plunder.

Now, the terrifying army from the west was defeated and a new population had moved into the pitiful ruin, slowly cleaning away the rubble and the bodies to make a new settlement. Convicts—over two and a half thousand—were led by a mixed cadre of nearly a hundred mercenaries and freed men. Their purpose was to turn Fallenhill into their training camp. The convicts were to become soldiers, trading military service for their freedom. That was what their leader Prentice Ash had promised his liege lady, the Duchess Amelia. He would take the broken wreckage of the Grand Kingdom's least men and turn them into a loyal, professional force that could defend her lands. No one knew where the invading army had come from except that it was somewhere beyond the grasslands of the frontier. And if one army had come, another could be waiting for its chance, or was already on its way. The duchess and the Western Reach were depending on Prentice to build a defense against that possibility.

For now, it was hard enough just to get huts built.

Convicts and masters had been at Fallenhill a week, and with the last tatters of autumn being swept aside by the coming winter rains, the entire company needed the long huts completed as quickly as possible. If they didn't have shelter soon, hundreds would sicken in the cold and damp, and many would die. Looking over the work on the second of four huts—each one nearly fifty paces long and built from stones dug out of the rubble, with roofs of salvaged wood and cut sod—Prentice came upon the two convicts arguing about whether or not the ruins in which they were building their new home were haunted.

"The only ghosts here are of Kingdom folk," he said without announcing himself. The two men jumped with surprise. "When they realize we've come to protect their land, they'll sleep easy enough."

The two men didn't seem convinced but nodded and tugged their forelocks, the sign of respect every convict owed to free men. It felt odd to Prentice to be on the receiving end. Less than a year ago, he had been a convict as well. After nearly a decade on a chain gang, he had won his freedom at last, and he wanted to offer the same chance to every convict in his charge.

"It makes you uncomfortable," said Sir Gant, coming up on Prentice's left side as the two convicts shuffled off to find other work to do.

"What?"

"Accepting their deference."

"I suppose so."

Sir Gant was Prentice's second in command, a free knight who had sworn his service to the duchess. Prentice had saved his life in battle and Sir Gant felt he had a duty of honor to the ex-convict who now commanded an army of convicts. Standing next to one another, the two men were easy to pick apart. Sir Gant was lean and slender, with red hair that was starting to grey at the temples. He had greenish hazel eyes and a hawk-like face with a beak nose. He wore a threadbare tabard, faded to an indistinct grey, over an arming doublet that had never been dyed. Prentice, on the other hand, was broad-shouldered and muscular. Since coming off the chain, he had regained much of the strength and vitality that the hardship of convict life stripped from a man. His hair was fair but darkening with age, and he had piercing blue-grey eyes. His face was hard-lined, with a determined set of the jaw and brow. He was wearing a quilted gambeson for warmth and protection, dyed a muddy brown, over simple trews and a shirt. Fine leather boots on his feet were the treasure he had promised himself after years as a convict; he was done enduring hard ground and bitter weather while barefoot and shackled.

"We need to start getting their shackles off," he said to Sir Gant as they walked the length of the hut, inspecting the work.

"You think they're ready for that?" A knight by birth, Sir Gant had the Kingdom nobles' typical attitude to convicts—they were untrustworthy to a man. He had serious doubts that Prentice's plan could even succeed, and he did little to hide that opinion.

"It has to be done at some point," Prentice said, explained his thinking. "Rogues have shackles, not my militia."

"What's to stop them just running off?"

Prentice shrugged. "Eventually? Hope."

Sir Gant looked even more skeptical.

"Every convict has the possibility that he will serve his time and go free, his sins purged," Prentice explained. "Half the settlers of the Reach have at least one convict in their family line somewhere. We keep that hope before them, and they'll have good reason to follow instructions and learn war as their trade."

"Eventually, you say. What about in the meantime?"

Prentice looked around him at the high walls. "One main gate, high walls, and nothing but empty frontier in every direction. It's as good a prison as any other."

Prentice could see his friend was just not persuaded, but there was no more value in trying to push the point. Either he could turn them into an army, or he couldn't. The proof would come in time. Sir Gant flicked at his long moustache and looked at the gateway where a gang of convicts was clearing away the broken remnants of the old gate, ready to build a new one.

"Best to keep mercenaries on the gate, I think," said Gant, and Prentice agreed.

"Free men only, for now. Taking off their shackles is one thing but trusting them to guard themselves might be a bit much to start with."

They shared a smirk. While they watched, someone emerged from the small crowd around the gate, heading straight toward them—a slight figure with a shock of strawberry blonde hair, dressed in striped trousers and a woman's bodice over a linen blouse. She marched right up to them.

"Greetings, Mistress Cutter," said Sir Gant.

The young woman paused and scowled at him.

"I don't answer to that name no more. You know that."

Convicted and transported for killing a man in a brawl, the woman had a brand under her eye that would forever mark her crime. Once, she'd been called Cutter Sal, but had taken to posing as a young man, using the name Cutter. For her loyal service, Prentice had given her a new name—Righteous. She had taken to it immediately, and woe betide any man who dared to call her Cutter still.

"My apologies," Sir Gant said with amused earnestness. "I was forgetful. I will work to remember in future."

"See that you do!"

"Did you want something, Righteous?" Prentice asked. She looked at him and the scowl fell away. Ever since he had given her the name, Prentice felt that there was a growing appreciation between them, perhaps even respect, or at least as much respect as the quarrelsome young woman knew how to give when she wasn't daring the world to knock the chip off her shoulder. Strangely, Prentice found he enjoyed her belligerent attitude, at least when it wasn't making trouble for him. She had...spirit; it was something he wanted in all his soldiers, if he could just harness it.

He nodded for Righteous to speak her message.

"Riders coming back in," she reported. "Looks like they've got a whole farmstead with them."

"We'd best go see."

Prentice had a dozen riders at his command, assigned by the duchess; he used them as rovers—part scouts and messengers, part hunters and frontiersmen. He'd also had to use them once to hunt down a clutch of escaped convicts who'd slipped their chain during the march. He had hated to do it, but there was nothing else for it.

Passing through the gate and its gang of convicts tearing down the broken beams, he emerged onto the road and meadows of the dale beyond. Not half a league away, horsemen were driving a large herd of shaggy cattle and, behind that, a flock of sheep that were in sore need of shearing. Prentice smiled and walked on down the slope, followed by Sir Gant and

Righteous. As the leader of the riders drew near, Prentice hailed him.

"Ho, Aiden, good hunting?"

Aiden was a lanky, sun-browned man who wore leather trousers and a homespun tunic. The unofficial leader of the rovers, he returned Prentice's greeting with a wave. "It was just as you said it would be. Abandoned farms and gentle livestock just scattered about. Wolves and the like have taken their share, but there's hundreds of head of cattle in the foothills just waiting for someone to round them up."

This was what Prentice had hoped. The invaders had driven the settlers out of the frontier, killing and rampaging, but they had not had time to loot all the livestock from the farmsteads. Eventually the settlers would return, particularly if they could secure the frontier against future invasions. In the meantime, there were animals running loose, and he had thousands of hungry men and women to feed.

"What about the sheep?"

"Easier to herd but in much worse condition."

"How so?"

"Most were in pens and paddocks. They ate the ground clean around them. Lots are starving, and they need shearing or else they'll risk getting flyblown come spring. They've gone a whole summer unshorn; we're lucky more aren't dead."

Prentice knew next to nothing about sheep herding, so he accepted Aiden's assessment with a nod. Odds were good there'd be more than a few shepherds among his convicts—or sheep thieves, at least.

"We also picked up a visitor," said Aiden, pointing back over the animals at a covered wagon that was rattling up the slope, pulled by a pair of lumbering bullocks. The two mighty creatures huffed and snuffled as they labored along. Prentice tried to make out the figure sitting on the driver's board.

"A sacrist," Aiden explained. "Church man and healer, he says. Says he knows you."

"Fostermae," Prentice said, recognizing the clergyman at last.

"He's good value," said Righteous, smiling.

Fostermae had treated Prentice's wounds after two savage combats in Dweltford only weeks ago. He was an earnest and devout man, bone thin with a rough-shaved tonsure, dressed in a simple robe and sandals. Prentice, Sir Gant, and Righteous greeted him as he drove his wagon up the road.

"I come bearing charity," the sacrist announced. "Cloth from merchants of the conclave. Though by the look of the flock you're gathering, you'll be making your own once you get them shorn."

"Not without weavers and looms, we won't," said Sir Gant.

"No home-spinners among your fallen charges?"

"Your charity is welcome," Prentice said, ignoring Fostermae's question. There was a good chance there were many convicts who knew how to spin and weave. About one in eight of the convicts were women, and spinning and weaving were a goodwife's skills. But that took time, and the poorly dressed convicts needed cloth now. "What word from Dweltford?"

Dweltford was Duchess Amelia's capital, but she wasn't there at the moment. She was on the march with the army of Prince Daven Marcus, crown prince of the Grand Kingdom. Baron Liam, her treacherous castellan, ruled the town in her absence. Liam hated Prentice and had even attacked the duchess herself, but he had the prince's favor and so retained his position. Baron Liam was a continuous worry in the back of Prentice's mind. The lesser nobleman had his own force of knights and a grudge to bear.

"The baron has not been seen in many days," said Fostermae, knowing immediately what news Prentice was seeking. "He keeps to his bed, I'm told. Nonetheless, he sends men about the town, looking for you. Every inn and rooming house have had a visit from his sworn blades. He's even sending men into the sewers, thinking you might have a secret hiding hole down there."

"Poor beggars," said Sir Gant.

Righteous was less sympathetic. "Work for filth, get filthy work," she said.

Sir Gant frowned but did not disagree with the sentiment.

"We've all done our time down there," said Prentice. At the end of the summer, he'd led a force through Dweltford's sewers to retake the town from a rebel. Sir Gant and Righteous had both been with him that night. "Seems the baron's occupied for now, but we need to be watchful. He won't forget about us. For now, though, we need to get those animals inside the walls."

He looked up the road to see the rovers herding first the cattle and then the sheep through the gate.

"At least we'll eat well for a while," said Righteous.

"Do you think we've got any butchers amongst us?" asked Prentice.

"More than a few, I'd wager," said Sir Gant. "Though maybe not the kind you want."

"Sure, there'll be a load who can wield a sharp knife," Righteous agreed.

"Yourself included, of course?"

Righteous poked out her tongue and Prentice laughed. Righteous was a well-trained and experienced knife-wielder, a former pit fighter. Her savagery with a short blade was well renowned amongst all Prentice's free forces.

"How long will you stay?" Prentice asked the sacrist, walking beside the wagon as it creaked its way inside the walls. Fostermae rubbed his hand over his head, thinking for a moment.

"If you'll let me, I'd like to see to your convicts. I'm not much of a healer, but I'm sure many will have hurts and injuries that could stand being looked to, even at my level of skill."

"A healer for convicts?" mused Prentice. "Whoever heard of such a thing?"

"Not me, that's for sure," chimed Righteous.

Fostermae shook his head, sadly. "It's not right," he said. "We put men on the chain, and women, too, to scourge their flesh and purge their souls. But we give them no succor, no prayer nor instruction. How can their souls be saved if Mother Church only ever turns its back upon them?"

Sir Gant made a surprised noise, and Prentice raised his eyebrows. Fostermae shrugged at their response.

"That's just how I see it," he said apologetically.

"You're a good man, Rector," said Prentice. "And you're free to minister and preach as long as you wish."

He and Fostermae shared a nod of agreement, and then the wagon was negotiating the gateway. Prentice held back to avoid getting caught in the narrow gap. He was glad to see the sacrist, and not just for the cloth he brought, which was sorely needed. Fostermae was correct; many of the convicts, if not most, were in need of a healer's help, even if just to treat their minor ailments. Prentice hoped Fostermae would be with him for a long while.

CHAPTER 2

Duchess Amelia awoke to the smell of campbread baking in a pot on the fire and the gentle sounds of her handmaid Kirsten getting dressed early, ready to serve her mistress. The duchess rolled over and sighed quietly. The tent around her was cold and she was glad of her bed, with blankets and comforter. She was not looking forward to getting out of it. Nonetheless, she pulled back the covers and stretched, yawning and shivering.

"Your Grace," said Kirsten, bobbing a curtsey, "I'm sorry. I hope I didn't disturb you."

"Not at all," said Amelia. "The smell of breakfast cooking roused me."

"Oh, I don't think it's ready yet. I can look."

"No rush; I'll dress before I break my fast. It will be good to be ready early for the day. Perhaps today the prince will call the march."

"Very good, Your Grace."

Kirsten bobbed again and moved quickly to ready Amelia's dress and shoes. The duchess smiled at the girl's earnestness. Kirsten was a young woman, given to fantasies of romance and courtly love, but she was diligent in her service, and her manners were impeccable.

"How old are you, Kirsten?" Amelia asked.

"I'll be seventeen before winter's out, Your Grace."

"Seventeen? It's coming time we found you a husband, don't you think?"

Kirsten looked up from the chest she was hovering over and beamed.

"Oh yes, please."

"Do you have someone in mind?" Amelia asked, cocking an eyebrow. Kirsten shook her head gently.

"Not really. There are many fine men here in the camp, noble and well placed."

"And none of them takes your eye?"

Kirsten looked down again. She had a shamefaced expression for a moment.

"Is something wrong?" Amelia asked.

Kirsten shook her head.

"No, Your Grace, I just...I do not wish to seem too forward or willful..."

Amelia was puzzled by her reticence. What was troubling the girl? "But...?"

"But the prince has come west with his entire court, it seems. So many fine gentlemen and ladies, and it's only been such a short time since we marched. I barely know even the names of most. I know there are many fine and noble young men in the Reach, men suited to my rank, but...well you married well, Your Grace and I...and the ladies of Rhales are all so finely dressed and courtly..." The rush of her words trailed off and she bowed her head again.

"I think I understand," said the duchess. "Why waste your arrows on rabbits when there are fine stags in the forest to hunt? You don't want to reach beyond your station but neither do you want to shorten your reach."

Kirsten's eyes went wide, scandalized by her mistress's blunt talk, but she nodded readily. Amelia understood the girl's hope and dilemma. She wanted to marry well but didn't want to be seen as having notions above her station. The duchess imagined it was a problem that confronted many a young woman of the court. Amelia herself was the great exemplar of marrying well. She was the daughter of a successful wine merchant, and her father's wealth had made the perfect dowry to attract the bankrupt Duke Marne, lord of the Western Reach. In spite of the calculation of their match, Amelia had grown to love her husband dearly in the short time they had together, and when he was poisoned, it had broken her heart. Now she was a young widow, scrambling to establish her rule over her husband's lands before ambitious men took them from her.

"There are, no doubt, many fine gentles in the court of Rhales," she said with a smile. "We shall see which of them is amenable to a fine and noble young Reacherwoman for his wife. Surely we can find a number in this wide camp."

Kirsten beamed and brought Amelia her slippers so the duchess could begin to dress for the day. Soon enough she had her gown on—a simple linen dress with black stitching on the bodice that befitted a widow mourning her dead husband. Her long, straw-colored hair was plaited and tucked under a silver coif with a black lace veil. Looking at herself in a glass, Amelia was pleased with her appearance. She did not believe she was ugly, but she knew she was no great beauty. She had no illusions on that score; it had been her family's wealth that had won her a high-born husband. Nonetheless, he had loved her. She knew that beyond doubt, just as she had loved him. Looking at Kirsten's fresh face and gentle manners, Amelia had no doubt she could secure her maid a fine match as well, even without a great dowry.

When she was dressed and made up, Amelia decided she wouldn't wait for her breakfast and stepped out of the tent to see what the morning held for her. A short distance away, stewards of her household sat around a large campfire. The warmth of it flowed over her as she approached, along with the smell of the campbread cooking in its pot, hanging from a spit. As Amelia approached, one of the stewards noticed her and they all stood, tugging their forelocks respectfully. The duchess knew each man, but one of them—a tall bull of a man with a mop of black curls on his head—was especially dear to her. He was Turley, an ex-convict like his good friend Prentice Ash. In the summer, Prentice and Turley had rescued the duchess from a force of invaders, and she had rewarded them with pardons for their efforts. Prentice, she had made an advisor, and Turley had become head of her household staff. He was not the thoughtful man that Prentice was, but he was shrewd and loyal, and his roguish good humor cheered her.

"Butter beer and fresh bread to break your fast, Your Grace?" Turley said, waving at one of the other stewards to serve the dish. A small silver tankard was filled from a pot sat warming by the fire, and a piece of the fresh-baked campbread was offered on a silver plate. Amelia took them both.

"A serve for Kirsten, too, Chief Steward," she said, and Turley saw to the handmaid's repast as well. Amelia broke pieces of the rough campbread and dipped them in her tankard. "What word for the morning, Turley?"

"Plenty of rumors, Your Grace, but little that I would trouble you with."

Turley was a font of information about the camp and the court. Servants gossiped, and it appeared that he had an ear in every conversation. Whatever happened, he seemed to know it was coming. He was a very handy man to have in her service.

"Will we march today?"

"It could be, but the prince has given no orders."

"He still dallies with the lodge?"

"So it seems."

Amelia looked to the northwest where she could just make out the wooden rooftop of a nobleman's hunting lodge over the tops of tents and pavilions. It was the only permanent building for leagues in any direction. The prince had marched west on the promise that the lodge hid a king's ransom in silver, looted from the Reach's own mint. Since arriving, the prince had spent almost every waking moment in the simple wooden construction, accompanied only by his closest entourage. Turley's sources claimed some silver had been found but nothing like the promised fortune. Now, the prince had men with picks and axes tearing the building apart from within, searching for secret hiding places.

Looking back from the lodge roof, Amelia cast her eyes over the camp. There were tents and shelters for nobles, brightly colored, with gilt fittings and pennants flying above. A chill morning breeze whipped amongst them, causing guy lines to hum, and the grey sky above seemed to drain them of their colors. The prince himself dwelt in a vast pavilion of royal wine-red silk with over a dozen "rooms" that took almost a day to fully erect or break down, and Amelia wondered how that was supposed to work on the march west. Even as she looked in that direction, a herald approached, wearing a doublet and hose in royal colors. He strode confidently and looked about ready to announce himself to her when Turley suddenly interposed himself.

"Going somewhere?" he asked the herald. The man pulled up short and looked up at Turley's towering form. He sniffed with disdain.

"Out of my way, servant," he said. "I would have words with your mistress." The man spoke with a Rhales accent, and odds were he had some measure of birth, probably a knight by blood.

Turley showed that he didn't care by putting his hand on the man's chest to hold him in place. "Wait here," he said. "I'll see if her grace is receiving visitors."

"I come with a message from the prince!" The herald looked past Turley to Amelia, standing not two paces behind her steward. She avoided making eye contact.

"I will inform her," Turley assured the man. Then, he turned on his heel and took one step to stand directly in front of the duchess, tugging his forelock with exaggerated politeness. "Your Grace, there is a messenger here from the prince. He begs leave to present himself and his message. Do wish to receive him?"

It was all Amelia could do to keep a straight face, but she managed to nod her assent. Turley whirled about and took a step back to the flabbergasted man.

"Her Grace will receive you," he said and stepped aside, giving the man the courtesy of a tug of the forelock. The herald stepped up, and it was clear from his expression he was annoyed at having been ordered about by a mere servant, but Turley's flawless manners would make him seem churlish if he complained.

"Your Grace," he said sourly and executed a perfect bow, "the prince would speak with you." He did not add the word urgently; there was no need. Any summons from the crown prince of the Grand Kingdom was urgent.

"I shall come directly."

The messenger bowed again and left. Amelia watched him go, and when he was out of earshot, turned to Turley.

"You ought not tweak his nose, so," she chided. "He is herald to the prince."

"And you are Duchess of the Reach, Your Grace," Turley answered. "These Rhales types walk around with their noses in the air. It's disrespectful."

"They are your betters, steward."

"Aye, Your Grace, but they are not yours."

Now Amelia did smile. He was offended on her behalf and defending her dignity. She nodded to him and bade him fetch Kirsten from their tent. Then, with her maid in tow, she made her way as quickly as dignity allowed to wait upon the crown prince, Daven Marcus.

CHAPTER 3

At the prince's tent, the duchess was informed that Daven Marcus was not present but was still in the lodge where he had been through the entire night. Amelia wondered if he'd even slept in his vast pavilion one full night since they arrived.

Upon being informed, she led Kirsten on to the lodge, and when they arrived, she was shocked by the condition of the building. Originally constructed from cut logs on a stone foundation, with wooden roof shingles, glass windows, and a long verandah down one side, it had seemed a sturdy edifice that could easily have lasted a century or more. Now, one wall was smashed apart, and the roof sagged inward. Windows were broken, and boards and shingles had been ripped up in the destruction of the prince's treasure hunting.

As she approached, Amelia found the prince and his closest courtiers standing a short distance apart from the damaged building. Although they all wore fine clothes, warm quilted doublets, and tabards in the bright array of colors that bespoke their noble houses, they were disheveled and obviously deeply weary. Many had dust or splinters in their hair. The duchess wondered if they had been up all night, watching or even participating in the destruction of this one building.

The prince alone looked energetic, though there was a hollowness to his features and dark circles around his eyes. He stood straight and noble in an arming doublet and trews of white linen, edged in red and gold. There were smears of dirt on the fabric, signs that he had been an active participant in the night's demolitions. There was only one woman with the group, and she hung attentively upon the prince's arm. Amelia knew very few of the prince's court personally, but this woman she could name—the Countess Dalflitch. Married to a count from a province in the northeast, she was thirty and childless, neither of which was as great a scandal as the fact that she was very publicly Daven Marcus's mistress. Amelia sometimes wondered if it was her marital status or her age that most scandalized the court. The prince was barely twenty-two; dalliances weren't uncommon for noblemen and royals, but an older woman was.

In spite of the woman's age, Amelia could not deny her obvious grace and beauty. The countess might barely yet be a young woman, but she was unmistakably the most beautiful woman of the court, with fine features, dark eyes, and porcelain skin. Her hair was a deep sable black and was never covered by a full hood or coif. She was wearing a warm dress of rich velvet green that was nonetheless cut to emphasize her cleavage. There was a golden chain hung with rubies at her throat. As the duchess approached, the countess laughed at something the prince said—a deep, earthy chuckle that put Amelia immediately on edge.

"You sent for me, Highness," she said, curtseying.

Daven Marcus looked down his nose at her. "I told you she was a dowdy little thing," he said to the countess on his arm, and Dalflitch smiled. Amelia kept her eyes down and her expression carefully neutral. She had long ago become accustomed to the prince's petty provocations. There was a long moment of silence, and Amelia imagined the prince was leaving her that silence in hopes she would humiliate herself by protesting his mistreatment. She wouldn't fall for that.

"I am growing sick of your failings, Duchess," he said at last.

Amelia wanted to tell him he could leave her alone, and then he wouldn't have to suffer any of her supposed failings. Instead, she schooled her face into an apologetic frown.

"I am so sorry to hear that, Your Highness. If you would tell me what offends you, I can correct myself."

"Where's my silver?"

"Highness?" That question surprised her.

"The silver that I was told was here, Duchess! There's barely a piece in ten of what I was promised."

Amelia looked at the broken-down lodge for a moment.

"Perhaps they exaggerated," she said. The prince had pardoned a cabal of merchants who had conspired to embezzle the duchy's taxes on the promise that they would tell him where it was all secreted away. That was what the lodge was supposed to be. It seemed that the merchants had not been truthful. "They were liars and thieves, Highness. I would not trust their word at face value."

"They were merchants," Daven Marcus snapped back, "which is of the same type as liars and thieves, I suppose. And you are a mere merchant's get, Duchess Piglet."

The courtiers around him tittered and chuckled every time the prince called her a pig. It was such a dull insult that Amelia wondered at their response. Even for sycophants, they had to be working hard to sound so appreciative of such lame attempts at wit.

"Regardless of their truth or lies," the prince went on, "the warrant to mint the king's coin was given to your dead husband, inept fool that he was. He allowed those swine to get their snouts into my father's taxes like it was their private wallow. The duke had one duty—to enforce the kingdom's law—and he failed. And now that failure is yours."

Amelia wanted to slap his smug face for calling her husband a fool. It took all her will to control her tongue as she drew her hands back within the winged sleeves of her dress so that he didn't see her clenching her fists in fury. She swallowed.

"If you will provide a full account, Highness, I will see that the taxes are paid to the last copper shaving. The king's taxes will be paid; the Reach does its duty."

Now Amelia straightened her back and looked directly at the prince. She knew that the prince had no idea how much money had actually been embezzled, and in fact, had no claim on the silver, even if he could specify the amount. The tax belonged to his father, the king. He was claiming it supposedly on his father's behalf but would spend it on himself and maintaining his army. By asking for an exact accounting, Amelia was reminding Daven Marcus that even though he clothed himself in the righteousness of King's Law, he was every bit as much an embezzler as the merchants who'd sent him to this lodge, and everyone knew it.

The prince sniffed theatrically.

"I'm sure you'd like nothing better than to have me pore over account books like a petty clerk, but I was not born in a pigsty like you were," he said at last.

He seemed ready to say more when there came the sound of heavy wooden wheels creaking and reigns snapping. The prince turned to look, and all eyes followed his to the vast wagon being slowly maneuvered around tents. The thing had enormous, iron-rimmed wheels that were broad across the rim so that they didn't sink into the ground, but it made the wagon so much more difficult to guide or turn. Atop the wagon was a siege gun—a vast bronze tube, carved like a dragon and open at one end. Fashioned in the shape of a mouth, the weapon's muzzle was as broad across as a man's chest. Two soldiers sat on the cannon, and another stood at the wagon's yoke, cracking a whip to drive a six-horse team, while another four men on the ground helped to guide the draft animals and keep the wheels away from obstacles like rocks and such. Every man of the crew was dressed in a tabard of royal red, with a rampant dragon on the chest, the livery of the Royal Dragon cannoneers.

"You see my displeasure now, I assume, Duchess?" the prince said.

Watching the heavy engine of destruction being wheeled toward them, Amelia had no idea what was displeasing the prince. "I am at a loss, Highness," she said quietly.

"No doubt. But consider this: my Dragon crews are proud men, and their task is difficult enough without being forced to scrabble in the mud to push their weapons into place by themselves. That is work for laborers, for convicted men."

With a flash, Amelia knew what the prince was talking about. He wanted to know where the convicts were—the two-and-a-half-thousand condemned souls he had marched through the mountains, the convicts she had entrusted to Prentice Ash to train into an army for her. The prince no doubt expected to use the convicts in his crusade, but traditionally, convict laborers in the Reach were the duke's responsibility, and they were leased out to landowners and village councils to use building up the Reach. They were a cheap labor force for the duration of their conviction.

"Are there no convicts to do the duty?" Amelia said, feigning ignorance.

In a moment of rage, Daven Marcus detached himself from the countess on his arm and surged at the duchess, seizing her by the chin and forcing her to look at the cannon and its crew.

"Do you see any convicts?" he shouted in her face. "Are there any here?"

"No, Highness," she gasped, swallowing in fear. Behind her, Kirsten let out a little gasp of shock.

"There are none! That's why you can't see them. Not a single, damnable one on my march. Why is that?"

Amelia wanted to say that it was hardly her fault if it took him weeks to notice that he'd lost two-and-a-half-thousand bodies from his little traveling court, but she kept her tongue on a better leash.

"I ordered that my army was to cross that lake and march west," he went on. "Now I hear that none of the convicts crossed. And my heralds inform me that it was at your order! Confess your rebellion!"

The prince's grip was painful on her jaw and made it hard to speak. Amelia wanted to maintain her dignity, but her voice came out as a whimpering cry.

"I ordered the convicts set to work, as with every chain that comes over the Azures," she said. "It is the duchy's duty."

Daven Marcus whirled her back to face him, not releasing his grip from her jaw.

"Duchy? Duty?" he shouted, so close that his spittle hit her face and made her blink. "What do you know about any of that? My chamber pot held more nobility this morning than you have in your whole family line. What do you know about duty?"

"Every convict who ever came across the mountains has been the duty of the Reach, subject to King's Law under the duke's discretion. A duty my husband faithfully executed every year of his dukedom. I maintained his honor and gave the orders he would have given. It is duty, law, and tradition." In spite of herself, Amelia let some of her true feelings come out in her expression, meeting the prince's anger with her own fury for just a moment. Daven Marcus stared into her eyes.

"Duty, law, and tradition," he repeated, grinding out the words. "You shouldn't try your little wits with such vast notions." With dismissive strength, he suddenly shoved Amelia backwards, releasing his grip. She staggered under the force of the gesture but was thankful that she didn't fall. Kirsten rushed to her side to help her, but as she straightened, she noticed that the prince's entourage all seemed amused by her predicament. She had no allies among them. Countess Dalflitch openly sneered as Daven Marcus returned to take her hand and put it on his arm.

"If you wish, Highness," she said, her eyes narrow, but forcing herself to maintain at least a semblance of deference. "I could send for the convicts to be brought here. It should take no more than a month to gather and transport them."

That was the last thing Amelia wanted to do, but she hoped the talk of a month's delay would prick Daven Marcus's impatience and make him forego the convicts altogether. He had other ideas, it seemed.

"I've sent word to your baron," he told her, raising his nose in the air. "He is to gather my convict rogues and bring them to the crusade, post haste. You will give no more orders for them, or I'll have my displeasure flogged from your back."

Amelia was pleased to hear that threat draw a handful of shocked gasps from the flock of sycophants. The prince had enormous leeway in their eyes, but having a peer of the realm flogged for his mere displeasure was a step too far for some of them at least. If Daven Marcus heard their expressions of shock, he didn't show it.

"Now, Duchess Sow, just stand over there and watch, quietly. I've arranged a demonstration for the court. A chance to witness the power at my command. You can have the honor of watching as well. A goodly experience for you, I think."

Amelia forced herself to curtsey and then turned to watch as the gun crew positioned the bronze dragon to face the hunting lodge. They wedged the wheels, and a smaller cart was pulled up, carrying sacks and large stone balls the size of a man's head.

"They will use stone cannonballs today," the prince opined loudly to all about. "When we face proper fortresses and castles, they'll use balls of iron." The entourage made appreciative noises of fascination.

As she watched, Amelia saw the cannoneers heft sacks from the wagon, each one sewn shut at either end. Two sacks were placed in the mouth of the bronze dragon and four of the men in red used a long, mace-like pole to shove the sacks all the way down the monster's throat. Then, a small step was put in place and two men awkwardly climbed it, carrying one of the stone cannonballs between them in a rope sling. Once they were directly in front of the cannon's muzzle, a third man standing atop the cannon used a rope with a hook to pull the ball into the barrel. Once it was in, the ones with the pole returned and toiled to push the ball all the way down. It was such a laborious process that, as she watched, Amelia wondered how such a device could be useful in war since it took so long to prepare a single shot.

"Is it true, Highness, that your ancestor, King Holber Stret III, banned any further production of these cannons?" one of the courtiers called, though Amelia could not see who it was. The prince seemed happy to have the question, as it gave him more opportunity to share his opinions.

"Yes, it is true. The only ones in existence are the ones in my father's armory, and these five he allows to me. They are all centuries old, dating from before the pacification. Holber Stret was a fool, and my fool father refuses to overturn his edict. Things will be different after my accession. This campaign will be but a foretaste for the rebellious Vec princes. When I am king, I will lead a full crusade that will bring the whole south back under our dominion."

Daven Marcus clearly had total confidence in his vision of the future, as well as in his assertion that the invaders from the west were actually from the Vec in the south, even though all evidence was to the contrary.

The cannoneers had completed their loading and scrambled away from their weapon, standing ready in a line. Their leader, holding a long pole with a length of smoldering string on the end called a long match, turned to the prince and awaited his permission.

"You might want to cover your ears, Your Highness," the man said before turning to the cannon and reaching the long match pole up to the touchhole on top of the cannon. The prince disdained the man's advice, and most of the courtiers did likewise. When she saw each of the cannoneers put their hands to their ears, Amelia decided to follow their example. In a short while, she was glad she had.

The long match lit the touchhole, and there was a spark that fizzed there for a moment, followed by a short pause where nothing happened. Then the bronze dragon erupted, tearing the morning air apart with a belch of fire and smoke that shook the very ground they stood on. Many courtiers cried out in alarm, and several staggered. The force of the explosion battered at them. Then, the stone ball struck the wooden wall of the lodge, and the logs were ripped to splinters. The air was filled with a rain of wood chips and dust. As it began to settle, the remains of the lodge became visible. At least half of the building was simply gone, obliterated by the stone ball that had itself shattered on impact.

Amelia put her hand on her chest. She could still feel the impact of the cannon blast inside her; it had almost driven the breath from her lungs. That was a single shot, and half the lodge was gone. And the prince had five of these monsters. What could stand against them? It wouldn't matter how quickly they fired if that was the result of a single shot. She was sure even stone walls would be ripped down by iron shot.

The head cannoneer looked pleased with himself as he turned to the prince once more.

"It's still half up, Your Highness. Would you like another shot?"

The prince smiled, his first true expression of happiness all morning.

"Until it's firewood," he said.

Amelia watched in fascination and horror as the loading and firing continued, and the entire lodge was blasted to bits. And from then on, every time the bronze beast shouted, every courtier present covered their ears.

CHAPTER 4

P rentice knew he was dreaming, if only because he was out in the middle of the night and couldn't feel the cold. He was walking amid the rough, newly built huts of his little camp. Around him, in the light of the banked fires, he could just make out the figures of convicts sleeping, each wrapped in blankets that Fostermae had brought in his wagon. It was nearly ten days since the sacrist had first arrived, and in that time he'd been back to Dweltford and come again, this time with two wagons. Now every man and woman had at least something to wrap himself in to ward off the night's cold.

But Prentice didn't feel that cold now.

In the manner of dreams, one moment he was standing near Fallenhill's new gate, and the next he was far to the west, walking amid the endless grass. Overhead, the stars wheeled at dizzying speed, and the moon shone as brightly as the sun. The Rampart, the ribbon-like band of light that stretched across the night's sky from west to east, was almost equally bright, but despite all the array of silvery illuminations, there were still dark shadows lurking among the long grass. From out of those shadows, a tremendous figure stalked forward on silent paws. It was a lion, as large as a pony and as white as fresh snow, and as it approached, its fur began to glow like the light from the sky. Eyes like opals shone with ancient wisdom in the creature's noble visage. This was an angelic being, older than men and wiser by far. Prentice had seen this creature many times in recent seasons, in dreams and visions, and he still wondered why it chose to speak to him.

"This is the boundary," it said to him, its voice rumbling in his chest like thunder. "If you will stand here, then you must learn the lessons of this land."

"Why do I have to stand here?" he asked. The leonine angel looked at him for a moment and then looked away, declining his question.

"Watch as they hunt," it said to him.

As he watched, a pride of lesser lions became visible in the shadows. They were stalking in the grass, and beyond them a strange herd of animals became visible. The herd was strange because it was not of one breed of animal but of a multifarious array. There were stags and bears, wolves and great serpents. Prentice even saw birds, such as eagles and vultures. And the pride of lions stalked them all. Watching them draw closer to their prey, Prentice began to see that every feline was white, like the angelic lion, though nowhere near as large or glorious. It was strange the way their color was revealed. Prentice couldn't tell if the creatures were changing color or if he was just coming to see them better as they emerged from the grass.

"Pay close attention," said the angel. "Only when the prey is close do they spring, and first they roar."

Suddenly, the lions all surged forward, wild-maned males and sleek she-lions, altogether. They roared, startling the prey.

"Now they fall upon the prey, and they rend, first with their foreclaws and then with the rear. At last, when they are close enough to feel the breath of the foe, they bite, and the fangs finish what the claws have begun."

Even in the dark of night, Prentice could see in detail everything the angel was describing. The impossible brightness helped, but somehow the angel's words made the scene even more vivid.

"This is the lesson you must learn," it said to him.

"I don't understand," he protested.

"If the fangs are swords and the claws are like spears, then you already understand enough."

With that, Prentice realized that he did understand. The lions, the pride, their form of hunting... it was a pattern that he could use, a pattern upon which he could model an army. It would be an army of polearms and swords, working in combination to be ready for anything the battlefield would throw at them. He saw it all in a single moment.

"You must lead the pride and teach them to hunt, but it is not your pride," the angel told him. "The she-lion must have her pride before the winter's end, or else she will lose her house. She will be ripped apart by dogs and eagles from within. Then, a serpent will come and crush her, and the dog and eagle with her. You stand on the boundary for her—dogs at one hand and a serpent coming for you too."

The she-lion must be the duchess, Amelia. Prentice knew it was true.

He looked behind him and saw a pack of slavering dogs coming out of the grass toward him. Their fur was dark and sleek, and their eyes glowed in the moonlight. In the distance, the lions continued to struggle with the wild melee, but none of that concerned these dogs. Prentice wasn't troubled by the dogs' presence until he looked about and realized he was alone. The angelic lion had gone. He stepped back in the grass, trying to keep the stalking pack at a distance, but as he did so, he looked down and saw that he had put his foot into a nest of sleeping rats. Seeing them, he knew they weren't what he needed. He couldn't fend off wild dogs with a mere pack of rats, no matter how savage the little beasts were.

"I need lions," he shouted, hoping the angel would hear him. The dog pack was so close he could hear them panting, could see their jaws slavering for blood.

"Rats hide in walls," came the angel's voice, echoing. "Shut the door and the dogs will wait outside. You must teach the rats to be lions before winter warms to spring or the pride will fail, and the she-lion will be first ripped apart and then crushed."

Angels certainly do not mince their words, Prentice thought grimly.

"And learn what it means to hear the lions roar. That is the beginning of battle for the pride, and you must uncover that secret. Every dog and beast will fear the lion's roar, but first you must learn." Then the wild dogs pounced, and Prentice recoiled in fear, starting awake from his dream.

Around him, he heard the sounds of the camp waking and realized it was almost dawn. He pushed off his blanket and sat up, reaching for his boots. He slept on the ground like the rest of the camp, much to Sir Gant's displeasure. The knight thought it unseemly for a commander to have no bed. Prentice offered to have one made for Sir Gant, since he was a man of rank, but the knight had declined. If his commander would have no bed, then neither would he. Prentice was determined not to sleep or eat better than his men.

He wondered at the images of the dream he just had. He was fairly certain he understood most of its meaning, and even without much effort, he found his mind expanding on the notion of the pride of lions as the basis for a military strategy. Before he had walked out into the morning light, he had a rough tactical and strategic structure he was convinced he could build a victorious army upon. But the angel's final words about the lions' roar were a mystery to him. He'd have to figure the meaning for himself somehow, but in the meantime, he had enough to begin with.

He fitted his weapon belt comfortably into place, then looked around to see who else was about. Prentice's weapon of choice was not a sword, but a sword-breaker, sometimes called a steel whip, though it had little flexibility to it. Not much more than a steel bar forged with ridges designed to catch and damage a sword's edge, it was essentially a baton with a cross-guard. Wielded properly, though, it was a deadly tool and the bane of a knight's longsword, capable of deflecting the longer weapon and even chipping and bending the blade. Prentice adjusted the weight and then headed off to find Sergeant Ranold and the others who were going to be his closest officers.

Soon enough Prentice had gathered up Sir Gant and Righteous, along with Ranold's corporal, a wiry, dark-haired man named Felix. They were looking for the sergeant and the mastersmith Yentow Sent when sacrist Fostermae drove his lumbering wagon past. The clergyman waved cheerily.

"Off again, Sacrist?" Prentice called to him.

"Your little settlement has no end of needs," Fostermae responded. "It looks like we could have a few days before the heavy winter rains come. I might make one more trip to Dweltford in that time if I'm quick."

"Your diligence is appreciated."

Prentice walked beside the wagon, discussing with Fostermae what the most urgent needs of the camp might be. He had already entrusted the sacrist with a purse of guilders. Duchess Amelia had sent Prentice north with a chest full of silver, which he had hidden in the ruins of Fallenhill's keep the first night they arrived. Money was the least of his worries.

As the wagon neared the gate, a crowd gathered to see the sacrist off. In his short time among them, Fostermae had won a good deal of affection from the drafted convicts with his earnest service to his faith and skills as a healer. The wagon negotiated the recently repaired town gates, and the crowd came a little way out beyond the walls to wave him goodbye. Mercenaries, knowing their duty, pushed through the crowd. Using long poles, they held the crowd at bay in case one of the convicts thought to make a run for it.

Fostermae's wagon was no more than ten paces out when Prentice realized that the tailgate was hanging unsecured at the back. There was a coil of rope visible on the backboard. The loose gate would bang and might even break during the journey back south to Dweltford, and things like the rope could be lost. He called for Fostermae to wait a moment and went to lock it into place. Hefting the thick wooden boards, he shot the iron bolts. Happy it was secure, he turned aside and was about to wave the wagon on when he thought about how the tailgate had hung underneath the level of the wagon and what it might have concealed. With a heavy sigh he crouched down and found two convicts secreted underneath the wagon, clinging white-knuckled to the boards.

"Come out of there," he said in a weary tone. The two men dropped reluctantly from their perch, and Prentice reached under to grab one of them and drag him out. He called up Corporal Felix and handed the man off. Felix took him in a tight grip.

"Looks like we execute some deserters today," said Felix grimly. Prentice ignored his words and looked back under to see the second attempted deserter had pressed himself farther back under the wagon so that he had almost reached the front.

"Stop that and come out," Prentice ordered the man.

The convict shook his head and, ferret-like, twisted about and pushed himself out from under the front of the wagon, just avoiding the bullocks. Once he was up, he sprinted off down the hill. Prentice stood and watched him flee.

"We'll have to get the rovers to go get him," he told Felix. The corporal nodded and shouted for his men to fetch a rider. It would be faster and easier to bring the man back on horseback than try to catch him on foot. Prentice looked at the other escapee, casting an eye down onto his iron fetters still locked around his ankles. "What was the plan? Just ride there all the way to Dweltford?"

"Maybe," the man responded with a petulant sneer. Prentice suppressed another sigh.

"You've both still got your fetters," he said, exasperated. "Soon as any free man laid eyes on you, you'd be dead. Reachermen don't suffer escaped convicts."

"Maybe we could have got them off."

"How?" demanded Felix, taking up Prentice's side of the conversation. The man scowled and said nothing more. Prentice just shook his head and headed to the front of the wagon. Fostermae had a guilty expression on his face.

"Did you know about this?"

"They begged me to let them try."

It was all Prentice could do to keep from cursing. He clenched his fist and gritted his teeth.

"Kindness is one thing, Sacrist," he all but spat at Fostermae, "but these men are convicted. They're thieves and murderers, every single one."

"You don't think they deserve mercy?"

"No one deserves mercy. That's why it's mercy. If we deserve something, then it's justice."

"That sounds like sophistry, to me."

"I have no intention of debating with you! When you come here, you do it under my authority or you don't do it at all!"

Fostermae lowered his head, seeming to accept the rebuke, but Prentice had no idea if he could trust him. He appreciated the sacrist's even-handedness in his Christian duty; there were few enough in the wider church who genuinely cared for the poor and downtrodden. But the law was the law, and as much as he had suffered under its judgements, Prentice did not want anarchy. Criminals should be punished. Rubbing at his neck, he looked down the slope at the rapidly retreating escapee. He was already hundreds of paces away. As he looked, Prentice saw movement beyond the fleeing man, down near the river almost a half a league away. Sir Gant came up beside him, along with Sergeant Ranold, who had finally been found, it seemed.

"Riders?" asked Ranold, also seeing the movement in the distance.

"A hundred, at least," agreed Sir Gant.

Prentice suddenly remembered his dream, and the warning about dogs and rats thrilled through him.

"Back inside," he shouted. "Everyone back behind the walls, now!" Corporals turned to start pushing the convicts back in, but slowly, not really seeing any danger yet. Looking back down the slope, Prentice watched the fleeing convict stop when he, too, noticed the approaching riders. The cloudy grey morning light gave no telltale flashes, but Prentice was sure the riders wore steel. They were men-at-arms.

"You too, Sacrist," Prentice ordered.

"What?" Fostermae was obviously confused by Prentice's urgency and looked downslope as well.

The riders had come to a halt, having reached a point where they could see the walls of Fallenhill clearly. Perhaps they were assessing the situation. They may not have expected to see the crowd at the gates and might have been planning their approach. The escaping convict apparently decided he didn't want to wait to see what they would decide, and he began to run obliquely across the field, away from the riders but not toward the walls. Two men-at-arms separated from the company and galloped after him. It took them almost no time at all to reach him. The first ran him straight down under his horse's hoofs. The convict tumbled on the ground while the second rider wheeled wide around him and drew a sword. When the stunned convict tried to drunkenly recover his feet, the second rider leaned in his saddle and hacked the man down with a single stroke.

CHAPTER 5

"Oh, dear God," Fostermae gasped.

"Inside, dammit. Get your bloody cart turned around!" Prentice ordered. Having seen the sudden violence of the newly arrived men-at-arms, most of the convicts were all too glad to be herded behind the safety of the walls, though a handful decided to make a break for it.

"Let them go!" Sir Gant bellowed at two corporals who started to chase after them. He looked to Prentice to confirm the order and Prentice nodded. Prentice was just glad that Gant recognized the danger they were all in, as well as the urgency.

The wheels of Fostermae's cart creaked loudly as he tried his best to get the vehicle turned in a tight circle. The bullocks groaned and bellowed in protest as he wracked them with his driver's whip.

"We have to get everyone behind that gate," Ranold declared. "If they decide to rush us before we get it closed, they'll make a mess of us."

Looking toward the riders, they saw that another small group—this one a trio—had detached themselves to run down the other convicts who were fleeing from the gate. The rest of the riders were watching, seemingly in no rush. Prentice tried to estimate the distance, certain that these knights were toying with them, seeing how long they could leave their charge. Once they spurred their mounts to the gallop, there would be bare moments before they were upon them. He looked over his shoulder to gauge his chances. He could make the distance, but not if the gate was blocked with the awkward cart. Then he realized that blocking the path to the gate was exactly what he wanted, but only on his terms. He turned back to Fostermae.

"Get down!"

"What?"

Not waiting to explain, he reached up and yanked the sacrist off the wagon. Fostermae complained at the rough handling, but Prentice ignored him, thrusting him into Felix's arms. He rushed to the bullocks' shoulders and tugged on the yoke, guiding them in a slow half circle across the front of the gate.

"What are you doing?" demanded Fostermae. Prentice answered his question, but speaking to Sir Gant and Righteous, who had emerged through the crowd that had rushed back through the gate.

"Once the wagon's across the gate, cut the traces and pull the yoke pin. Get the bullocks inside."

"What for?" demanded Righteous.

"I want to block the gate so they can't bring a ram up without clearing the wagon away first," he explained. "Anyone who comes near, we get to shoot or throw rocks at." It was a haphazard defensive work, but from the grin on her face, Righteous seemed to like the idea of throwing rocks at knights. The bullocks were slow, but when the wagon was in place, the overconfident attackers still stood waiting, like the slavering dogs in Prentice's dream, slowly stalking while the rats were looking to hide in the walls. They would see their mistake soon enough.

While others got the bullocks free, Prentice clambered into the wagon and grabbed the rope. Wanting to work as quickly as he could but forcing himself to go slowly to keep his hands from shaking, he tied one end of the rope to the far side of the wagon. Crouching with his back open to the attackers, it took all Prentice's will not to keep looking over his shoulder. At every moment he expected to hear the drum of hoofbeats and feel the thrust of steel between his shoulder blades. At last, the rope was tied off and he threw the coil over the wagon.

"Tie this to the yoke!" he shouted. "Get the bullocks to pull it over."

From above him, he heard voices cry out and looked up to see dozens of convicts standing on the ramparts, pointing down at the knights. Prentice looked back and saw that another pair had detached themselves from the company and were urging their mounts to a trot, heading up the road. Had they figured out what he was trying to do? Even if they had, why were they being so casual? He had a moment of insight and wondered if the leader of the knights wanted to capture some convicts first and perhaps interrogate them before assaulting the walls directly. It would have been a sound tactic, rather than a wild headlong charge at the first sign of the enemy, if that were ironically not exactly the tactic the situation called for.

The wagon groaned and rocked, dragging sideways slightly, then fell back onto its wheels. The bullocks lowed discontentedly. Prentice rushed around to find that the panicked animals were refusing to pull the load with a crowd of frightened men all shouting around them. Sir Gant pulled on the yoke pole, but the beasts refused to move their feet.

"The things are affrighted," Righteous said to Prentice. She had Fostermae's whip in her hand.

"Of course, they are." Prentice charged into the gate, waving his arms. "Back! Everyone back! Give them room!"

The way began to clear.

"Whip them bloody if you have to!" he said to Righteous. Then he slapped Sir Gant on the shoulder and pointed to one end of the wagon and the small gap between it and the wall. "You watch that end; I'll watch this. As soon as you hear the wagon go over, sprint for it and shut that gate. Don't wait for anything!"

Gant nodded and drew his longsword in a swift stroke, taking a ready stance where Prentice had assigned him. Prentice ran to the other end and worked his own weapon out of its sling. The weight of the sword-breaker felt good in his hand, even though it seemed so much shorter and less impressive than Gant's elegant blade.

Prentice heard the sound of hoofbeats mixed with the groaning wood of the wagon. Men on the walls shouted, and the driver's whip cracked again and again. Then, one of the knights wheeled out around the wagon in front of Prentice. The man was clad in plate and mail, wearing a conical steel bascinet helmet with a full, snouted mask. His tabard was striped in alternating blue and two tones of green, but there was no other heraldry on it. He had an arming sword in hand and a shield with a quartered blue and red pattern. The shield was Baron Liam's colors, making it clear whose man this knight was. In the calm inner part of his mind, Prentice realized that his camp of convicts had been found. In all likelihood, it was Liam himself who was commanding the force of knights, sending little forays up from his line of men-at-arms.

Then the knight in front of him lowered his sword to point at Prentice's chest and there was no more time for thought. Spurs touched the destrier's sides and the knight surged forward, the trained beast springing up to a high charge almost from a standing start. Prentice watched, waited for his moment, and deflected the deadly thrust with his sword-breaker, diving aside as he did so. The knight wheeled almost in place after his charge missed and drove his heels in for another pass. Prentice dodged this assault as well, but he knew he was now wildly out of position. Two passes and he was all but completely separated from the safety of the gap between wall and wagon. Prentice looked to get back to that safety, but the knight was ready for him to try that move. The man turned his mount across to block the way.

This one knows what he's doing, Prentice thought and softly cursed the man's competence. Prentice drew in a deep breath to help himself keep calm. He remembered the wild dogs in his dream and realized that if this kept up, the knight would run him down all too soon. He needed to end it. As the mount was spurred to its third charge, he waited, shifting as subtly as he could to keep himself in the way of the horse, not the line of the rider's slashing blade. If he timed his move wrong, he'd be trampled under the iron-shod hoofs. Waiting until the last possible moment, he launched himself across the line of the charge, ending up on the knight's shield side, and instead of rising, he kept himself in a low crouch, lashing out with his sword-breaker, catching the mount on its knee. There was a sickening snap of bone and the poor beast screamed in pain as it stumbled on that side. Prentice hated to be so brutal, but he had no other hope.

The knight showed he was a skilled horseman, keeping his saddle cleanly as his mount went forward, ready to tumble dismount as he had trained for years. Prentice had no intention of allowing that. The knight was controlling the fall, slowing the motion, which gave Prentice time to leap at him from the ground, and using the sword-breaker like a bar, he wrestled the man out of the saddle before he could jump free. Riding the knight to the ground, he kept the armored man off balance and dragged him backwards, with the steel baton gripped with both hands under the chin of the man's helmet. Only the armor's gorget prevented the knight from being choked. Once he'd wrestled his opponent down onto his back, Prentice slipped the sword-breaker out from under his chin, and with a swift, wheeling strike, brought it crashing down on the pig-faced helmet before the knight could get his sword or shield into a defensive position. The impact rang on the steel like a bell. Prentice didn't stop at only one hit, and rained blow after blow on the helmet until the steel plate was deformed and stoved in. The knight in the armor was surely unconscious and likely seriously injured. Prentice stood and drew in a deep breath, feeling his heart hammering in his chest, though whether from fear or the wild exertion of his attack, he couldn't say.

In the momentary pause, he heard two noises at once. One was the resounding crack of the wagon finally being tipped on its side. The other was the hoofbeats of the other knight's steed. Whatever had happened to Sir Gant, the rider who'd gone to his end of the wagon was now out in the open again and wheeling around to hunt new prey. Prentice looked behind and realized that as it had been pulled over, the wagon had shifted so that it was closer to the wall and at an angle. There was no way for him to get back to the gate from this side. He checked where the other knight was and saw the man riding in a wide circle, clearly looking for him. From the wall above came shouted warnings.

"Here they come!"

Prentice didn't spare a moment to confirm what those words meant; he was sure he knew. The whole company was coming. He dashed along the side of the wagon, determined to reach the other end and get to the gate before the lone knight ran him down. He could hear the rising drumbeat of the approaching company, but he shut it out of his mind. The lone knight nearby spurred to a charge and Prentice paused near the wagon's upturned wheel. He waited until the rider was nearly on him, then used his sword-breaker to guard his legs while he ducked his head under the wagon's wheel. If the knight had aimed low, the sword-breaker would have caught the hit, but as it was, the knight aimed for his head and the man's sword struck sparks from the wheel's iron rims.

As he'd hoped, the knight continued his charge a few paces, as if Prentice was a mere training dummy. The man thought to simply toy with him until he was eventually run to ground. Knights of the Grand Kingdom tended towards an arrogant disdain for men on foot. Right at this moment, Prentice didn't care about respect or disdain, only that the rider had given him a short window to act, and he used it, running about the front of the wagon to the gate. He found it already closed, just as he'd ordered Sir Gant to do. He rushed into the small space created by the wall and the wagon and spun about, ready for the knight's next attack. There would be no more charges; the small space had him trapped, exactly like one of the rats in his dream. In a strangely calm part of his mind, he wondered why the angel would bother to bring a vision if he was to die before he could share it with anyone.

Then he heard a thump on the ground behind him. Glancing swiftly over his shoulder, he saw a rope thrown from the ramparts.

"Grab it, you daft bastard," Righteous shouted at him. He smiled and stepped back to twine the rope around his free hand, holding the sword-breaker out to guard against any swings from the knight. Seeing the prey escaping, the knight rushed his destrier into the gap, rising in the saddle to slash at Prentice as the rope heaved him into the air. The slash bit only empty space, and soon enough, Prentice found himself being manhandled over the edge of the rampart.

"You left that damned close," said Righteous, a stern look of disapproval on her face. She was the first of a crew of convicts who'd hauled him up on the rope. He flashed them a smile of bravado that he didn't feel in his heart.

"I had faith in your sense of timing," he joked. Many smiled, but Righteous only thumped him in the chest.

"Fool!" she said and then turned on her heel and pushed away through the crowd on top of the wall. Prentice was surprised to feel her disapproval bite deep in his mind for a moment, but that swiftly turned to anger. What had she expected him to do? Besides, wasn't cheeky bravado exactly the way she faced the world? He blinked for a moment, getting his confused emotions under control. Then, drawing in another, deeper breath, Prentice threaded his sword-breaker back into its sling. His heart was still hammering, and he felt his hand tremble for a moment. To cover that motion, he looked down off the wall and pushed his way along to where Sir Gant was looking out at the approaching company of riders.

"I didn't like leaving you out there," said the knight, "but I knew you wanted the gate closed."

"You did the right thing," said Prentice, clapping Gant on the shoulder, but when the two men's eyes met, his smile slipped for a moment.

Gant nodded. He understood. Then he looked at the fallen knight.

"You certainly did for him."

"He didn't leave me much choice."

"No doubt. You'll have won yourself some admirers on this side of the wall, I'd say though."

That notion caught Prentice by surprise, and he looked around him at the other men standing on the wall. True to Sir Gant's point, a number of the men were looking at him with a measure of respect he'd not seen before in the typically sullen convicts' expressions. No doubt seeing him beat a knight into the dirt made it clear what side Prentice was on.

CHAPTER 6

The knight lying prone on the ground was still not moving, and his injured mount was whimpering pitifully as it limped to its master and tried to nudge him awake. The man's companion rode around to check on him, and convicts on the rampart hissed and jeered at him. The knight pulled up his visor and glared at them. Prentice wondered if the man was about to shake his fist at them, but the knight kept his dignity.

"Look to your friend," Prentice called down. "He needs a healer."

The knight on horseback gave no answer but carefully re-sheathed his blade and then dismounted to check his wounded comrade. While he did, the rest of his company rode up. Amongst them, just as Prentice had anticipated, was a knight in the finest white plate armor under a red and blue tabard. Baron Liam. His coif of dark hair was unmistakable as he rode bare headed. His distinctive helmet, with its large, gilded antlers, was hooked to the back of his saddle. The antlers had come from the bestial Horned Man, whom Prentice had slain as a convict. Since it was impolitic to give credit for a victory to a convict, the story had been put about that Liam had slain the enemy champion and he had been given the horns as a trophy. All these features made Liam unmistakable among his men, but without them Prentice would never have recognized the baron. His face was brutally changed, twisted by a savagely broken jaw, an injury Prentice had given him barely half a season earlier. It probably hadn't even healed fully yet. No wonder he didn't wear his helmet; he probably couldn't, even if he wanted to. He must have been in no little amount of pain.

"Hi ho, Baron," Prentice called out. "You should have sent word you were coming; we would have prepared you a better welcome." The entire company of knights looked up, several having to open visors or even remove helmets to do so. Baron Liam looked up with a hateful scowl.

"Open up, convict," he ordered bluntly, his words twisted and poorly pronounced. The injury also affected his speech, it seemed.

"No convicts here," Prentice said. Several of the men around him chuckled, but Prentice wasn't joking. Whatever his recruits had been, whatever they were, in his eyes they were no longer convicts. "I'm a free man, for a start."

"You're a cur with all the honor of a dog turd under my shoe," the baron spat back. Several convicts jeered again. One man relieved himself over the wall, but it went nowhere near the knights on their horses. "I am baron of these lands. You'll open the gate to me, and you and your mob of escaped vermin will surrender to the king's justice. That is a command."

"Give all the commands you want. I've got a warrant here and the duchess' signet giving authority over Fallenhill to me. I don't have to open the gates to anyone but her."

That caught Liam by surprise. The horse under him must have sensed his tension. It moved about and he had to take a firm hand on the reins.

"I am sent by the Prince of Rhales. He supersedes your bitch duchess."

"And when he shows up, I'll open the gate to him as well. Until then, you can wait out there."

Many of the knights held whispered council with their baron, obviously discussing their options. Prentice was enjoying throwing insults at Liam, but ultimately he knew the conversation was pointless. They couldn't open to Liam without a bloodbath. Two thousand men should easily overpower a hundred knights, but only if they acted together. At this point Prentice's men were more likely to scatter than fight, and the knights would run them down. The angel's message was completely correct. Lions could stand and fight; rats hid in the walls.

Liam drew his mount a short distance from the foot of the wall. Two of his men left their horses to recover their fallen comrade. Inside his armor, the defeated man was utterly limp, and the other two were forced to carry his full armored weight between them.

"He's dead," someone on the wall shouted. "The captain killed him outright."

There was more mockery and hissing, but Prentice could feel eyes on him, assessing him. Wearing no more than a jerkin and with what to most only looked like a steel baton, he had defeated a knight in full armor and on horseback and come away from the fight with no more than bumps and bruises. While he hoped they were impressed, Prentice knew in his heart he had been fortunate. If the encounter were repeated a hundred times, he wouldn't expect to succeed so well even one time out of every ten, if that. And it was odd to hear himself called captain.

For a time, many of the knights rode back and forth in front of the walls, apparently assessing the possibilities for assault, while Liam and a handful of horsemen stayed looking at the gate. Soon enough several riders returned with one of the escaped convicts slung over his saddle, arms bound. The knight threw the man to the ground and then several dismounted and proceeded to tie ropes to his hands and feet. The other ends of the rope they tied to their saddles.

"Go find Yentow Sent," Prentice told Sir Gant. "Fast as you can. See if he's got a crossbow, a bow. Hell, a javelin or a dart. Something, anything."

Gant rushed off, but even as he did so, Prentice knew he was going to be too late. Liam was going to have the captured man drawn, pulled apart by horses. As the ropes were tied off, two riders mounted and walked their horses apart to lift the man into position. As the tension began to bite into his limbs, the dazed man began to come back to himself, feeling the pain. He grunted and groaned as the knots bit into his wrists and ankles.

"Let him go, Liam," Prentice shouted.

"This is appropriate punishment for rebels," Liam slurred back, his twisted features sneering. "And it is the fate every man in there can expect." He nodded to his riders, and they began to walk their horses apart. The bound man gave out an agonized cry.

"These men aren't rebels," Prentice called over the sound. "They're convicts, and everyone still wears their shackles. They're not even escaped. Every man is still under law!"

"And yet the gates of Fallenhill remain closed to me. If they will follow you in your rebellion, then they will suffer a rebel's fate."

There was a soft but sickening snapping sound as one of the tormented man's joints dislocated suddenly. He screamed in fresh agony, and then, mouth still open, his voice choked off as he passed out from the pain.

"I am not without mercy," Liam offered, his expression showing just how much he was enjoying his cruelty. "If they will seize you right this moment and throw you down off that wall to me here, I will have no need to punish them. They can return with me to Dweltford and the chain. They can purge their souls and serve out their conviction within the law. They need only give you over to me. From there."

Prentice cast a glance around himself. Several of the faces that had been looking to him with admiration seemed suddenly doubtful, as if considering the baron's offer. He narrowed his eyes as he looked from one to the next.

"Any of you trust him to keep his word?"

One by one the men who met his gaze shook their heads and turned away. Prentice looked back down on the knights below.

"Not going to happen, Baron," he shouted.

Liam glared up at him for a moment, and then his eyes narrowed in pure contempt.

"So be it," he said. He nodded at the two knights, and they spurred their horses to sudden surges of power. In a savage spray of blood, the man between them was ripped apart, limbs from torso. He bled so quickly from torn arteries that he was dead even as the destriers were brought up short, only mere paces into their charges. The grass was splashed crimson, and looking down on the scene from above, a growl of fury rippled through the crowd on the battlement.

"You have only yourselves to blame," Liam told them dismissively. "And you will count his fate merciful when your own turns come. You will beg for so swift a death. You all will."

Prentice suddenly felt tired. He nodded his head sadly and turned away, pushing past the men around him to the stairs. He suspected they were looking to him to know what to do next, but he had nothing for them. Not yet. As he headed down the stairs, he met Sir Gant rushing back the other way.

"This is all he had," Gant said, holding up a small crossbow designed to be shot one-handed from horseback. It would be used for hunting birds and small game. Prentice had wanted something he could use to end the tormented man's suffering before the execution, but this was probably too small anyway. A shot from that, unless supremely accurate, would only have added to the man's sufferings.

Prentice put his hand on Gant's shoulder and shook his head as he moved past. Up on the wall behind him, the convicts he planned to free continued to shout and hiss at the knights beyond the walls. And they watched. He didn't need to watch; he knew what would happen next. Liam would want to move the fallen wagon and bring up a battering ram for the gate. Prentice knew he'd need to set a guard over the gate and get stones up on the wall to throw down on anyone trying to clear the wagon. That was the next step.

But first, he was hungry. He hadn't even broken fast yet. He wanted a drink of water and something to eat. And he wanted to try to forget the image of a foolish, desperate convict being torn apart to satisfy a vile nobleman's bloodlust.

He didn't like his chances.

CHAPTER 7

S ome days later, Daven Marcus gave orders at last for the army to march west. Rumor had it that after searching the lodge and having it demolished for target practice by one of his cannons, he had then ordered men to scour the nearby lands for any sign that there might have been silver still hidden somewhere close about. Convinced that the amount he found hidden in the lodge was not enough, he wanted to make sure that there wasn't a more significant buried treasure being missed. Only when he was finally convinced did he give orders for the march to commence.

Men in royal livery were appointed wardens to the march, and they ranged up and down the camp with lists of order, determining where each noble was permitted to travel in relation to each of the others. Some nobles had unchallengeable positions; their prestige was secured by their birth. Most, though, existed in a competitive flux, their relative importance being much harder to judge. Was a baron from the Reach as important as a baron from the court of Rhales? Rhales was the prince's court and therefore had precedence, but they were travelling through the Reach, and respect to the local lands was equally due. The prince could easily have ended the confusions and uncertainties if he were so inclined, but other than the exceptions of those who actually traveled in his immediate company, he simply did not seem to care. And so, the royal wardens did a brisk trade in bribes and favors as nobles competed to be placed ahead of rivals or nearer to others with whom they hoped to make alliances. The politicking of the court extended everywhere, even to the question of who walked where.

Amelia had no choice about where she rode in the column. As the soon-to-be-announced fiancé of the prince, she was forced to accompany him in his immediate party, though every day she found Daven Marcus showed her virtually no attention at all. She was left to Kirsten's company as the prince's closest entourage all followed his example and ignored her as well. Despite this lonely prestige, no amount of negotiation could gain Amelia's baggage any preference in the march. She was sure it was on Daven Marcus's direct orders, so that while she was at the front, her tent and clothing was forced to take a place far to the back of the column. It meant that each evening while she arrived early at camp, her tent would still be another hour or more away and she was forced to wait. It was a petty annoyance, and Amelia took it as such.

Turley was the only other person the duchess spoke with in the first few days of the march, but even though he walked at her stirrup, it was not seemly for her to hold a conversation with a steward. The gossips had enough to work with, considering her low-born past, and she had no desire to start more rumors by public fraternizing with a servant. As it happened, the duty of having to govern her traveling household meant that Turley was often away from her in any case, tending to servants' needs and her baggage.

Soon after luncheon on the third day, as a chill breeze blew across the line of march from the northwest, forcing Amelia to wrap herself tightly in a dark woolen cloak with a white, rabbit-fur collar, Turley returned to her from the baggage with a message.

"With your permission, Your Grace," he said, tugging his forelock, "a Reacher nobleman seeks an audience."

"Who?" Amelia asked, glad of the distraction.

Under her cloak, she was yet wearing her linen dress with black edging and her black lace veil, which hid her face and matched her melancholy. Beneath that outward show of mourning though, she was in fact a little bored. Missing her husband and honoring his memory were important, but she wanted to talk about something more than the pretty dresses of the court ladies, a topic which seemed to endlessly fascinate Kirsten.

"A Viscount Wolden, Your Grace, of the Griffith Pale."

The Griffith Pale was a stretch of land on the southern border of the Reach, surrounding the town of Griffith, close to Mur River and the border with the Vec. Amelia almost gave immediate permission for the viscount to approach but knew better. Nodding to Turley, she geed her horse, Meadow Dancer, forward and drew nearer to where the prince rode on his own steed. She pushed past several Rhales noblemen and ladies, and when she was only a horse length from Daven Marcus, she called to him.

"Noble Prince, might I crave your indulgence?"

The courtiers around the prince turned to look at her with a kind of disapproving curiosity that seemed so stiff and forced that she almost wanted to laugh at them. She knew none of them by name, but also knew that as Duchess of the Western Reach, she officially outranked all of them. Only the prince himself was her superior in this company.

"What do you want, little Reacher girl?" the prince asked loudly, refusing to even turn his head to face her.

"Highness, I have received a request for an audience from a Reach nobleman, Viscount Wolden. Would you have me present him to you as well?" Amelia chose her words carefully. The prince had every right to refuse to let the viscount approach his party, and if so, Amelia would have no choice but to deny the nobleman an audience, at least until the end of the day's march. She hoped to head that off by playing to the prince's conceitedness.

"A viscount?" Daven Marcus sniffed. "Did you have cobblers and seamstresses you wanted to show off as well?" His entourage laughed obligingly. From the other side of the prince, the Countess Dalflitch spared her a pitying look, and Amelia clenched her teeth in anger, glad her lace veil concealed her expression. The prince's contempt was something she had come to take for granted. The countess was another story.

"You are right, of course, Highness," she said as sweetly as she could. "I will receive him myself and spare your dignity."

"See that you keep him downwind, little sow," the prince called after her, still not looking in her direction. "A Reacherman too close so soon after luncheon. It's like to turn the gentler stomachs of my court."

Another dutiful ripple of laughter.

Nothing would suit me better, you preening cockerel, Amelia thought.

She smiled to herself as she turned Meadow Dancer away. Although Daven Marcus had enjoyed another round of mocking her, he had implicitly given her permission to meet someone outside his entourage, which was what she wanted. Once she returned to her customary place at the back of the prince's party, she gave Turley a nod and he rushed off to escort the viscount forward.

Even for a Reach nobleman, Viscount Wolden was not richly dressed. His woolen cloak was a simple dun color, with no embellishments or embroidery. Under that, he wore a suit of plate and mail of an older fashion, with no gilt or fluting. Nonetheless, the viscount's tabard looked newly made, the colors bright even in the overcast light of the chilly afternoon. There was a green bull's head sewn on his left breast, and the white cloth was edged in grey. He wore his wiry, brown hair long, so that wisps that resisted being tied back flew about his face in the breeze. No more than thirty, he had an earnest expression under his thick beard. He bowed in the saddle as he approached, and Amelia accepted his bow with a nod.

"Well met, Viscount," she said honestly and politely. The duchess was always acutely aware that she was being watched. "While I welcome your company, I must tell you that the prince has determined that he will not be receiving any audience this afternoon and so I cannot present you, if that was your hope." She was surprised by the viscount's response.

"Oh, Your Grace, I had no such aspirations," he said, putting a hand to his breast. "Of course, I hope for an audience at some time on the march, but I would much rather wait until I had something worthy to present to the prince."

"You don't think you need present anything worthy to me?" Amelia asked him. It was a reflexive question, defending her own honor with a subordinate, but she immediately regretted its sharpness. For his part, Viscount Wolden bowed his head apologetically.

"I do have gifts, Your Grace, but they are with my baggage. I should have thought to have them ready when I sought your audience."

"Do not fret yourself, Viscount," Amelia said, trying to sooth the man's honor after pricking it needlessly. "You are a liegeman to the Western Reach, and you have the right to your duchess' attention. The noblemen of the Reach have ever proved themselves loyal and steadfast."

The viscount straightened in his saddle, and that pleased Amelia. She didn't trust the nobility, not fully, because no matter how they seemed to her, they would always have one eye on their own honor and ambition. She'd learned that bitter lesson with Baron Liam, whom she now regarded as an outright traitor. If ever she got herself out from under the prince's thumb, she would bring justice to the baron for assaulting her. Nonetheless, men like the viscount were loyal to a point, and it was wise for her to foster that. If she could tie their honor and pride to her service, she could better trust their loyalty, she was sure of it.

"Your words are kind, Your Grace," Wolden said to her. "I hope you are enjoying the army's march." He looked at the sky and the open grassland around them. Overhead was grey with clouds and the grass waved forlornly in the cold breezes. Amelia followed his look and then looked back to him.

"I like the journey well enough," she said. "But I will like it better when we find the invaders who harmed our lands and punish them."

The viscount nodded and gave her a grim smile of approval. Amelia wondered at his expression for a moment and then looked away again. It seemed to her that there was a distinction between the nobles of the Reach and those of the prince's court, the ones from Rhales, but the more she thought about it, the more she found that it wasn't as she expected it to be. Rhales nobles looked like they considered themselves superior to everyone they met. Even the least born knight from the prince's court showed her little more than snobbish disdain. Western Reach nobles seemed less concerned with her ignoble birth and more concerned with how she ruled. That was why the viscount seemed to approve now, Amelia realized. He was prepared to treat her as a mere courtly lady, making agreeable conversation and being polite, but he was happy to see she had her mind focused on vengeance for her people. The Reach wanted her to be for them, she was sure of it, and in her private mind, that was what she wanted as well. She had taken up the role of duchess as a way to honor her dead husband, mourning him and ruling in his name, but as every day passed, she had a growing need to protect the people she ruled—protect them from the invaders from the west and from the disdain of the nobles from the east.

Amelia realized that the viscount was making more pleasant conversation and she wasn't saying anything. As she listened, she felt there was an unspoken tension in the viscount's voice.

She looked to her other side at Kirsten, to see if her maid had a similar sense, but Kirsten had her face sternly focused forward, as if ignoring the viscount entirely.

"My lord, I am thankful for your company," she said, turning back to Wolden. "But I sense you have something you wish to say and are holding back. Do not fear to speak your mind, I encourage you."

Wolden seemed to swallow, and Amelia wondered how serious the issue he wanted to raise could be.

"Your Grace, I know you remember Sir Carron Ironworth," he began.

"Prince Mercad's knight commander? I do indeed remember him."

In truth, Amelia doubted she would ever forget him. At the Battle of the Brook, he and Prentice Ash had rallied the broken Kingdom army and turned sure defeat into a victory. Sir Carron was a hero with decades of service to his name; the Brook was only the latest in his long list of heroic deeds.

"When Daven Marcus became crown prince, he dismissed Sir Carron as knight commander," said Wolden. His expression darkened, and it was clear he disapproved, though he knew better than to say so, it seemed, which was right. A viscount did not openly criticize the decisions of a prince, not if he ever wanted to advance in favor.

"Doubtless the new prince wants to bring a new commander to the fore," Amelia said, politely. "Sir Carron has earned his rest, surely?"

"Sir Carron has earned a place among the angels, by my measure, Your Grace."

"Then what troubles you, My Lord?"

"The prince has not appointed a new knight commander."

It was a simple statement, but the viscount's tone carried an unmistakable tone of disquiet. Amelia looked up at the clutch of nobles riding not ten paces ahead of them. That was too close for her comfort, if the viscount was thinking to criticize the prince.

"The prince is doubtless waiting for the right candidate," she said and immediately saw the problem. If the prince had no replacement for Carron Ironworth, then why dismiss him?

"There is some talk around the court as to who the replacement might be."

Amelia had a sudden suspicion. Was Wolden angling for the position himself? If so, then approaching her was the wrong way to go about it. Perhaps Wolden hadn't heard the stories, but the prince had made it clear to his closest courtiers that he didn't trust Amelia to tell him that grass was green or that the sky was blue. There was no possible way he'd listen to her advice for choosing a knight commander.

"Do you think you know a worthy candidate?" she asked warily, hoping he wouldn't suggest himself.

"It is not for me to say," he responded readily, to Amelia's deep relief.

On the other side of her, she heard Kirsten sniff quietly, a disapproving sound. The duchess's handmaid was politely keeping out of the conversation, but it seemed she suspected the viscount's motives as well.

"But there is something you do wish to say?"

"When we marched with Prince Mercad, Sir Carron knew to keep order among the knights and to look to the lords of the Reach for the lay of the land. None of these things are happening on this march."

"Perhaps the prince is simply turning to others whom you don't know."

"I've spoken with many Reachermen of noble rank, Your Grace. Not one has been consulted. I don't doubt our prince. His royal bearing is unmistakable. But we nobles, for all our birth, we are..."

The viscount paused, apparently reaching for the right word. Amelia didn't envy him. Regardless of rank, no one in the

Grand Kingdom was supposed to show misgivings for their superiors. She had exactly the same problem with Daven Marcus. He was prince and free to mistreat her any which way he chose.

"Speak with care and I promise to hear you," she said, turning to him. For the first time on the march, she regretted wearing her lace veil. She wanted to look him in the eye to show her sincerity.

"We nobles are like eagles," he said at last. "We are proud creatures by nature, preferring our own nests. We do not do well gathered as a flock. Although we long to hunt our Grand Kingdom's enemies, if we are not shown a strong hand by the falconer, our eyes turned by hoods and blinders, then we will tear at each other and even at our rightful masters. We are loyal, but we require a firm hand. Do you understand my meaning, Your Grace?"

Amelia put a hand to her mouth to stifle a gasp. Wolden's words made perfect sense and were an excellent metaphor for the behavior of nobles in the court, but that wasn't what shocked her. When the prince had arrived at her castle in Dweltford, she had experienced a terrifying vision during his welcome feast. Amelia had seen the great hall torn apart by strange, supernatural beasts, all doing battle with each other, and amidst the melee, she had seen the prince and his entourage transformed into strange, eagle-like birds, sickly and mad, tearing at each other. Viscount Wolden brought the vision back into her mind so forcefully that it was almost like being slapped in the face. She sniffed and blinked her eyes to keep tears from forming. It might be forgivable for a mourning widow to weep in public, but Amelia didn't want to show any sort of weakness so close to the prince. It would only encourage his cruelties.

"Have I offended you, Your Grace?" asked Wolden and Kirsten sniffed again.

Amelia straightened herself in the saddle and squared her shoulders, rubbing quickly at her eyes beneath her veil. "Do not concern yourself, Viscount," she said quickly. "A sudden memory of my departed husband came upon me, nothing more."

Wolden seemed immediately embarrassed. "I will withdraw at once, Your Grace. With so many happenings in the Reach, it is too easy to forget you are yet in mourning. Please forgive me."

The viscount began to let his horse drop back, but before he had gone, Amelia turned to him.

"Thank you for bringing this to my attention, My Lord," she said. "I will think upon what you have said."

Wolden bowed his head once more, and when he was a sufficient distance behind them, wheeled his horse away to return to his appointed place in the column.

"Impertinence," Kirsten said when the viscount was gone. Her tone was harsh.

"You think so?" Amelia asked her.

"Of course, Your Grace. To ask for an audience while we are on horseback and then to present hogwash about the prince not leading properly. As if the crown prince of Rhales needs the advice of a hayseed frontiersmen to govern his court and his army."

Kirsten concluded her criticism with a huff that made Amelia want to smile. As a handmaid, it was part of Kirsten's duty to keep an eye on protocol and courtesy, but sometimes Amelia wondered if she was too fixated. Perhaps she was trying to protect her mistress. Amelia was only noble by marriage, after all. If she were too familiar with lower orders, it would merely feed the idea that she didn't deserve her rank as duchess. With court ladies like Countess Dalflitch mocking her at every turn, Kirsten's concern for the niceties might not be misplaced.

The cold breezes continued to buffet the march, and as she hunched in her woolen cloak, Amelia considered Viscount Wolden's concerns, one notion standing out particularly. He had spoken to many of the Reach nobles, and none were in the Prince's confidence. Wolden's worry was military. He and his fellow Reach aristocracy wanted their chance to find glory in battle. But as duchess, Amelia thought about the problem politically. The Reachermen were not being listened to by their prince. That was an opportunity. If she could make them feel that *she* listened to them, trusted them to act for the good of the Reach and the Grand Kingdom, then she would have another tool, another weapon in her battle with the prince. If she could cement their loyalty to her, then the prince would have to rely on her to call on them. For now, the prince took them for granted and took her for granted. She had no honor in Daven Marcus's sight. But if the Reach honored her—truly, devotedly honored her—then the crown prince would have to be more careful lest he generate more unrest in the Reach and lose half his army. At the very least, it might make him stop calling her a sow. When the army reached its camp for the night, while she was waiting for her baggage and tent to arrive, she planned her next moves.

CHAPTER 8

"Spears?" Yentow Sent, Prentice's master smith, spat out the word as if it tasted disgusting in his mouth. "For nearly a year I have traveled and waited for the silly special noblemen's license to make the finest swords this hinterland province has ever seen, and now you ask me to make mere sharpened sticks? Perhaps you'd like me to fashion a few pitchforks as well? My journeymen are the best weaponsmiths in the world, but I'm sure they can turn out a shovel or two, if you'd like!"

Prentice sighed heavily.

Yentow Sent had cause to be proud. He, his journeymen, and apprentices were undoubtedly the greatest weaponsmiths the Reach had ever seen, having come from lucrative and competitive markets in the far south. It was also true that they had been prevented from forging swords, specifically longswords, because such blades were reserved by Grand Kingdom law to be wielded only by men of the rank of knight or above. Sword-making was only legal for those smiths who had noble warrants. Prentice had one such warrant, signed and sealed by the duchess herself, so now, at last, Yentow Sent could forge swords on Kingdom territory.

But Prentice didn't need swords, at least not longswords. Longswords were the weapon of a knight. It took years of training to master those blades, certainly if you wanted to meet another knight on the field as an equal. Sir Gant, for example, had been given his first training blade before the age of ten. But Prentice remembered his dream. He needed to build a new kind of man-at-arms, one who fought completely as a part of his company, like the lions in the pride. And he needed a different set of weapons.

"Pikes, not spears," he corrected the angry smith.

"A difference without a distinction," came the reply.

Prentice drew in another breath and worked to calm himself. He looked around at the other faces gathered with him. Yentow Sent had his three journeymen. Sergeant Ranold and his senior corporal, Felix, were present, as were Sir Gant and Righteous. Prentice had gathered them to explain his plan for training the new militia. They were meeting on the one stone gallery of Fallenhill's burned-out keep. Once, the short tower had been a home for the baron and his family, but the invaders had torched it, along with the surrounding town. Its wooden floors were gone; now, it was just a hollow column of four walls open all the way to the sky. In the bottom, Yentow Sent had set his apprentices to clearing away the wreckage and setting up his new smithy and workshop. One floor above, reached by the keep's stone stairs that hadn't burned away, was this single gallery, running along the length of two of the walls. From here, they could look down at the rapidly forming smithy. Further along the gallery, the humble craftsmen had laid out their blankets and slept uncomplainingly upon the stone. When he'd first seen it, Prentice had wondered if everyone from Masnia in the south was so modest in their living conditions.

"We are in a siege, Master," Prentice told Sent, not for the first time in the meeting. "We need to make this rabble into an army and do it soon. I don't doubt your skill, and I mean no disrespect to your dignity. But I have to ask you for what I need, whether it challenges you or not."

Yentow Sent huffed, but before he could speak, Sergeant Ranold interjected.

"Perhaps if you could explain your plans in detail, it might make more sense. Could we go through it again?"

Felix and Gant made noises of agreement, and Righteous shrugged. Whatever happened, she was along for the ride. Sent's journeymen were utterly po-faced, but that was because they were waiting to follow their master's lead. When Sent finally nodded his agreement, the journeymen were equally willing to pay attention. Prentice crouched down, spread a sheet of vellum on the stones, and began to sketch his ideas with a charcoal.

"Like a lion, we hunt on the battlefield in a pride," he began and hoped he didn't sound crazy. His entire idea had come from a dream, given to him by an angel. A commander who thought he received messages from God had better be right, otherwise he was just a madman, and madmen made poor leaders. He pressed on. "We teach them all to fight together. No one leaves the safety of the pride. No wild charges and no honor duels."

Ranold and Felix seemed to have no problem with that idea, but Gant's lips twisted into a frown under his thick red moustache.

"When a lion strikes, it's claws first. That's the pike and halberd."

"Like the invaders from the west?" Gant asked.

"Longer," Prentice averred. "At least half as long again."

That troubled the knight. "A man can't wield a shield with a weapon like that."

"We won't use them."

All the trained men looked uncomfortable at that notion. Prentice tried to reassure them.

"The point is for them to engage their enemy at a range he can't hit back. And not one to one. Every man stands together to form a hedge, and behind him another row of steel, and behind them a third, fighting over the shoulders of the man in front."

"A wall of blades to fight through before you even get to the first man." Ranold and Gant nodded now, beginning to see the idea.

"What about a man in full steel?" asked Gant. "Plate and mail will take a battering, but the best knights, with the finest new plate, will be able to bully through even a host of blades, especially if they start hacking at the wooden hafts, say with a battle-axe."

"That's right," said Prentice as he kept sketching, drawing new figures in between the men he'd drawn wielding long polearms. The new ones had swords and shields. "Once a lion has bloodied its prey with its claws, when it is close, then it locks on with its fangs. That's our swordsmen—every third man in the front and second lines."

"You have swords in amongst the pikes?" asked Ranold. "How's that different from a crowd of knights? They all fight with whatever they like. That's not an ordered company."

"It will be the way we do it. We'll have them evenly spaced and they'll have one task only—to tackle the knights that get close. Like I said, no one charges off to their own individual glory. These swordsmen stay close, supported by their comrades with the poles. Claws bloody them, and the fangs bring down the prey."

"I thought you said you couldn't train proper swordsmen?" Sent chimed in, sensing the conversation coming back to his preferred topic.

"These won't be knights with longswords," Prentice assured him. "We couldn't train them, and even if we could, we couldn't afford to garb them. We don't have time or resources to make that kind of plate and mail."

"So how do they fight a knight in that kind of armor?" asked Gant. "You already admitted such a man could push past the pike and halberd."

"We give them shields, helmets, and brigandines. And we teach them to fight in amongst their comrades. A swordsman becomes a master by learning the skills for every condition. We don't have time for that, so we won't try. We'll teach them to fight in the pride, and first, to fight armor. They won't have longswords; that's a weapon for the open field. The fangs will fight in the press of the company. They'll need long blades but single-edged for chopping, with strong points for thrusting through seams and joints. No flourishes, no artifice, just coldly calculated techniques. We keep it simple and make sure they master that simplicity."

"It could work, I suppose," Gant agreed, showing no enthusiasm for the idea.

Prentice looked to Ranold and Felix. They seemed equally unenthusiastic.

"Maybe," said the sergeant with a shrug.

Suddenly Righteous chimed in. "'Course it'll work," she said with her usual bravado. "It'll be like an alley fight when the walls are tight on both sides. Fancy techniques don't count for nothin' then, I swear. In *that* close, it's speed and reach every time. Four times out of five, even strength don't come into it! I've taken out bulls two and three times my size in places like that."

Prentice smiled and felt a surprisingly deep admiration for the girl brawler. For all her brash manner, he knew she was telling the truth because he'd seen her do it. She'd even saved his life that way once.

"Perhaps you are right," Sir Gant nodded.

"Of course, I'm right," said Righteous. Prentice watched the men around him share a look. Righteous was always defiant, sensitive to any possibility of disrespect, even though she had already proved herself so many times, especially to Prentice. He wondered if there was some way he could show her he respected her so she'd stop being so belligerent before she caused real trouble that he'd have to deal with.

"Do your lions roar?" asked Yentow Sent, cryptically. The question brought the last words of Prentice's dream back to his mind in a rush.

"I don't know," he said distractedly, staring at his drawings and trying to fit the concept of a lions' roar into his plan. "We need to learn what it means to hear the lions' roar."

Yentow Sent spoke quietly to one of his journeymen in the lilting Masnian tongue. The man nodded and went off. Prentice barely noticed him go.

"What does it mean to hear lions roar?" asked Sir Gant, picking up the question. Righteous and Ranold had nothing to say about it.

Felix was more in tune with the idea. "Lions don't roar on the hunt," he said. "They roar to announce their rule, mark their territory. It scares away other hunters and terrifies their prey."

"Don't that just make them run off?" asked Righteous.

"Sometimes, but some prey freezes. I don't know the whole of it, just what I heard from a rover once in a tavern."

"Mark their territory before the prey even sees them," Prentice mused, and they all looked to him, waiting for an explanation. "During the Battle of the Brook, there was a moment when the two forces paused, lining up to face each other."

"I remember," said Sir Gant. That was the stage of the battle just before he'd lost his squire, the enemy hacking the poor youth to pieces.

"And when we were there, Turley said that all we needed was twenty or thirty crossbows to turn the tide. We could have driven them back before they even got to pike distance, before the claws even struck. We could've roared at them!"

"With crossbows?" asked Sergeant Ranold. His skepticism was obvious. "Not only do you want to mix swords and pikes, but you want crossbows to march beside them?"

"Not beside," said Prentice, warming to the idea. "With them, in the ranks."

"That's madness."

"Perhaps not in the ranks, not to shoot. But they could stand to the front or on the sides, and then if they face a charge, they can retreat into the body of the company. When the enemy withdraws to reform, the crossbows come out to roar again and harry them away. Would you want to reform a charge under bow shot?"

Ranold shook his head.

"You don't want crossbows," said Yentow Sent flatly and with such certainty that every eye turned to him. His long index finger stroked the side of his nose thoughtfully.

"I think I do," Prentice replied, feeling his irritation rise again. Sent *and* Righteous? Did he have *any* close underlings who wouldn't contradict him constantly. Sent held up a hand.

"I can do better for you. A true roar, as of a kingly lion."

Everyone watched the smith, waiting for his explanation, but the Masnian only stood silent, patiently waiting for his journeyman to return. When the under-smith returned, he was carrying a heavy object wrapped in a felt blanket. He hefted it up the stairs and presented it to Sent, who pulled back the cloth with a flourish.

"This."

It was a long piece of wood, carved like the body of a crossbow, but instead of cross arms and a bowstring, it had an intricate trigger mechanism, wrapped with a long string, and a slender steel cylinder on top. It took a moment's examination, but Prentice soon devised its purpose.

"A hand cannon?" he said, almost incredulous. Cannons and bombards were not unknown to the Grand Kingdom, but they were always seen as weapons of siege—slow to move and difficult to aim. Attempts to produce versions that could be carried by a man to the field had met with mixed success. If an iron ball from a hand cannon struck home, it slew a man outright, or could easily tear a limb away. But cannonballs were heavy, and the time it took to load the next shot was far too slow. Grand Kingdom armies disdained such weapons as more trouble than they were worth.

"This is something new," explained the weaponsmith. "It is called a serpentine."

Looking closer, Prentice realized there were clear differences with this new weapon. Normally, a hand cannon was a short, fat tube of iron or bronze, about the length and width of a man's forearm and usually mounted on a long staff for aiming. The typical device was heavy and unwieldy. This weapon that Sent called a serpentine had a much longer and thinner barrel and was more like a heavy crossbow, which would potentially be much easier to use.

"It must fire a small ball," Prentice mused. "How much use is a mere pellet of iron?" He looked at the other fighters around him. Felix and Ranold had no opinion, and Righteous was only mildly curious. Sir Gant showed the contempt that all Kingdom knights had for weapons of range. A man of birth fought face-to-face in the Grand Kingdom.

"Let me show you," said Sent, and he proceeded to lead them down to the ground floor where with a few quick instructions, he had two pieces of flat steel, each the thickness of a knight's breastplate, leaning against a strawbale. With his typical deliberate manner, Yentow Sent poured grains of a dark powder down the barrel of the serpentine, followed by a piece of rag and finally a small iron ball. He used a long poker to hammer the whole mix into the bottom. Then he lit the long string from a reed-light an apprentice brought to him. Apparently soaked in some kind of fuel, the string formed a long-match that smoldered away, neither burning out nor bursting into full flame. When he was ready, he turned to Prentice.

"Take your charcoal, if you would, Captain," he said, "and mark a cross on the steel for me to aim at."

Again, Prentice was surprised to hear himself addressed by rank, but he quickly went to the front plate and put a charcoal cross on the steel.

"Now, if you would stand back."

When Prentice was out of the way, Sent hefted the serpentine to his shoulder, exactly as a crossbow was aimed.

"For a long battle, a pole can be used to rest the barrel and reduce the weight," he explained. "For this demonstration, I can hold it."

Yentow Sent sighted along the barrel, and everyone present watched to see what would happen next. The smith clasped the trigger lever, and the spring-loaded mechanism thrust the burning end of the long-match into a pan with a small amount of the powder in it. There was a small flash and puff of smoke and then suddenly a loud retort, like a roll of thunder cut short or the loudest kind of crack of a log on a fire. Smoke burst forth from the barrel, and the sound echoed around the stone walls of the keep. High above, roosting birds took flight in panic. As the smoke cleared, Sent put the serpentine on the ground and smiled at the others. When they met his eyes, he nodded in the direction of the steel plate. They looked, and there were quiet gasps of surprise and appreciation.

There was a hole punched through the plate steel, no more than a finger's length from the charcoal X. Prentice went there and put his finger through the hole. The edges were jagged and sharp. He pulled the first plate back and found the second had a heavy dent. If the second one had been a piece of armor on a man's chest, that man was surely knocked off his feet and maybe even had a broken rib to boot. But the man who wore the first piece was dead, his heart or lungs pierced by a single steel ball the size of a child's marble. Pulling the two plates apart further, he found the little ball sitting on the ground, deformed by the force of its impact.

"That's an accurate shot," said Felix, coming with the others to examine the damage to the target. "I'd accept that as accurate from a marksman at that distance."

"And I am far from an expert shot," said Sent. He projected a smug satisfaction, and all his underlings were smiling. They were all proud of the serpentine and what it could do.

"How accurate is it?" asked Prentice, twisting the deformed shot in his fingers thoughtfully.

"Out to a hundred paces," Sent said confidently. "And I am sure a man practiced in the use could load and shoot at least as fast as a crossbowman."

Prentice did calculations in his head. Against a charge, that might mean two rounds of shooting before the enemy closed the gap. Men with these could fire their weapons twice and then retreat into the body of the pikes, halberds, and swords for protection. And that was assuming that a charging enemy formation wasn't simply brought to a standstill by iron shot ripping into them. Horses could probably run them down in the reload time, but how many horses would charge into a burst of fire and smoke like that?

"How many of these can you make?"

"How many do you want?"

"Twenty. Twenty per hundred men."

"You have two thousand men. That's four hundred serpentines."

"Can you make them?"

"As long as we have steel to work with, and time. Then there's the alchemy of the powder. I know the secret, but it is not simple to produce."

"Do whatever you have to." Prentice looked back at the punctured steel. This was the lion's roar; he was certain of it. He wondered if he would have time in this siege to master it. If he could bring such weapons to bear against Baron Liam, then the knight's advantage would be significantly reduced. He looked back and saw Sir Gant staring in disbelief at the same spot. Gant frowned when Prentice met his gaze, and Prentice nodded. As impressive as seeing the damage here was, he knew Gant was imagining what it would be like to feel that ball pierce your breastplate and make a ruin of your chest. He hoped when the time came, the knights following Baron Liam would be similarly shocked.

CHAPTER 9

Duchess Amelia felt a little sorry for her head steward when she told him her plan. If she wanted to woo the loyalty of the Reach nobles, she had to make a show of her respect for them. Since her husband died, she had only reacted to circumstances, responding to the actions of different powerful men. First, she had marched with Crown Prince Mercad to defend the Reach. Then, she had been shut out of her town and castle by Sir Duggan's treachery. Prince Daven Marcus had put an end to that, only to become the worst tyrant of them all. When she thought about it, she felt a little like a dumb cow being led around passively by a ring in her nose. It must seem like that to the nobles of the court, especially Daven Marcus's cronies, and those trying to curry his favor, but it wasn't even remotely true. What she needed now was a way to show it. To that end, she planned a feast for the Reachermen, and that was the plan that was giving steward Turley such a headache.

Armed with nothing but the duchess's authority, he had to acquire meat and drink for hundreds, along with a way to cook it and serve it. At the end of the first day after she had told him what she wanted, he reported back to her with bad news.

"You're saying it can't be done?" she asked him.

"I'm saying it can't be done tonight, Your Grace," he said. In spite of his apologetic demeanor, he still had his characteristic gleam in his eye. "Not tomorrow night neither, if I'm honest. But with a bit more time, your feast will happen."

"Because you can't get meat and drink?"

"Nor means nor men to cook it and serve it."

"Does Her Grace not have a household of servants with her?" Kirsten asked in some disbelief.

"Her Grace has servants enough to serve her and her needs, not to feast a hundred or more knights," Turley answered. "And where do we sit them? Did you see a stack of banquet tables in the baggage train? We're more than seven days walk straight west from the Dwelt. A fast rider might get back to the castle in Dweltford in three days, probably four, but then there'll need to be time to get things ready, and then there's the slow walk to catch us up while the prince leads us ever westward."

Kirsten sniffed in offense at being spoken to so rudely by a servant, but Amelia had to grant the soundness of Turley's reasoning.

"Can nothing be purchased from the merchants already with us?" she asked without acknowledging her displeasure.

"Some, but most of what's here is already spoken for."

"Does my name count for nothing? Is there no merchant seeking the favor of his ruling lady?"

"There's talk as how you don't have much like for merchants, Your Grace," Turley said, and for once he seemed genuinely shamefaced. "Most think it's 'cause of the merchant cabal that were in bed with Sir Duggan's conspiracy, but others say you must be ashamed of your heritage, being a duchess but born low."

"Impertinence!" Kirsten hissed. The handmaid started forward a step and Amelia wondered for a moment if she was going to hit Turley, but she recovered herself and merely glowered at the steward. "Who are you to speak so?"

"It's not my words, Your Grace," Turley answered the question as if Amelia had asked it. "I'm only telling what's being said."

"And you repeat this blather in Her Grace's presence?"

Amelia wondered if Kirsten was offended by the words because they were an insult to her nobility or because they made a kind of sense. After all, what Kingdom noble who had risen from the common ranks would want to be reminded of the fact? A merchant's daughter turned duchess? Wasn't that the basis of the prince's contempt for her?

"But the worst thing is coin, if you'll forgive me, Your Grace. I'm offering your word and your credit, which is all good, by and large, but the prince is paying silver. And silver guilders speak to a merchant's heart. Sure, they do."

"The prince is paying silver," Amelia repeated.

My silver, she thought. *He's buying the Reach right out from under me and using my coins to do it.*

For a long moment she sat and watched the firelight shadows through the cloth wall of her tent while a soft rain was falling outside. That was another issue she'd have to deal with. With his vast pavilion, Daven Marcus could feast fifty every night, and if he wanted to make a more impressive display, he could no doubt rearrange his tent to fit twice or even three times that. She had no such shelter in which to host her feast, and a rainy night after a winter day's march was not a pleasant time for an open-air banquet.

"Am I making a mistake, trying to do this?" she asked. Kirsten obviously thought it a rhetorical question, politely not answering. Turley took her words at face value.

"I wouldn't say so, Your Grace," he said, his expression again showing its typical swagger. "Just will need some planning and some finagling is all."

His confidence made her smile.

"I'll leave you to it then, Steward," she said, dismissing him. He tugged his forelock and left her tent. She heard Kirsten tut under her breath as he left. "You don't approve of him?"

"Forgive me, Your Grace," Kirsten said. "But you allow him to be too familiar."

Amelia frowned and looked down at the dresser next to her. On one side were her brush and combs, and her looking glass; on the other was a stack of paper and parchment, a pot of ink and two quills, freshly cut. An excellent metaphor for her place in the Reach and in the prince's court. On the one hand she was a duchess, a noble lady, meant to seek beauty and the things of a wife and, ideally, a mother. On the other hand, she was the liege of the Western Reach, her beloved husband's heir and, it seemed at times, the only one with any concern for his legacy.

Kirsten was correct, of course. She did allow Turley too much familiarity. But how could she explain to her perfectly polite handmaid that at this very moment she needed that familiarity. She needed someone she could trust and who would stand beside her, lend her their strength, even when she was too weak to be Duchess of the Western Reach, noble and imperious. Often, that was when she needed their strength the most. More than anything, she longed for someone who could stand beside her, stepping in close when she needed and then stepping back when rank required. Prentice knew how to do that, and she missed him terribly. The truth was, she longed for a husband, a companion against the depredations of life. As she thought about it, she realized that if he were not such a vile monster, she would have accepted Daven Marcus's proposal without hesitation. If he were even half the man a prince should be, she would throw herself at his feet and all but beg to be his. And she was even willing to marry him now, venal brat that he was, for the sake of the Reach and to protect her people. First though, she had to consolidate her own power. In her heart she was sure that was the only language the prince would ever understand. Love was no more than a game to him, as was war and rulership. Only naked power would give him pause, she hoped.

"Let's set to making our guest list," she said, turning her mind to the next task in her plan.

"Will there be any Rhales nobles invited?" Kirsten asked in a studiously neutral tone.

Amelia turned and saw that her handmaid had taken up embroidery again, sewing pink roses onto a length of linen—cloth for her wedding. Since assuring Kirsten that she would seek a member of the prince's court as a suitor for her, Amelia had barely given it another thought. She felt a pang of guilt and realized that she was failing in her duty to the young woman. Kirsten was on the looking glass side of the dresser, one of Amelia's duties as a lady.

"Well, we will have to invite his highness as a matter of protocol," she said, smiling. "Perhaps we should send to the herald of the march for the full list of members of the court to see who else might wish to attend a feast to celebrate the heroes of the Reach."

"As you wish, Your Grace," was all Kirsten said in response, not looking up from her stitching.

Amelia was sure she saw the girl smiling to herself, though. She pulled a new letter sheet and opened the ink. The next thing to do was to pen the request to the herald of the march and devise some appropriate gift to send with it. For all that they despised the grasping greed of merchants and the lower classes, every nobleman of the Grand Kingdom expected to be shown respect with gifts equal to his station. Amelia could not help but sneer inwardly. You could not buy a nobleman, but you could certainly bribe yourself one, as long as you called it a gift.

CHAPTER 10

"**N**ever get yourself involved in a winter siege."

Prentice could see Ranold was uncomfortable, and he knew it wasn't because of the small force encamped in front of the gate at the bottom of the slope. The hundred or so knights who'd ridden up with Baron Liam had been joined by an equal number of household guards and lesser men-at-arms, ranking commoners trained for war, but not high enough born to win a knight's spurs and ride a horse into battle. The whole force had set themselves to guard the front gate, sitting in bright tents beneath their war banners. For days they had done nothing else but set up their camp, arranging the space to their liking, making sure they had fuel for their bright and warm fires and shelter for themselves and their horses.

Kingdom knights always enjoyed comforts when they could, but Prentice knew there was another reason for this patient approach. It was winter, and just as Ranold observed, a winter siege was bad business. Usually, it was as bad for the sieging army as it was for the besieged. Sickness could rip both sides to pieces without either of them ever having to face each other in battle. Even the most well-prepared sieges became a race between hunger within the walls and infirmity without. And this was far from a well-prepared siege. Prentice and Ranold were doing an accounting of their position, and Prentice knew Baron Liam must have done a similar assessment in recent days. Much as he loathed the baron, Prentice had no illusions about the man's skill as a warrior and leader in war. Liam must know what he and Ranold knew, his two-and-a-half-thousand would-be soldiers had nothing like the stores they needed. Prentice had hoped for Liam to spend the winter healing and moping, but the baron had found him in less than a month.

"Digging out the wells will only take a couple of days," Ranold said. The two of them were standing on the ramparts over the town gate. In front of them was Liam's camp, behind them the ruined town with its long stone barracks with leaky peat roofs. Fallenhill's old wells were all silted up and full of fire wreckage. Prentice's people had been fetching their water from the nearby streams. Now that they were shut behind the walls, they needed the wells functioning again as quickly as possible.

"Good. Pretty soon we'll have to get to work slaughtering the livestock."

That made Ranold frown.

"You're sure you want to kill the lot right now?" As a mercenary campaigner he knew that meat on the hoof was easier to keep.

"Not all, but much of it," said Prentice. "Even if we wanted to keep them, we can't feed them all. There's a little grass in here, but hardly any straw or grain."

"We're going to want that grain for ourselves," Ranold agreed. "But even if we slaughter the lot, how do we keep it? We haven't anything like the amount of salt we'll need."

"We'll have to set up a smokehouse. At least we won't want for charcoal."

"We'll be needing that fuel for our hut fires, too, before the winter's out."

Prentice looked down, kicking his toe at an uneven flagstone and shaking his head thoughtfully. He had a myriad of problems and most had their own simple solutions, but every one of those solutions was thwarted by his one main problem—the patiently set up camp of knights downslope from his gate. Yes, Baron Liam knew his business very well.

A chill wind blew across the battlements, and the two men looked west to see a new bank of dense grey cloud blowing in. There'd be more rain soon.

"How are we doing with corporals?" Prentice had ordered the two thousand men split into forty contingents of fifty men each. Over each contingent was a corporal, chosen from Ranold's mercenaries, or in a few cases, one of Prentice's own men who were known as the Rats of Dweltford.

"Fifty men's as many as I'd like for a corporal. So far, they're keeping order, but like you said, everything's nice and easy for now. Once we're all hungry, once you start rationing...?" The sergeant shrugged.

"We'll need to keep them busy."

"In the rains of winter? Good luck with that."

Prentice appreciated Ranold's honesty. The man was a mercenary, and as long as he was paid, he'd accept almost any orders, but he wasn't afraid to speak his mind and share his experience. Prentice knew the theory of war as well as any man; before he'd been accused of heresy, convicted, and transported, he'd trained at the famous Ashfield Academy, which produced the knights of the church. And there had been no better student than Prentice. Nonetheless, he had only ever experienced war as a convict, a part of the rogues foot, thrown into battle like fodder for knights. He needed the experience of men like Ranold, who'd led men and fought from the position of command.

"We'll have to give them tasks and march them everywhere we can. Every time the rain stops, I want them out marching, even if it's just up and down and around the walls."

"Be a dog's breakfast, you know."

"At first," Prentice agreed, but he was sure this would help with another part of his plan. He wanted soldiers who could maneuver on the battlefield in complex patterns. The way he imagined his company fighting meant he needed to be able to line them up precisely and position them with flawless timing. If they were all used to fitting in with each other in the confined space inside the walls, then that would be good practice. On the other hand, it might just lead to frayed tempers and fist fights, or worse.

"And last thing, you sure about the fetters?"

Since arriving, not one of the convicts had been kept on a chain, but they all still had their shackles on their ankles. A convict would wear those iron shackles for the duration of his conviction. They were bound with a forged link, and it took a smith's hammer and chisel to remove them. Prentice knew from experience there was nothing a convict hated more as a symbol of his condition than those fetters, with their ring for a chain to go through.

"We're all in this together now," he told Ranold. "If those knights get in here, they'll put us all to the sword, convict and free man, with no distinction. I want them all to know that I'm in here with them."

"You're not worried?"

"About what? Escape? Baron Liam's made it clear what he thinks of any convict trying to flee! We don't need to work too hard to keep them here."

"You don't think familiarity will breed contempt?"

"Knights march farthest and fight hardest for the kings that share the hardships of the march with them and fight in the front rank."

"These men aren't knights," said Ranold. "And, begging your pardon, but you're no king."

Prentice smiled ruefully. "True enough, but the principle's the same. The lions that lead the pride are the strongest, the most powerful. Knights and nobles know that, but they hide from it behind laws that say only the highest born can ride a horse or wield a longsword. Those men down there, my men, have already shown they don't respect law. So, we teach them to respect strength, and we show them it's worth their while."

"And we do that by cutting their shackles off?"

"That's one way. We'll find others."

"So how do you want to do it? Just line 'em up?"

Prentice thought about it. As he watched the little encampment in the middle of the burnt ruins and felt the first whispers of rain blowing in, he noticed the slight, strawberry-headed figure of Righteous making her way to the wall. His mouth twisted in a half smile.

She always makes me smile, he thought and wondered why for a moment. He turned back to Ranold.

"We'll make it a reward. Tell every corporal to arrange his contingent into five ranks of ten men each. Each rank picks a first from amongst themselves. The first's job will be to help keep order. He sees that his ten are looked after and that every task given to his ten gets done."

"A corporal under the corporals?"

"We'll call them firsts for now. Once they're picked, the corporals have to teach their fifties to line up straight and march in ranks," Prentice explained.

"Easy enough."

"And challenge enough, for some. Once they get that done and can march across from the west wall to the east, then they get to march straight to Yentow Sent's workshop and have their fetters off. But don't tell them that, not until they do it the first time. Just say that there's a reward."

"The reward for acting like a proper set of recruits is to stop being treated like convicts? Good thinking. That could properly work." Ranold nodded approvingly.

"If we want lions, we need to give them cause to rise to it. If we keep treating them like rats and curs, they'll only ever act that way."

"I'll pass the word and we'll see who can get his fifty set right first." Ranold turned to go. As he left, Righteous came up behind him and the two swapped places on the rampart.

"You need to come with me," she said without preamble.

"Is that right?" Prentice found Righteous an unexpected pleasure, bringing a smile to his face almost reflexively, but at moments like this her brashness also annoyed him. Couldn't she see he needed to be respected?

Prentice was fairly sure what he liked about her. She'd once been a pit fighter for noblemen who enjoyed the decadence of two half naked women fighting for their entertainment. Even after being convicted and transported, not to mention raped by a pack of convict overseers and hiding as a boy amongst men, she still had a belligerent spirit ready to fight the whole world. She was a true wild thing and would die before she ever let herself be fully broken. Her heart resonated with the same inner fury as Prentice's, it seemed to him—the will to never yield. Nonetheless, her quarrelsome attitude and lack of respect, especially in front of others, gave the wrong impression. It made him look weak, and as he'd just been discussing with Ranold, lions don't follow weakness.

"You coming?" Righteous had made to go and seemed surprised that he wasn't following.

"If you want me to do something, then you need to do two things," he said to her. It was time to set her straight.

"What's that?"

"You call me captain, and you ask."

"And if I don't?" she asked bluntly. Her expression was openly angry, much angrier than usual. It was an odd day when Righteous wasn't looking for a fight, but Prentice could see that this was something else. Still, he pressed the point.

"You'll do it, or you can go out the gate and make your own way in the world." He looked over the battlement at Liam's camp. "Perhaps the baron needs a washerwoman. You could ask him."

"Never," she said through gritted teeth, eyes flashing fury.

"Then you know what to do."

Righteous sucked her teeth and her eyes narrowed even further as she stared at him. She looked to be assessing how serious he was and weighing whether she wanted to make a fight of it. The wind blew a wave of raindrops through the air between them. Soon enough the coming storm would be pelting the battlements, but Prentice refused to move a single step, his eyes fixed on hers. At last, she nodded.

"Captain," she said coldly, "please would you come with me? There's something you need to see."

"Lead the way," said Prentice.

Righteous scowled as she turned, and Prentice felt himself release a breath. That had gone better than it could have, and he realized that the idea of her leaving the camp had disconcerted him. Even with her belligerence and disrespect, he did not want to lose her. The idea genuinely unsettled him.

He followed her as she left the battlements.

CHAPTER 11

"Are you going to tell me what's going on yet?" Prentice asked Righteous. She shook her head and kept marching ahead. Soon, they were walking between the huts, and the rain came in full, thumping dully on their roofs.

"Just in here," Righteous insisted. She pushed aside the leather curtain that covered one hut's entrance and ushered him inside. It was dark, with just a few tallow candles for light in the overcast afternoon. The entrance was on the end of the long, narrow hut, so that the walls made a corridor-like barracks that stretched some distance into the gloom. There was enough space for rush-and-straw mattresses to line the walls and leave a tight passage to walk down the middle. The roof was not high enough to stand, so they both stooped.

"This is the women's hut," Prentice said.

Righteous only nodded and offered no more explanation. Instead, she waved for him to follow her, leading him past the rows of empty bedding. About three hundred of the convicts under his command were women, and they had fallen naturally to the tasks of womenfolk in any settlement. Without needing orders, they had begun cooking and sewing, tending to camp chores. They had naturally congregated together in this hut, the first one built, and the arrangement suited Prentice's plans fine. As he followed Righteous further inwards, he could see that one or two women were in bed, but that was to be expected.

Among more than two thousand convicts, some were always going to be sick. With winter still coming on, he hoped they weren't a precursor of many more. He wondered if that was what Righteous wanted him to see, but she didn't stop for them.

Farther still there was a clutch of women bent over, one holding a tallow candle melted in place on a plank of wood. In their midst was another woman, lying down on a bed of rushes. As Righteous and Prentice approached, the women made space, and Righteous knelt next to the one on the bedding. She spoke softly a moment and then gestured for Prentice to join her. He went down on one knee.

"This is Tressy."

Tressy was a scarecrow-thin creature, clad in the typical rags all the convicts wore. Clothing would have to be another priority. Every convict had a blanket now, but that wasn't going to be enough indefinitely. Tressy had one piece of linen wrapped around her shoulders like a shawl and a blanket of wool across her legs. Someone was going without their blanket for this woman's good. Tressy's hair was a dark mat of a color Prentice couldn't really make out in the poor light. She had a patch of cloth pressed to the right side of her head and face, and it seemed wet. It took a moment to realize it was a poultice, doubtless made of some mix of herbs by the women around her.

"Are you hurt?" he asked.

Tressy nodded.

"Show him," Righteous urged gently.

Tressy hesitantly moved the poultice aside to reveal a savage wound. With the light and the mess of the poultice, it was hard to distinguish at first, but slowly, Prentice came to see that it was two cuts. One started on her face and went up into her hairline. The other all but severed her right ear from her scalp. The flesh of it hung loose, and there was a smell of rot that didn't bode well. The longer he looked, the more Prentice became convinced that she'd lose her ear for sure, and that was only if the infection didn't take her life outright. The woman with the candle held it closer for him to see, and tears of pain that glistened in Tressy's eyes.

"She needs Fostermae's care," he said absently while he studied the injury.

"They wouldn't send for him at first," Righteous explained. "I made 'em though."

Prentice nodded. He had no disrespect for an herbalist's craft. He was satisfied the poultice would be a good one. Most goodwives knew some herbcraft, but this girl needed a healer's care if she was to survive.

"How did this happen to you?" he asked gently.

Righteous silently urged Tressy to speak, but the girl refused. She pressed the poultice back in place with a whimper and turned away.

"Her man done it to her," said one of the other women. "He found out she'd been laying with more than him, and he took it for an insult." They all nodded on Tressy's behalf. Prentice felt a sudden surge of fury.

"How's that?" he barked more harshly than he intended, and all the women around him flinched. In the face of their fear, Righteous took up the story.

"Lots of girls have taken to trading favors, giving what a woman gives to get a little more on their plates. A woman's got to survive in an army camp full of men. You can't be shocked by that, you being ten years on the chain. Convicts are no different!"

"What's his name?" Prentice demanded through gritted teeth, and he saw a strange mixture of relief and panic flow through the women's expressions.

"What do you want to know that for?" Righteous asked, eyes narrowed.

"So I can drag the bastard to the gates and geld him in front of everyone before I throw him over the wall!"

"You can't do that!"

"The hell I can't!" Prentice was already back on his feet and ready to charge out of the hut the minute he found out the man's name. Righteous also stood up, and as they both stooped for the sake of the roof, she looked him dead in the eye.

"You'll shame her!" she almost shouted at him, and Prentice was shocked to see his own emotions reflected in Righteous's expression. "Drag him out and he'll call her a whore in front of God and man. That's why he cut her face—to mark her so that any man about who sees her will know the story. And now she's got no beauty, she'll go alone for the rest of her life."

"'You'll die a spinster,' he said when he did it," Tressy said with a soft, shaking voice. "He said it's what a whore deserves."

The fury in Prentice burned, but it was a cold thing, like the driving wind and rain outside, but Righteous's anger was a scorching flame. It burned wherever it found fuel until it burned itself out, getting her into trouble. Prentice never let his emotions get him into trouble. The rage roiled inside him, but he could still think; it was a sword in its sheath, cold-forged, sharpened, and controlled—safe until it was drawn forth, and then there was blood. Looking from Tressy to the women trying to care for her and then to Righteous, standing against him without an ounce of fear in her eyes, he knew they were right.

"What do you want me to do?" he asked quietly, quelling his seething emotions under iron-hard control.

"First, of all, leave this bastard to me," said Righteous, and from her tone he could see she already had a plan. "And when it's done, trust me that it was done right and don't make a king's case of it."

Prentice nodded. He could see the poniard in Righteous's belt, the dagger he had given her when they were fighting in the streets of Dweltford. And he knew she could be trusted to take vengeance on Tressy's abuser.

"Next, let me teach the women to use a blade. Give them some tricks and ways to keep safe."

"You want to teach them to fight?"

"The men are learning. Why not the women? You think there aren't any out there now, wearing trousers and learning to march? There are lots of girls like Tressy, but I'll bet there's some like me, too."

Prentice nodded as he thought about what Righteous was saying. He didn't like the idea of women who were sleeping around being taught to think and act like street fighters. Some would surely be strong enough to hold their own, but he was training soldiers. Fighting men weren't going to back down just because their latest fancy waved a dagger in their face. The whole thing could lead to bloodshed, perhaps even a lot of bloodshed. Then he looked at Tressy and realized blood was already being shed. This was not a problem he had expected to have. He was trying to train an army, not set laws for a new settlement. He looked again at Righteous, and he knew he could trust her and how far. She was a child of violence, but she was no fool. He led her a short distance away, out of the hearing of the other women and spoke quietly.

"You know she might not live."

Righteous looked back toward Tressy. She shrugged. "No point worrying about that until it happens."

"Take out that poniard I gave you," Prentice told her, making his decision. Righteous drew her dagger. "You take that to Yentow Sent and tell him this is what I say. Any woman that comes to him and asks gets a blade like that the same day she asks. The cost comes out of my purse."

"And the other business?"

Prentice met her eyes. "You take care of it," he told her. "But you make it clean. Not torture."

"You happy with an execution?"

"Everyone here is a transported convict. And this? This calls for an execution. That's Kingdom law and Reach law."

Righteous nodded, an eager, predatory expression in her eyes. Prentice caught her by the arm.

"Mark me, make it clean, Righteous. I see any signs otherwise on the body, any indication you took an extra pound of flesh, and I'll teach you some of the lessons I learned at the hands of the Inquisition's interrogators. I promise you."

For the first time, Righteous's expression showed a moment of doubt, and Prentice knew she believed him. She might be a wildfire, but he was steel; fire did not frighten him. He moved back to Tressy and the women clustered around her. Kneeling, he put a hand on one of hers.

"Tressy, Righteous will explain what's going to happen now," he told her. "But when this business is done, I want you to look for a husband. No more doxy life. Find a man who'll have you and cleave to him. Sacrist Fostermae will do the vows for you, I'm sure. And if any show doubt because of your scars, you tell them you have a dowry of a hundred silvers to carry past their doubts."

"I don't have no dowry, sir," Tressy said back, barely more than a whisper.

"You do now," he reassured her. "It's sitting in the camp treasury, waiting for you and a husband." The women all looked at each other, astonished by Prentice's promise. He stood up and was about to go when Tressy called after him.

"Master Ash, sir, is it true that you used to call her Cutter?"

Prentice looked to Righteous and nodded.

"But now you call her Righteous? You gave her a new name?"

"That's true," he said.

"Can you give me a new name, like you gave her? A new name without the stain on it."

Prentice bowed his head for a moment.

"You don't need a new name, Tressy," he told her finally. "You just need..." He trailed off. He knew what she needed, but he couldn't give it to her. She had to find another man for that. He had duties to fulfil already, obligations to his duchess. He moved off, and Righteous followed at his shoulder.

"You couldn't give her a new name? Would it be that tough for you?" she demanded, but in a hushed tone.

"You earned yours," he answered. "Let Tressy earn hers."

"For a moment there I thought there might be a kind heart somewhere under all them scars."

"No. It's just scars, all the way down." He looked at her, and for a moment all the guardedness was gone between them. He was a man who had just had to order the death of one of those in his charge because of the abuses of another in his charge. And she was a scarred woman who wanted justice for a friend who was suffering as she herself had once suffered. It was as intimate a moment as Prentice had had since being transported west over the mountains.

You don't just make me smile, he thought. Then he pushed the leather curtain aside and stepped, blinking, into the rain.

CHAPTER 12

I t took four more days, but when it was done, Amelia was ready to swear that Turley was a miracle worker. The night before, he had asked her permission to take her baggage ahead, which she had given, even though the prince's heralds still had her people marching behind. For the whole day she had ridden Meadow Dancer and tried not to fret. She had no idea what exactly her chief steward planned, and knowing all the challenges he faced, she could only imagine failure.

What she found made her marvel.

First, the army camped early, barely the third hour of the afternoon. It was the earliest the column had stopped since they left the hunting lodge, and if Turley had made that happen, it was a wonder in itself. When she and Kirsten went looking for their tent, they found it set up some distance from the rest of the camp, near a stand of dead trees. Small stands of a half a dozen trees together were common enough in the grasslands, and these had clearly died many years ago; their wood was grey and hard. Somehow though, Turley had conspired to hang an array of cloths of various colors from their branches so that an effective shelter was created, a de facto pavilion that could comfortably keep more than a hundred people protected from the rain. Nearby to that, but a safe distance from cloth and wood, a fire pit had been dug, easily fifteen paces long, and there were already whole sides of beef and pork turning on spits being tended by potboys stripped to their loincloths against the heat of the coals.

There was only one table, and not a very long one at that, but it had a fine linen cloth, a candelabra with genuine wax candles, and a number of chairs. As soon as she saw it, Amelia realized she would sit as host and then have guests come and go from the other chairs throughout the feast. She could invite nobles to sit with her for a time. That befitted her station as ruler of the Reach, and she was pleased. One of the chairs would also have to be left empty for Prince Daven Marcus. He was invited as a matter of course. It would have been unforgivably rude to not invite the prince to a feast on his own march, but she didn't expect him to attend.

"Does it meet with your approvement, Your Grace?" Turley asked when he saw she had arrived.

"It's astonishing," she said earnestly, not even bothering to correct his misuse of language. The afternoon was already almost dark as night, the heavy clouds in the sky closing out the light. But looking up she saw a dozen oil lanterns hanging from the dead tree branches. At least one had colored glass that cast beautifully festive light. A thin breeze blew under the cloths, causing them to whip and flap, but when it passed, the heat of the firepit quickly reasserted itself. "It's like a winter festival of the fey."

"That's a fine thought, Your Grace."

"What do you think, Kirsten?"

"I think it will make for a pleasant evening."

It was sparse praise, but knowing how much she disapproved of Turley, Amelia was glad Kirsten afforded him even that much. She had few enough true allies on this march. The last thing she needed was for them to be at odds. If she could get Kirsten to see Turley's value to her, that would be a worthwhile effort.

"I made sure your chest is ready in your tent, Your Grace," Turley explained. "There should be time for you to clean away trail dust and change, if you felt the need."

Amelia heard Kirsten tut to herself and almost wanted to slap the girl. Yes, it was rude for a steward to discuss his mistress's ablutions with her, but he was being dutiful and serving her as well as he knew how. And he had achieved more than she had dreamed. Loyalty and service were worth more than good manners. She just wished she could persuade her handmaid of that.

Looking around herself one more time, she smiled. This would work.

"How many have accepted invitations?" she asked.

"I...haven't been able to make the numbers true, Your Grace," Turley answered, and his tone sounded embarrassed.

"Can you not keep a basic count?" Kirsten scoffed. If her contempt offended him, he didn't show it.

"I've kept a count to over seventy, fine folk and the like, but that's the only ones who sent replies by heralds or servants. A lot sent notes back, just like the invites you wrote, and I can't tell what they said, not always. I don't have my letters that good."

He couldn't read. Amelia gritted her teeth. Why hadn't she thought of that? Kirsten rolled her eyes with haughty disdain, and fearing she would say something cruel, Amelia spoke quickly.

"We'll have to see to that, won't we, Steward?" she said.

He tugged his forelock dutifully. "If you say so, Your Grace."

Dismissing Turley, she went to her tent to change. For the evening, she chose an overgown of heavy black velvet trimmed with white lace, but visible underneath was an embroidered shift in Reach blue and cream. On her head she wore a silver coif, held with a long, sapphire-topped silver pin. She contemplated wearing her lace veil but decided it would not suit the aim of the night's feast. Even though she still felt to mourn her husband, the point was to celebrate the strength of the Reach and its leaders.

"We must make sure you are dressed in your finest, too," she said to Kirsten as the girl wove her hair. "After all, you'll need the best arrows for your bow."

Kirsten smiled but did not say anything.

When both women were ready, it was just after sundown. Amelia led them back to the feast area. A fine, misting rain was falling, but thankfully there was little breeze to blow the drops under the canopy. Already, a crowd of nobles had gathered, all dressed in household colors and fine jewelry. Silver was the prevalent precious metal of the Reach, so most of the nobles wore it, but the richest had gold, and it marked them apart. Already some had plates with meat, and Amelia was pleased to note a few other foods, including cheese and some kind of bread. Turley had excelled with the menu as well, it seemed.

When she reached her table, she found Turley waiting by her chair. He pulled it out for her, and she sat herself down, projecting as much dignity as she could.

"Quite a number of the guests have asked to present themselves," Turley said quietly in her ear. "I didn't know if you wanted to eat first, Your Grace, but they've been pressing me something fierce. Like greedy piglets fighting to get at the teat."

It took all Amelia's self-control not to laugh. The image of the dignified nobles around her as greedy piglets was almost too much. Then she remembered the prince's insults, calling her a sow, and the urge to laugh died away instantly.

"Steward, you will not compare my guests, the worthies of the Reach, to farm animals," she rebuked him. Almost as soon as she said it, she regretted it. She sighed inwardly; she was too young to have to play the bitter dowager.

"I apologize, Your Grace," Turley replied, accepting her rebuke with a tug of the forelock, his tone not sounding in the least bit chastised.

His loyal good humor amused her, and this time Amelia allowed herself a little smile as she considered the main question. It would reinforce her rank in front of these men if she forced them to wait while she ate before speaking with them. Certainly, it was within her rights as the ruler of the Western Reach. But the point of this feast was to win the Reachermen more firmly to her side. Did they want to see a friendly face that put them first, or a stern face that held to its dignity? Unable to pick between the two options, Amelia decided to try for a measure of both.

"Fetch me a plate," she told Turley, "and let it be known I will receive guests in order of rank. You'll have to enforce that carefully. More than one will want to jump the line."

"Yes, Your Grace." Turley moved a step away and then stopped. "Uh...sorry, Your Grace but...the order? What order is that?"

Amelia nearly rolled her eyes and had to fight not to smile too broadly. It wasn't his fault. Why would a man of Turley's station know the differences between the noble ranks? But more than that, it delighted her to have someone near who wasn't watching every insignificant interaction of rank and who wasn't obsessed with every little advantage or slight, as she felt she had to be.

"Earls first," she told him. "Then viscounts and barons. Knights last of all." He tugged his forelock and turned away again. The Western Reach had only one earl, a handful of viscounts, and then a number of barons. After that were hereditary knights and the raised.

Of course, mere title was not always enough to measure a noble; a baron might have won more fame or served the Kingdom in a way that an earl might not, and that could complicate matters, but there was nothing Amelia could do until she had time to meet them all and assess them for herself. She was thankful that the prince and his court weren't likely to attend the feast. The differences in rank were even more complicated when comparing a Reach noble to one from the Western Court in Rhales, or even more so the King's Court

in Denay. A baron in Rhales was superior to a baron of the
Reach, but did that mean a Rhales baron was the equal of a
Reach viscount? And how did one compare the achievements
of a Reach noble who'd fought in battles against Vec invaders
to the tournament victories of a Rhales champion who'd never
seen war and therefore never been defeated in single combat?
It boggled the mind. When she thought about it, Amelia was
suddenly surprised—not that nobles fought honor duels to
resolve such questions, but that they weren't fighting duels
constantly.

Turley returned quickly with a silver plate bearing two slices
of roasted meat and a small roll of black bread. Using a silver
knife, she cut herself a sliver of meat and had just put it in her
mouth when she looked up to see Viscount Wolden standing
before her table. As their eyes met, he bowed low.

"Your Grace."

"Viscount? Are you the first to present yourself?" After
warning Turley to be careful, was the very first nobleman a
line-jumper?

"I have the sad duty to bring Earl Derryman's sincerest
apology, Your Grace," Wolden said with solemnity. "He is sorely
afflicted with the gout and is unable even to ride his horse. His
chirurgeon has insisted that he not leave his bed until the sores
are fully treated. He has asked me to attend in his stead, and so
I present his sorrow."

Derryman was the only earl in the Reach and would naturally
have been first to present himself. The viscount acting in his
stead was in the right position. Amelia turned to Kirsten, who
stood by her chair. The maid already had her own plate and was
picking at her food. Amelia wondered how she came by it; she
hadn't seen Turley fetch it for her.

"Kirsten, make note that we must send condolences to Earl
Derryman," she said loudly enough for anyone standing near to
hear. "He will be missed at this feast."

Wolden bowed again, formally accepting the compliment on behalf of the absent earl. The complexities of courtly behavior were never ending, it seemed.

"Lord Wolden, if you will accept my apology," Amelia went on, "I have not yet had a chance to speak with the prince on that matter you brought to me." In truth, she had no idea how to even raise it with the prince. It was another question that vexed her.

"I appreciate that you keep it in mind," Wolden replied. "I thank you for the generosity of your feast on this important march, Your Grace, and will make way for others to present themselves. Perhaps, if it suits you, we might speak again later."

"I look forward to it."

Wolden withdrew, and Amelia was pleased at his formality. Another nobleman, also a viscount, approached to present himself next, and he followed Wolden's example, being formal and precise. Reachermen had a reputation amongst Kingdom nobles for being ill-mannered and brutish, crass frontiersmen one and all. But receiving each noble in turn, Amelia was struck at how formal they were. She wondered if the viscount's example had set the standard or if the Reach had simply suffered an unjustified reputation.

CHAPTER 13

It seemed to take at least an hour, and the crowd at the feast had swelled significantly when Turley noted that the next in line to present themselves was a knight. Amelia raised her hand to signal the presentations should stop, at least temporarily. At her instruction, Turley used the hardwood rod he carried as a sign of his authority to bang loudly upon the table. The sound carried out into the night, stilling the voices around the feast. Every guest turned to look. When she was sure that everyone was looking at her, Amelia stood and surveyed them, forcing herself to meet their curious eyes in the lantern light and the flickering of the flames. She especially noted the few women amongst the crowd. Though the prince marched with his whole court, most of the Reachermen had not brought their wives with them, and none of the women at the feast had been presented to her yet. She didn't know any of them, and that saddened her. As duchess, she should have been receiving ladies and maids, seeing to the duties of a wife and mother for her duke. Instead, she was a widow on a military march, her second in a year, while trying to play politics to fend off the cruel advances of the crown prince of the realm. She missed her husband, and the pain of that was suddenly so fresh in her mind that she wanted to cry.

No, she told herself.

She had wept enough. Now she would be strong. Her lands depended upon it. These men and women in front of her depended upon it. In the Reach, they mined iron to make steel. As the duchess, she would be like that iron. Let her enemies beat upon her; she would be forged into steel.

She hoped.

"Noble Reachermen," she said, projecting her voice as loudly as she could, hoping it didn't sound as nervous in their ears as it did in hers. "I thank you for joining me tonight, and I apologize to you all."

That caught their attention. Amelia watched as many looked about themselves for a clue; what was she apologizing for?

"This meagre meal on such a miserable evening when we would all rather be by our hearths is poor thanks and deficient tribute. Wine should be spiced and warmed on a night like this. I am embarrassed to offer such a feeble shadow of a banquet to such worthy company."

She cast an involuntary glance at her steward when she said that, hoping he didn't take offence at her words. She didn't think this feast was a feeble shadow of anything; by her measure, Turley had achieved a minor miracle putting this celebration together while they all marched farther and farther west, beyond the frontier of civilization. But she was wooing her nobles, and that required flattery.

"But I remember my dear, beloved Marne and how he would have laughed to hear tell of hearths and spiced wine. He would have said this was a lovely night to be out and offered everyone another round of brandy. In a moment, we will broach some casks and drink to his memory."

Amelia was pleased to see many nod and smile at the mention of her deceased husband. It was his legacy she most wanted to preserve. Ultimately the Western Reach belonged to the Grand Kingdom, so as Prince of Rhales, Daven Marcus was its rightful liege, but Amelia was damned if she was going to let him treat her husband's people the way he treated his own courtiers, especially the women, and most especially the way he had already treated her. The Reach was a duchy because of the courage and skill her husband had shown in winning it. Prince Daven Marcus was a brat next to her Duke Marne.

"Some days I feel that I am too young to be a widow, but then I remember, I am not alone. None of us deserved to lose our liege so soon. He was taken from us, and if you have not heard, it was by treachery."

She paused a moment to let that notion grow in their minds.

"Poison," she declared loudly into the thoughtful silence. "Given to him by the merchants who conspired with the traitor Duggan."

There were angry sounds among the crowd at this revelation. By now the story of Duggan's betrayal would be widely known, but Malden and the other merchants' roles were something she had only learned herself very recently.

"A dog called Malden, one of those who stole Kingdom silver which our prince has reclaimed, used poison brought from far Masnia and planted in my beloved's food. I have judged him and sent for his head. His paid men are dead or on a chain already. Let the word go forth now. Tell your magistrates and remember when you yourselves sit in judgement over your lands. This is how the Western Reach answers treason. No man or woman stands above this law. What say you?"

The grumbles and sounds of anger grew louder. There were shouts for the merchant's execution, calls for hanging, for beheading, and judicial torture. Amelia watched, pleased at their reaction. For so long she had felt like an outsider among these people. They were born to the nobility, and she had bought her way in, at least that was how the gossip went. But this was something they could share, something they had in common—the love for her husband and the horror at the way he had been taken from life.

She took her cup from the table and held it up so that the firelight glimmered on its silver surface. When she was sure every eye was upon her, she turned the cup over so that the wine spilled out on the table and the ground. It was a nobleman's gesture of contempt, emptying your cup while this person was being discussed to show categorically that you did not drink with them or to them. You despised them too much to take the risk that someone might think otherwise. Amelia was delighted when she saw every Reacherman, man and woman, do the same, emptying their cups. She even saw one or two go a step further and invoke the more ancient gesture of taking a sip from the cup and then spitting it upon the ground before throwing the rest of their cup after it.

"Now let us drink and offer a prayer to the memory of our beloved duke," Amelia proclaimed, her voice echoing in the night. "May he dwell in the comfort of our Lord while his murderers burn in hell. Brandy, as he would have drunk on this perfect night to be abroad in his beloved Reach."

She nodded behind her, and Turley stepped up with a linen cloth over one arm and a silver-bound glass decanter in his hands. He filled her cup. Elsewhere among the feasting nobles, stewards and serving boys broached casks and filled every offered cup with brandy. During the planning for this night, when Turley had come to her to say he might be able to lay his hands on some casks of brandy, Amelia had remembered her late husband's fondness for the drink, and this toast had formed in her mind, this entire gesture. It pleased her no end to see it working. She waited patiently until every cup was filled and, despite the coldness of the wintery night, she felt warm in the love of her husband's people. Her people. Soon enough there were nods from the stewards to say that every cup was filled.

Amelia lifted her goblet and was about to toast her husband when a noise to her left caught her attention. She turned to see a pair of men in red and gold royal livery emerge from the darkness carrying a table. It was richly carved and covered in gilt. Without a word, they placed the table next to hers, then stepped away. They were followed by two other men, dressed the same, one carrying a throne-like chair to match the table and the other a red cloth, which he spread upon the tabletop after first wiping away the misting raindrops with his sleeve. It was clear these were royal stewards from the prince's household, and that meant the prince himself was joining them. Amelia lowered her cup. It would be rude to drink a toast now. She was sure that Daven Marcus had picked his moment deliberately, and it was all she could do to keep from cursing out loud.

The steady stream of royal stewards came back and forth until the royal table was set and ready for his highness. With gold cutlery and plates glinting on the red cloth, it seemed to glow in the firelight. Its richness made Amelia's own table seem beggarly by comparison. At last, the stewards ceased, and the empty chair waited. From the same dark edge of the feast, two heralds with brass trumpets in hand stepped into the light. Their tabards had the royal eagle stitched on the chest in gold. The two stepped up beside the newly set table and put their trumpets to their lips. A clarion blast rang out, so loud in the watchful silence that it hurt Amelia's ears and, despite her best efforts to keep her reserve, she flinched from the sound. As she did so, she realized that every one of the nobles around her were now watching in stilled silence. The prince had waited for the perfect moment and stolen the entire attention of the feast from her toast. It was at once a petty and brilliant move. When they had finished their fanfare, the paired heralds lowered their instruments.

"Attend now, attend," they shouted ritually. "The prince, Daven Marcus, Prince of Rhales, approaches."

Daven Marcus emerged from the night with the Countess Dalflitch on his arm. He wore a heavy, fur-lined winter cloak, pulled closely around his body, and a golden coronet on his head. Tiny, misting beads of water settled about him, causing the gold to glitter even more than usual in the firelight. Dalflitch also wore a cloak, but hers was open, revealing the richness of her dress beneath, a ruby-colored velvet with a neckline that plunged far more than was decent. About her neck the countess wore rubies, and diamonds hung from her ears. She was a picture of affluence and beauty, and Amelia churlishly hoped that the woman's indecent dress left her feeling chilled in the brisk conditions.

Knowing their courtly duty, every noble present went down on one knee. As a privilege of her rank, Amelia remained on her feet but bowed her head. When she lifted it again, she saw that the prince had arrived at the head of a small array of Rhales nobles, all of whom she had invited but none of whom had replied to her invitation. Another petty slight. She ignored them and moved to present herself to the prince, handing her goblet to Turley first.

"It is a pleasure to have you join us, Your Highness," she said, curtseying formally.

"Yes, I'm sure it is," he replied, looking down his nose at her. Amelia waited at the bottom of her curtsey, as politeness required. The prince did not give her leave to stand, instead surveying the gathered nobles for a long moment.

"God," he said at last, "isn't this a dismal little excuse for a revel?"

Amelia thought he was asking a rhetorical question, but when she looked up, she saw by his expression that he meant the question to be answered.

"It was the best that could be arranged on the march," she answered. Especially since the prince and his nobles were pouring money into merchants' coffers to make sure only they had the finest things available to the prince's army—money that was Amelia's by right, taxes embezzled by Duggan and Malden, which the prince had seized to line his own pockets. Amelia worked to keep her expression neutral, hiding her inner resentment.

"I suppose," the prince conceded with a sour expression. He looked down at Amelia again and seemed to notice for the first time that she was still curtseying, as were the entire company, all on one knee. "Oh, stand up, the lot of you."

Amelia straightened up. The prince took hold of his golden cup and waved it about ostentatiously.

"There was about to be a toast, wasn't there?" he asked loudly. "What are we drinking to?"

"Duke Marne, Highness," Amelia explained. "My late husband."

The prince cocked an eyebrow, as if puzzled.

"You do not think the first toast should be to the king? As his heir and emissary in all things in the west, I would be remiss to not remember my father's health and blessing first."

Amelia wanted to slap him. The only way he could know that they had not already toasted the king was if he had watched and chosen his moment specifically. He hadn't come only to steal attention away from the wayward duchess of the Reach; he was going to make sure he humiliated her as well.

"Forgive me, Your Highness," she said through gritted teeth, "I am remiss. Perhaps you would lead the toast to King Chrostmer, your father?"

"Of course, I will."

Amelia waved to Turley to fill the prince's cup. He moved forward to the prince and bowed his head, waiting for the cup to be offered. Daven Marcus rolled his eyes to his compatriots, as if being served by the duchess's steward was funny to him. Then, with the manner of a man indulging a precocious child, he held out the cup. Turley poured the brandy, then bowed again and stepped back. The prince sniffed at it.

"Ugh, I can't toast my dear father with that," he declared and tipped the whole cup on the ground. Amelia refused to feel the bite of this little insult, but she was surprised when she felt the shifting mood behind her. Could it be that they stood with her? When the prince insulted her, did they feel it too?

The prince waved for one of his own stewards to pour him a drink, and the steward filled the prince's cup with a rich, brown liquor. It was obvious this whole act had been staged. It would not have mattered what the duchess had served; Daven Marcus was going to find it beneath his dignity and throw it out. When his cup was filled, he lifted it. Turley moved quickly to hand Amelia back her cup so that she could toast with the others.

"My father, King Chrostmer the Seventh."

"The king!" toasted the assembly, including every one of the prince's entourage, who had all conveniently brought their own full cups. The only one who had no cup was the countess, who looked to the prince's cup as if expecting him to share with her, a most intimate act. The prince kept his cup to his lips however, draining it to the dregs. Since the prince drank his cup dry, protocol required that everyone present do the same. Daven Marcus smacked his lips loudly when he had finished drinking.

"Now, that's better. What were you going to drink to again, Duchess?"

"My husband," Amelia said quietly. "But it seems my cup is empty." It took all her will not to throw her goblet at him in a fury. Her fingers twisted around the silver stem until they ached.

"And you have no more? Oh well. Perhaps another time I shall invite you to a feast of mine and you can see how it's properly done."

Daven Marcus made his way to his chair and sat. He gave the golden plate to one of his stewards and the man ran to fetch fresh cuts of meat. Watching as the prince fussed over his fork and cup, making a show of ignoring her, Amelia realized that the evening's humiliations had just begun. Nevertheless, she made her decision. Let him do whatever he wanted to her; in her heart she was sure he had misjudged her nobles. Perhaps these shows of disdain and contempt impressed nobles from Rhales, perhaps even in the court of the king in Denay, but they had little currency with Reachermen. Amelia was almost certain of that. Even less than a year ago, the nobles of the Reach might have seen her as an upstart, a merchant's daughter who thought to buy her nobility. But now they would see her dignity in comparison to the self-indulgent privilege of the crown prince.

She was resolved. She was the Duchess of the Western Reach. When the prince insulted her, he insulted them, and they would stand with her, she would make sure of it. They would stand with her because she stood with them. All she had to do was make sure they could see it.

CHAPTER 14

Amelia watched the prince at his table, wondering at what he was doing. Even wrapped in his cloak and the simple lamplight, he was resplendent, surrounded by gold and red. As he picked unenthusiastically at the meat on his plate, she was struck with the thought that he had probably already eaten before coming. When he dropped his fork with an exaggerated sigh, as if the meat also was beneath his refined taste, she became sure of it. He had come to spoil the feast, not partake. He was here to play dog in a manger. The countess standing beside him leaned in and said something quietly in his ear. Whatever it was amused him, and he chuckled. Then he looked directly at Dalflitch, as if only just noticing that she was standing where she was.

"Grenough," he called to his steward, "the countess needs a chair. Fetch her one of those."

The prince waved at Amelia's chair and the one beside it. Without even looking, Amelia knew which one Grenough would pick. It would have been arranged beforehand. She watched as her seat was taken from her plain-looking table and placed next to the prince. He looked down on it, as if his steward had just placed a chamber pot next to him.

"I suppose it'll do," he said and gestured for Dalflitch to sit.

She giggled and carefully arranged herself in her cloak as she sat down so that her bust was still prominently displayed. She smiled as she pressed against the prince's arm. Amelia wanted to cringe. The woman was nearly thirty, if she was a day, yet she was giggling like a fresh maid and disporting herself like a tavern doxy. It made Amelia think of her own handmaid. Kirsten sought the attention of a worthy man, but even for the prince, Amelia was sure she wouldn't stoop to such a petty display. Casting a glance in her maid's direction, she saw that there was a puzzled look on her face. Perhaps Kirsten was shocked at the whole silly show. There were always rumors about the debauchery of the Rhales court. Certainly, the nobles that the prince had brought with him showed no disapproval, but from the expressions on the faces of the other Reachermen, Kirsten wasn't alone in her shock. Then, the mood soured further, and around her she heard displeased mutterings.

Looking back to the prince's table, she saw that he was standing again and had removed his cloak, ostentatiously throwing it at his steward. As he turned back, Amelia saw the front of his doublet and realized what had stirred everyone's ire. The elegant jacket was fine velvet, dyed royal red and deep, midnight blue in alternating squares. The red was from the royal heraldry and the blue was the Reach's own field color. Mixing heraldic colors was common when two noble houses joined together in marriage. By combining the two on his doublet, Daven Marcus was unsubtly announcing his intention to marry Amelia, bringing the Western Reach under the direct control of the royal house. But that was not the only heraldic message proclaimed in his clothing.

On the prince's chest was the royal eagle, stitched as usual in gold, with its wings spread wide in the elevated attitude. Underneath the eagle, the doublet continued its theme of melding two noble houses, as there was a white lion sewn there. But here, the marriage theme was given a sharp sting. The lion of the Reach was white and always portrayed rampant, rearing up in power. The lion on the prince's doublet was the right color, but it was dormant, lying down, with its head down, asleep.

As she looked, Amelia realized that the lion's tail had been tucked between its legs, the position called coward. No house willingly displayed that heraldry; it was forced upon nobles for acts of dishonor. Normally in a noble marriage, the heraldic animals would be displayed side by side, signifying the melding of the two family lines. By displaying the eagle above the lion, the prince was giving his family preeminence. That was not too controversial; after all, he was the crown prince. But by displaying the Reach lion dormant and coward, he was publicly claiming that the duchy was weak, lazy, and cowardly. He was insulting the duchess and everyone of her household, and by extension, every noble who owed her fealty.

In other words, every nobleman in the Western Reach.

Amelia could barely believe it as she watched Daven Marcus standing proudly, chest thrust out, letting the entire crowd see his insult. Surely, he didn't think such contempt would win their loyalty? She knew the prince despised her and loathed the Reach as anything but a resource to line his purse, but this was folly. Did he think he was putting them in their place? Amelia scanned the faces of the Rhales' nobles behind him, and their smug smiles made it clear they knew what he was doing as well. Behind her she felt as much as heard the swell of disapproval, like a ferocious dog growling to defend its territory. If Daven Marcus heard it, he only seemed pleased, smiling broadly. Then he sat back down next to the countess, who pressed into him once more. His eyes surveyed the crowd one more time.

"It seems you were right my dear," he said, ostensibly to the countess but loud enough to be heard by the entire gathering. "They don't appear happy for my upcoming nuptials."

"Oh Daven," the countess said with another giggle. She spoke more quietly than he, but still loud enough for Amelia and those close to hear her. "I only said that perhaps you shouldn't bring me for such a moment."

"Why wouldn't I? You are the most gorgeous of all the ladies of the court and look truly fine upon my arm. Why would a prince not wear such a dazzling adornment?"

At least she has half a wit in her head, Amelia thought and knew that she was losing control of her facial expressions. Amelia's thoughts would surely be obvious, but she almost didn't care. The arrogant peacock had brought his mistress to the announcement of his wedding and was making sure everyone knew that he had done it deliberately. Short of making her kneel in front of him and eat from a dog's bowl, she couldn't think of a way he could disrespect her more. And then she smiled; she could not help it. He was making it easy for her. He insulted her and he insulted her people altogether. With his contempt, he obliterated the distinction between Amelia and her nobles. They were all tarred now with the same brush.

Her smile was short-lived, though, as Daven Marcus looked over his shoulder at one of his entourage.

"What say you, Lord Robant?"

A disdainful-looking young man with short brown hair and a finely trimmed beard answered the prince's question. "I should have thought a cheer for your coming wedding would be appropriate. But I wonder if this feast has the right mood for it?"

"It *is* a dismal affair," Daven Marcus agreed, "even without the rain and the cold."

"I would not blame them, your Highness. As you say, it is dismal cold and wet, and worse yet, they all suffer under the hand of a..." Lord Robant paused and looked directly at Amelia. "Under the hand of...their duchess."

There it was. The prince was despising the Reach because it was ruled by a woman who didn't deserve her rank. He wanted them to spurn her to earn his respect. It was a strangely ugly way to go about it. Even if they blamed her for everything the prince did, he had still insulted them to their faces. How important did he think his respect was to them? Amelia looked around her.

Most seemed angry at the prince, but some few cast sidelong glances at her, and she felt a sudden tinge of worry. The whole point of this feast, the effort, the difficulty and the expense, was to cement her loyalty and respect among the Reach nobility. The prince was going to undo all of that if he could. He was making a ham-fisted job of it, and there seemed little risk he would succeed, but Amelia knew she would not let him. In her mind she searched for a way to make sure his contempt for her stirred her people's loyalty, not rejection. Her eyes met Viscount Wolden's for a moment, and all she could think of was his question about the disorder of the march.

"Your Highness, the Reach naturally exults to hear news of our engagement," she said, lifting her voice to be heard while trying to still sound sweet. Even as she spoke, though, she could hear the edge in her voice. "But we do yet labor under an uncertainty that concerns many."

The prince cocked an eyebrow while he waited for his steward Grenough to refill his goblet. Amelia pressed on, baiting her trap.

"When the invaders came out of the west last summer, your late, lamented uncle, Prince Mercad, marched to defeat them with his heroic knight commander, Sir Carron Ironworth, as leader of the army. He showed by fine leadership what it was to direct an army of the Grand Kingdom to honorable victory. Many of the nobles gathered here fought with that army, shedding blood to defend the Reach and the Grand Kingdom. Since you have dismissed Sir Carron from the court, perhaps you could choose a commander for this march from amongst those who have already proved their worth."

Amelia met the prince's eyes and smiled, happy with the position in which she had just put him. He could choose one of the Reach nobles as commander and risk insulting his closest flunkies from Rhales, all of whom probably thought they were entitled to the honor. Or he could look the Reachermen in the eye and tell them he didn't think they were worthy, that these men who had already defended the Reach and fought off an invading army weren't good enough in the prince's eyes. Her confidence dimmed slightly when the prince returned her smile.

"Did you hear that, Robant?" he asked loudly, holding Amelia's gaze. "I thought Ironworth was a pompous old carthorse that was long overdue for pasture. Was I wrong?"

"He was strong in his day, Highness," Robant answered. The disdainful young lord picked some piece of thread or fluff from his fine velvet doublet. "But his day was long past, as you say."

"Just like my fool uncle," said the prince. Again, Daven Marcus threw insults around. Amelia wondered if anyone enjoyed his respect if he even despised his own uncle. "But they did fight off the first foray."

"Proving how little the so-called invasion must have been."

"So true, Lord Robant, so true. So why do they keep looking to broken-down nags to ride instead of true thoroughbreds?"

"I don't think they can help it, Highness. After all, what can a people following a swineherd's daughter know about leadership? What would she know about anything but lying on her back and pumping out litters of piglets?"

Amelia blinked in surprise at Lord Robant's words, but before she could think to say something, she started at a shout from nearby.

"Enough! This cannot longer stand!"

She turned to see Viscount Wolden striding out of the crowd to stand beside her.

"You insult our duchess, dog!" he declared loudly, his face contorted in fury. "The prince may speak as he wishes; it is the right of his rank. But you are beneath her. As her sworn man, I insist you apologize!"

"Or what?" said Lord Robant.

"Or I will demand satisfaction. Which will you give?"

There was a moment's silence during which Robant and Daven Marcus exchanged a knowing look that unsettled Amelia.

"Satisfaction then," said Robant.

From that moment, things moved fast for Amelia. Lord Robant stepped around the prince's table to stand in front of Lord Wolden, while seemingly from nowhere a pair of arming swords were fetched by a steward. The crowd moved back from the two men, making space in front of the tables. The spits were lifted from the fires and the servants cleared the meat and dishes away swiftly. Both blades were simple affairs, with straight cross guards and steel discs for pommels. Lord Robant took one, testing its edge with his thumb, then swung it experimentally. Lord Wolden accepted the other and lifted it in salute to Amelia.

"With your favor, Your Grace?" he asked.

It took Amelia a moment to even understand what was happening, it was all so sudden. Was she supposed to have a kerchief to offer him? Or a ribbon? She had nothing of the sort to hand. Thinking hastily, she turned to Turley standing by and snatched the linen cloth from his arm. Holding it out to the viscount, she shrugged a little apologetically. The cloth was finely woven, but hardly a true lady's favor. Nevertheless, Wolden smiled to receive the gesture and tucked the cloth into his belt. Then he turned to salute Robant.

"With her favor," he said.

"It's not the smallest prize I've ever fought for," Lord Robant said archly, giving the prince and his entourage a smug smile. "But it's small enough."

"Rogue," Wolden spat. "You'll eat those words! Lay on!"

The two raised their swords in guard and the duel began. For a moment they circled, then Wolden sprang forward, striking hard. Robant parried and deflected the attack. The two parted again, to resume circling. Wolden came on again. Reachermen began to cheer him on, and he pressed Robant harder this time. When they parted, though, Wolden was forced to jump back out of the way as Robant swung a low cut at him. They faced each other yet again, and it seemed to Amelia that Robant was backing away from Wolden. That encouraged her, and she felt hopeful as Wolden surged with a long series of consecutive strokes, forcing his opponent onto the back foot.

"He'll be in trouble in a moment," she heard Turley mutter under his breath. She assumed he was talking about Lord Robant, but when she glanced at his face, there was a tension in his expression that worried her. She looked back in time to see Wolden push Robant back against one of the cook fires. Wolden seemed in control, but at the last moment, Robant checked his opponent's blade and absorbed his momentum. Lord Wolden was suddenly pulled off balance and Robant turned in place, hooking his opponent's leg and tossing Wolden into the fire. Sparks and burning coals burst into the night as Wolden crashed through the blaze. On the other side he beat at himself, half cutting, half tearing away his tabard which was smoldering and threatening to catch flame.

Robant made his way casually around the fire, keeping his sword comfortably in guard. There was a sound behind Amelia, and she looked over her shoulder to see the prince standing up from his seat again to get a better view. She noticed his entourage watching eagerly as well, like a flock of hungry vultures, longing for blood. She was vividly reminded of her vision not so long ago while sitting at the high table in her own great hall. The entirety of the prince's entourage had seemed like a flock of twisted carrion birds, and the prince himself as a great sickly eagle, more vile than they. Now, even though they were only men and women, they felt to Amelia as they had in that vision—predatory and diseased in their hearts.

As Amelia looked away, she noticed Kirsten watching the duel attentively, and she remembered her promise to find the handmaid a suitor at this feast. There was little enough chance of that now. Kirsten wanted a Rhales courtier for a husband, but so few had even bothered to attend, and those who were here had come to give the prince an audience to play to, to watch him humiliate her. There was no way Amelia would be able to arrange anything with the prince's flunkies, and even if there was a Rhales courtier who might have been favorable for a match, she was loath to offer Kirsten up to one of them. Far better to find her a match from among the Reachermen, someone like Lord Wolden. Kirsten would be disappointed, but she would be better for it. Such a match would help solidify Amelia with her liege nobles as well. Amelia shook her head. On the one hand she faced the memory of a horrifying vision, the true meaning of which she still did not understand. On the other were her duties to her maid and to her entire household. Behind her she felt the weight of the dignity and expectation of the entire Western Reach. And in front of her, two men fought for her honor. It was as if her thoughts were walls, and everywhere she turned, she was trapped by them.

A sudden resounding clash of steel told the duchess which of her thoughts demanded her immediate attention, and she watched as Wolden staggered away from Robant. The viscount was flexing his left hand, and there was blood on the side of his face. Amelia had not even seen the hit, but she wondered why that wasn't the end of it. Blood had been drawn; the matter should be resolved. Lord Wolden looked at her, and even in the flickering light of the fire, she could see the uncertainty in his eyes. He felt outmatched, she was sure of it. Then he set his face in a hard expression. His injured hand went down to the cloth tucked in his belt and his lips were moving, though no words were coming out.

Was he praying?

In that instant, Amelia realized that he was going to die for her honor. She wanted to cry out, to put a stop to the duel, but even if the rules of chivalry and dignity hadn't made it impossible, it was already too late. Wolden drove forward, thrusting for Robant's chest. The two blades engaged and Robant turned his over Wolden's. Once his line was clear of the viscount's guard, it was over, and Robant's point thrust straight down into Wolden's belly. The force of the thrust, combined with the momentum of Wolden's charge, drove the steel straight through his torso, so that more than a handspan of blade emerged from his back with a spit of gore. Robant withdrew the blade with a savage tug and more blood rushed out with it. Wolden sank to his knees and fell sideways, his eyes unfocussed and his face white even in the poor light.

Robant leaned down over his defeated opponent. "You have your satisfaction," he said with a tone so cold it made Amelia shiver. She hugged herself without thinking. The Rhales nobleman snatched the linen favor from Wolden's belt and used it to wipe the blood from his blade. He walked back to the prince's table, pausing as he passed Amelia to hold out the cloth to her.

"Did you wish this back?"

Amelia looked at the fine linen, marred by the crimson stains. She felt her fists clenched against her sides as her arms pushed tighter around her. Even if she wanted to take the cloth, she couldn't make her arms move. It was all she could do not to weep for the fallen viscount. Why did so many men around her have to die?

"No?" Lord Robant asked at last. He shrugged. "I've no use for it." He tossed the cloth at Turley, who caught it and held it in his fist. Robant continued back to the prince's table. He bowed to his liege. "With your permission, Highness, I will withdraw."

"A moment, Robant," Daven Marcus said. "I think it's clear enough that the Reach is now under the rule of men, not doddering geriatrics and slatterns. Men are rewarded when they do well." The prince lifted his goblet and drained it, then held it out to his man. Robant accepted the golden trinket with a bow.

"Perhaps I could take the cup as my heraldry," he said. The prince smiled at the idea but shook his head.

"I think your father would rather you kept the family livery."

"True, Highness, but the cup *and* the dolphin? It has a nice ring to it, I think."

"Indeed, it does."

Daven Marcus looked to the countess and took her hand.

"But if you've had enough, we might make an end to the night as well."

The countess stood to join the prince, and with seemingly no signal, the two heralds who had been standing patiently at the edge of the feast put their trumpets to their lips and blew another blast.

"The Prince," they cried out in unison. "The Prince withdraws."

The entire assembly went down on their knees once more. Amelia curtseyed and everyone waited as Daven Marcus led his mistress, his champion, his entourage, and all his servants away from the feast. There was silence then, with only the sound of the fires crackling quietly. Viscount Wolden coughed suddenly, a hideous, wrenching sound cut off by an agonized groan. Swiftly, there were calls for squires to fetch a chirurgeon or a healer or just a physic. Men rushed forward to bundle the fallen noble in a cloak and take him to a tent to try to warm him. Amelia watched them go, certain he would not survive the night.

"I want to go home," she said to herself but not caring who heard.

"Your Grace?" Turley asked, loyally attentive but with a bitter tone in his voice.

"Escort me to my tent, Steward," she told him, using the formality to keep herself from collapsing in tears.

"Very good, Your Grace."

Kirsten fell in beside them as they made their way back to the duchess's tent and helped Amelia ready herself for bed once they were there. Throughout the whole process, Amelia never said a word. When she got into her cot, she pulled her cover about her head and readied herself for the tears. But they never came, and she fell asleep dry-eyed and cold despite her blankets and furs.

CHAPTER 15

"That's another touch, I think."

Prentice cursed under his breath as Sir Gant stepped back and set himself in stance once more, his wooden practice sword held loosely and comfortably.

"Tell me again why I'm doing this?" Prentice asked as he set his own practice weapon in guard and readied for another pass.

"Because you foolishly believe that as a commander of men you need to master the longsword. As if knights you face on the field would respect you more if you used their weapon against them."

Prentice scowled. Gant's assessment was brutal but essentially correct. The longsword was the distinctive weapon of the knight and the nobility. If he was going to command the duchess's militia, he didn't want to do it with her bannermen looking down their noses at him. But there was another motivation buried deeper in his thoughts. When he had trained as a knight for the church at the academy in Ashfield, he had learned the longsword there. It was the only legitimate way someone of Prentice's low birth could have studied the long blade, and since the inquisition had unjustly cast him out, he'd never since had a chance to handle the exclusive blade. By mastering it, some part of him wanted to reclaim what had been taken from him. He knew it was foolish in a way, a mere vanity, but inside himself he couldn't ignore the drive for it.

Foolish felt like the right word now, especially as he and Sir Gant sized each other up for the next pass. They'd had easily three dozen engagements in this sparring session, and Prentice had been lucky to win one pass in five, if that.

"The longsword is a harsh mistress," Gant had said when Prentice asked for the practice. "Neglect her and she will abandon you—that what my master always said—and you have neglected her for a very long time."

Prentice came in with a series of high cuts, hoping to draw Gant's guard up to make an opening. As soon as he swept low to get under his opponent's sword, Gant stepped in, checking the attack and switching to a half-sword grip. Prentice found his attack intercepted and Gant's wooden blade reversed so that the point of the cross guard had stopped only a finger's breadth from his eye. In a real duel, Prentice would have been knocked out by the blow, the steel point of a real cross guard driven into his face. He disengaged, shaking his head and acknowledging Gant's touch.

"Shall we take a moment?" the knight asked.

Prentice nodded and reached down for a cloth to wipe his face. The weather was cold, but combat training always raised a sweat. He didn't want his skin to chill. Gant grabbed a wooden jug full of water and drank straight from the spout, then offered some to Prentice. He waved it away.

"Your instincts aren't bad," Gant said, reading his mood. "You know how to move in a melee, and that will always stand you in good stead. It's just your specific longsword techniques that are lacking."

"Are you trying to cheer me up?"

Gant shrugged and sat down. Prentice sank next to him, and the pair watched the encampment at work around them. Things were moving with an encouraging sense of orderliness. It had taken a day or so for the first corporal to get his cohort in order, five lines of ten men, each with a line "first" appointed. When that cohort got to march to Yentow Sent's workshop and have their fetters off, word quickly got about. From that point, it only took three days before every cohort could line up, ready to learn to march in order. It was a busy time for the smiths, striking off nearly two thousand sets of shackles.

Now every cohort had tasks to perform every day, except when it rained heavily. There were always some of them learning to march, and more and more of those had long practice poles to learn the discipline of marching with weapons. Others were set to clearing the ruins, dredging every useful thing out of the wreckage. Stones and bricks, as well as any unburnt wood, was the most common, but there was also a good deal of salvageable iron—from pots and pans to nails and tools. And a vast amount of charcoal was gathered as well to use as fuel, since they couldn't collect any wood while they were under siege. Prentice and Sergeant Ranold devised other tasks to keep the men busy, including building ovens into the walls of the barracks huts to heat them against the winter chill and hauling stones up onto key points of the walls to hurl down on any invaders. A smokehouse was also being built that would allow them to preserve their meat, since they had almost no salt. Once it was done, Prentice was going to order the animals slaughtered.

And always, there was the ubiquitous guard duty, especially on the ramparts. Prentice never had fewer than two cohorts on the walls on watch against Baron Liam's besieging force. Everyone cursed that duty, standing unsheltered in the cold wind, especially at night, but they had braziers set up for light and warmth, and harsh duty or not, it was necessary.

A roll of drums sounded, and Prentice and Gant watched as the entire encampment swarmed. It was time for duty changes. Every cohort ordered themselves to march to a new duty. The recruits on the wall marched down for a rest near a fire. Sentry duty was always followed by a rest. Their replacements moved up the stairs with much less enthusiasm. The plan to have every cohort move at once to learn how to maneuver around each other already seemed to be yielding fruit. Contingents moved well, and only very occasionally did two groups interfere with each other. Inevitably, there were always some instances of pushing and shoving, but corporals moved quickly to quash that behavior. From where he sat, it seemed to Prentice that even the line firsts were starting to take the lead as well to keep conflict to a minimum.

"I heard that we lost someone recently," Sir Gant said. Prentice was still on watch for deserters, even with the siege, but he knew that wasn't what Gant meant. "One of our number was found face down next to a slit trench, I'm told. Went out for a slash in the night and never came back."

"I heard," was all Prentice said. The dead man had been found with a single puncture wound in his neck, and that was all the evidence he needed to know that he was Tressy's attacker. Righteous had done as she promised and obeyed his order; it was a clean, professional kill.

"Do we need to hunt for a murderer?"

"I don't think so."

"Very well."

Gant clearly understood something other than random violence had occurred and seemed mostly happy to trust Prentice in that. He did have one objection, though. "In the longer term, it will be better to do justice in public, though. Rumors have a habit of twisting uncertain facts. Discipline is better served by open application."

Prentice gave him a stern look. The knight shrugged.

"It's true," he said.

Prentice knew he was right, but if they started having public floggings, the recently unchained convict recruits might take it upon themselves to revolt, and that they couldn't have.

"We'll have to decide a standard for unshackling the women," he said, realizing that was another issue he'd have to address.

"I hadn't thought of that," said Sir Gant. "How are we going to do it? The men are only freed in trust. They're earning freedom with service."

"We can have women serve as well."

"You don't mean...?"

Prentice looked Gant in disgust. "Certainly bloody not!" he declared. "There's a hundred home crafts we could use from goodwives."

"But not that?"

"I've already said I don't want whores in this camp. I'll make sure Righteous spreads the word among the women so that they all know."

Sir Gant thought about that for a moment. "You know many of them were probably whores before they were transported. It's not an exiling offense, but criminal women often find themselves in the trade."

"Well, they can find themselves another trade."

The two sat quietly for a moment more.

"You seem to know a lot about it," Prentice said, allowing himself a wry flicker of a smile.

"I'm a knight, not a saint," Gant replied readily, accepting Prentice's ribbing. "And when you pay for a bed on the road, sometimes it comes with more than a blanket for warmth."

Prentice chuckled but didn't push it any further. He was only bantering. He didn't want to humiliate Gant.

Slowly, the chaos of changeover began to calm as the cohorts settled to their next tasks. Prentice was about to tell Gant he wanted to spar some more when a convict came running from the direction of the gatehouse. A skinny youth with downy facial hair, he leaped over the broken ground and skidded to a halt in front of them. He reached up to tug his forelock, then stopped and half bowed before stopping again. He had no idea how he was supposed to relate to his commanders.

"Uh, m'lords, I mean, um...sirs, captains, uh..."

"Something you want to tell us, lad?" asked Prentice. The youth eagerly nodded.

"The gate. They need you at the gate."

"Run and tell them we are coming," Sir Gant told him. The young man stood watching as Gant and Prentice stood up. Gant's expression hardened. "Now! Run!"

The youth dashed away while they retrieved their practice swords. Gant seemed in no hurry, but Prentice had been waiting for Baron Liam to do something, so he marched toward the gate at pace. Sir Gant had to trot a moment to catch up.

"Are you worried?" he asked.

Prentice gave him a cold glance. Gant was a fatalistic character. As a knight, it was his duty to risk his life on the battlefield, and his years as a wandering sword had hardened him to the daily worries of life. He knew his responsibilities and would die to fulfil them, but beyond that, he hardly spared a thought. Prentice knew the freedom that kind of fatalism could bring. It was how he had survived so long as a convict, doing his best to never think past the immediate problems or needs. But now he was the captain, the leader in charge, and every problem ultimately fell upon his shoulders. If he failed to deliver the duchess an effective fighting force, it wasn't just he who suffered. A failure meant leaving the young duchess vulnerable to being exploited by rapacious nobles, and it meant leaving the Reach's people vulnerable to exploitation as well, not to mention invasion by savage forces from the west. And then there were these men he had offered freedom to through service. If he failed them, they ended up back on the chain, assuming they even lived. He was supposed to turn this pack of rats hiding in the walls into a pride of lions.

"Yes, I'm worried," he said tersely, forcing down the temptation to be envious of Sir Gant's freer attitude. Gant surprised him.

"Good," said the knight.

Prentice wondered if he wanted to say more, but they were already on the steps and headed up to the ramparts, with many of the men around them. It wasn't the time or place for long conversations. As they reached the top, Prentice looked down to see a line of knights on horseback, in full armor, waiting at the bottom of the slope in front of the gate. He looked for Liam, but he didn't seem to be one of the knights. To one side there was a small company of men-at-arms, also standing ready.

Pushing their way along the wall, Prentice found Righteous and Ranold standing directly above the gate, looking down on the toppled wagon that still blocked access. It was the first time he'd seen Righteous since Tressy's attacker had been found dead, and they exchanged a serious look that Prentice hoped let her know he considered the matter finished. After that moment of seriousness, she looked back out at the gathered attackers and then flashed a smile.

"It was about time they tried something," she said in her most cocksure tone. Several of the men around them smiled at that. Ranold had already given orders, it seemed, and many of the men had heavy rocks ready to throw at any attackers who came near.

As far as Prentice was concerned, Righteous was correct. It *was* time for them to try something, and he just wanted to see exactly what that would be.

CHAPTER 16

The knights advanced their mounts slowly up the slope in a line until they were within bow shot of the wall. They held for a moment at that distance, surveying the ramparts. Prentice and his men watched them.

"What are they doing?" asked Righteous.

"Waiting to see if we've got archers up here to shoot at them," said Sir Gant.

"Makes sense," Ranold said, nodding. "We should get some of Master Sent's serpentines up here. That'll give 'em a scare."

Prentice shook his head. "We gain too little by using them for this. Better to keep the secret for now."

There were mystified looks from many nearby men. They had heard the loud bangs coming from the workshop, but outside Prentice's closest officers and Yentow Sent's smiths, no one knew much about the serpentines. Prentice wanted to keep it that way. One serpentine wasn't much more than a noisy and powerful crossbow. A force equipped with dozens would be a terrifying surprise to unleash on an unsuspecting enemy.

Watching the knights, he noticed that several of them had unwound lengths of rope with iron hooks. An order was barked and the whole line started forward, the high-stepping mounts jingling in their tack and barding. Then the company increased its pace, and as they neared the fallen wagon, the men with ropes and hooks began to swing them around their heads while the others drew swords and began to ride wide of the wagon on either side. They began to circle back and forth around and behind the knights with ropes, who had to ride quite close to throw the heavy hooks. They were also forced to halt their mounts to land the throw, making for tempting targets. As soon as they were close, stones began to fall from the rampart, but they did little good. The knights were close enough for a throw, but their armor made them difficult targets to harm. The stones heavy enough to do real damage to their steel plates fell far short, doing little more than dropping straight down onto the upturned wagon, no matter how strong the man who tried to throw them. The rocks that were light enough to be thrown the distance were too light to hurt a man in well-tempered steel. Pieces half the size of a man's fist rang off the metal as they struck, making the knights inside curse, and one of the horses shied, nearly throwing its rider. These riders would have bruises to show for this confrontation, but it was clear the stones were doing little real damage.

Prentice was about to order the men to stop wasting their time when there was a sharp rattle and a curse from farther along the rampart to his left. Looking, he saw one of his men holding a bleeding wound in his forearm. As he watched, a dark streak rose over the edge of the wall, clattered as it struck the crenellation, and deflected crazily, knocking another man backward as it struck him in the crown. The struck man cursed and clutched at his head, but it was only an unpleasant cut.

"Crossbows!" hissed Ranold. Prentice looked over the edge of the wall to see that while the knights had been riding about and hooking the cart, the small company of men with them had advanced some distance on their flanks and brought some crossbows up with them. Now the handful of men hid themselves behind pavises, heavy shields that archers used to protect themselves between shots, more like small wooden walls than a true shield. Two of the men-at-arms ducked out from behind their pavises, shot their quarrels, and then hid again to reload. Prentice and those around him ducked behind the ramparts, and the two shots bounced harmlessly from the stone.

"Perhaps we should get some wood shields of our own if we're going to be up here too much longer," said Gant, flicking at the ends of his moustache.

"Good idea, sir knight," Ranold agreed, a note of sarcasm in his voice.

Prentice looked back down at the knights, three of whom had managed to hook the wagon. They had the other ends of the rope wound around their saddle horns and were using their destriers' strength to start pulling the wagon away from the gate. Prentice looked to Ranold.

"The rope we used to tip the thing over, is it still to hand?"

"Near enough, I think."

"Fetch it."

Ranold took two men with him and headed off the battlements. Prentice looked back. He needed to delay the knights pulling on the wagon.

"A silver to any man who can knock one of them out of his seat!" he shouted. "A guilder and a jug of mead with his meal tonight!" Prentice had no idea if there was any mead in the whole camp, but he would scare some up as a reward if he could. He was pleased as chunks of stone began to rain down on the three knights with renewed enthusiasm. Odds were good they'd never knock a man from his saddle, but Prentice only needed to slow their progress long enough for Ranold to get back with the rope. Soon enough the sergeant returned, the two men with him carrying the lengths of strong cable between them.

"Make two loops," Prentice told him. "One a lasso, broad enough to reach both ends of the wagon. Make the other one a small loop for a hand or foot to lower down and pull back up."

The two men blinked in surprise for a moment at the odd instructions, but Ranold cuffed one of them on the shoulder.

"You hear the captain; set to. And some of you lot, help them."

Other men stepped up, and together they began to form the thick rope into the two specified loops. While they worked, Sir Gant drew beside Prentice. He looked in his captain's eyes and read his intention.

"This is a goodly plan," he said quietly. "But it is not a captain's task."

Prentice was going to argue, but from his other side he heard Ranold speak equally quietly.

"He's right. You need to order others to it. Ordinary men can be replaced; you cannot."

At one level, it surprised Prentice at how easily they had predicted his intention to undertake the dangerous task himself. And their objection was reasonable, but he bristled at the thought. He loathed the idea of ordering other men to take a risk like this and not going himself. However, if he was going to command men on a battlefield someday, he would have to get used to it. He grabbed hold of the looped rope, handing his practice sword off to Sir Gant.

"Right, I need two volunteers," he said loudly, every eye watching him. One man stepped up without hesitation, but no others. The men around had a good guess what Prentice was planning. "I said two!"

Still, no one else came forward.

"There's a guilder and a jug in it for you as well," shouted Ranold. He looked to Prentice to see if the captain approved the reward. Prentice nodded.

An older man pushed his way forward.

"I could'na hit the side of a barn with a rock, but I can climb fair enough for a pot o' mead."

Prentice waved the two men closer, and the stirrup loop was loosed so they could each put a foot inside and be lowered down together. When they each had the rope in one hand, Prentice laid the lasso across their shoulders.

"You need to get this hooked around both ends," he explained to them. "The wheel at the back and the heel of the yoke pole at the front. Only one won't do, it's got to be both. We're going to give them a tug o' war..."

"And you don't want to lose 'cause a wheel popped off," the older man interjected.

Ranold cuffed him across the shoulder, but Prentice just smiled.

"That's right."

Others took up the cable to lower the two men down while they twisted and bumped against the wall, hanging on for their lives. Prentice looked at the watching faces along the top of the wall.

"Get on this rope," he ordered. "The moment they get the two ends tied away, I want those horses to know they're in a fight. The rest of you take up some stones. If one of those bastards comes near on his pretty mount, I want to hear his armor sounding like a mad bell-ringer's favorite chime."

The two volunteers were already near to the bottom when a flight of crossbow bolts bit into the stones nearby. The older man held on tight, but his partner flinched and lost his grip. The younger man fell the short distance to the ground and cracked his head against the wall. He cursed and held his head, dropping the lasso. The older man slipped down behind the wagon and proceeded to fit his side of the lasso under the boards at the back.

"You alright?" someone called from the top of the wall at the younger man. He looked up, blinking even though the leaden sky was far from bright. He waved at them, as if to say he was hale, but there was a drunkenness to his movements that made it clear he was anything but. He staggered toward the front of the wagon, but voices above called him back; he'd forgotten the lasso. Their calls made him swivel about, trying to puzzle out what was wrong. He was at the front of the wagon now, vulnerable and almost fully exposed to both the crossbowmen and the knights on horseback. The three pulling on the ropes stared at him for a moment before one called to his comrades. The other knights seemed not to have noticed him yet, so intent were they in riding their circuit around their fellows. A crossbow quarrel rammed home in the wood of the wagon after ruffling the dazed man's hair. Bewildered, he spun around again, confused by the sensation on his head.

Above him, the shouting grew more desperate. The crossbowmen would have his range any moment. Some told him to take cover while others yelled and pointed at the rope still lying on the ground. Then, there was the sound of hoofbeats. One of the circling knights had noticed the vulnerable man and was charging in with a mace held ready. Pieces of rock dropped from the wall, most missing their target, but some ringing off the steel of the horse's barding. In spite of the rain of stones, the destrier never shied, and in a short moment the knight towered over his target. Then the mace fell, and the injured man's pain and confusion came to an end as his body slumped to the ground.

There was a moment of silence as the knight wheeled his horse on the spot and looked behind the wagon. He sighted the older man, who had just finished looping his part of the lasso well under the corner of the wagon. It was clear the knight meant to be thorough. Before he could spur his horse forward, however, the shouting from the wall suddenly renewed with a different, more hateful edge. Along with the hollers and curses, there came a fresh rain of stone. This time few of the thrown rocks missed, the target being so close. Horse and rider's armor clanged like a bell, just as Prentice had ordered. The knight was almost knocked from his saddle by a number of hits, and the horse shied from one strike that rang on its head. Simply to keep his saddle, the knight was forced to withdraw, hounded away by jeers and questions of his parentage, along with some overly optimistic throws.

With the knight gone, the older man grabbed the other half of the lasso and dragged it to the yoke pole. He seemed to spare a moment's glance for his fallen comrade before working to tie off the other end of the wagon. Although there was no one there to strike him down now, that meant he was vulnerable again to the crossbowmen. He was more cunning than his dazed companion had been, though, and he managed to keep himself more in cover behind parts of the wagon while he fixed the rope in place. Suddenly, he looked up with a twisted smile and waved his hand.

"Pull that loop tight and get it tied off on the ramparts here," Prentice commanded. The wood of the wagon creaked as the lasso tightened around both ends. On the ground, the older man rushed to the stirrup loop.

"Make it quick, you mongrels!" he shouted at them as he put his hand through the rope and waited to be hoisted up. On the battlements, men heaved to lift him up. The crossbowmen, seeing their prey escaping, fired swift volleys; they must have been working their fingers bloody to get the bowstrings pulled and set so fast. One of their quarrels skipped on the top of the crenellations and bit into a man's thigh, but no one on the rope flinched from his task. They got their man up onto the wall and there was a cheer. Prentice made to clap the man on the back, but even as he did so, the older man collapsed on the stones. There was blood all down his legs; one of the crossbow bolts had buried itself in his back. He was already pale when Prentice rolled him over.

"Figured if I got both ends on, I'd be up for claiming both rewards," the man gasped as Prentice leaned down close to him.

"You earned it."

Prentice reached into his purse and pulled out two guilders, pressing them into the man's weakening grip. He smiled.

"Me ma always said I'd never have two silvers to rub together," he said, his voice fading. "Said I was too stupid to make an honest living. She was half right, I guess." He groaned in pain and clutched at his stomach.

Prentice didn't know what to say. What could he say to a man who he'd just sent to his death?

"Don't waste two jugs on it," the man whispered. He was pale and sweating now, and he seemed to be losing the strength to even lift his head. "But if you could pour a cup o' that mead on me grave, that'd sure be grand." Then he lowered his head and his last few breaths rasped out of his chest.

Prentice stood. Men pressed close on every side, but he hardly knew they were there. His thoughts were cold and black, like the surface of deep water at night. On the ground, the knights had resumed pulling at the wagon, ropes creaking with the strain. Two men helped the third with the bolt in his thigh down off the wall. Ranold ordered them to find Fostermae to care for the wound, then detailed others to take away the body.

"And he gets buried with those coins," Ranold ordered them. "When the sacrist's done with the healing, I'll bring him to say the rites. If those silvers aren't in his hand when I get there, I'll skin your hides and make me a new pair of boots, see if I don't. I've marked your faces and I'll find you."

Somewhere, under the coldness in his mind, Prentice realized that Ranold's threat was probably useless. The coins would be stolen soon enough; they were in a camp full of convicted criminals, after all.

"That's a tug of war they're going to lose," said Righteous, looking down at the knights with their hooks and ropes. She had an expression of grim satisfaction.

"They'll get that rope cut eventually," said Gant evenly.

"Probably do it at night," added Ranold. "In fact, I don't know why they didn't do this whole thing at night. Be a damned sight harder to hit them with rocks in the dark."

That was a good point. Prentice's brows narrowed as Ranold's comment wormed its way into his bitter thoughts. Two men were dead, and he was responsible. But they'd succeeded in their mission, and if he'd gone instead, as he'd planned, then likely he would be dead in their place. He felt relief at that thought, but the relief made him feel like a coward and a bastard. He could feel the cold fury inside of him, screaming for vengeance, longing to punish the knights, the crossbowmen, Baron Liam and, ultimately, himself. Yet, still winding through the blackness of these thoughts, Ranold's words seemed to tease his mind with their significance. There was something else he was missing.

Sir Gant stepped close to him.

"It's not your fault," he said. "Men die in war. It is what it is."

Prentice knew that he was trying to be comforting, as well as trying to keep his commander from doing or saying something foolish in a moment of anger or grief, but he barely even heard the knight. He stared down at the armored men and horses, no longer tugging hard on the ropes but still riding about in circles.

"Makes for a nice parade, though," said Righteous, and her words cracked the dark ice on the surface of his thoughts as Ranold's observation found the light of Righteous's comment.

Breaking from his grim reverie, Prentice realized what was happening. His head whipped about as he looked back over the encampment at the far walls.

"What is it?" asked Gant.

"It's a diversion," Prentice answered through gritted teeth, eyes searching back and forth.

"Damnation!"

Prentice turned to Ranold. "Get a cohort down at the gate in case they're trying to sneak men in to open it from the inside. Then put two extra cohorts up on the walls right now," he ordered. "Have them spread the word. Liam's sending men over the walls, I'm sure of it." He snatched his practice blade back from Sir Gant.

Ranold ran straight for the stairs while Prentice pushed his way through the men and sprinted along the rampart. Behind him, he heard Righteous call out in surprise, but he ignored her. He hoped she and Gant had the sense to go the other way around. He had to find out where they were coming over the wall. Somewhere there was a corner, an unexpected angle where men on the wall wouldn't notice a force sneaking up, especially if they were distracted by the action at the gate. Wherever that spot was, Baron Liam was there, making his move.

CHAPTER 17

Fallenhill's walls were simple stone curtains that followed the bowl of what had once been an upland meadow. The ramparts were interspersed with towers, but these were not the complex structures of larger towns and cities. There was no interior to these towers; they were simply solid platforms built from cut stones. The only way to the tower tops were short staircases from the battlements. So as Prentice ran along the town wall, he leaped up the little sets of stairs and stopped in each tower's top to look for any other force of knights that might be coming over the walls. Soon enough he was almost halfway around the circuit of the walls, his heartbeat drumming in his ears as much from fear as from his breakneck speed.

"Where are you?" he muttered to himself. Looking back, he saw Ranold arranging lines of men with bills at the gate, ready to fight any attempt to force it from the inside. Still, he hadn't found any sign of someone coming over the walls. Then, as he was jumping down the steps from one tower back to the wall, he caught a movement just inside the tree line of a little wood at the back slope of the town. He stopped and crouched behind the crenellations in case Liam had other crossbowmen with him. Searching the shadows beneath the trees, Prentice was sure he could make out horses. The longer he looked, the more detail became clear. Then there was a flash of light, and he realized someone had built a fire to warm themselves against the winter chill. That confirmed it for him. Someone was watching from the trees.

Leaning out, he searched the ground in front of the wall for a ladder or something similar. There was nothing. He rushed along the rampart to the next tower and was partway up the steps when he heard a metallic sound, like a knife scraped on a stone. He dropped flat against the stones and crept up to the tower top. There was no one there. Then the scraping sounded again, and Prentice realized it was coming from the other side of the tower, where the wall turned away to curve around the back of the town. He looked over his shoulder to try to signal to Ranold or Gant at the gate. It was then that he realized he was in a blind spot; the curve of the wall and the rise and fall of the ground made it difficult to see or be seen from the gate. Liam had chosen the perfect point to sneak men over the walls.

Clever bastard, Prentice thought begrudgingly.

Creeping forward, he looked down from the tower top at the wall on the other side where he found the ladder he was expecting. It was laying right against the corner between the tower and the wall, and it reached the rampart where the steps down from the tower top left a small gap, a cleft just large enough for a man to hide in. It was the ideal spot to climb the wall. Only someone looking straight along the rampart from that side would see them. Or someone looking directly down from above, as Prentice was. He carefully leaned out over the edge of the tower to look straight down and saw a man in plate and mail guarding the top of the ladder. He was a knight, with a longsword drawn. He was pressing himself back into the gap between the steps and the crenellations so he could surprise anyone rushing down the stairs, but that was what had given him away as his armor scraped against the stone.

Prentice ducked back. He had to get to the ladder and remove that guard, but there was no way he wanted to fight one to one against a knight in full armor and with a live blade using only a practice sword. Plus, there was always the chance that whoever

was watching under the trees would send more knights up the
ladder if they had to.

Why haven't they done that already? Prentice wondered. He
didn't have time to call for reinforcements of his own. Whoever
came to help would not win the race against any knights under
the trees. He had to take the ladder and its guard now, and
he had to do it fast. Whispering a short prayer, he slid up
onto the crenellation stones as quietly as he could, forcing
himself to stay calm by drawing in a long, slow breath. Then
he seized the moment, pushing himself swiftly to his feet and
jumping straight down on the knight, landing feet first on his
pauldron-armored shoulders. The force knocked the man over,
while Prentice used him like a springboard, leaping from his
shoulders directly at the walkway on top of the wall. He rolled
as he fell, as well as he could, knowing that if he misjudged the
angle, he would roll straight over the edge. That fall might not
kill him, but it would likely cripple him if it didn't. He regained
his feet with a handspan to spare, but the desperate maneuver
had caused him to lose his wooden sword. The dummy weapon
clattered on the edge of the wall before tumbling over.

The knight had fared worse though, being flung to the stones
by the impact of Prentice's jump. The salet helmet he was
wearing had no visor, and it looked like he'd smashed his nose
when he fell. The man grunted in pain and spat as blood ran
from his nostrils onto his mouth. He'd also lost his grip on his
sword in the fall, and the steel blade rang as it spilled against
the rampart stones. Rolling his shoulders to test if they were
injured, the knight forced himself to his feet, but by the time he
did so, Prentice had retrieved the man's sword and was pointing
it at him. When he saw he'd lost his prime weapon to his
assailant, the knight snarled in fury and plucked a bodkin from
its sheath at his belt, ready to fight. Prentice had no intention
of letting the man bring his reserve weapon to bear and stepped
in with a swift combination of strikes. His technique was good,
and he forced the man back against the crenellations, but the

knight was happy to take all the slicing cuts on his armor, the longsword blade having no chance of penetrating the polished steel.

At the end of Prentice's combination, when the two men had ended up close to each other, the knight exploded forward suddenly, throwing a series of tight swings and thrusts with his dagger. Prentice sprang back, parrying desperately, the longsword blade ringing on the man's gauntlets. In only his jerkin, he had no armor to absorb even one cut. The knight paused for a moment, and from the grimace on his face and the way he moved his left arm, it seemed Prentice's drop had done more damage than he'd first supposed.

"Shoulder giving you some trouble?" Prentice taunted him. The knight sneered back at him.

"I'm going to kill you for that, convict."

"Free man," Prentice corrected.

"Dead man!"

The knight charged again, using his armor to press away Prentice's defense with the purloined longsword. It was clear the man thought to drive Prentice off the wall, and Prentice knew his best chance was to try the same. He let the knight come on, not having to fake being hard-pressed by the assault. When they were both near the edge, Prentice dropped one hand from the sword, and catching the knight under his arm, tried to use the armored man's own momentum to hip-throw him over the edge. The knight was ready for such a maneuver, though, and swiftly shifted his weight, breaking Prentice's grip. Prentice had to jump away again to avoid a straight thrust aimed at his midsection. As it was, the bodkin point bit through his jerkin, tearing the leather. The knight was getting closer. The next pass would likely be the telling one. And this fight was taking too long.

"Prentice!" shouted Righteous, coming over the tower, dagger in hand. Prentice knew the voice and didn't need to look. The knight was surprised by the feminine tone and cast a glance in that direction. It was all the opening Prentice needed. Putting one hand on the longsword's blade, he half-sworded his weapon, reversing his grip, just as Gant had done to him in practice, and hammered the blade's pommel into the knight's injured face like a mace blow. Teeth were knocked out and the man staggered back. Without a pause, Prentice dropped, and using the sword's crossguard like a hook, caught the knight behind the knee, tripping him up. Unable to stop his fall, the man's arms pinwheeled as he tumbled backwards, struck the edge of the wall, and fell headfirst to his death.

When he was gone, Prentice rushed to the ladder. Looking out to the woods, he saw a number of knights and men-at-arms coming slowly out from under the trees, apparently unsure if they should rush to reinforce their man. Their hesitation was his salvation.

"Help me with this," he demanded of Righteous, hauling on the ladder.

"Just throw it back," she told him but came to help, nonetheless.

"To hell with that. Let them make another one. Besides, we could use the wood."

Righteous shrugged and put her hands to the rungs, helping to pull the enormous ladder up over the rampart and let it fall inside the wall. The advancing men stopped when they saw the ladder being removed. Prentice was glad to see it, but there were still the others inside the walls somewhere. Before he could go looking for them, Righteous slapped him across the face. He looked at her in shock.

"What is wrong with you?" she demanded.

Damnation, how many different ways did this woman want to disrespect him? "What?" he demanded.

"Do you want to get yourself killed?" she insisted in return. "Going blade to blade with a knight in full plate, and you just in your shirt?"

"I've seen you do it," he retorted, defending himself in spite of their difference in rank, too surprised by the rebuke to be angry.

"I jumped one from behind in the dark!" Righteous countered. "The first thing he knew about me was my point in his eye. You all but challenged this one to a duel! I'm surprised you didn't salute him and exchange genial trees."

"Genealogies is what they're called," Prentice corrected. By tradition, knights in tournaments and duels would often list their ancestry to prove themselves worthy and sufficiently noble to meet their opponent.

"I don't care what they call them," she insisted. "Stop risking your life in fool ways! There's folk in here need you alive, you know."

He was about to tell her to mind her place when a scream echoed across the walls, followed by the sound of clashing steel.

"There are others," said Righteous.

"And they're in the workshop."

The two of them sprinted to the nearest stairs and rushed toward the workshops where the sounds of fighting were getting louder.

CHAPTER 18

The morning after her feast, Duchess Amelia emerged from her tent to find Lord Robant standing waiting for her with four men-at-arms wearing the prince's colors. The young nobleman stood by the fire while her servants did their best to work around him, preparing her breakfast. Robant was wearing a felt cap with a long pheasant feather in it, and when he saw her, he tipped the cap like he was greeting an old friend.

"Lord Robant," Amelia said, trying to conceal her surprise. She cast her eye warily over the armed guards standing by. "What is your purpose here?"

"Duchess, the prince has sent me to inform you that you no longer enjoy the freedom of his camp. You are to confine yourself to your tent until you receive instructions from him."

Amelia blinked, trying to understand Robant's words.

"My Lord...I'm sorry, Robant, but what rank exactly do you hold with the court? We've not been formally introduced."

"No, of course," Robant replied. He removed his cap and sank into a deep bow with one sweeping gesture. "Your servant, Duchess. Robant, son of Wren, born fourteenth baronet of Golburne and raised in Prince Daven Marcus's service to the rank of baron. So, I am the first Baron of Golburne, it seems."

"Daven Marcus raised you to baron?" Amelia asked, arching her eyebrow. Daven Marcus had raised her own retainer Sir Liam to the rank of baron, and it had only served to make the man more ambitious and headstrong. "The prince seems to make a habit of raising barons."

"Ah yes, your man as well," said Robant, obviously also thinking of Liam. "Baron is, of course, the highest rank the prince can bestow without his father's warrant. He's raised four barons and a baroness just since he became crown prince."

"You seem unimpressed by your own ennoblement."

"I am one of five, all raised in less than a year. It hardly seems impressive."

Amelia could barely believe the man's audacious vanity. Her father worked his whole life to amass the money that became her dowry. Without it she would never have been able to marry her husband, and she would never have achieved the rank of duchess. The prince was raising people freely, and all Lord Robant could think to do was disdain his largesse.

"You think me arrogant?" Robant asked, seemingly reading her thoughts in her expression.

"Indeed, I do," Amelia sniffed. "You imagine yourself, a mere baron, to have the right to restrict the movement of a duchess—the Duchess of the Reach in fact, liege lady of the very province in which you stand."

"I do not imagine myself anything, Your Grace. I am simply the tool by which our prince exercises his will. I only carry his instructions, no more arrogant than the quill he would write them with, if he chose to write them down."

"Truly? You see yourself as no more than a tool in Daven Marcus' hand?"

"In this case? Yes. The authority which restricts you is not mine, but his."

"And what of last night?" Amelia asked, and she made no effort to hide the bitterness in her tone. "Were you no more than his tool then?"

Baron Robant gave her a long look, showing no deference. It was rude, but the man's natural charm, combined with his authority from the prince, seemed to give him license to defy convention. His eyes drilled into her for a moment, then a wry half smile danced over his lips.

"The prince instructed me to be provocative last night, that is true. But your man chose to settle the matter with steel. He chose to give up his life. You can't blame me for that."

"Viscount Wolden is dead?" Amelia put her hand to her mouth. She had not yet heard of the Reacherman's fate.

"He passed sometime last night," Robant confirmed, happily. "A sacrist was called to administer the rites before dawn."

"You killed him to help the prince make a point? How could you do such a thing?"

"Which one? Obey the prince or fight the duel?"

"What difference does it make?" Amelia said, horrified at the casual way the baron discussed Wolden's death. Robant shrugged his shoulders.

"Obeying the prince requires no explanation. He is the prince. As to the duel, when a man draws steel on another man, when he offers a challenge that is answered, then he has taken his fate into his own hands. His death is his own. I shed no tears for the viscount, and neither should you. He died well."

"He died in agony."

"Many men do."

There was a calmness in Lord Robant's words and demeanor that frightened Amelia, but then reminded her suddenly of Prentice. He spoke of life-and-death matters with the same directness, the same certitude. In that moment, Amelia realized who Lord Robant was, at least to the prince. He was Daven Marcus's man, just as Prentice Ash was her man, both skilled in combat and cold in battle. She wondered if Robant was like Prentice in other ways. Did he have ambitions, or did he keep all his emotions on a leash, enslaved to the single purpose of survival? In spite of his styled hair and fine, almost effeminate clothing, Amelia knew that Robant was likely the most dangerous man in the whole of the prince's army, except perhaps for the man who held his leash—Prince Daven Marcus.

"Can I inform his highness that you will be obedient to his orders?" Robant asked.

Amelia forced her emotions down and met the man's gaze with a cold mask.

"Your Grace!" she said.

Robant blinked in confusion for a moment. "I don't under...?"

"I am Duchess of the Western Reach," she interrupted him. "Prince's authority or no, you will address me as 'Your Grace,' or you will feel my displeasure. It will visit itself upon you with more than a single steel edge, I promise you." Amelia didn't wish to give up her dignity for this cold-hearted popinjay but wanted her threat to carry the whole of the fury she felt in her heart. She wanted to shake him, undermine his confidence, if even for only a moment. No matter how good a duelist he was, she could call enough of her own men-at-arms to take him prisoner. It was the prince's march, but these were her lands. It pleased her when he gave the prince's guards a quick, nervous glance. Then he bowed formally.

"Of course, Your Grace," he said. "May I convey your compliments to the prince and your undertaking to obey his command?"

"You may, Lord Robant. And directly. The business of princedoms and duchies does not endure lollygagging."

"As you say," he said, pausing for emphasis, "Your Grace."

Robant straightened from his bow and nodded to the prince's men who took positions on either side of Amelia's tent. They were more symbolic than anything else. If she wanted to force the issue, a sizeable portion of the army could be roused to fight for her freedom. But that would be rebellion against the prince and thus the crown. So, while they couldn't force her to do what the prince wanted, their presence was a symbol of his power. More than that, they would doubtless report back on every bit of her business—who she saw, who she spoke with. With a final nod, Robant strode away without waiting to be dismissed. Amelia was watching him go, quietly fuming, when Kirsten came up beside her.

"The prince did not send us a lesser man to be our jailer," said the maid. "It does not seem the worst fate to fall under his power."

It took Amelia a moment to realize what she was saying. With a puzzled frown, she looked at the young woman. Kirsten admired Robant. No, more than that, she desired him. Amelia could see it in her eyes. In some part of her, Amelia knew that Kirsten's reaction was perfectly natural. The girl was ready to marry, and Baron Robant was a dashing man of rank who seemed to have no wife, at least as far as they knew. But wherever that rational understanding came from, it was swamped in waves of indignation that rushed through her thoughts.

"He is not for you!" she snapped at her maid so vehemently that Kirsten visibly recoiled. "He'd never look twice at you anyway!"

It was a harsh thing to say, and it made it sound as if Amelia thought Kirsten was too low born for the arrogant baron; but it was not her duchess's opinion that was at issue. Knowing the prince and the baron's contempt for Reacherfolk, Amelia was certain that Robant would think Kirsten was beneath him. In truth, it was likely even the meanest Rhales courtier would disdain her. A quiet, rational part of Amelia's thoughts knew that Kirsten wouldn't understand it that way, that she would inevitably take the hard words to heart, but the duchess was too angry to stop herself. She was furious with the prince, furious with Robant and the whole western court, and furious that her own handmaid would find such a man attractive. And since she could not loose any of that fury at the prince or the baron, her maid took the full force. Covering her face with her hands, Kirsten withdrew without asking permission, all but running off into the camp.

Watching her go, Amelia felt herself torn in so many directions at once. She wanted to rush after her and apologize for her harsh words, but she also wanted to rebuke her for the public rudeness of leaving without permission. She wanted to withdraw back into her tent, to gather her thoughts, but that felt like an acceptance of defeat. With one order, the prince had turned her tent from a personal refuge into a prison cell.

"Still, he tries to make me into his princess in a tower," she muttered under her breath, remembering the way the prince had all but imprisoned her in her own castle in Dweltford. One of the servants standing discretely nearby heard her speak.

"Did you want something, Your Grace?" the woman asked politely.

"Send for my steward," Amelia told the woman, thinking up an order on the spot to protect her dignity. The woman curtseyed and left immediately. Amelia sighed and, making a point to not look at the prince's guards standing nearby, went back into her tent. "I suppose I'll have to think of some task for Turley when he gets here," she muttered to herself and closed the entry flap behind her.

CHAPTER 19

"Christ blind you, convict!" one of the knights cursed as he was frog-marched toward the gate. The fight at the smithy had been short and brutal but ultimately one-sided. Five knights in full plate had snuck over the wall using the ladder Prentice found. They'd headed straight to the smithy, only to be confronted by Corporal Felix and his cohort of recruits. Expecting that an attack at the gates might have led to a breach, the corporal had marched his fifty men to the smith and had live weapons issued to them so that he could lead a counterattack if needed. Five crashed into fifty, and even heavily outnumbered, fine armor and superior training meant that eleven recruits were slain or severely wounded before the knights were stopped. One of the knights was killed, and another was so gravely injured that he would likely die from his wounds, though Sacrist Fostermae was doing his best to keep the man alive.

Prisoners now, Prentice ordered the knights stripped of their armor and weapons. Enthusiastic ex-convicts took the orders further, removing the men's doublets and hose as well. Held under armed guard, the three healthy noblemen shivered in their smallclothes as misting rain fell from the darkening twilight sky. Fostermae was arranging a canvass hammock to hang beneath a pole for the injured knight.

"What do you plan to do with us?" the cursing knight demanded as he was pushed toward one end of the hammock pole.

"We're sending you back," Prentice told him. "We have no use for prisoners."

"We could put 'em on a chain," said Righteous, eyes narrowing with contempt. "Let 'em work as convicts for us."

"No! As long as I have the rule, there'll be none but free men in Fallenhill," said Prentice. From the expressions around him, that declaration got a mixed reaction. Some clearly liked that Prentice was so against conviction, but others seemed as though they wanted the chance to exploit these high-born men the way they themselves had been exploited as convicts. Prentice couldn't fault them—not completely.

"You don't rule here, convict," countered another of the prisoners. "You're just a rebel and doomed for it. Baron Liam has the sovereign right here. He will see you all hanged and burned for this."

Prentice reached into his belt and plucked out the duchess's signet ring, the ring she had given him as a sign of her authority. He put it on his finger and thrust it at the prisoner's face.

"See that? Look closely. That's the signet of the Reach from the hand of the duchess herself! Tell me I don't have the right here."

"You stole that," the knight retorted, refusing to believe.

"Ask the duchess," said Prentice. "See if she agrees with you."

In the fading light the man scowled, but the shadows of his face showed a certain doubt as well. Prentice gave orders, and the wounded man's hammock was lifted so that the pole was on the shoulders of two of the prisoners. Then, the two men's hands were tied to the pole. The third walking man was made to carry the body of his slain comrade, the corpse's hands tied around him so that it sat across his shoulders like a macabre bandoleer, after which the whole group was pushed toward the gate.

"At least let me ransom my harness," one of the knights on the pole called to Prentice as they marched. "I have money; I can pay. That armor has been in my family for a century."

Prentice drew close to the man.

"What was your purpose, coming over the wall? Five of you couldn't have expected to take the gate by yourselves, let alone the whole of our camp. Especially with your comrades outside drawing us all to the front rampart like that. What was the plan?"

The younger knight cast a black look at his comrades, both of whom were struggling to look back over their shoulders while their escorts poked at them to keep them marching.

"We were to take you prisoner," he said tersely.

The answer genuinely surprised Prentice. "Me?" he asked. "Why would you think I'd be there, not on the battlements? Do you imagine I'm that much of a coward that I'd run and hide at the first sign of armed men at the gate?"

"It wouldn't surprise us, cur," said the man on the other end of the pole. Righteous drew her dagger and used the pommel to clip the man across the head. He cursed and ducked, almost dropping the pole as he did so. The man in the sling groaned in agony at the sudden motion.

"Have a care, Righteous," called Fostermae, still leaning down over the wounded man and ministering to him, even as they walked.

"We didn't expect to find you there," the younger knight said, continuing to speak after a moment of quiet. The hardness of his tone made it clear that he resented how poorly their plan had played out. "We were supposed to find a hiding place and wait for darkness, to take you in your sleep."

A sound enough plan, Prentice thought, nodding. "You expected the best hiding spots would be in the burned-out keep?"

"We expected to find your sleeping quarters there."

"Shut up, fool," the knight carrying the corpse shouted over his shoulder, but he didn't turn or look back. The young knight sucked his teeth and spat in a gesture of contempt.

"Whatever we expected, no one said anything about a smithy full of armed rogues ready to do battle!"

Prentice contemplated the man's words and then nearly burst out laughing. Liam had expected that Prentice was living in the ruins of the keep because that was what he would do. The old baron of Fallenhill had lived there. A castle was where a liege lived and ruled. Liam imagined Prentice was making himself a petty lord of a broken fiefdom, so he naturally assumed Prentice would set himself up in the keep. He couldn't help but smile at the thought.

"I've answered your questions," the knight said to him. "Will you ransom my harness now? It is my family honor."

"You stole over the walls like thieves. You planned to take me in the night, like assassins. What honor do you think is left to ransom back? And what would you ransom it with?"

"I have guilders."

"We have silver in abundance," Prentice told him lightly. "This is Fallenhill." He waved about at the walls. The knight hung his head, choking on his fury. He muttered something under his breath that Prentice couldn't hear but could guess at. The whole company of prisoners and guards were nearing the gates.

"Swear yourself to me," he said suddenly.

The knight looked up, too astonished to be angry. He shivered in the cold. The other prisoners turned around despite their guards, expressions of disbelief on their faces. Even Righteous and Fostermae were amazed by the idea.

"You are a convict," the young knight said directly.

"Freed man," Prentice corrected. "And I already have a knight sworn to me. You came as assassins. Swear to me, under the duchess, and your service can ransom your honor." He presented the ducal signet again. The knight looked at it and then past Prentice to his two comrades, both of whom had stopped to hear his answer. His expression hardened and his dark eyes narrowed as he looked Prentice in the face.

"You have a nothing sworn to you," he said, voice dripping venom. "Barely a knight at all, and he traded what little he had to follow a rebel. For what? Did you give him a dog's bowl to eat at your feet? Do you feed the cur from your own plate? Keep the armor. I'd rather my family's shame!"

The other knights made noises of approval and Prentice shook his head. He hadn't really expected any other answer.

The darkness of the wall loomed over them, shutting out the last of the grey twilight as they reached the gates. Men held rushlights, while others stood by the gate bar. Sir Gant was waiting there as well.

"How goes it outside?" Prentice asked.

Gant shrugged. "Quiet. Some time ago they stopped trying to right the wagon and the riders withdrew. The crossbowmen stayed on a time, taking pot shots. I think they just wanted to empty their quivers. They never hurt anyone else." He looked over Prentice's shoulder at the prisoners. "A diversion, was it?"

"Seems that way."

"Clever."

"Not clever enough," Righteous chimed in.

"And we're giving them back?"

"We can't keep them," Prentice said flatly. "They won't last a night amongst this lot." He knew that the men around him would hear what he said, but he didn't think they would care. It was the truth. The gates were opened, and the prisoners were pushed through.

"Tell the baron he'll have to do better next time," Righteous shouted at their backs, and that raised a light cheer.

"Next time you'll be begging for our mercy," one of the knights spat back. His words only raised jeers.

"That was the young one, I think," said Gant as the gate was drawn closed again. "His confidence seems...undimmed."

Prentice nodded, turning to head back to the huts and get some dinner. Corporals began to order their men back to their duties, clearing the area around the gate. Men who were due to do watch duty on the wall tromped up the stairs with the usual lack of enthusiasm, but there was a wariness in their eyes. They were on edge. The danger of the baron's force just on the other side of the wall was suddenly so much more real to them. When he noticed it, Prentice was glad. He couldn't afford for any of the recruits to become complacent. It made him smile to think that Liam had, in a sense, done him a favor. He'd given the recruits cause to be careful, to be diligent.

You should have expected that, Liam, Prentice thought. Of course, Baron Liam thought convicts were less than dogs, so their motivations were irrelevant to him.

"Fool," he muttered under his breath.

"What was that?" asked Gant.

Before Prentice could answer, a confusion of noise arose from across the walled space. The two men looked over in the darkness to where the livestock were herded. There was nothing to see, but as the noise increased, they could tell it was the lowing of cattle, as well as bleating sheep and goats. There were flashes of firelight, and suddenly the lowing rose to a cacophony of panicked animals cries. Then the firelight grew and spread, sending crazed shadows across the walls. Sir Gant watched, puzzled for a moment, but his attention was drawn when Prentice spat out a venomous burst of curses.

"Cunning bastards!" Prentice said through gritted teeth. "They'll trample everything in here."

"What?" asked Gant. "What's happening?"

"The cattle! They're stampeding the cattle!"

As soon as Prentice said it, it was clear Gant understood. The lights were flames that had been placed among the livestock, driving them mad with fear. Most likely, they were bundles of straw, soaked with pitch to burn longer and tied to the tails of several of the animals to produce maximum chaos and panic.

Sergeant Ranold appeared out of the dark just as Prentice spoke. He comprehended the danger immediately, as well.

"We have to get those fires out," he said. Gant seemed ready to agree, but Prentice shook his head.

"We'll never get men in amongst them now. It would be a death sentence."

"Will we even be able to keep them in the pen? It's just a low stone wall."

As if waiting for someone to ask the question, there came a grating noise that made it clear the stacked stones that fenced the herd was falling, and soon enough the first beasts from the edge of the panicking mob of animals started to stumble and bolt out of the dark.

"They'll trample us all if we don't get them under control," Ranold declared.

Prentice looked about in the dark, trying to think what could be done. Ranold was right, but there was no way to calm the animals while some of them were dragging the fire around with them. Wherever they fled, they would bring the panic with them. In the darkness they would trample over everything, breaking their legs on the half-cleared ground as they did so. They would smash into the huts and gore each other with their horns. Already some were charging amongst the crowds of convicts nearby. Men leaped aside and some slapped their hands on flanks and shoulders to try to redirect the maddened creatures, but it did little good.

"Torches!" Prentice shouted over the growing din. "We need torches and poles to fend them off!"

"Fire is panicking them, and you want to add more?" said Sir Gant in disbelief.

"We'll never get them calmed now! They'll run until they escape or are exhausted, and with nowhere to escape to, they'll crush themselves and everything else in here that gets in the way. We can get flames and poles around the huts and that's where we'll make our stand. Fend them off!"

"I'll get the drummers to sound the call," said Ranold, and he rushed off into the darkness.

Prentice hoped the drums would be heard over the growing din. He slapped Gant on the shoulder, and pointing into the night, the two men rushed to the huts, gathering up every other man they found on the way, calling all to make their stand together. Between the fire and the shadow, with the noise and the growing threat of being trampled or gored by an enraged beast, Fallenhill was transformed into a hellscape. As he dodged and hid, always pressing towards the barracks huts, Prentice remembered the two convicts who had argued over whether Fallenhill was cursed. It must have seemed so to the populace, chained and burned by the invaders in the summer. And now again, fire was bringing terror and slaughter.

Prentice shook his head. Curse or not, Baron Liam had done his work well. Prentice had seen through his first ploy, but that had only made him smug. He wanted to curse himself. He ducked back behind the remnant of a stone wall as a man was catapulted out of the dark with a scream of pain. Two frenzied cattle thundered past, narrowly missing the stunned man they had knocked to the ground. Prentice reached for the man and lifted him up. The stunned casualty groaned as he was hefted up, and the tone rose to a harsh cry as Prentice tried to move him by one arm. Likely the limb was broken, or the joint dislocated. Doing his best to cause the man no more pain than necessary, Prentice half dragged, half lifted his charge and they staggered to a growing field of light where men and women with torches stood around the barracks huts. Already there were handfuls of injured there, their bloody wounds visible in the torchlight. Prentice laid his man down against a wall and stood again, his jaw clenched in rage. Someone he didn't recognize handed him a training pole, and he stepped away to help fend off any of the cattle that came this direction. It would be hours yet before any of them were truly safe, but at least now there was a plan to survive the night.

Liam had done his work well.

CHAPTER 20

One day into Amelia's imprisonment, the full winter rains began to hammer down, quickly turning the whole camp into a quagmire. Mud churned under the feet and hooves of the army and court. The heavy drops drummed on the tents and ran in rivulets, flooding the ground. Even by mid-morning, Amelia was almost thankful to be confined to her tent, with no duty drawing her out into the wet weather. By the afternoon, she even began to feel some pity for the four men-at-arms assigned to watch her, standing all day in the rain as they were.

That evening word came that Daven Marcus had ordered the march to resume the next morning in spite of the rain. Amelia could scarcely believe that the entire company would ride west in such foul weather, but so long as the prince wished it, she knew no one would dare to question. Rumor was that some of the ladies of the court had complained that the muddied ground would stain their gowns, and in anger, the prince declared that the whole company would have to move on in the rain then. That was the story Turley relayed to her, but Amelia doubted it.

"It seems unlikely our crown prince would inconvenience himself just to make a point to ladies of the court," she said as he stood inside the tent flap, wet clothes and hair, his legs splattered with mud past his knees. "Whatever the true reason, we will be ready to leave in the morning as the prince instructs."

Turley tugged his forelock and nodded.

"Have you heard word of what will become of Lord Wolden's body?" Amelia asked.

"No, Your Grace."

"Find out. I assume his body will be sent back to his holdings and his family, but I will pay my respects before he is taken home."

"Yes, Your Grace." Turley's lips twisted into an uncertain frown. "You…um…might find that difficult, Your Grace."

Standing at Amelia's shoulder, Kirsten tutted as usual at his impertinence, but the duchess ignored her.

"Why do you say that?" she asked him. Turley sucked his teeth before he answered.

"Them guards the prince's man put outside," he explained. "They've made themselves at home, well and truly. They kicked your people away from the fire and are questioning everyone who comes near, high or low. They likely won't take to the notion of Your Grace leaving your tent."

"You think to tell the duchess where she can or cannot go?" Kirsten demanded, indignant. Amelia held up her hand and did her best not to find it tiresome. Turley was doing no more than speaking the truth, and Kirsten's only objection was that the words came from the mouth of a retainer. The murderous Robant had said much the same to her a day ago, and it was all Kirsten could do not to fawn over the man.

"Nevertheless, steward," she said to Turley. "Go now to whoever has charge of Lord Wolden's body and tell them to arrange a moment for me to pray for his departed soul. Then warn my household guards that I will need an escort for the visit. That should give Robant's men pause. And if not, you have my liberty to let it be known that it was Baron Robant acting on behalf of the prince who interfered with my duties to my people."

"Very good, Your Grace."

There was a twinkle in Turley's eye as he accepted her instruction. He understood clearly how she wanted to play the game. That pleased Amelia for a moment, but then she remembered that it was Wolden's death that had made this 'play' possible. The mortal remains of such a loyal man should not be a piece in a game. The duchess's thoughts soured immediately and remained that way long after Turley had gone to do her bidding. She fell asleep chewing them over still.

Turley returned the next morning before she had even awakened. Kirsten found him waiting outside the tent flap. The rain had not stopped, but he was relatively dry from waiting under the awning. When she admitted him, he presented the noblewomen with two hooded, oilskin cloaks, one for each of them to protect them from the rain. He assured her he had some similar protection for himself.

"I've spoken to the viscount's people as well, Your Grace," Turley explained. "They've received the prince's leave to depart the march this morning, but they will await your respects afore they make off."

Amelia was pleased. Turley's industry impressed her, and she wondered when he found time to sleep. Then she remembered he had survived many years as a convict. A steward's duties were probably much less daunting.

Turley withdrew, and she and Kirsten finished dressing, finally fitting the heavy, water-resistant cloaks about their shoulders. Ready to face the rain, Amelia stepped from her tent and was surprised to find a carriage parked literally in front of her, not ten paces away. It was a dark wooden box with an arched roof, drawn by four draft horses. It stood on spoked wheels and had a single door in the side. She wondered how she had not heard it arrive, especially as she listened to the rain drumming on its roof panels. Turley was standing by the step at the door, wearing a straw hat that dribbled water from its brim to soak his shoulders. A face appeared in the carriage door's little open window—Lord Robant's. He was wearing his broad-brimmed, felt cap.

"Your Grace," he said smoothly, "a pleasure to see you this pitiful, wet morning. Out of concern for your wellbeing, the prince has commissioned this carriage to carry you into the west."

Out of a desire to keep me continually imprisoned, Amelia thought, but she forced herself to smile politely.

In the distance between her tent and the carriage, two rows of soldiers formed rank like walls to keep her from turning in any direction but toward the carriage. One rank was Robant's men but the other was made up of hers. The two faced each other, and Amelia fancied she could see hostile looks passing between them. She wondered if Turley had deliberately set them like this and was almost immediately certain he had. It was his way to assert her authority. As she stepped out into the rain, Robant opened the door of the carriage and stepped out politely, holding out his hand for her.

"Your Grace."

Amelia ignored the baron's hand and looked instead to her steward. He immediately offered his own hand, and she took it to step into the carriage, deliberately not looking to see if Robant took offence. Her small pleasure at disdaining him was dispelled when she realized she was not alone in the carriage. Pressed back into the far corner of the dark space was another woman, the Countess Dalflitch. Amelia blinked in shock.

"What are you doing here?" she demanded, too surprised to bother being courteous.

"The prince insisted," Robant said from behind her. "He wishes to see all his most important ladies safely bestowed."

Dalflitch said nothing but gave Amelia a smile so condescending it was all but a sneer. Amelia seated herself in the opposite corner from Dalflitch, ready to raise an objection with her jailer, when she heard Kirsten's voice outside the carriage door.

"Am I permitted to ride inside as well?" Kirsten asked demurely. Amelia was about to demand that of course her maid would ride with her, but Robant beat her to it.

"I insist," he said and held out his hand. As she stepped into the carriage, Amelia was sure her handmaid seemed a little flushed in the cheeks. Doing her best to control her annoyance, Amelia leaned back out the doorway while Kirsten settled herself in the carriage's cramped confines. "Turley," she called.

Turley slipped past the armed men still forming the belligerent honor guard and was about to step up to the carriage when Robant stopped him with a hand straight on his chest.

"You aren't riding in there," said the baron, meeting the steward's level gaze.

Robant was tall, but Turley was taller still. Nonetheless, the nobleman showed no indications that he was the least bit intimidated by his lesser. Each man held the other's gaze in a moment of cold confrontation, and then Turley turned his expression to its usual, roguish grin.

"Of course not, m'Lord," he said, jauntily tugging his forelock under his straw hat so that fresh droplets cascaded from the brim. "I'll be riding on the back step at my grace's beck and call. That's why I'm wearing my new good hat." He nodded to the rear of the carriage.

"Take your hat off when you address me, servant!" Robant ordered. Turley's expression went cold again, his mouth a hard, pursed line. Nevertheless, he was about to obey the baron's order to expose his dry head to the open rain when Amelia called him.

"Do not lollygag, steward."

Turley's smile came back in a flash, and he ducked his head again. "The duchess summons me," he said, giving Robant a mocking wink.

Turley made his way around the baron, and as he did so, Robant turned his head to watch him. From her perch at the carriage's door, Amelia could see Robant smiling at her steward's back as if he enjoyed Turley's sense of humor, but the nobleman's eyes were like hard, dark pieces of glass. He seemed equally as likely to break any moment into a delighted laugh or a murderous rage. In spite of herself, Amelia shivered at the sight; thankfully the cold weather gave her good excuse.

"Give word to the drivers," she told Turley, forcing herself to drag her eyes off the dangerous Robant. "We will stop with the Viscount Wolden's retainers and pay our respects."

"Your Grace appears mistaken," said Robant. "These drivers do not answer to your instructions. I fear you cannot tell them where to go, when to start, or when to stop."

"Again, Lord Robant, you propose to tell the Reach's liege what she may or may not do?" Amelia said lightly.

"Again, Your Grace, not I but the prince."

Robant punctuated his words with a little bow. Amelia turned immediately to Turley.

"In that case, steward, run directly to the viscount's people and offer my apologies. Say that the crown prince esteems the lives of Reachermen so cheaply that he cannot allow me a moment to pay respects to one slain in honorable combat. Say that he regards the Reach, its duchess, and her people so lowly that he thinks it a worthless endeavor to show them even common courtesy."

"Very good, Your Grace." Turley stepped away, ready to rush off with the message, but Robant caught him by the arm before he could leave.

"Your man would be at risk if noble ears heard that message," he said to Amelia with an underlying tone of threat.

"Nobles of the Reach would know the truth of the words," she said calmly, and this time it was her turn to meet Robant's eyes. Watching the baron's face closely, she could see him thinking through the implications. It was probable that the prince had given instructions that she was to be kept in the carriage throughout the day in order to maintain her imprisonment. But there was no legitimate way Lord Robant could block her from sending messages or giving her servants instructions, not with her armed houseguards standing mere paces away. And her message, if sent, would certainly embarrass the prince and draw attention to her condition. Finally, Robant finished weighing the situation.

"Very well, Your Grace," he said, bowing again. "We shall stop a moment for you to pray with the viscount's remains. He did, after all, die for the sake of your honor." He twisted the last two words like a knife, but Amelia would not shrink from the blame.

"And at your hand," she reminded him. "Perhaps you would like to pay your respects as well?"

Robant's mocking smile hardened, and he pushed Turley toward the rear of the carriage, releasing his arm with a shove.

"Take your place on the backstep, steward. And let me hear no more from you for the rest of the day!"

Turley trotted to the backstep as instructed, splashing through the mud, and Amelia withdrew within the carriage, pulling the door closed for herself as she did so. Sitting back on the cushioned seat, she looked across at her maid and then to the countess, who returned her look with a smile.

"Did you wish to say something, Countess?"

"He plans to break you, you know," said Dalflitch, her painted lips smiling but with no apparent malice in her tone. "The prince, I mean. Robant is just his highness' attack dog. He follows orders. But Daven Marcus doesn't like your willfulness. He means to cure you of it."

"Is that so?"

"There's little point fighting him. He is the crown prince, second highest man in the Grand Kingdom, and one day, its king. Why be willful? He will only win in the end, regardless."

"I am the soul of meekness," Amelia responded, though she knew her tone was anything but meek. "I have no will of my own, only the will of my people—the will of the Reach."

"The prince says they're *his* people, and he will break them to his rule, just as he will you. He means to marry you, to make you first a princess and then a queen, and then your precious Reachermen will be the people of a princedom. Why make it hard on yourself?"

Amelia was about to answer her, but the wagon suddenly jolted forward, and she was forced to reach out for the nearby side panel to keep from losing her seat. Once they were moving, she relaxed again. She looked to the countess and tried to remember what she had wanted to say. Suddenly, it seemed so pointless. Dalflitch was correct, mostly. Come what may, the prince meant to marry her, and if not him, it would have to be someone, someday. The Reach was a frontier; it needed a lord. The Grand Kingdom would settle for nothing else. Why shouldn't it be a prince? But Daven Marcus disgusted her, and if she was going to have to endure his "love" for the rest of her life, she would do it for and by the strength of her people and for the memory of her first, true love, Duke Marne.

She sat back and looked away from Countess Dalflitch. Someday soon she would be a princess, married to the Prince of the West. She would not demean herself, bandying words with her future husband's mistress. The bouncing and rocking of the carriage over the muddy ground promised a day's journey that would be uncomfortable enough. Amelia fixed her eyes on a blank spot on the opposite panel and tried to compose some words in her mind, worthy of Viscount Wolden's remembrance.

Her man. Her people. Her duty.

CHAPTER 21

"A cursed charnel house." Prentice couldn't help muttering under his breath, looking out over the carnage as the grey light of morning filtered down through the sputtering rain. Fallenhill was in ruins again.

Just before dawn, a heavy downpour had emerged from the west, drenching everything and finally dousing the flames that were driving the livestock to panic. The cloud-banked sky hid the rising sun, but as the night's darkness paled to grey day, the wreckage was everywhere to be seen. The cattle stampede had crushed and trampled everything inside the walls, including the cattle themselves. At least eighty of the beasts were dead or dying, having cast themselves in every direction trying to escape. Of those that still lived, many were lamed, legs broken from charging over collapsed walls and fallen beams that hadn't yet been cleared from the ruins. Mournful lowing thrummed through the air, and the smell of blood spilled, splashed, and smeared in seemingly every direction filled the nostrils. Even with the rain, it would be late in the morning before the noisome stench was sluiced away into foul puddles that pooled amongst the winter grass.

The defense of the barracks had been a success of sorts, with most of the men and women there surviving, but an end of one hut had been collapsed by several bullocks that managed to climb the rough ground nearby and plunge through the sod roof, tearing that bit of the low building apart in a panicked tumult. Flames and poles had made an effective deterrent around the rest of the huts, giving most of the men and women of Fallenhill a measure of refuge during the night. There were myriad cuts and bruises, not to mention a number of serious injuries. It was the dead that most concerned Prentice, though.

"Do you have a count and a list?" he demanded of Sir Gant.

As soon as the beasts started to calm, Prentice had sent his knight lieutenant out to tally the dead. It was mid-morning and Gant was returning from his task, filthy, grim-faced, and wet to the skin. Prentice met him in the rain, just as chilled and soaked through as Gant appeared. He could feel the cold pressing into his bones, but he ignored it.

"Not finished yet. Some folks were far scattered in the chaos. But at least fifty lie lifeless out there."

"Fifty?" Prentice hawked and spat on the ground.

"And then there's the wounded," Gant followed up. "We'll lose a dozen more, I'd wager, with injuries too dire to treat."

Prentice shook his head and turned away in disgust. He rubbed his hand through his hair and icy water squeezed out to run down the back of his neck. He grunted at the discomfort.

"It is bad," said Gant. "But we did much better than we might have."

The calm part of Prentice's mind knew Gant was right. For all the carnage and destruction, they'd survived the night better than they deserved to. But that only added to the fury that thundered in Prentice's thoughts. Liam had outwitted him completely. The whole camp had suffered brutally, and they didn't even know fully how much yet, but they deserved much worse. Because of him. No amount of inner calm could suppress the turmoil he felt as he looked at the dying men and beasts and the wreckage, knowing it was his fault. He'd smugly expected Baron Liam to attack straight on, to besiege the gate with battering rams and try to make an honorable fight of it. Prentice could feel his self-control slipping. He had rapists and thieves inside the walls and a force of murderous, cunning men waiting outside the gates. The storm inside him threatened to sweep him away. He was seized by a sudden desire to take his sword-breaker and charge out the gate to Liam's camp; to fight his way toward the baron, falling under a storm of knights' swords. He shook with the effort it took to keep himself in place. For a long moment he did nothing else, eyes staring unfocused at the camp walls. Then, he realized that Gant was talking, and he hadn't been listening.

"What did you say?"

"Sergeant Ranold," Gant repeated. "He is one of those we lost. They found his body. Looks like he fell and hit his head on a stone, and then some cattle trampled his leg and hip. He bled into his body in the night."

That news broke the spell of Prentice's fury, and he felt himself sag suddenly. The night's fatigue and the cold of the rain all fell on him in a single rush, and he sank down to sit on the stones, hanging his head in his hands.

"What do you want to do?" Gant asked him. His tone was full of uncertainty. For a long moment, Prentice ignored him. He had no reassurance to give. "What are your orders?"

At last, he looked up and saw Gant's expression. The knight was worried, but Prentice thought not for himself nor for his captain. For the camp. A crisis like this needed a leader, someone who could look the destruction in the face and not flinch. But, for the first time since he'd met then Sir Liam and Duchess Amelia at the quarry in the south, Prentice was almost certain he did not have the strength he needed. He looked around him and back at Gant's earnest eyes, and inside himself he felt nothing but flinching. He wanted to run away. For a decade he'd been a convict, and it had never scared him like this because he'd never been responsible for anyone else but himself. Liam and his knights, with their swords and maces, were nothing to fear compared with the thought of the lives that were ended now because he had been outfoxed.

Too bad, the calm voice inside him said. The steel in his soul that never flinched from the fire or the chill reasserted itself. *Pity yourself tomorrow,* it said to him. *Today needs orders.*

"That meat won't take a day to start rotting in this rain," he said flatly, gazing at the dead and dying cattle. Gant looked over his shoulder in surprise, nodding.

"The herd's gone, or all but," the knight agreed. "And there's not a sheep or goat alive either. It's a waste."

They had to save what they could.

"We need to get to stripping the carcasses as fast as we can," said Prentice. "Every bit of meat and offal, anything that can be eaten. We'll take horn and bone as well, and any scraps of hide that might be tannable."

"How will we store it?"

Prentice shrugged. "The huts that have ovens built already can start drying the meat immediately. We don't have enough salt to preserve it all at once, but we'll do what we can. The forge fires will work for smoking as well."

The workshop forges, placed as they were in the foundations of the tower keep and surrounded by stone walls built to withstand siege, had escaped the night's disaster unscathed, as had anyone who'd hidden there.

"Master Sent will not respond favorably to that idea, I think," said Gant.

"He will if he wants to eat a week from now," Prentice snapped so angrily that Sir Gant blinked for a moment. Prentice pushed himself back to his feet. "I need to speak to with Corporal Felix, find out who takes over his company now that Ranold's died. Damn, that's a loss to us."

Prentice knew he sounded cold, assessing the sergeant's death only from the perspective of its impact on his own plans, but that coldness helped shore up the walls of his own self-control. Then a thought occurred to him that threatened to tear it all down again.

"Righteous?" he asked. Through the chaos of the night, he'd not given the young widow the least thought, but the sudden notion that she might be among the dead struck him hard, so hard that the intensity surprised him. Why was her safety so important?

"She survived," Gant reassured him with an odd expression. "She survived the night with the women's hut. They did well, from the looks of it. Now she's got them out treating wounds and tending to the dead."

Prentice was glad to hear that, and with a surprisingly difficult effort of will he put his concern for Righteous back on a shelf in his mind. He told himself it was because of the brutality she'd suffered in her life that he had a soft spot for her and probably always would. With that thought, he turned his thoughts to his other duties. He was about to give more orders when a call came from the gate. It surprised him to realize that there were still men on the battlements doing guard duty, except, of course, that the walls had probably been the safest place to endure the night's terrors—ironic, given how loathed battlement duty normally was.

"What do you wager the baron has come to invite us to surrender?" he asked Gant bitterly as he headed off toward the gate.

"I don't have much left to wager with, you know," the knight said, looking about at the destruction. "And neither do you."

"I lived ten years on a chain with less than this to my name, and it was enough to slay the Horned Man and break his army!" Tired from fighting with his own doubts, Prentice felt no interest in soothing Sir Gant's

"That's true enough," said Gant, and despite Prentice's angry tone, he seemed less troubled than he had a moment ago.

CHAPTER 22

The rain had receded to a light drizzle. Baron Liam was on his charger, his polished plate armor bright even in the dismal, cloud-cloaked light. His injured face was twisted in a garish smile, as if he his expression was painted on like an actor's. Prentice imagined that the baron would probably look that way for the rest of his life, his scars deforming his once-handsome expressions so that no emotion would seem sincere again, except perhaps for hatred. With Liam were a dozen other knights, and looking down from the wall, Prentice was sure he could recognize at least one of the prisoners they had released the night before.

Hells bells, Prentice thought. *Was it only yesterday they had captured those armored men coming over the walls?*

"Did you have a difficult night, convict?" Liam shouted. "It sounded like hellish strife."

Prentice heard men next to him muttering grimly. He wanted to throw a witty retort back at the baron, something Turley might have said with his usual cheek, but nothing came to mind. Liam was right, it had been a difficult night. Prentice was bone weary and just wanted to sleep.

"It was a long night, Baron," he called down, not bothering to hide the fatigue in his voice. "Thank you."

"The knights you sent out stripped yesterday said you seemed to have everything under control in there. I didn't want to believe them, and when we heard that noise, like a battle all through the night, I half hoped your men had risen up and slain you. Alas, you live."

Prentice sighed and looked away from the proud knights below him. His eyes lighted on the besiegers' camp and he saw that it had grown substantially. There were more animals than there should have been. Liam's men must have gathered much of the abandoned livestock from the nearby countryside, animals Prentice himself had planned to claim before the siege. It made sense, but as he looked, something about Liam's words caught Prentice's attention. The baron should be so much more smug, hard as that might be to imagine. If Liam had such a huge herd of cattle and knew that Prentice's smaller herd had stampeded itself to death inside the walls, he would be gloating; Prentice was sure of it. If he wasn't gloating, he must not know, and if he didn't know, that raised an unpleasant question.

"You've gathered quite the farmstead down there, I see," he shouted, pointing at the camp. He wanted to prompt Liam to confirm his suspicion.

"My vassals," the baron shouted back. "They've been crawling out of the holes where they hid from the invaders and bringing their goods with them, eager to pay for my protection, as they should. I've got a baker and a brewer, and there's even been a deputation from the silver miners in the hills. They've been working hard, it seems."

Liam's pride talking about the little settlement growing at the foot of the meadow was unmistakable. But he still wasn't gloating about the suffering inside the walls. Prentice leaned close to Gant and spoke in a whisper.

"Go now, just you, and do a walk of the walls. Look for any sign that men got over the walls last night and then got back again."

"What's your thinking?" Gant whispered back.

"Liam doesn't know about the stampede; I'd swear to it. Which means his men didn't set the fires among the cattle."

"But that would mean..."

"Someone in here did it."

Gant cast a suspicious glance around him. Prentice put a steadying hand on his shoulder. "One problem at a time. Go first and make sure we didn't miss something. If one of Liam's men is lying dead under a cow, or there's a rope hanging over the side of the wall, I need you to find it. Otherwise..."

Prentice let his meaning hang in the air and Gant nodded. He moved off quickly, head down, making his way along the battlement.

"I'm sorry, Baron," Prentice called down to Liam, who had been saying something to his men. "I must bid you good day. Duty calls. You couldn't imagine the responsibilities that fall upon true leaders."

It was a lame jab, but Liam obligingly took offence, nonetheless, standing in the stirrups, eyes blazing with fury.

"Those walls are your prison, convict! And I am your jailer! Enjoy your miserable last days; they will be few enough. When I come for you, I will claim Fallenhill as the seat of my new barony. The prince will grant it to me, do not doubt. And on that day, I will see you flayed and butchered alive. You will beg me for death before we are done."

"If you say so, Baron."

Turley would have had something much more cutting and certainly cleverer to say, he was sure, and for the first time, he wished his good friend was with him. Then he shook his head. Wherever Turley was, Prentice was glad he was there and not caught in this rat trap.

He left the battlements and returned to the grim cleanup inside the walls. Behind him, Liam shouted a handful more insults. He ignored them, but the venom in the baron's voice troubled him. As long as the siege held, Prentice's people were doomed to hunger, and with the livestock slain and the rain rotting the meat, that hunger was now looming on their horizon like another winter storm. But that wasn't what troubled

Prentice. Liam's hatred for him was the real danger. Up until now, Liam's superior attitude and disgust for all lower-born men had kept him from seeing the one tactic that would win him Fallenhill in a single moment. In truth, all Liam really had to do was offer amnesty. If he offered to forgive these convicts their debt to the Western Reach and the Grand Kingdom, and they'd have Prentice's head on a spike over the gates in a trice.

With that thought, coupled with the notion that there were traitors inside the walls who had set the fires among the livestock, Prentice found himself watching every man or woman around him with a near paranoid distrust. He was as trapped as they were, just another rat inside the walls, but what if the other rats decided to fall on him? Right now, they were afraid of trampling each other like the herd had in its stampede. But if Liam promised to give them an escape?

So that was the race Prentice was in—against Liam's pride, his hatred, and his strategy and tactics as a knight. Prentice had outrun Liam's strategy, just, but he was confident he could do it again. The baron's cunning and hatred were the two that he had to outrun now. If, even for a moment, Liam's hatred got its nose in front in the race, if he let his pride drop just a little, he'd offer amnesty in exchange for Prentice's head, and then it would be over. The rats would turn on the leader of their pack and trample each other to get to him. And if it turned out that the stampede fires hadn't been lit by Liam's men but by someone inside the walls, the whole race was being sabotaged and all bets were off. The thought turned Prentice's stomach, and he hawked and spat to get the taste of bile out of his mouth.

"Right, let's get some graves dug," he called to men standing about, listless and exhausted from the long night. Under his breath he added, "And maybe a spare one for me, just in case."

If any of them heard him, they didn't say anything about it.

CHAPTER 23

For all that she hated having to share her journey with Countess Dalflitch, Amelia found she was glad to have the carriage to ride in. The heavy winter rain she heard outside must have been drenching the rest of the march to the bone. The carriage's door held the only window, and for the most part they kept it shuttered against the rain. It made the air inside stuffy and unpleasant, but in those moments when the showers abated enough to open the shutter, every person she saw riding or marching looked miserable and waterlogged.

Through the morning of that first day there was virtually no conversation in the carriage, which suited Amelia. After her initial jibes, Dalflitch settled into her corner of the carriage, so relaxed that for much of the time the countess looked to be asleep. While Amelia enjoyed the quiet, her mind drifting with the creak of the axles and the sound of the rainfall, Kirsten seemed to find the quiet air more oppressive and difficult to accept. She spent much of the morning casting suspicious glances in the countess's direction, and in the few instances when she felt constrained to speak to her mistress, she whispered, as if they were sharing the carriage with a wild animal she was afraid of waking. For all her apparent disinterest, Dalflitch must have noticed Kirsten's discomfort as well, as near noon, the countess gave a bold, throaty chuckle.

"It's alright girl," she said, turning suddenly to look at Kirsten. "I don't bite. Not girls, at any rate."

"Perhaps she's just uncertain how to address you," Amelia responded, not bothering to look in Dalflitch's direction. "What is the correct title for the slattern lying in her mistress's betrothed's bed, would you say?" Amelia meant to insult the countess, but the woman showed no ire, only sighing quietly.

"The proper form of address is 'My Lady,'" she said.

Amelia sniffed derisively and waved an equally dismissive hand.

"Isn't your husband still alive?" Kirsten asked. Amelia would have rather Kirsten not speak with Dalflitch, but it occurred to her that she actually knew virtually nothing about this woman who seemed so important to her future husband.

"Yes, my husband lives," Dalflitch confirmed. "What of it?"

"Then how can you...? I mean, with the prince?" Kirsten pressed.

"How can I what?"

"With the prince..."

"What with the prince?"

Kirsten's meaning was obvious, but she was clearly too uncomfortable to say it out loud. It infuriated Amelia that Dalflitch was being deliberately obtuse.

"You're a married woman," she snapped. "My maid wants to know how you can so publicly cuckold your husband?"

"My husband is not with the court," Dalflitch responded.

"Not surprising."

"Why? Do you think he would challenge the prince over my honor?" Dalflitch laughed again. Something about the notion seemed funny to her, but Amelia couldn't imagine what.

"You hold your husband in such contempt?"

"My husband is nearly seventy," Dalflitch said breezily. "And even if he were not, and even if he had been the kind of man to issue a challenge for honor, what man in the Kingdom could challenge the Prince of Rhales?"

The countess's point was fair of course; no man could legitimately challenge the prince. Amelia still found herself disgusted at Dalflitch's contemptuous attitude. It was true that Duke Marne had married her for her family's money, but they had loved each other earnestly, nonetheless.

"We are not that different, you and I, Duchess," said Dalflitch, and Amelia felt her eyes go wide in furious surprise.

"You insult me to my face?"

"Oh, hardly. I married my husband for his rank and position, as you did yours."

"I loved my husband, and he loved me!"

"I don't doubt it. Certainly, you make enough show of mourning him. What are you? Twenty? And dressed every day like a dried-out crone."

Amelia knew the countess was trying to shock her with her brazenness, and she forced herself into dignified silence. Next to her, though, she heard Kirsten having to stifle a shocked gasp. Absentmindedly, Amelia fingered the black lace of her veil a moment. It reminded her of the past year's tragedies, and she felt a hardness in her heart.

"My husband is barely more than half a year dead!" she said through gritted teeth, knowing that her expression did nothing to hide her contempt for this vain woman.

"Exactly," was all Dalflitch said, as if her point were made for her.

"Are you saying her grace has mourned enough?" asked Kirsten.

It was unusual for her to speak out of turn, but feeling her emotions start to run out of control within her, Amelia was thankful for her handmaid's involvement. Dalflitch surprised her by considering Kirsten's question seriously.

"I don't know how it is out here in the far west, what rural traditions hold sway," she said at last, "but in Rhales she'd be remarried by now."

"Already?" Kirsten's tone was shocked, but there was a breathless, excited undertone to it.

"Of course. She's what? Twenty summers with only one husband?" Dalflitch was speaking directly to Kirsten now, virtually ignoring Amelia. Such a breach of etiquette should have offended her, but Amelia was just glad not to have to speak with the countess for a moment. She clenched her jaw with the effort of keeping her dignity.

"By Rhales' standards, Her Grace may as well still be a maid," the countess declared.

"I'm still a maid," said Kirsten.

"It shows."

"Oh." It was clear that Kirsten didn't know if she was being insulted or sympathized with. Amelia was sure she knew.

"My dear," said Dalflitch, suddenly sounding like a kindly aunt or older sister. "The truth is that with your mistress' power and influence, you should command the attention of a dozen suitors. More, if we count the petty nobles of the west."

Kirsten seemed taken with the idea, but she still had one question. "How would I know which ones only wanted marriage for advantage?"

"All marriage is for advantage."

Amelia couldn't help but snort in disgust at the countess's pronouncement.

"No?" asked Dalflitch, cocking one eyebrow. "Your first was for that purpose, was it not, Your Grace? And will your next one be any different?"

Her next? Amelia glared at the countess.

"Her grace will marry the prince," Kirsten explained as if the countess didn't realize. Dalflitch tilted her head to look at Amelia, and Kirsten turned to look as well. There was a strange look of realization in Kirsten's eyes that Amelia found disconcerting and annoying.

"Daven Marcus' reasons for wooing me are his own," Amelia said coldly. "As you yourself said, who would oppose the will of the Prince of Rhales?"

"And yet his will is to your advantage."

Amelia met the countess's eyes and, in that moment, realized why the licentious noblewoman was being so hateful. She wanted what Amelia would have; she didn't want to be the prince's mistress, nor even his consort. The countess wanted to be the princess, and of course, one day the queen. As she thought about it, Amelia realized that Dalflitch probably didn't even want Daven Marcus himself. It was the rank she craved. Looking into the ambitious noblewoman's eyes, Amelia suddenly knew that this woman was willing to endure his many depravities, his self-love—anything—for the chance at her ultimate prize. And that meant, in Dalflitch's eyes, this rural duchess from the Kingdom's most parochial frontier was her greatest rival. It was all Amelia could do not to laugh out loud at the thought. She would just as soon help the countess marry the prince as challenge her for the privilege. Kirsten and Dalflitch were speaking quietly, and Amelia realized that she'd been ignoring them.

"Did you wish to say something, Your Grace?" Dalflitch asked when she noticed Amelia staring at them both. Amelia only shrugged, but she didn't hide her smile.

"I will sit quietly for a while, I think," she said. "But by all means, continue your conversation."

Dalflitch gave her a puzzled look, which pleased Amelia. Let the countess wonder at her thoughts for once.

As the day's journey went on, the conversation, the sounds of the wagon and rain, and even the stuffiness of the air all receded into the background as Amelia considered the possibilities offered by Dalflitch's ambitions. She was sure the prince had the two of them in the same carriage for a reason. Perhaps he thought it would stir up rivalry for him, making Amelia start to compete for his affections. Or he might simply have thought to insult her. That had been her first instinct; Daven Marcus's idea of diplomacy seemed to be to abuse and insult people until he got what he wanted.

But Amelia found herself wondering, what if she could make an ally of Dalflitch? The woman was already in the prince's bed, something that made Amelia shudder every time she thought of it. Why fight the countess for a prize she didn't want? And Dalflitch? The woman wanted the crown, but Amelia knew there was no chance of that. Whatever her beauty or skills at love, she was just a woman, and that was far too little advantage against the dowry the Reach would bring to the prince. Silver and iron were the prince's greater loves. Then there was the matter of the countess's marriage. It was possible that the prince might have enough influence with the Mother Church to have her marriage annulled, but if he genuinely wanted that, Amelia was certain he would already have done it. It was a large favor to ask of the church.

No, whichever way she sliced it, Dalflitch would never be Daven Marcus's wife. So then, what use could the countess be to her? Amelia would be happy to leave the prince's bed to Dalflitch. Let him marry her, get an heir on her, and then go back to his mistress. She doubted that would suit Dalflitch, but if Amelia showed she was happy to remain in the Reach while the countess and prince held court in Rhales, that might suit the ambitious woman. The whole idea seemed farfetched to Amelia, but she had to admit, it offered the seductive possibility of getting out from under the prince's thumb. Of course, there was little chance the king would approve of such an arrangement, nor would the church, most likely. Thinking again of the church brought Amelia up short. What would God think of such an arrangement? A woman trapped in such a loveless, calculated marriage might be excused socially if she accepted it, but would God forgive her if she planned such a defilement of the marriage bed right from the start? And that thought brought back memories of her husband. Marne was a romantic. He married her for money but loved her for herself. He would have despised such a calculated relationship.

Oh dearest, Amelia thought. *You are gone, and this is the estate you have left me. I have no defender now.*

That wasn't true. Prentice was still in the east, building her militia. And there was the vision and what it purported. Truly the prince and his courtiers were like carrion birds, picking at her and her lands as at a carcass. If the vision was true, then she needed lions to defend her. That was what Prentice and his soldiers were supposed to be, and perhaps Turley. But Turley was the only one here, and as protective as he was, he was not enough, not against the prince's flock of carrion courtiers. Perhaps the time had come to make some allies among the nobles of Rhales, and Dalflitch was her best first choice. It was far from moral, even far from likely, but it was the prime path she could see ahead of herself.

That evening, when the march stopped, Lord Robant arrived quickly to escort Countess Dalflitch to the prince's tent while he informed Amelia and Kirsten that their own tent was not yet arrived, let alone set. It was meant as a slight, but Amelia welcomed the chance to talk privately with her maid.

"You and the countess seem to be growing close," she said quietly once the carriage door was closed again. Kirsten's expression took on an uncertain cast.

"Do you disapprove, Your Grace?" she asked, nervously twisting the hem of her sleeve in her fingers. "I was only seeking to be polite."

Amelia raised a hand. "Do not worry," she said gently. "You did nothing wrong."

Kirsten relaxed visibly.

"I know the countess sees me as an enemy," Amelia went on. "A rival, I imagine."

"How can you be a rival? She is married." There was a gossipy breathlessness to Kirsten's words, as if she was more excited by the rumors of the countess's immoral behavior than offended by the fact of it.

"I do not know what she thinks, and we would do well not to fall to gossiping about her motives."

Kirsten looked down, accepting the rebuke.

"Nevertheless, I do not hate the countess in return," Amelia went on. "She enjoys the prince's favor for now, and it would not be seemly to disrupt the peace of his court with pointless rivalry."

"You do not mind his dalliance with her?" Kirsten looked up again, and her eyes were wide as saucers.

"I don't..." Amelia hesitated. What could she say in response to that? What would her maid think of her if she simply accepted her future husband's debauchery as if it were nothing? "I think the countess is right, at least in part, when she says that it is not our place to question the prince or his actions."

"With respect, Your Grace, that's not what Countess Dalflitch said."

It was not like Kirsten to question her so openly, and Amelia wondered for a moment what was going on in her handmaiden's head.

"It is the meaning I choose to take from her words," she chided. "And you would do well to do the same."

"I will stop speaking with her," Kirsten offered.

Amelia shook her head. "That will not do. She is the prince's favorite, and you are his betrothed's maid. If you are rude to her, you could provoke trouble far above your station. Instead, I think you should let friendship grow between the two of you if it should seem possible. It might be that you could form a bridge between myself and the countess."

"And what of the prince?"

"What of him? However he chooses to make use of me or of the countess, those are his matters, and he answers for them to his father and to God. Whatever the prince chooses to do, Countess Dalflitch and I will have to come to our own accommodations."

Kirsten nodded, accepting her mistress's instructions. Before either woman could say anything more, there was a knock at the carriage door and Turley was there to escort them to their tent. As they walked through the dark and rainy night, feet squelching on the wet grass, Amelia had a moment of misgiving. Some part of her knew it was wrong to accept the prince's dalliance with Dalflitch with such a calculating attitude. It was immoral, and she worried suddenly that she was being drawn into the shabby, carrion-bird morality of the Rhales court. Worse, she was teaching her maid to do the same. She felt like a drowning swimmer, dragging a companion down with her. Yet what else was she to do?

The cold and wet made the inside of their tent uncomfortable to sleep in, but even if it were not, Amelia would not have slept well that night.

CHAPTER 24

Two more miserable days' journey passed in the stuffiness of the carriage. Following her mistress's instruction, Kirsten made a clear effort to engage the countess in conversation. While Dalflitch showed some initial reluctance, Amelia was surprised at how quickly the two women struck up a rapport. Their conversations mostly circled around fashions and court gossip, subjects that of course fascinated Kirsten. It was an interest the countess seemed to share. Kirsten made a creditable effort to involve her mistress in the conversation, and Amelia knew she wasn't making it easy on her, but she could not rouse the least interest in court fashion. She spoke hardly at all.

Nonetheless, she listened closely to the gossip which Dalflitch willingly shared, not because she enjoyed gossip, but because the tales the countess told helped her fill in the empty spaces in her knowledge of the Rhales court. The salacious details of a suspected affair between a court lady and a young knight were of supreme disinterest to Amelia. But finding out that the knight was able to get away with his dalliance because of his father's influence over the wool trade in the lady's husband's home province was an important thing to note. If that knight or his father became an enemy, then a tax on any of their woolens imported to the Reach would be a way to attack them.

These were the thoughts that occupied Amelia as she rode quietly in the carriage until around noon on the third day when the vehicle lurched suddenly sideways, and all three ladies cried out in surprise as they were forced to grab at the side panels to keep from falling. When the unexpected motion finally stopped, the carriage was still canted at a wild angle, so that they could not sit comfortably. From outside, there were angry shouts and quickly there came a knock at the door. It opened and Turley leaned in at an awkward angle.

"Forgive me, Your Grace," he said and tried to tug his forelock, but taking his hand off the sides of the carriage made him nearly fall backwards. He righted himself and, repositioning his balance, attempted the gesture of respect again. "The carriage has become bogged. For your comfort, I can help you and your ladies to get down, if you would like."

"Am I one of your ladies now?" Dalflitch asked with her usual, sardonic tone. Amelia ignored her.

"Bogged, you say? Is it dry enough for us to get down?" she asked him.

Turley nodded happily.

"I'd say so, Your Grace. There's spots nearby with green grass and solid ground. Even the rain has held up a bit for now. I can fetch your weather cloaks from the luggage, as well, and leather covers for your ladies' feet."

Covers were overshoes made of waxed leather, designed to keep water out of the kind of footwear favored by courtly fashion, such as the slippers all the ladies in the carriage were currently wearing. They were neither dainty nor fashionable, but that only made them more appealing to Amelia at this moment.

"Please fetch those things," she told Turley.

He nodded. "I'll have them brought right away. But I suggest I stay to help you ladies down. The door's not in its usual place to the ground right at this moment."

Turley's bright attitude made Amelia want to smile. From outside she could hear carriage men cursing as they argued the best way to right their vehicle, but Turley was clearly enjoying the undignified disruption to the journey. He was doing his best to show no disrespect, but his pleasure was clear. Amelia looked to see if her companions noticed it and was surprised. Kirsten looked like she hadn't yet recovered from her fright, still too unnerved to worry about recovering her dignity. Amelia had hoped to see some indignance in Dalflitch's countenance, some sign the countess had been disrupted by events, but there was no such impression. Instead, she wore the same expression of entertained equanimity with which she seemed to approach everything in life. In fact, the countess gave Amelia the impression that she was enjoying Turley's amusement as much as Amelia was. That thought annoyed the duchess for some reason, and she peremptorily held out her hand to demand assistance.

"Help me down," she ordered coldly.

Turley ducked his head again and the undignified process of exiting the canted carriage began. The entire procedure was long and slow, complicated by the ladies' skirts and head coverings, but Turley worked carefully and was able to exert his bear-like strength easily to lower each woman in turn to the ground where another servant quickly escorted them to a nearby hummock of grass.

After long hours in the dimness of the carriage, the overcast day seemed strangely bright, even despite the heavy greyness that stretched from horizon to horizon. The covers and oilskin cloaks were brought, and though there was a chill in the air, there was no rain to speak of. Amelia found the whole outdoor moment pleasantly refreshing. Looking around, she could see that they were in the midst of a wild, green grassland. For a moment she tried to find the mountains on the horizon, then realized that she could not. In fact, there seemed to be no distinguishing features in the landscape at all. If it weren't for the rest of the column marching and the trampled grass going back in one direction to show where they had come from, Amelia would have had no way of choosing east from west, or north, or south, especially with the sun hidden behind the clouds.

That thought gave her a moment's nervousness. Then, as she looked away from the direction they had come, Amelia realized there were features she could pick from the terrain ahead of them. Looking at the gentle rise and fall of the plain, she realized that the grasses were dipping out of sight in places into small depressions in the ground. Looking farther, she saw that the depressions seemed scattered everywhere ahead of their path. Some of them were quite large, and in their midst was a darkness that took her a moment to recognize. They were pools of water. If the sun had been out, she imagined they would be glittering brightly, but under the grey sky they were dark and ominous. Looking back, she realized it was one of these strange pools that had nearly upended the carriage. The driver had misjudged the edge of one of the impressions and the wheel had sunk deep.

"What are these odd ponds, steward?" she asked.

Turley shrugged. "Not sure, Your Grace. They're odd, sure enough, and the long grass makes them hard to see until we're close up."

"Our drivers do not know how to recognize bogs and mud holes?"

"I don't think they are bogs, Your Grace," Turley corrected her, at least remembering to keep his voice down as he did so. "The ground here isn't muddy like a bog. It's more like clean sand, like you get in a fast brook. And there doesn't seem to be much water, just these shallow pools all about under the grass."

"Not a bog, and yet our wheels are bogged," Amelia mused. "Is that not strange?"

"I'd have to agree with you, Your Grace."

A gust of cold wind blew past them, heralding the possibility of fresh rain, and Amelia suppressed a shiver under her cloak.

Looking to the other two ladies standing nearby, she noticed that Dalflitch was watching her closely. The countess's eyes slid back and forth between her and Turley, and Amelia knew that the gossipy noblewoman was trying to puzzle out the nature of her familiar relationship with her steward. She sighed inwardly. The last thing she needed was this rumormonger spreading a story of the duchess having an affair with a servant.

"That will be all, steward," she said, formally dismissing Turley for the benefit of Dalflitch's watching eyes. "Be sure to remain nearby. When the carriage is righted, I want to be underway immediately."

"The very moment, Your Grace."

It didn't take too long for the carriage to be pulled onto solid ground, and the ladies were safely inside before the rain started again. That night, the entire army took much longer than normal to camp since scouts struggled to find a space suitable for so many people amid the grassy pools. Nevertheless, Amelia was not left waiting about as she had been on previous nights. Instead, she and Countess Dalflitch were summoned, even before their carriage had stopped for the night, to an audience with the prince. The two noblewomen were guided through the darkness by a chain of wardens of the march holding flickering torches aloft in the dark. Each man in the chain marked a safe path between the half-hidden ponds and pools.

"There have been a number of accidents already," a herald assured them. "Mostly one only gets wet, which is little enough danger in this constant rain, but at least one fool has drowned himself."

"Drowned?" asked Amelia.

"Ended up tangled in the long grasses, somehow, they say. He couldn't get his head free of the water. Silly fool."

"And you give us this guidance because you think we're fools like him?" asked Dalflitch. Even in the flickering torchlight, Amelia saw the herald shudder in a moment of sudden panic.

There was no way he had meant any such insult to the two
highest ranking ladies on the march. For Dalflitch to take
umbrage was the pettiest abuse of power imaginable. But the
prince set the tone for his entire court, and Amelia was certain
the herald was aware of how petty Daven Marcus could be. The
man had to be terrified of being accused of insulting the prince's
mistress.

"I don't think, My Lady," the herald answered at last,
swallowing heavily as he did so. "I merely follow the instructions
given to me by my betters."

"As it should be," said Dalflitch. The two ladies continued
wending their way through the torch-lit path in the darkness.

"Why do that?" Amelia asked her when they were out of
earshot.

"Do what?"

"Why terrorize the man? You know he meant no insult."

"Terrorize? Why duchess, you make it sound as if I had the
man soiling his breeches." The countess's voice was tinged with
laughter. "I was merely reminding him of his place."

"You think he was forgetting it?"

"I think he was looking down his nose at a dead boy. I helped
him remember that no matter who was beneath him, there were
still better above him."

Amelia wasn't sure if she doubted the countess's motives or
respected them. The herald had been showing contempt for a
youth who had lost his life in a wasteful tragedy. But was it
right for the countess to heap contempt upon contempt? How
would Dalflitch like to be on the receiving end?

"I suppose if you get ideas above your station, you expect to
be reminded?" she asked.

The countess didn't even turn to look at her. "Of course,"
said Dalflitch.

"Very good," said Amelia. "I will make sure to do so when I
feel you need reminding."

The countess's head snapped in Amelia's direction, and even with the firelight shadows dancing on the woman's face, her hateful anger was unmistakable.

"Daven Marcus is over us both," she hissed through gritted teeth. "He will keep us to our places, you can rest assured."

This was the most naked Dalflitch's ambition had ever been, and Amelia found it somehow comforting, as if it was the final symptom a physician needed to diagnose the disease. She smiled to herself.

"Even the prince has a place within the Grand Kingdom."

"Until he replaces his father on the throne," Dalflitch retorted.

"After that, too," Amelia went on. "When he dies, he must answer to God, who is above all." Amelia wasn't exactly sure why she invoked the Lord. Although she counted herself a godly woman, she was not a creature of great faith, she did not think. Perhaps it was the mystical visions she had been receiving, or perhaps it was just that she hated the notion of Daven Marcus being sovereign over all he surveyed with no fear of judgement or rebuke.

"Yes, even kings and princes answer to God," said Dalflitch slowly. The countess began to visibly recover her bearing as she did so, reasserting control of herself. Amelia couldn't help but admire the woman's will. "We will all be judged for our actions, one day. Until then, we will all have to be watchful for our own places, as well as those of our lessers and betters. I will have to defer to your judgement, I think, Your Grace. You know at least as well as I what it means to be out of your place."

Amelia knew Countess Dalflitch meant to remind her of her common birth, to put her in her place even as she threatened to do the same back. The insult barely landed, though; its sting was like a mere insect bite to Amelia. Instead, she was struck by how much she suddenly understood Dalflitch's position in court. She was the prince's mistress, which gave her power and influence above her station, but that was entirely dependent on

Daven Marcus's good will. Her place was utterly vulnerable to the whims of a petulant man-child. It reminded Amelia of her own uncertain grip on her own power. In that moment, despite her other feelings for the countess, Amelia found herself pitying her, and she wondered if everyone in the Grand Kingdom, from the greatest to the least, felt this insecurity. Was all social status just a shifting sand that threatened to suck them all under, like the boggy pools all around them in the grass? Was a king more secure than a yeoman? She remembered something Prentice once said about the brutal but simple concerns of convict life. Food and rest, these were all that a convict thought about every day. It was a vile existence, but in a perverse way, it was the most secure in the entire Kingdom. That notion troubled her.

At last, Prince Daven Marcus's tent loomed out of the dark. The entire pavilion had not been set for want of solid ground to raise it on, and a veritable company of heralds stood around the edges, holding torches aloft that guttered and danced in the winter wind. Amelia and Dalflitch were ushered inside where the usual flock of courtly sycophants was gathered, with a mix of Reachermen scattered among them. Amelia noticed that many of the western nobles whom she knew by face, if not name, looked at her almost pleadingly, and she realized the entire tent seemed to have a much more earnest air than usual. The cruel jests and petty maneuvers had been replaced by sincere conversation.

"I beg your forgiveness, Highness, but it is not a river," said someone Amelia could not yet see through the crowd. "It is a salt marsh."

CHAPTER 25

Daven Marcus had come to the Western Reach with his mind already made up. From the moment he arrived, Amelia had seen that. Not only had he formed his contemptuous opinion of Reachermen, their fallen duke, and the rest of the frontier nobility, but he also was convinced he knew the origin of the invasion he had come too late to fend off. The invaders had come out of the west, but the prince insisted that was a transparent ruse. There were no kingdoms or nations in the west, no people at all, except perhaps the odd hermit starving to death under a sparse tree in the vast sea of grass. No, the prince was certain the "western" invaders actually came from the south, from the Vec Princedoms, the hereditary enemies of the Grand Kingdom.

Historically, the Vec had once been the southernmost provinces of the Kingdom, ruled from Denay, the same as the rest of the inner provinces and the same as the Reach. Then, nearly two centuries ago, the southern nobility had risen in rebellion, declared themselves a confederacy of princes, and driven the Grand Kingdom back across the Mur River. Since then, the river had remained the general border between the two nations. Now and again, forces from either one would cross the river to raid, and twice the Grand Kingdom had undertaken crusades to take the Vec back, but both had failed. In the last century, the Kingdom had contented itself with expanding

across the Azure Mountains into the vast west, especially when
the Dwelt River was found, a broad watercourse that ran north
to south along the same line as the mountains, eventually
joining the Mur River. Just over ten years ago, the Vec had
united under a king—a rare enough event—and that king had
struck up the Dwelt to conquer the Grand Kingdom's western
flank. Because of his heroism and leadership in the campaign
to drive those forces back, Amelia's husband Marne had been
made Duke of the Western Reach. All that had happened when
she was still a child and, therefore, before she was married, but
she knew the tales.

Everyone in the Grand Kingdom knew them, including
Prince Daven Marcus. The prince had come west to be the next
hero of the Reach, and the tale he expected to be told was a near
mirror of the previous. Convinced that there were no peoples
in the western grass, the prince insisted the invaders must be
from the south. And he followed that insistence with a claim
that made perfect sense to him and confused all the men of the
Reach—the Veckanders must have come north by river again.
Since they had not come up the river Dwelt, then there must
be another river, another tributary of the Mur, farther to the
west. Now that they had found this land of grassy pools, Daven
Marcus was taking it as a sign that he was correct. But the hidden
salty ponds showed no signs of flowing water, and that was the
bone of contention in the royal tent this night.

"A salt marsh?" asked Daven Marcus, standing on a wooden
dais, his throne behind him. "Whoever heard of such a thing?"
All the nearest courtiers shook their heads and frowned to show
how much they shared the prince's distrust of that news.

"A wetland where little grows, Highness," said the voice that
had raised the objection. Amelia still could not see who it was
behind the crowd. "Because of the salt in the water. Like the
ocean."

"You should be careful. Second flood is a heresy," the prince said in his usual casual tone, but a ripple of tension washed through the entire room.

Even the prince's closest confidants seemed to Amelia to shiver with disquiet for a moment. Heresy was a black stain that could drag down the most noble of men. Her retainer Prentice had been convicted of heresy and transported west to fight and slave until he died for the crime. Amelia didn't fully understand the theology that made second flood a heresy, but she knew that no one present wanted to be connected to it or any other teaching condemned by Mother Church.

The man who had been speaking of a salt marsh must have been cowed into silence by the prince's implication. The crowd parted as everyone looked to see if he would continue his speech, and Amelia was able to see who it was—Earl Derryman, the nobleman who had been too ill to attend her feast. It seemed he had become well enough to attend tonight's gathering, though he looked to still be in a good deal of pain. A tall, heavy-set man with a full belly and touches of grey in his brown hair, Amelia could see the earl rocking back and forth slightly as he tried to stand still, which made her think his gout was causing him distress. She felt a sudden rush of compassion for the man and decided to come to his defense.

"Far be it for any Reacherman to speak heresy, even in his heart," she declared loudly. All faces turned to look at her. "I know little of this second flood of which you speak, Highness, but I am certain Earl Derryman rejects it without hesitation, as he would every heresy, known or unknown."

The earl looked at her for a moment, surprised by the interruption, then turned back to the prince and bowed uncomfortably.

"The Duchess is correct completely, Highness," he said and there were words of agreement from around the gathering. Amelia hid her smile and moved quickly to stand in front of Daven Marcus, curtseying to present herself. When she looked up, the prince was looking down on her with a strange smile, and when his eyes slid away from her, she looked to see that Dalflitch had moved up to curtsey beside her. He looked back and forth between them, and it seemed to Amelia that he was no more pleased to see the countess than he was to see her. It was a strange development that puzzled her, though it was not unwelcome. She expected the prince to call Dalflitch up to stand beside him, as he usually did, but he did not. Instead, he looked back to the earl. She didn't look to confirm it, but out of the corner of her eye, Amelia was certain she noticed a frown on the countess's face, as if the prince's disinterest confused her as well. It was all Amelia could do not to grin.

"What, then, is this salt marsh you speak of, Earl, if it is no thing of heresy?"

"Only what I have sometimes seen near the sea and some rivers," the earl explained. "Water that comes shallowly onto the land but not in flood like winter rains create. Then, as the waters retreat slowly, much is left behind along with the salt, especially if near to the great waters, like the ocean beyond Denay."

"You admit then, Earl, that these salt marshes occur near rivers?"

"Yes, Highness. I said as much."

"So, even with your protests, you confirm the truth of my statements. Perhaps your only purpose is to draw some attention to yourself, to be noticed among your betters?"

Amelia knew this game all too well, and though she would have liked to help the earl further, there was nothing for her to do, at least nothing that would not risk making everything worse.

"I am only your humble servant, Highness," said Earl Derryman, and he bowed painfully again.

"Yes," agreed the prince, sourly. "You Reachermen are nothing if not humble." That drew an approving titter from the sycophant chorus. "Withdraw Earl. We have heard what you have to say."

Derryman backed away, keeping his face down, hiding his wincing expression as he did so. Even as he was absorbed back into the audience crowd, the prince beamed, an expression full of delight that made him seem suddenly handsome and charming. With a simple shift of his expression, Amelia watched her tormentor transform into the royal heir everyone wanted for their kingdom. It was his greatest weapon—a face he could wear that Amelia knew was as false as an actor's mask.

"What do you think, Duchess, of the excellent news?" he asked her.

"I have spent my day in a carriage, Highness. I have been given no news."

Daven Marcus scoffed theatrically. "Trust a sow not to notice her feet are wet when she's walking through mud."

More titters. Amelia thought she heard a derisive noise from Dalflitch beside her as well, but she refused to look at the countess.

"You mean the puddles, Highness? What my earl said heralds a 'salt marsh'?"

"Puddles?" The prince laughed, seemingly with real enjoyment, unselfconscious for a moment. It was a surprisingly pleasant thing. "More than mere puddles, little Duchess. The pools you see all around us are the proof I am right. I was always right."

Amelia suspected he wanted her to ask about what, but she held her tongue. Daven Marcus looked down at her for a moment, waiting for her to speak. Then he went on anyway.

"The river farther west! The second river. We've found it!"

"Forgive her, Highness," Amelia heard Dalflitch say next to her. "It was dark when we arrived. It was not possible to see the river."

The prince frowned suddenly, and a shadow passed over his entourage, all their expressions souring as one.

"No one's seen the river yet, Countess," Amelia said, guessing the source of their discomfort. "Only the puddles. But as our prince and the earl have said, it is a good sign that there is a river somewhere ahead of us."

The entire tent fell to silence for a moment as everyone watched to see how the prince would react. His intent had been to make Amelia seem small and stupid, speaking to her as if teaching a child; she was sure of that. That was always his intent when he spoke to her these days. But Dalflitch's move to help in the mockery had been misjudged, and now it was Amelia who could talk down to her. No one knew how Daven Marcus would respond.

"A good sign?" He mused, repeating Amelia's phrase. "More than a good sign, wouldn't you say, Lord Robant?"

"I have never needed a sign, Highness," replied the baron from the other side of the prince's dais. Amelia looked to see him standing arrogantly off by himself, as if too good for the rest of Daven Marcus's flunkies. Too good or too dangerous. "You assured us that there is a river in the far west, and your word is always enough for me."

"The waters do not encourage you?"

"Only that we are drawing close to the prize. I am eager for the fight, of course."

Daven Marcus laughed again, and the cloud in the room cleared once more.

"I can always rely upon you, Baron."

Robant bowed to accept the compliment.

The prince went on. "Tell me, how are you finding your new duties? Not too onerous having to wet-nurse little girls?"

"I didn't realize you wanted me to nurse them, Highness," Robant quipped, feigning shock. "That might be a burden beyond my manly capabilities."

The prince enjoyed the joke and his sycophants laughed with him. Behind her, Amelia sensed a much more mixed reception. There was an air of impatience, she thought, but she couldn't be sure. It felt like she was standing amidst a bored crowd at a theatre, all watching the stage and hoping the show would begin to entertain. But there was also a sense of tension, of frustration. At least that was what she thought she felt.

"But you are having no problems?" Daven Marcus went on, eyes fixed on Amelia.

"The ladies have been most compliant, Highness, but some of the servants have been..." Robant paused deliberately, leaving the possible implications hanging in the air.

"Difficult?" asked the prince, not breaking his gaze from Amelia's eyes.

"Dense, Your Highness."

"Dense?"

"Slow to learn."

"You had to teach one of them a lesson?"

"Only this afternoon."

It was obvious the entire conversation was for Amelia's benefit. She was sure no one present could miss that.

"Did he learn the lesson well, do you think?" asked the prince and Amelia felt a sudden, grim premonition. The prince seemed to leer at her, and she remembered him as the cackling, diseased bird of prey he had been in her vision.

"It was a wet lesson, but it was one he will never forget," the baron answered enigmatically, and in a rush, Amelia remembered Robant's conflicts with Turley and connected them with the tale the herald had told, of someone drowned earlier in the day. In her mind, the two notions locked like pieces of a puzzle. She gasped involuntarily at the thought that the "fool" the herald had spoken of might not have been a youth, as she had imagined, but was in fact her steward.

Was Turley dead in a pool of water somewhere nearby? She had not seen him for hours.

"Something troubles you, Duchess?" the prince asked, his smile twisting to a predatory cast. "Perhaps you are worried for your servant? You're so close to some of them, I hear."

Amelia looked at Dalflitch next to her; for certain the countess would have told the prince about Turley. Only moments before she had been pleased at scoring a petty point over this woman. Now Dalflitch was watching her with the same sort of smile as the prince. Not as hateful perhaps, but just as predatory. Amelia felt suddenly alone, and her fear for Turley was clutching at her chest. Behind her were the nobles of the Reach, the worthies she hoped to win to her, but not one of them was stepping forth to support her at this moment.

"Duchess?" Daven Marcus pressed. "Nothing to say?"

"I...I..." Amelia felt herself stammering, reaching for words and not finding them.

"No? That's good, I think. Women are better seen than heard."

The sycophant chorus tittered and nodded, approving their prince's apparent wisdom. Their spinelessness offended Amelia. The prince and Robant and Dalflitch—they might all be hateful predators, but the rest of Rhales court were contemptible, like the flies that gathered around a horse's rear. She loathed them, and that hatred helped her steel herself.

"I'm sorry..." she began. The prince tried to take her apology as a cue to dismiss her, but she spoke straight over him, violating proper protocol in her fury. "I'm sorry that your Baron Robant was such a nervous puppy that he had to come to you with a problem over a mere servant."

Amelia invested that last word with a contemptuous tone of strength she didn't actually feel. The contempt was real, but the strength felt false. The thought that they were talking about her sworn man, about Turley, lying face down in a grassy pool, was breaking her heart. She would vent her contempt for them all, but if they had slain her man, let them see what she thought of them, if only for a moment.

"I would have thought the Baron too much of a man to trouble a prince over the business of a lady's servant," she said. "Perhaps he is better suited to nursing after all. In the morning, I'll send to my other servants and see if they know of any women who've recently birthed. We can find Lord Robant an infant to practice with. Who knows, once he gets a babe to his nipple, he might find he has a talent for it."

Amelia was savagely pleased to see the usually cool-tempered Robant's face go red with rage.

"You little..." he began, his teeth clenched, but the prince's raised hand cut him off. Behind her, Amelia could hear quiet chuckles, and that pleased her. They wouldn't back her against the prince, not yet, but they would side against his favorites, at least. For his part, it seemed her outburst even amused Daven Marcus as well. She could almost feel sorry for Robant, suddenly alone in his humiliation. The prince was a fickle patron to have.

But the pleasure she felt over her little victory did not last long, could not last. The audience wound on into the night, the prince expounding on his theories of a Vec invasion via a river in the west, which still sounded to Amelia like the fantasies of a young boy who dreamed of repeating and then exceeding the heroisms of his ancestors. Before the gathering was dismissed, Daven Marcus promised that he would lead them into a re-conquest of the entire Vec princedoms, then on to a crusade against Masnia farther south, and even to sail across the eastern ocean to legendary Aucks. It was ridiculous, at least to Amelia's ears. Wherever the invaders came from, she was sure it was not the Vec. Nonetheless, every courtier of Rhales and every Reacher noble present listened to the prince and accepted his assurances. They had found water, after all.

For her part, Amelia wanted nothing more than to leave this meeting that seemed so pointless to her and find out for sure if her fears were warranted. She needed to know what had happened to Turley. When the prince finally grew bored of the sound of his own voice, dismissing the gathering en masse, she left his pavilion and strode recklessly through the dark paths lit by warden's torches, pausing only to take directions to her own tent. When she reached it, she stormed inside and all but fell upon Kirsten, demanding to know where he was.

"I've not seen him this evening, Your Grace," Kirsten replied, obviously taken aback.

"Send for him immediately!" she snapped, her calm worn thin by waiting.

The handmaid curtseyed in panic and fled the tent.

Amelia slumped onto her bed, and as she did, she heard the ground under it squelch with water. She wondered if everywhere around her in this salt marsh was equally waterlogged, or if her tent had been deliberately placed near to one of the treacherous ponds. Would the water act like a sinkhole and swallow her up with her tent in the night? That thought prompted her to think about how many wagons would be lost journeying west from here. And then she remembered the Royal Dragons. Surely there was no way the enormous, cast-bronze cannons could be driven through this wet land. An image in her mind of the massive weapons bogged the way her carriage had been made her bark a single, bitter laugh, but there was no joy in her amusement. She sat worrying at the blanket on her bed, waiting for Turley, or news of him. She fell asleep that way, with no further news.

CHAPTER 26

"Father, we surrender the soul of Sergeant Ranold of South Bannerton to you, as we consign his remains to the earth from which we all come. We cannot say for certain if he was a good man, or evil, but he was a loyal friend and comrade to us. You, Father, judge the hearts of men as only you know the heart."

Sacrist Fostermae intoned the prayer for the dead while the winter rain pelted the little gathering. There'd been a string of burials now for days, and the sacrist had prayed at each of them. Despite the inconvenience it caused, Prentice had insisted on individual funeral rites for each person who died in the assault and the stampede. He'd seen too many convicts worked to death and thrown into a mass grave or left to wild animals at the side of the road. He was resolved that anyone he lost would at least have the dignity of their own funeral, and he ignored the grumbling complaints of the men who drew grave-digging duty in the winter's chill.

As Fostermae finished his prayer, most of those present turned away immediately while those who'd come to pay their respects and the diggers began to hurriedly toss mud into the hole that was already a quarter filled with rainwater. They worked quickly, and as soon as they were done, Prentice dismissed them. The drenched, ragged men rushed away to find a spot out of the rain.

"Is that the last of them?" Fostermae asked Prentice, his teeth chattering with cold. He absentmindedly flicked water away from the bald pate of his tonsure.

"That's it, Sacrist," Prentice told him. "Go get yourself a spot near one of the ovens."

Fostermae bowed and retreated towards the nearest hut. No matter their actual position on the faith, no one would keep Fostermae from their company. He was the camp's only healer of any real power, and he gave his service freely, working himself so hard that he was always wan with fatigue. Prentice watched the man shiver in the cold and wondered if he'd have to bury him soon, too. At least he wouldn't have died from a knight's sword or a trampling hoof, just from hunger and siege sickness. Prentice found little comfort in the thought.

"Well, we finally got him in the ground," said Corporal Felix in a sour tone. The corporal was the last of the mourners remaining, besides Prentice himself. Prentice knew why he was angry.

"Officers go in the ground last," he said, reiterating his decision. "That'll be the way with the Reach militia. First to rise and last to sleep. No Reach commander rests until his men are rightly bestowed, even in death." He knew Felix understood his reasons. To build loyalty in his men, Prentice wanted them to know that they were important to him and to his officers. He also understood Felix's resentment. Between repairing the damaged hut and rushing to preserve as much of the lost meat as they could, burials had been too long delayed. Sergeant Ranold's broken body had started to putrefy, and in the damp weather, the rot was moving swiftly. Felix no doubt felt it was poor respect for an honored comrade.

"What's the word from the rest of the corporals?"

"They'll have me as sergeant," said Felix. With Ranold dead, the remaining mercenaries had to decide among themselves who would take command of their company. Prentice had assumed the role would automatically fall to Felix, but it seemed mercenary appointments were as politically fraught as those of knights and nobles. There had been a few earnest, late-night conferences, apparently.

"You told them I'd still pay Ranold's share to divide among them? I won't take a dead man's pay out of the company coffers."

"They were glad to hear that, but..." Felix's eyes strayed involuntarily in the direction of the locked town gates, barely visible through the sheeting grey of the rain.

"But they're not too concerned with extra silver in their purses when there's nowhere to spend it?" said Prentice, thinking Felix's thought for him.

"There it is."

"Are we looking at mutiny?"

"No," said Felix, reflexively. Mutiny was the one true mercenary sin. Even a whiff of it was enough to ruin a company's reputation. Vec princes, who most often used mercenaries, were known to kill whole companies when mutinies had to be put down. Nevertheless, they did happen, and Prentice would not be surprised to see one coming from Felix's men. They were stuck in a losing siege, without enough food, in the cold of winter, and with a rabble to command that knew as much about soldiering as Prentice knew about flying like a bird.

And his suspicion was based on more than just the poor renown of blades for hire. After the night of the stampede, he and Sir Gant had made a thorough check of the ground and the walls. There was no sign of a point where other knights had infiltrated from Liam's forces. That meant the likely source of the stampede fires was someone already inside the walls, one of his people. That made it an act of deliberate sabotage. Prentice found himself keeping his hand on the hilt of his dagger these days out of habitual paranoia.

"If it's settled for now, we can get back to training," he said.

Felix's expression did not improve under the brim of his hat. Made of black felt and with a feather that now drooped in the rain, it had been Ranold's. Felix had inherited it. Prentice wondered if Felix hoped it would give him an air of legitimate authority over his fellow corporals.

"It'll be a bitch of a job, getting them out into the rain," the corporal protested. "It'll be enough of a task getting the other corporals to poke their heads out."

"They'll come out if they want to eat," Prentice replied.

"As long as the food lasts."

"That may not be as long as we might hope, either," came Sir Gant's voice from nearby. He and Righteous were approaching, their feet squelching on the mud. The rain appeared to be letting up, but a chill wind still blew. When Prentice turned to look at them, Gant gave him a respectful nod while Righteous just smirked.

"We was waiting to speak to you," she said cheerfully. "But since you seemed to lack the wit to come in out of the rain, we had to come out here. Truly, I've known blind, three-legged goats have more sense than you do."

Sir Gant rolled his eyes, but Prentice let the comment pass. He knew he gave Righteous more latitude than anyone else in the whole camp, but he found he couldn't help it.

"What about the food?"

"There's been theft already. Quite a bit, actually."

"We set guards over it?" Prentice asked Felix.

The newly promoted sergeant nodded.

"Bet it's the guards that are stealing," said Righteous.

Prentice knew she was probably right.

"Is it bad?"

Sir Gant scowled, but then his expression softened, and he shrugged.

"It can't be good, but what can we do? Even if we keep every morsel under lock and key, we'll be running out in just a handful of weeks. I would guess that most of the thieves simply do not trust us and are trying to secure a small supply for themselves."

"It's what I'd do," said Righteous. When she saw the other three looking at her, she held up her hands. "IF! IF I was thieving. If...! I swear I'm not."

Prentice believed her. Even so, he hung his head and let the water drip from his face for a moment.

"How long?" he asked.

"As I said," Gant answered, "in mere weeks, all the legitimate food will be gone."

He didn't have to explain what "legitimate food" meant. They were all soldiers or former convicts, and they knew what hunger drove folk to do. Between them, they all knew the taste of sawdust bread, of boiled grass, or stewed shoe leather. And if they couldn't break the siege, then there was still one more dreadful form of meat on the hoof. Prentice knew the minute he heard tell of one of his people eating the flesh of a man, he would go and give himself straight into Baron Liam's hands, pleading for mercy for them or at least a quicker death. He would not drive his people to cannibalism. He couldn't.

"I wasn't talking about food," Prentice said, and then he lifted his head. He looked at each one in turn. "How long before someone in here figures out that I'm the solution to the problem? I'm the key that turns the lock on that gate?"

They had no answer for him. As he looked between them, Prentice was confident he could trust these three. Gant and Righteous would die for him, he was certain. Felix was not so loyal, but his professional pride was strong—strong enough that Prentice was sure he'd die for it. So, these three weren't the problem.

But there were two and a half thousand others in the camp with them, most with the vilest criminal backgrounds. How long until one of them got the notion in their head?

As it turned out, the answer was two days.

The weather hadn't broken, although the storms had receded to leave overcast days of persistent drizzle, and so the recruits were driven from the relative comfort of their rude huts and made to march. Many now had their practice poles, and the initial stages of formation drilling had begun, with much complaining as blisters on hands from carrying the hardwood lengths were added to sore feet and aching backs on the list of the recruits' sufferings. Prentice was with Sir Gant, watching the last cohort of fifty recruits receiving their poles from Yentow Sent's journeymen when a runner came from the gate wall. The two of them went to see what was happening this time.

In front of the gate, the siege knights had hauled a cart with a crossed pole fixed in the back. A man in rags was tied there, like a thief on the cross. His arms were bound to the crossbeam, and his body and legs had bands of cord holding him to the pole. He had a rag tied around his mouth. Beside him on the back of the cart stood another man, dressed in a common jerkin and a heavy leather apron. He was wearing a mask made from a sack. The cart's occupants were accompanied by a knight in mail under an oilskin cloak. When Prentice emerged onto the battlements, the knight threw back his hood.

"You convicts, illegally hiding in Fallenhill, hear this," he shouted, apparently giving a prepared speech. He pointed to the man tied to the cross. "This fellow was one of yours. He was caught two nights ago attempting to flee. Baron Liam has tried him and sentenced him to death by vivisection."

Prentice gritted his teeth and he heard men around him suck in shocked breaths. This man was going to die as brutally as the victim who'd been drawn by the two horses on the first day of the siege.

"Baron Liam reminds you that he has been patient with you all, hoping you would do what is right for once in your worthless lives, but he wants you to know that his patience is not limitless. Soon, he will assault these walls, and everyone within will fall to his swords."

That was nothing but a vain boast, Prentice knew. Liam had nothing like the forces he would need for an assault, but Prentice had to wonder how many of the former convicts around him knew that. How many would believe this claim, despite what Prentice told them?

"The baron is a hard man," the pronouncement went on. "A man of iron will. He is determined in his course. However, since he is a man of faith and sacrists have counselled him to mercy, he is willing to offer one more chance to you. Whichever of you, man or men, lays hold of the heretic Prentice, falsely called Ash, and hands him over to the baron, will find the mercy of Mother Church. All others will share this man's fate."

It was a while since anyone had bothered to indict him of heresy, but it was true that that was the crime for which he had been transported over the Azure Mountains. The "falsely called Ash" accusation was new to him, though. Prentice had gained the battle name Ash from the invaders out of the west. They said that whatever was burned, no matter how hot the fires of war, Ash always remained. When the enemy had denounced him with this epithet, it had been a mark of respect to a worthy foe, and Liam had been insulted that the title went to Prentice. Liam thought he was the invader's most respect-worthy foe.

The knight finished his speech, and just before he pulled his hood back over his head, he gave the executioner a nod. The strong man nodded in return and drew a sharp, wickedly curved flensing knife. He pressed the fingers of his free hand into the prisoner's exposed armpit, clearly looking for the seams of his shoulder joint. Then, he took the flensing blade and began to amputate the man's arm.

The captured convict's eyes bulged in agony, and he screamed so loudly into his gag that every man could hear it. Even with the rain falling, the spray of gore from this first injury was vivid, covering the victim, the executioner, and the cart in watery crimson. The first amputation was surprisingly swift, and when it was finished the severed limb stayed tied by its straps to the crossbeam. Whoever the executioner was, he knew his business, there could be no doubt about that. The prisoner hung his head, weeping from the pain.

"Stay here to starve or be boned like a chook," someone behind Prentice muttered and he felt himself tense, his fists clenching.

"Ain't much of a choice, is it?" said a second voice, and the menace in it was unmistakable. Prentice didn't even bother trying to turn in time as he heard feet shuffling behind him. Instead, he sidestepped and twisted as he felt a hand try to push him from the rampart in a shove. Another pair of hands had just missed his ankles, doubtless thinking to tip him up over the crenellation stones. His unexpected step had made them miss. Turning in place, he pulled his dirk from its sheath, bringing it up to threaten a hard-faced man with pox-scarred cheeks.

"I got one of them too," said the man, and he brought up a fighting knife of his own. Behind him, the other assailant had snatched up a training pole to use as a weapon, but he couldn't bring it to bear yet because his partner in crime was in the way.

"I ain't getting' vivisected," declared the second man. "That's no way for a man to die!"

"The baron won't pardon you," Prentice argued through gritted teeth. "He's going to kill us all, no matter what."

But they were not going to listen to him. Pox-face swung his dagger, and Prentice ducked back. Behind him he heard others getting out of the way. They were not coming to his aid, but at least they weren't helping his attackers. The pole man tried to thrust over his friend's shoulder but only ended up waving the length of wood in the air. He pulled the over-balanced weapon back to try again, but before he could get a better grip, Sir Gant stepped up behind him and thrust him through with his longsword. The man gave a single gurgling cry and fell to the stones. His pole clattered down the inside of the wall to the ground, and the sound of it made pox-face look back in surprise. Prentice used the distraction to step in swiftly and plant a tripping kick behind the man's knee. The convict fell, and as he did so, Prentice caught him and twisted him in his grip so that the man ended up kneeling with Prentice behind him, holding him by the throat. He pointed his poniard at the man's face.

"Drop the blade!" he ordered him. The man struggled for a moment, but when he realized he was caught fast with Sir Gant standing in front of him with his longsword drawn, he released his knife.

CHAPTER 27

"Did you really think it would be that *easy?*" Prentice said in the man's ear. On the battlement in front of him, the other convict that had joined in his attempted rebellion was face down, bleeding to death on the flagstones. Prentice looked over his shoulder at the men standing behind him uncertainly. Spitting rain from his lips as he did, he barked orders at them.

"You two, take him!"

He stepped away from his defeated assailant, throwing him on his back as he did so.

"Hold him fast! You, fetch a rope!"

Men blinked for a moment. Everything had happened so suddenly. Only a moment before they had all been watching the horrific execution still going on before the town gate. Now, the pitiable fate of the knights' prisoner was forgotten. They looked from Prentice to the pox-faced man at his feet and then to the other man dying in a puddle of his own blood, Sir Gant standing over him.

"What are you waiting for?" Prentice bellowed at them, and his voice echoed off the walls so that even the executioner paused in his vivisection. Men finally burst into action. Two leapt onto Prentice's prisoner and held him by the arms. He struggled, but his feet slipped on the wet stones, and they never let him get his balance. He tried to argue with his captors, but Prentice used his dagger to cut away a strip of the dying man's clothes and stuffed that into pox-face's mouth, gagging him. It did not seem long until the man sent to fetch rope returned with a coil, but in that time, others had heard something was going on, and among those who rushed up the steps or gathered on the ground inside the walls were Sacrist Fostermae and Righteous.

When the rope arrived, Prentice tied a quick, simple slipknot on one end and pulled the loop over pox-face's head and around his neck. The man tried to struggle free, but the two men held him fast and the struggle forced him to his knees again, close to the edge of the rampart. Prentice tied the other end of the rope around a crenellation stone. He was about to kick the noosed man off the wall to hang when Fostermae's voice called to him.

"Captain Prentice, what do you do?"

Prentice looked down at Fostermae, still on the step some distance away. The sacrist was having to lean out a distance to be seen around the crowd that filled the entire walkway between them. Frost-cold fury burned in Prentice's heart, the icy killer instinct he felt in the midst of battle. Nevertheless, there was a quiet part of him that wondered at how swiftly this flock of spectators had gathered. Not long from being convicts, there was a good chance they would identify more with the man with the noose around his neck than with Prentice, poniard in hand, and a knight with a drawn longsword at his back. Perhaps there was a wiser way to handle the whole situation?

Prentice did not care.

This bastard and his mate had tried to throw him to a vivisector. One was dead and this one was going to follow him, dancing from a noose. As he looked to the sacrist, he saw the expressions on so many other men. They were watchful and afraid, it seemed.

Good, he thought. Let every man fear the consequences of trying to usurp him.

"I am executing a mutinous traitor, Sacrist!" he declared loudly. "He is about to suffer a similar fate to his partner in crime."

"Without a chance to pray first?" asked Fostermae, and that cut through Prentice's fury for a moment. He had committed to proper burial rites and practices for his men. Even in his rage, he could not say no.

"Alright, be quick!"

The sacrist pushed through the crowd, taking a moment to look down at the now dead man still lying on the stones, then stepping around the narrow space until he crouched down in front of the man on his knees. He reached for the cloth stuffed into his mouth.

"May I?" he asked Prentice respectfully before he pulled it out. Prentice nodded his permission and the sacrist drew the cloth forth. Immediately pox-face started begging for his life.

"Mercy! Please, mercy," he cried. "I was just scared. I'm sorry! Please. I'm sorry."

Fostermae shushed the man and then, with one hand on his shoulder, looked at Prentice, a questioning look on his face. It took a moment for Prentice to realize that Fostermae was asking for mercy for the man. Prentice shook his head. Surely, he wasn't serious.

The man just tried to kill me, Prentice wanted to say.

And that wasn't just murder, it was usurpation. It was mutiny against a commander, one appointed by the liege of the land, which meant it was also treason against the Throne. There were no higher crimes. If he were tried in front of a ducal magistrate, there were good odds he'd end up being cut to pieces like the poor sod on the cart outside the walls. He had to be executed, or others would think there was no strength in Prentice's leadership. They were criminals, and criminals cared about nothing but strength. Crimes had to be punished, or crime would never cease. Prentice wanted to say all this, but he had no intention of trying to justify his decision to the sacrist—not in general and especially not in front of his men.

He looked away in disgust, and as he did so, his eyes scanned across the watching faces. He saw fear there, the bitter dread of convicts suffering at the hands of a callous power that cared nothing for them. They didn't care what the man on his knees had done. All they knew was that one of them was about to die, swinging from a rope in the wet and the cold, bitter and alone, like so many of them already had. Prentice wanted to explain it to them, wanted them to see the difference between this and the general tyranny that ruled over convicts, but he suddenly knew this wasn't the way. They would never understand like this.

As he looked them over, he saw Righteous, her eyes ablaze with anger, and finally his sight lighted on Sir Gant. The knight still had his sword in hand, almost all of the blood washed away from the blade by the rain. His expression was a flat mask, offering neither support nor opposition, but in his eyes, Prentice felt he understood the problem. Gant gave the barest of shrugs that said he had no solution to the conundrum.

Prentice turned back to the sacrist, now on his knees and holding the condemned man's hands in prayer, but still looking at him with an earnest, dignify plea in his expression. Pox-face himself had his head down, weeping quietly. Prentice drew in a deep breath, and even with the cold air and rain, he felt hot under the weight of every eye that watched him closely. He took hold of the rope and used the slipknot to haul the man's head upright.

"What's your name?" he demanded loudly. Prentice loosened the loop slightly to allow the man to speak clearly. "Tell everyone your name."

"Markas," the man stammered.

"Louder."

He cleared his throat and said it again, more clearly. "Markas!"

"What did you just do, Markas?" Prentice asked him. "Tell everyone what you did."

"I...I tried to throw you over the wall."

"Why?"

"So we could go free."

Prentice scanned the faces around him again for a moment, looking as many in the eye as he could, one after the other.

"If any of you, even one of you," he told them, "thinks that the baron is going to show you mercy if you just give me to him, think again! Look around you."

Some of them blinked in surprise, but Prentice continued to prompt them, and they began to do what he said.

"Look at the men around you, women too. Think of how many you know, how many are your friends. Baron Liam has slaughtered more convicts than you could name in his time. I've seen him do it! He hates me, but you are nothing to him."

Prentice pulled on the rope and the slipknot tightened again. Markas choked and was half pulled off his knees by the force. Prentice held him in that painful position.

"There's no mercy out there, not even the mercy of a quick death."

He brought his dagger to Markas's throat and held it there, letting everyone see it. Then he drew it around behind Markas's neck and used it to saw the rope, cutting it free from the stone it was tied to. He still hadn't released the slipknot, but there was no way now its victim could be hanged by it.

"Militiaman Markas," Prentice shouted, toning his voice like a pronouncement. "You are guilty of treason and mutiny, guilty without excuse. But mercy...?" Prentice paused and looked at Fostermae. "Mercy is like food and drink and a place to sleep. We all need it."

Prentice released the rope and Markas fell forward, having to catch himself before falling off the edge of the wall.

"Your sentence is death, but I hold it suspended. You'll wear that noose around your neck every day until I release you from your sentence. The sentence hangs over you now. One more crime—anything—and it will fall upon you. Steal, rebel, sneeze in the wrong bloody direction, and you will be a dead man! Do right, obey your commanders and serve, and then when you complete your service, that noose will come off your neck as well. Do you understand?"

Markas rubbed at the skin under the rope around his throat, looking over his shoulder at Prentice. He nodded but said nothing.

"Answer the captain!" Sir Liam barked, and Markas jumped.

"I understand. I understand, sir." He tugged at his forelock.

"Sir? Do I look like a knight to you?" Prentice demanded, leaning in close.

Markas shook his head sheepishly, not sure what the right answer was to Prentice's question. Prentice was surprised at the reaction in himself, but suddenly in his heart he felt the old revulsion for knights. With rare exceptions like Sir Gant, knights were vile in Prentice's eyes, men who had other men literally cut to pieces just to make a point. No matter how far he rose in society, Prentice never wanted the honors given to knights. He never wanted to be one of them, which meant the officers of his militia would need some other gesture of respect, some other way to show honor.

"Do you know your right from your left?" he asked loudly.

Markas nodded, and his face showed how the question confused him.

"Then make a fist with your right hand!"

The man did as he was told.

"Now take it and put it over your heart."

Markas obeyed.

"That's our salute," Prentice told him. "Every lesser man gives it to every man senior to him, no matter his birth. And every senior man returns it—the lower first, and then the superior. Every man gives the respect, and every man returns it, because some of you are only just freed men now, but some of you will rise to be corporals and one day some to be sergeants, even bastards like Markas. One day someone will replace me as captain—not by blood or rank, but because he's marched and trained and fought with us. That's how it will be with us! Birth be damned. I will measure a man by his actions and his service. *We* will measure that way. We are the lions of the Reach, and any man who marches and roars with the pride, hunts and dies with us, we will never despise! Markas, you are a spared man, escaping from judgement two times—once as a convict freed to serve and again today. Salute and serve, and one day you will be free."

Markas drew his fist to his breast as Prentice had explained and held it there. Prentice made his own fist and thumped it to his chest to return the salute. When he released his hand, he noticed that Sacrist Fostermae was smiling up at him. Something in the cleric's expression made him uncomfortable, and he looked away to see that all around him, throughout the little crowd, every man present had put his right fist to his heart, saluting their captain. He looked from face to face, and every one of them met his eyes with respect, holding their gesture of honor—even Gant and Righteous. It was so humbling that Prentice found it hard to swallow.

"Right," he said, "that's enough of this folly. All of you go, find something useful to do."

"You heard the captain!" shouted Gant, and suddenly corporals and firsts were bellowing orders and driving cohorts to tasks.

Prentice nodded and watched the crowd break up, stepping aside for Fostermae to escort Markas away, apparently planning to make sure the man's throat would not swell from its mistreatment. Two men were detailed to carry away the man Gant had killed, and in a short while, Prentice was alone on the wall. He looked out and saw that the executioner had finished his butchery; his victim had mercifully expired at last.

Mercifully? Prentice wondered. Was mercy in such short supply that bleeding to death with your limbs flensed away could qualify for the term? He had just shown mercy, a better kind, he was sure, but he had no idea what it would mean for him in the long run. Would his men lose fear of him because one who had attempted to betray and kill him was wandering around, still alive? Would his mercy look like weakness?

"I'd have killed him," said Righteous, coming quietly up behind him and apparently reading his thoughts.

"I nearly did."

"I still could, if you want. Just like I did for Tressy's man. Quiet in the night again."

"No!" Prentice said vehemently, whirling on her. "Mark me, Righteous, I mean it! No more hidden judgements and secret punishments." He was reminded suddenly of the cellar where the Church Inquisition had chained and tortured him. A burning rage flushed through him, threatening to overwhelm him. He all but shouted at Righteous in his fury. "Never again! No secret interrogations in cellars and dungeons. No daggers in the night! We will never be like that. So, you don't touch him. I meant what I said. His sentence is suspended!"

She seemed to shrink back from him slightly, partly afraid, which was strange enough in her dealings with him, but there was something else in her expression as well. Whatever it was, Prentice was too full of wrath at that moment to puzzle it out. He glared at her and she nodded, then clasped her fist to her chest in salute.

CHAPTER 28

For the next two days, Amelia's life was its usual story of confinement, from tent to carriage to tent again, tedium upon boredom, but she hardly even noticed. Kirsten had returned the first morning with no news of Turley. Each evening when they stopped and each morning when they began the journey again, Amelia sent her handmaid out, like Noah's dove, but no sign of him was found. By the second morning she began to dread that Turley was dead, and she rode that second day in silence, barely aware of the conversation between Kirsten and Countess Dalflitch. Kirsten, for her part, seemed to do her best to care for her mistress, but Amelia's apprehension shut out all comfort. She knew she was being unfair to Kirsten, but she felt a harsh sense of loneliness she could not shake off.

The evening of the second day, Lord Robant arrived with orders to escort her to the prince once more as soon as the carriage came to a halt for the day.

"We have only just stepped down from our journey, My Lord," Amelia tried to protest half-heartedly. "Are we not to be allowed even a moment to refresh ourselves?"

Robant bowed graciously and smiled. As he did, Amelia thought she saw him flash a glance at Kirsten, standing beside her, although it was difficult for her to be sure in the dancing lamplight.

"The prince was insistent," said Robant. "You, Your Grace, the countess, and your maid. All are to attend."

Next to her, Amelia could feel Kirsten's nervous excitement, and she was impressed the girl kept her calm as well as she did. She was rocking gently from foot to foot like an eager child but managed a simple, demure curtsey to accept the baron's escort. Amelia knew Kirsten was drawn to Robant but now started to wonder if it was an attraction the baron returned. Had the prince truly summoned Kirsten, or was that Robant's doing? And if it was, did he truly have a legitimate interest in Kirsten, or was he simply exploiting a young woman's obvious infatuation? And if he was, to what end? Was he just acting the rake, thinking to bed a pretty maid like so many unscrupulous noblemen in every court from Denay to Masnia? Or did he think to seduce Kirsten away from her? The questions sat in Amelia's mind like toads, ugly and distracting.

Her first instinct was to ask Turley what he thought of Robant's motives, but that only reminded her that he was gone, face down in a salt pool somewhere behind the march. That thought made her even more frustrated, but when she considered it, she felt miserably vile. Turley was dead, murdered in this vast empty wilderness, and all she could think was how it affected her politically. It took all her will to steel her resolve and keep her expression neutral.

"Of course, Lord Robant. Every instruction from the prince comes with the force of insistence. We would not think to deny his highness even for a moment. Please, lead on."

As Robant guided them from torch to torch through the windy night, Amelia noticed that the pools were fewer and larger than other times in their journey through the salt marsh, and she wondered if that meant they were nearing the prince's river. After a short journey across the trampled grasses, Robant led them up a steep slope of stony soil. It was awkward, and it took all their concentration to keep from slipping as they clambered, unladylike, to the top of the rise. Amelia resolved to make the climb by herself as a point of pride. However, Kirsten didn't hesitate to accept Lord Robant's offered hand, and when she showed a moment's difficulty, the baron directed a nearby warden to escort Countess Dalflitch. Amelia knew she had provoked it, but she nonetheless felt the pointed rejection as the baron made no effort to help her. Robant, Dalflitch, and the rest of the little escort were waiting at the top of the rise by the time Amelia finished the short climb. She'd had to scrabble a fair part of the distance, and her hands were scratched from the rocks, which were dusted with a chalky white dirt.

"This way, Your Grace, ladies," said Robant, pointing along the rise. As Amelia looked, she realized the rise wasn't a ridge in the land as she had first supposed. It was, in fact, one side of a causeway, a raised road built above the soft marshland the army and court had been struggling through for days. Easily ten paces wide, stretching from the west to the east, it was an impressive piece of engineering. She looked down at the ground beneath her feet. It seemed to be made of sandstone, crushed and packed. Amelia wondered how far it stretched, but in the darkness there was no way she could tell.

"Impressed, Your Grace?" asked Robant as he led them by the light of a line of torches placed along the causeway. Somewhere up ahead, a pair of larger fires burned, likely braziers. Amelia expected that was where they'd find the prince and his flunkies. "The royal scouts found this road earlier this afternoon. They returned with word and then tried to follow it west. They traveled over a league, but night fell before they reached its end. What they found, though, was remarkable."

"Indeed, My Lord?" asked the countess. "How so?"

"Ah, it would not do, My Lady, for me to say. I am sure the prince would like to tell you himself. I would not steal his thunder."

"You are so loyal," breathed Kirsten and, not for the first time, Amelia felt a petty urge to slap her handmaid.

Soon enough, they reached the royal entourage, and the prince made his usual welcoming gibes, criticizing Amelia for being late.

You put me in a carriage, she thought. *It's not my fault your imprisonment is inconvenient.* But she did not say anything out loud. She didn't have the heart for another exchange of barbs.

"What say you, Duchess, of my discovery?"

His discovery? It was all Amelia could do not to sneer.

"It is an impressive edifice, your Highness. It looks like a perfect highway for an army to march upon."

"Indeed, it is. Positive proof that I was right."

Amelia wondered how the road proved the invaders were from the Vec but didn't ask. She couldn't be bothered. Even in the dark, the vulturous gaze of the prince's closest courtiers only accentuated her bitter loneliness. She would gladly have gone back to the carriage for another month rather than suffer the hateful attentions of the court.

"But this is not all, is it?" the prince continued, exactly as Amelia expected. "The news is even better than this."

"You have found the river, Highness?" Dalflitch asked, accepting the prompt.

Daven Marcus's expression darkened for a moment, and Amelia didn't bother to hide a bitter smile. How many times would the countess make mistakes like that before she learned to let the prince star in his own stage plays? Amelia could almost pity the woman her missteps if she wasn't such a dangerous slattern.

"Better than a mere river," the prince explained, his smile reestablishing itself. "A lake. A vast expanse of water that an entire army could sail. Scouts tell us that it stretched from north to south, horizon to horizon. These marshes are the lake's fringe."

"So, there is no river?" Amelia asked despite herself. Was the prince about to acknowledge he was wrong? Daven Marcus's smile said otherwise.

"Of course, there's a river, you silly sow. It's somewhere to the south. My cartographers tell me it must flow into this lake there from a shared headwater with the Murr."

"Shared...?" Amelia didn't understand what the prince meant.

"Wherever the Murr River begins, there's another river which flows in a different direction," Daven Marcus explained with exaggerated patience. "That river runs into this lake. So, you see how simple it is. The Vec princes sail up the Murr, debark their armies and carry their boats to this other river. Then, they sail all the way north to this lake and build this roadway out of the marsh. The western end of this causeway is a jetty for the invaders, do not doubt it."

Despite the prince's claim, it didn't sound simple to Amelia. Nonetheless, his courtiers all smiled and nodded at his self-vindication. Dalflitch naturally joined in, and Amelia was annoyed to see Kirsten also smile with seeming admiration in the dancing firelight.

"If it is as you say, Highness, then it must have taken them years to build this road," Amelia mused, distracting herself with the details because the prince's triumph was too bitter to have to endure at this moment. "And where would they have found the stone in the soft ground of this marsh?"

"Obviously, they brought it here," said a courtier Amelia couldn't name.

"That would make it take even longer," she mused, happy to argue if it meant she didn't have to think about Turley or anything else for a moment. "Even as much as ten years. They must have been building it since King Kolber's invasion."

That was the thought that genuinely confused her. Kolber had united the Vec princes under him, but it had been an unstable alliance. As soon as his son threatened his throne, the whole coalition had collapsed. Amelia knew this from reading the books Prentice had suggested to her to learn about war and politics. Kolber's invasion had taken the combined might of most of the Vec, and keeping that alliance together had proved too difficult for him. This vast road in the wilderness would take just as much cooperation from the princes, if not more. That would mean a second, secret coalition that had somehow survived Kolber's betrayal and death. Such a thing made no sense to Amelia. No matter what Daven Marcus said, she could not believe this was the work of the Vec princes.

Naturally, the prince saw it differently.

"Yes, building it for years," he said, and his eyes narrowed on her. "All this time, preparing their next invasion, and your husband, tasked with protecting the Grand Kingdom frontier, knew nothing about it. The useless duke, that's what they should call him. Too distracted bedding milkmaids and farm animals to do his duty."

Anger flared in Amelia, and she felt her hands clench painfully as she forced herself to keep quiet. If she spoke now, she would only give the prince the satisfaction of knowing he had offended her.

"So, you see, you can change your dress now, Duchess," the prince said, and that caught her by surprise.

"Change my…"

"Yes, of course," Daven Marcus smiled at her benignly. "You don't have to doubt anymore. I am the Reach's true hero."

"True hero, Highness?" Amelia wanted to ignore the prince's words, but they made no sense to her, and whenever that happened, there was too often a dangerous sting in them, a hook hidden in the bait.

"I am vindicated," he boasted. "Proven completely correct. You can stop mourning the fool old man you used to be married to and begin to celebrate our upcoming nuptials. Marne is gone, and his undeserved reputation has been washed away in the reality of this road into a lake. I have proved the truth of the threat to your lands, and tomorrow I will march in triumph to the other end of this road. I will capture the Veckander jetty, making the Reach safe forever. When I return, we will wed. No

more of these black lace veils and mournful looks. Put ribbons
in your hair! Wear your brightest gown. Skip and dance for
joy, as the betrothed of a prince should. Then, as my princess, I
will give you the wedding present of sailing with me in triumph
south to the Vec. You will get to watch me turn their treachery
back upon them."

There were huzzahs and shouts of congratulations. Amelia
felt her head churn with her objections to Daven Marcus's
words. She wanted to defend her dead husband's reputation and
deny any joy at the prospect of marrying the prince. She wanted
to question the likelihood that the Vec had built this road since
the collapse of King Kolber's invasion of the Reach, not to
mention the strange notion of building the road at all when
they'd shown they could just mount an invasion straight across
the Murr whenever they wanted to. From the swirl of thoughts,
though, she plucked one objection virtually at random.

"Sail south, Highness? How will we do that?"

The prince's condescending smile only broadened further.

"In the Veckanders' own boats, of course. They brought an
army north on the water and that army never went home. That
means their boats are sitting there, waiting to be used. We will
use them."

Amelia shook her head. There were so many assumptions
underlying this plan that she wondered how even the most
sycophantic courtier could accept it. She was about to ask
another question, but he interrupted her.

"Enough, Duchess. Your cow-like dullness wearies me. Go
and prepare for our wedding. And enough of hiding yourself
away like a sequestered nun. Move about the camp and let your
joy be seen. You are to marry the greatest man in the history of
the Reach. Act like it!"

Some part of Amelia still wanted to object, but she found
she didn't have the heart for it. The prince was triumphant.
There was no way to object to the wedding, and she had not
done enough to win the Reachermen to her side. His claim that

he was the greatest hero the Reach had known was laughable, but he was the crown prince, who would argue with him? She hung her head and accepted his dismissal without a word. The prince dispatched Robant to escort them back, and even without looking up, Amelia could sense the emotions of those around her. Robant seemed his usual smug self, and Kirsten all but bounced with excitement, doubtless at having a date set for her wedding to the prince. Only Dalflitch seemed unclear in her demeanor. Amelia flashed a quick glance at the countess, and it seemed the prince's mistress had a shadow over her countenance that wasn't only the product of the flickering torchlight.

"Take care, Your Grace," Lord Robant said when she nearly ran into a torch pole she had not seen because her head was down.

"Where is my steward?" she said, turning suddenly on the baron.

"I've not seen your man in days," Robant replied ambiguously.

Amelia shook her head. She was tired and had had enough of mystery and maneuvering.

"But you know where he is, don't you, My Lord?"

Robant paused and his habitual half smile turned to a cold, predatory grin.

"The last I saw of him, he was face down in a puddle of water. Perhaps he was drunk."

"Perhaps you put him there!" Amelia pressed.

Robant shrugged and gave the other two ladies present an apologetic smile, looking charming once more. When he looked back and realized that Amelia would not let him equivocate, the coldness returned to his expression

"He was an arrogant lout who refused to learn his place."

"And you taught it to him?"

"Pffh! I don't discipline mongrels that refuse to be housebroken," he said. "I leave that to my kennel master. A dog's leavings are a servant's problem, so I set some servants to the task."

"You had my servant killed?" Inside herself, a part of Amelia was crushed to have her fear confirmed, but she hid that part away behind an icy façade. "I will have you answer for that."

"How? The last man who came at me on your behalf paid for the folly of it with his life. What lesson do you think the Reach learned from that mistake? Do you think there are any who'd challenge me over the question of a belligerent servant's life? Even if he was a..." Robant paused to make his implication clear. "A *favorite* of yours?"

"Tomorrow the prince will take me to wife," Amelia spat back, fury burning her cheeks and threatening to erupt out of her. If she'd had a knife or similar weapon to hand, she was almost certain she would throw herself on him. She wanted nothing so much as to tear this arrogant fop down. "How do you think he will respond if I ask him a favor on our wedding day?"

"Do you think you have earned yourself even a fraction of that much esteem, Your Grace?" Robant was not in the leastwise frightened by her threat.

"Best you get yourself pregnant with an heir right quick," Dalflitch added, twisting the knife. "Your dowry will get you into the prince's bed, but an annulment is obtained easily enough if you fail your duty to him, as you did to your previous husband."

Amelia whirled on the countess in a fury.

"Aren't you afraid that the prince's bed will be too crowded with both of us in it? What use will he have for you if I'm there to serve his needs? Not afraid of being kicked out on your arse, are you?"

Kirsten gasped at her mistress's loss of decorum. "Your Grace?" she breathed in shock.

"Oh, shut up!" Amelia said, turning on her next.

Robant had just admitted to having Turley murdered, Dalflitch was lying with the prince while her own husband was back in the heartland somewhere, and all Kirsten could think to be shocked by was Amelia swearing once. The duchess turned on her heel and strode into the dark. When she realized that she had no idea where her tent was, she called over her shoulder.

"Come, Lord Robant. Be a good lackey and show me the way to my bed. I'd call for my servant, but I can't trust that you won't have them slaughtered for some petty slight. So, the low duty must fall to you! Do not shirk, Baron. You would not want it said you were less reliable than a mere steward, would you?"

Robant hissed at her, his dark eyes narrowing, but he stepped up to show her the way. Amelia followed in icy silence. She knew she had slipped and allowed them all to succeed. She'd forsaken her dignity and confirmed all their worst stories about her. Before dawn, she was sure Dalflitch would have spread the tale about the entire court.

Amelia didn't care.

Her liegemen lacked the will to come to her defense, or else were slaughtered with casual indifference for their loyalty. Servant or noblemen, death seemed the fate of any who were too diligent in her service. Back in the east, her last trustworthy man Prentice Ash had not sent her word since the prince had marched, despite the company of riders she had gathered expressly to carry messages back and forth. Had he betrayed her as well? Was she now totally alone?

Soon enough, the whole struggle would be over. The prince would marry her, and she would have to endure his attentions, as cruel as they were, at least until he got an heir by her. Once he did, she would likely be banished from the court. She could imagine no more desirable fate. She would take her son and raise him with no purpose but to hate his father with all the passion she could muster.

By the time they reached her tent, the duchess was shaking with cold and fury. She didn't wait for her maid to help her undress, but lay on the bed in her dress, the one she had chosen to mourn her husband.

She knew it would be the last time she got to wear it.

CHAPTER 29

When she arose the next morning, Amelia found that
Kirsten was not in her tent. Rather than send for her,
the duchess dressed herself. She put on her summer dress of
duck-egg blue, ignoring the cold, and tied her own hair in a
plait under her hood. Following the prince's instructions to the
letter, she left off her lace veil and put a silver and onyx chain
around her neck. She pulled leather covers over her slippers
and emerged from her tent quickly before her maid returned.
Amelia still felt some of her anger from the previous evening,
and she could not guarantee she wouldn't rehash the whole
thing with Kirsten, given the opportunity. The prince had let
her out of her isolation, and strangely that made her long for
nothing so much as some solitude, away from Kirsten, Dalflitch,
and Robant. She half expected to have a confrontation with
Robant's guards to win her freedom, but it seemed the baron
had already informed his men of the prince's orders. The
guards were nowhere to be seen. A serving girl offered her some
porridge from the fire for breakfast, but Amelia waved it away.
She wanted to see the camp.

Meadow Dancer, Amelia's roan mare, was tied to a stake
nearby, and she was glad to find her there. Rubbing her neck
affectionately, Amelia saddled her herself and climbed up gladly,
refusing the offered help of a groom who was seeing to the
hoofs of other mounts nearby. Seated in the saddle, the duchess

sighed and took a moment to enjoy the sensation before geeing her mount lightly to a gentle walk through the camp. It might be nice to go for a proper long ride later, she thought, to let Meadow Dancer stretch her legs, but for now Amelia had another purpose. She wanted to see the causeway.

The tents of the prince's march were strung out in front of her in the bowl of a long, shallow depression in the grass. Her tent was high on a gentle slope, and she could see the causeway far away at the other end of the depression. Beyond that was a copse, an oddly dense cluster of trees that seemed to have grown at the edge of the largest of the salt ponds Amelia had yet seen. The little wood could not have been a hundred paces from east to west, and likely the same north to south, yet it seemed strangely dense, like a piece of ancient forest that had been plucked from somewhere else by the hand of God and dropped in the midst of the grasses. Strangest of all was the water around it. How could trees so large and seemingly ancient grow in the midst of salt water? Why were they not poisoned?

Pondering the mystery of the trees, Amelia headed to the causeway, eager to see it in the daylight. She pulled her cloak hood over her head, even though there seemed no threat of rain, and some of the cloud cover even seemed to be breaking enough to let shafts of light through at times. She didn't want to meet with or speak to anyone. She just wanted to be out and about anonymously for a time.

One end of the causeway was some distance east of the camp, the raised road simply sloping gently down to the same level as the grassland. The five brass cannons of the Royal Dragons were already positioned at the foot of the ramp, ready to be deployed to the ships the prince planned to capture. Their gunners and crews paid Amelia no heed as she rode past them.

At the foot of the ramp, she turned Meadow Dancer to walk up onto the causeway. Looking down from the saddle and the height of the road, she felt strangely high above the surrounding land. From her vantage, it seemed as if she could see a great distance in all directions. The Azure Mountains were some vast distance far out of sight to the east, and not being able to see them reminded her how far she was from her home in Dweltford. All she could see in the east was the seemingly endless grasslands. North and south, the lumpy terrain of the saltmarsh stretched out, little grassy hummocks interspersed with depressions that hid the deadly waters where servants were consigned to die. Only the line of the causeway itself existed to divide north from south in the watery wilderness.

The sameness of each other direction was overturned to the west, though, and as Amelia rode that way, she was astonished at how clear the difference was. The yellow-grey grass and swamp of the marsh continued west for some distance in her sight, but beyond that flashed the unmistakable silver of sunlight reflecting on water. It was all but invisible from the ground, the uneven marshland acting like sand dunes to hide its presence, but from the causeway, atop her horse, it was vivid. The whole of the west was water, so much that the prince's use of the term lake seemed like another of his follies. How was this not a sea?

The raised road ran west, straight as an arrow's flight cutting through the marsh, and Amelia rode it alone, enjoying the solitude and fascinated by the alien landscape, so different from anything in the Grand Kingdom, or indeed in any land she had ever heard of. Finally, she saw a small group of people ahead of her, two men and a woman, all standing together and looking westward. As she approached, Amelia recognized the woman as Countess Dalflitch from her hair and rich dress, and she resolved to ride past without speaking. When she tried to however, one of the men standing there, a warden of the march, called her to a halt.

"Sorry, m'lady," he said politely, rushing in front of her horse to bow and block her path in one gesture. "Prince's order. No one else is to ride out west after him today."

"The prince is out there?" she asked.

The warden nodded.

"Indeed so. He rode out with his scouts and closest courtiers. They are looking to see the other end of the road so as to make the best plan to take them Veckander ships that are there."

"There are ships there?"

"So says the prince. Once he's seen their disposition for himself, he'll decide what forces he needs for their capture and send for them to come up the road. That's why he's ordered it kept clear, so there's no interference."

Amelia nodded. That made sense, almost more than she expected from the prince. She half-expected he would ride alone to whatever ships or facilities there were at the other end of the causeway and command them to surrender, the way he had commanded her castellan to return her usurped castle when he arrived in Dweltford. That had been just before the arrival of winter, but it seemed such a long time ago.

The duchess wheeled Meadow Dancer around and was about to start back when Dalflitch appeared at her side.

"You despise him so much, don't you?" she asked. There was a flatness to the countess's voice that surprised Amelia, as if her own misery was reflected in Dalflitch's heart. The idea made her want to scoff, but after her outburst the night before, she also wanted to be careful not to repeat her mistakes.

"What difference does it make to you?" she asked, not deigning to look down, her eyes fixed on the causeway's far end. "If anything, I'd have thought it was to your advantage."

"I thought that, too," the countess admitted candidly, "but it isn't turning out that way. I imagined at first it was the distraction of the crusade that kept him from my nights, but not so."

"Perhaps he pines for my love? Has that not occurred to you?"

Dalflitch smiled at that, but there was a wistfulness in the expression rather than her usual disdain.

"We are both too wise for that thought, wouldn't you agree, Your Grace?"

There was an unexpected candor to the countess's tone, and Amelia found herself looking around to see who else might be listening, expecting another verbal trap. The two wardens were out of earshot.

"If we are too wise to think the prince longs for my love," she answered, "then surely we are wise enough to see why I disdain him."

Dalflitch nodded but said nothing for a moment. Then she looked Amelia straight in the eye. "At first I thought it was a strategy in love," she said. "I laughed at night in his arms to think you were my rival—a widow with a vast, rich land as a dowry and you couldn't figure your way into his affections. You were playing too hard at being difficult to woo. I was sure I could take him away from you, even with your riches."

Amelia felt herself stiffen. How dare this debauched woman boast of her contempt straight to her face? Dalflitch had not finished, though.

"But I was wrong, wasn't I? Completely wrong. Even when he declared he would marry you, it was me on his arm at your feast. He had that doublet on. Everyone knew he had declared himself for your hand, and still I was so proud to hang on his arm. I thought it was my kisses that would sway him in the end." She shook her head. "So wrong. I'm just a piece of furniture to him, something he expects to find waiting in his bed at the end of the day. Except, no more. He threw me from his bed this morning with a command never to return. He made his use of me, as it suited him, and my beauty and my kisses have availed me nothing. And I have suffered for the privilege of his attentions, much as you have."

Amelia wanted to ride away, but she felt a sudden, unexpected rush of compassion for the countess. She was shocked that the prince had cast off his mistress so suddenly, but she knew from experience that the prince had no hesitation being callous and even violent with women. She had little doubt that Dalflitch had been on the receiving end of her share of assaults and now was cast off, just as Amelia knew she would be herself once the prince had an heir by her.

"Why did you do it?" Amelia asked. She'd been trapped into the prince's attentions by the circumstances of her husband's death, but Countess Dalflitch had sought them out. "Why put yourself through all this? His disdain and other...depredations?"

"Because this is the game we play, isn't it?" Dalflitch explained, her lips still twitching in a wry, self-mocking smile. "We play for the attentions of the best man available, and I have outplayed myself. I thought to outplay you and become the princess, but after last night I will forever be one of the prince's former whores."

"So why accept that role? Your husband still lives, you said. Why not return to him?"

"Because he knows. He stays away from court for the shame I have brought him. Everyone knows; I made sure of that. So confident. An annulment can be such a simple thing...supposedly."

"You thought the prince would annul your marriage for you?"

"Have the church do it for him, yes."

"And you still wanted to be the prince's wife?" asked the duchess, unable to overcome her disbelief. "Even knowing him as you do, as we both do? Even after seeing how he treats women who are no longer any use to him?" Amelia was shocked to see a tear in the countess's eye and hear her voice catch in her throat for a moment. With a sniff, the noblewoman wiped the tear away.

"I was to be the exception. Besides, I have already endured too much, sacrificed too much. The whispers and rumors. The contemptuous glances. To climb this high? I wasn't about give it all up because the handsome prince turned out to be something of a brute behind closed doors."

It was a harshly cynical assessment of Daven Marcus and his relationships. For the first time ever, Amelia realized that Dalflitch was neither a naïve girl, dreaming of winning the heart of a prince, nor a slattern, unable to keep faithful to her husband. Rather, she was closer in nature to Amelia than the duchess cared to admit; she was another woman who sought to better herself in a society that frowned on ambition in anyone born lower, women especially. What separated the two women was what they were prepared to do for their advancement. Dalflitch had cast off all limits in her ambition, and so was unable to content herself with her first husband. Whereas Amelia had fallen in love with her duke, Dalflitch had seen in her husband just another rung on a ladder that still went up. Whatever way she first gained Daven Marcus's attentions, he would have been an irresistible challenge—the highest rung yet, destined to one day become the top of the ladder itself.

Some part of Amelia said she should disdain this woman who had gambled her virtue for advancement and was losing both, but she couldn't do it. Time and again in the court she watched the ambitious trade virtue and honor for place and power. It was hard to fault the countess for doing what everyone around her was doing as well, even though she was so much more brazen about it.

"What will you do now?"

"I do not know. I came out here this morning because I knew Daven Marcus was riding past. I thought a show of devotion might cause him to relent and allow me back into his affections."

"It didn't work?" Amelia asked, already knowing the answer.

"He looked right through me," said Dalflitch, "as did all his closest courtiers—men who once waited hours just to ask me to whisper a word in his ear, and now they could not distinguish me from the grass on the side of the road."

Amelia nodded. She could imagine exactly what that had been like. She'd been through it herself often enough.

"Lord Robant did speak to me, though."

"Indeed?" That surprised Amelia.

"I am no longer welcome to ride with you and your maid. I am to find my own means to travel. I am not banished from the camp, but the prince does not expect to see me, either."

"What will you do?"

"I do not know. I am a lady without means in the middle of a wilderness with no patronage and a cuckolded husband far away who will not look for my return. When you lay your whole fortune on the turn of a card and lose..." The countess shrugged.

It was a succinct summary of her condition, and Amelia could not fault it. The duchess wanted to sneer, wanted to lord her position over her rival, but a rival for what? For affections which she loathed? For a status she was doing everything she could think of to avoid, or at least diminish? Amelia remembered how, only days ago, she had thought to befriend Dalflitch as a defense against the prince. Now, when Dalflitch had nothing to offer her, she found herself *more* drawn to the woman, not less. Was it the fact that no one else around her named Daven Marcus for the monster he was? With Turley gone, no one, not even her own maid, would speak a word against the crown prince. And even Turley had had a servant's circumspection. Dalflitch was the first person to be openly honest with her since the crusade westward had begun. Was that worth enough to her, Amelia wondered, that she would forget all the humiliations at the countess's hands?

"How will you survive?" Amelia asked her.

"I have my jewelry. That will buy my food and perhaps transport back east with a merchant, at least as far as your town. Once they learn of my estate, even the low born will gouge me for the price of every cup of water."

With no influence and no income, only the wealth she carried with her this far out into the wilderness, Dalflitch was a hair's breadth from starving to death. She knew it, and Amelia knew it too.

"If you can find nowhere else," the duchess said, still staring ahead, "I will give orders to my servants that a plate be made available to you at my fire. You will not starve."

Dalflitch cocked a sharp eyebrow, and her usual expression of contemptuous superiority reasserted itself momentarily.

"You want to keep me around to gloat over?"

"If I wanted to gloat, it would be over the thought of you dead in one the puddles hereabouts," Amelia retorted, looking directly down at the countess for the first time in the entire conversation. "I sought only to keep you from starving. If it does not suit you, you are welcome to find your own way in the world. You've certainly had a great deal of practice at that."

"Such gracious charity," Dalflitch responded but managed to keep herself from sneering.

"Gracious or not, it is the charity you need, fallen countess. Accept it, or don't; I will give the order to my servants, and you can avail yourself as you choose."

Amelia turned her head away and geed Meadow Dancer to a canter, leaving the countess behind. She wanted to hate the woman, fiercely wanted to, but she could not do it, and she'd had enough of trying.

CHAPTER 30

R iding back along the causeway, Amelia was thinking to
continue east into the grassland. She wanted to find some
open country with no one around and give Meadow Dancer
her head, to experience the wind on her face and the joy of
motion of a horse at a gallop. When she was passing the camp
and the little saltwater woodland, she noticed a man emerging
from under the trees—a large nobleman in a fine gambeson she
recognized immediately as Earl Derryman. Having noticed him
coming from a strange place and clapping at his lower legs to
beat sand and water from his hose, Amelia planned to ride on,
giving him no more thought. But as she did, something about
the earl seemed odd, and her mind worked of its own volition
to puzzle out what it was. Then she realized: Derryman wasn't
limping. In fact, he was moving swiftly and quite painlessly.
For all the march west so far, the earl had been afflicted with
gout, unable to ride and barely able to walk. Now here he was,
gamboling like a man less than half his age.

In the rational part of her mind, Amelia knew there might
be any number of explanations for the earl's change of step,
all of them innocent or simple. But the days of isolation, the
endless mockery and machinations of the prince, and of course,
Turley's murder, all worked on her mind to suspect some sort
of treachery. She imagined that the earl had deliberately faked
his illness to deceive her in some way. It was ridiculous and

paranoid, but her calm inner mind would not let her shake it off.

When she reached the ramp down from the causeway, she didn't guide Meadow Dancer off over the grass, but turned her head back toward the center of camp, looking for the earl. She wasn't exactly sure what she intended but vaguely imagined she would watch him from a distance to spy out evidence of possible treachery. It didn't work out that way, though, for as she rode around a large tent with fluttering green ribbons on its corner posts, she came face to face with the earl, not ten paces distant. He was looking straight at her and saw her the same moment she saw him. Hoping she didn't look too surprised or suspicious, Amelia schooled her expression to polite disinterest and made to walk her roan straight past the man. He, however, was clearly pleased to see her, although there was a troubled undertone to his expression, a knotting of the brows and downturn of his lips.

"Your Grace," he said and bowed deeply. She received his bow with a nod. "It is fortuitous to see you here. If you will forgive the forwardness, I would ask an audience."

"Certainly, My Lord," she said. What else could she say? "What would you like to discuss?"

"Not here, Your Grace," he said more quietly, stepping closer as he did so. "In your tent, if it pleases you. It is a difficult matter to raise."

"Very well, Earl. I was not planning to return so soon, but if you would accompany me, we can deal with your matter directly."

He seemed about to object, perhaps out of politeness, but then nodded and took a place next to her stirrup as she rode. It was a place of humility, the position normally occupied by a servant or lesser bondsman, and that made her uncomfortable. Perhaps he was only showing loyal humility, but her paranoia would not let her believe it. For the entire short journey back to her tent, her mind raced, trying to think what treachery the man might be plotting. Surely, if he intended her harm, it would make more sense to lure her into the marsh; there were any number of secret locations to dispatch her there. Here in camp, even in her tent, she could call for her house guard in a trice, foiling any violence—unless her house guard were part of the betrayal. Since Viscount Wolden's death, none of the remaining nobles had declared for her, not openly, even when they showed her approval. Daven Marcus had insulted them with the mocking heraldry on his 'betrothal' doublet, and since that night, still no one had spoken out. She was alone, her loyal retainers falling away, or murdered, one at a time. Her one hope, Prentice Ash, was so far east he might as well have been in another world, and who knew what had become of him. With all the other pressures she faced, Amelia realized she'd forgotten about Baron Liam and the prince's order to round up all the convicts. She cursed herself for a fool and wanted to cry. The reins fell from her hands, and she let Meadow Dancer wander.

The prince had ordered Liam to scare up all the convicts, and there were still no convicts with the march. That meant that they were either on the way or still in the Reach. None of the riders she'd set as messengers had come to her with word from Prentice and his militia. What did that mean? How had she let the worries of the court make her forget? Prentice planned to offer the convicts their freedom in exchange for service as soldiers. Liam had orders that would not let one of them off the chain. It was inevitable there would be conflict. Suddenly Amelia was sure that they were all slain. Liam hadn't returned because he'd found the convicts and killed them. Prentice would never surrender; she was sure of that. After his decade on the chain, he would prefer death, she was certain. And Liam would have no mercy for any mere convict who resisted his authority. They were all dead. It had to be.

"Your Grace, are you well?" asked Earl Derryman beside her.

"Not really, My Lord," she answered distractedly, unable to banish the terrible scenes that were swirling in her mind, images of convicted men slaughtered by knights, by sword and hammer and axe. She remembered a night, months ago, when the invaders from the west had tortured an entire village to death—men, women and children—while she and her guards had hidden in a church for their own safety. That had been the day she met Prentice, though he wasn't called Ash then. Her memories of that dreadful night and its aftermath mingled with her imaginings to fill her mind with horrors that threatened to overwhelm her.

Amelia swallowed and sat up straighter. She was Duchess of the Reach. She did not have the luxury of self-pity. Setting her face hard, she willed iron into her spine, holding her seat with a dignity she did not feel. Try as she might, she could not banish the horrors and terrors in her mind's eye, but she refused to let the world around her see it. Her heart might be broken, and the man at her side might be coming to kill her, but she was carved from alabaster, pale and unflinching.

"If you would take the rein for me, Earl," she said.

He nodded and took the reins over Meadow Dancer's head, leading the horse the short distance to Amelia's tent. When the roan was handed off to a groom, he helped her down and followed her into her tent. There was no one inside, but that did not surprise Amelia. Since Turley had gone missing, she had grown used to Kirsten being about the camp looking for him. Even though Lord Robant had confirmed Turley's death, it seemed Kirsten was maintaining the habit of absence. Amelia wondered if the girl was out gossiping, seeking out rumors. She had urged Kirsten to become closer to Countess Dalflitch, a supreme gossip. It was hardly the young woman's fault if some of the habit had rubbed off on her.

Amelia took a deep breath and turned to face Earl Derryman, trying to ready herself for whatever dread surprise he brought with him. She was surprised, therefore, when the earl went down on one knee, smoothly, with the practiced ease of a lifelong courtier.

"My Lord," she said. "Do not trouble your gout with such politeness on my account. We are in private."

"We are, Your Grace, but my gout no longer troubles me."

This was it, she thought.

"How can that be?"

The earl's brows creased, and he looked askance, as if he were trying to remember something that eluded him.

"Do you believe in prophecy, Duchess Amelia?"

What was that? Prophecy? What was he talking about?

"I have learned my catechism and know some of the scriptures. The prophets of lost Israel spoke the words of God and wrote them down. Is that what troubles you, My Lord? I am little skilled to answer a theological question. A sacrist would be better suited. Surely you have a chaplain of your own?"

"Do you believe in prophets today?" Whatever Derryman was talking about, it had nothing to do with the scriptures.

"I've seen wise women make predictions at harvest festivals, silly stories to thrill unwed girls. And there are wild men who count themselves holy, who sometimes wander from town to town, offering prophecies. Most sacrists drive them out as madmen, if not outright heretics."

"My family believes in prophets, Your Grace. We have held a teaching, quietly, never in disagreement with the Holy Church, but not widely known. We think that prophecy comes from an angel, sent by God, to give men and women words or dreams as they need."

Amelia felt her knees go weak, and she sat down on the only chair in the tent. She remembered her vision—the sight of the prince and his cronies as vulturous monsters fighting an impossible, many-headed snake and being defended in the melee only by white lions that protected her like guard dogs. It had been so vivid, almost more like reality than her day-to-day experiences. The thought that it might have been an angel speaking to her from God rather than a madness she could not explain struck her so heavily that she believed it completely and immediately. Her vision was from God, she was sure of it, but what did it mean?

"Why do you speak to me of prophets, My Lord?"

"There is a prophetess in the wood in the saltwater, Your Grace."

Amelia blinked in surprise. Of all the things she had feared or anticipated from this meeting, these words were not even close. She searched his face, and his dark brown eyes showed he was in deadly earnest. He meant what he was saying.

"How do you know this, My Lord?" Amelia was so full of wonder and uncertainty that her voice was barely a whisper.

"Almost as soon as we arrived here at this camp, my servants and even some of my own sworn swords began to speak of how ill-omened that little wood was. By this morning, the notion had spread so that they were sitting around the breakfast fire telling tales of lights under the branches in the night. Some were swearing never to go near it. Not even a day in its shadow, and they were terrified of fey and grumpkins already. I was not having it, Your Grace."

He frowned in a practical manner, like a dutiful uncle prompted to discipline a wayward child. It made him seem quite endearing to her.

"As my father always said, Your Grace, the only way to deal with a silly superstition is to confront it and show it for the folly it is. So, after I broke my fast, I told my servants I was going to walk the wood from the east to the west and then back and from the north to the south. That would put paid to their nonsense. I wasn't about to have the camp lose a valuable source of firewood because of a few nervous servants. Do you have any idea what merchants are charging for wood just to cook our food?"

Amelia was surprised to realize she had no idea people were paying for firewood, but as she thought about it, she also realized that, with so few trees in the grasslands—only one or two every league or so—there were no easy supplies of fuel close to hand. Merchants would make a fortune charging high rates for a product that cost them next to nothing to acquire back in Dweltford. She knew it was the kind of deal her father would have traveled a hundred leagues for, but as she thought about it, she was also reminded of the cabal of merchants who had helped Sir Duggan embezzle her late husband's fortune and paid for him to be assassinated. Now, other merchants were gouging her coffers and the coffers of her nobles for the sake of firewood. Suddenly she understood vividly some of why merchants enjoyed their poor reputation.

"I marched into the wood, and it was unthinkable how soon I was lost," Derryman continued. "I must have been walking in circles. I'd followed a small path in, but it was so dark under the tight woven branches, it might as well had not been day. I'd walked half around it on the outside, I knew its parameters, but within, it defied reason. More than once I stood still and tried to judge my location from the sounds of the camp, but I could not hear it. As impossible as it sounds, it was as if I was the only mortal for leagues about. Then I met her."

"Who?"

"A wizened old crone, hair so white it would shame the clouds and wrinkled like the bark of an ancient willow. Her skin was papery and her eyes deep sunk and dark as the pools of water about the grassy marsh."

"A witch, you mean?" Amelia felt herself drawing back from the earl's story. She hadn't believed in fae tales since she was a girl, and witches living in the midst of old forests were exactly that. Did the earl think she was a child to frighten with a fireside tale?

"Not a witch, Your Grace," he insisted somewhat indignantly. "Nor a true sorceress. I would not need to report such a person to you, Your Grace. I would send for a sacrist and have the evil rooted out.

"No, this was a prophetess. She greeted me by my own name, though I had not told her, and she did so in the name of our Lord. She said she had a true spoken message for me and asked if she could pray for my wellbeing. I told her I would be glad just for directions out of the copse. I also warned her to be watchful of unscrupulous types, since there are so many marching with us, it seems, if you'll forgive me, Your Grace."

Amelia wasn't sure if she was surprised or pleased to hear him speak so critically of the company the prince's march had drawn.

"So, she told you the way out?" she prompted him to continue the story.

He shook his head.

"No, Your Grace. She held up a soft leather bag. At first, I thought it was her coin purse, and it made a noise like coins when she jiggled it on her palm. But when she poured it out, it held only a few stones. She said these were the only thing of value she possessed, but no one would take them from her before time. Then she put them back and offered me the bag. 'Take one,' she said."

"And did you?"

"I wasn't going to, but then I did. No sooner had I put my hand in the bag and taken one in my fingers than she reached out and touched my leg, here." He pointed to his right calf. "Just a finger touch, and as she did, she beseeched the Lord to heal me. I swear, Your Grace, at that very moment, the pain left me. My gout was gone, all of it. You see me walking, standing, and kneeling."

"So, she is a healer?"

"And a prophetess. When I withdrew the stone, a simple grey thing, indistinguishable from a thousand other such pebbles in the world, she prophesied, telling me that soon I will die but leading a just charge against evil, defending the Reach."

Derryman practically beamed at her, and Amelia wondered if the man were mad.

"It pleases you, My Lord, to be healed and told that you will die in the same breath? Are you sure you are thinking clearly?"

"You don't understand, Your Grace, but please let me explain. I buried my second wife last summer. I loved her dearly. She came to me in the autumn of my life, long after my dear Sarah, my first, had passed on. Now Lilya is gone as well. My greatest friend in life, your husband Marne, was taken from us in the same season. It seemed the time, and with my sickness, I was ready to ride one glorious charge into the teeth of battle. Now I know that I will receive exactly that, and for the defense of this land, our land, which I love."

"But you are healed, strengthened again," Amelia protested. "Why seek death at all?"

"You would have me go home? Sit a few more years in a chair by the fire and watch the world forget me? Do you know of even one bannerman in your service who would squander newfound strength in such a way? Would you want one who did?"

No matter which way she turned the idea, Amelia could not make it make sense to her. Life was precious; honor and reputation were fleeting, at least to her. Then she paused and realized that wasn't true, not really. Since word had come to her of her husband's death, she had worked continually to protect his legacy with her defense of the Reach, delaying the prince's advances, and unmasking Duggan's treachery and the merchants who'd worked with him. Amelia had done all these things because she loved Marne and wanted to protect what was left of him in this life, even if that was only his memory and honor.

She nodded slowly and gave Earl Derryman a gentle smile. Everything he'd told her was strange, but it was a long way from the dread notions she'd had in her mind when they met in the middle of camp.

"I hope you will forgive me, Earl," she said quietly, "but I pray that your life will not be so short. Your service to the Reach favors me. Nevertheless, when the time to face your last charge comes upon you, I have no doubt you will meet it with valor and honor, and I will do whatever I can to see that the Reach pays you the respect your life deserves in memory."

"You are very kind, Duchess Amelia."

Derryman pushed himself to his feet and bowed once more. He was still a heavy man, but the freedom in his movement made him seem fifteen years younger. Why long to die in the face of such vitality?

"I am a lonely widow, My Lord. It would cost me the little love left if I added bitterness to the recipe." A thought occurred to Amelia just as she was about to give the earl leave to withdraw. "Why tell me this tale, Earl? Please do not mistake me; I was glad of it and your company, but you seemed so intent on sharing it with me before anyone else, it seems."

Derryman smiled.

"Because she told me to."

"She?"

"When she spoke her prophecy over me, she told me that the first person I should share the news with was you yourself, Your Grace. She said you would need to know."

Amelia blinked her eyes, bewildered by the notion. "Why?" she asked.

Derryman simply shrugged. "She did not say."

He made to withdraw, and she nodded to give him leave. His hand was on the tent flap when he turned back.

"With your permission, Your Grace, I know you have lost much with the death of Duke Marne. You are widowed too young and mourn his passing. The Reach mourns with you, more than you might guess. You say you are lonely and have cause to be bitter, but you have more friends than you know."

He bowed once more and departed, and Amelia was left alone with her thoughts. For a moment she considered saddling Meadow Dancer again and taking the long ride in the grass she'd planned before, but before she could stir herself to call a groom to prepare, a servant poked his head through the flap and asked to announce a noblewoman. Amelia gave her permission, and in a moment, Countess Dalflitch stepped into the tent.

Amelia sighed inwardly.

"Twice in the same morning, countess; has something happened?" she asked coldly. "Did we become confidantes overnight without my noticing? Perhaps while I slept?"

The countess curtseyed, the sincerest gesture of respect the predatory noblewoman had ever shown.

"Not yet, Your Grace," said Dalflitch with a knowing half-smile. "Not yet."

CHAPTER 31

"Not an hour ago you were the spurned lover, bereft and on the verge of poverty," Amelia said icily. Something about the countess's demeanor annoyed her. The old confidence was back, the pained self-awareness hidden away once more. "Has the prince taken you back? Is that why you're here?"

Dalflitch smirked, but there was also some surprise in her eyes.

"If he had, Your Grace, I wouldn't come to you with it like this," she answered. "I would wait until you found out for yourself in an audience with the prince. That way the surprise would be greatest and the impact most cruel. That is Daven Marcus' way, and he would expect no less of me."

Although the countess's directness annoyed her, Amelia had to agree with the woman's assessment. It was exactly the way Daven Marcus would want her to find out if he did take Dalflitch back into his bed.

"Your honesty does not endear you to me," she said. Honesty didn't justify cruelty.

"I would not expect it to, Your Grace." Dalflitch had her eyes down in the correct manner, her show of courtesy absolutely flawless. It made Amelia realize just how calculated every previous disrespect had been if the countess was capable of such politeness when it suited her.

"Nonetheless, perhaps I might find a way to enter your affections, if I make an effort."

"Even if it were possible, why should I let you?"

"You have no reason to," Dalflitch conceded. "But I hold out hope, even so."

"Why?"

Dalflitch looked up and met Amelia's eyes for the first time since entering the tent. Her expression was so calculated, such a mixture of ideas and emotions, that Amelia wondered if anyone could ever trust the woman.

"When you offered me charity this morning, Your Grace, I spurned it. That was a prideful mistake and I apologize for that."

This caught Amelia even more by surprise than Earl Derryman's tale of the prophetess. There was no doubt her expression showed it, but Dalflitch made no mention or comment. She merely continued with her explanation.

"It appears my estate is even worse than I imagined. After we spoke, I sought to buy myself a horse. I traded a diamond-and-amethyst-studded pendant in the shape of a leaping fish for a broken-down embarrassment of a nag and was told to be thankful for it. That jewel should have bought me a pair of fine destriers; a knight's horse at the very least. But the way merchants are charging this far from the Kingdom, I doubt my little purse of trinkets will last me a week. I will be relying on your charity just to eat before you board the first ship to sail south with the prince to the Vec. And what will become of me then?"

"You don't think you'll be given passage on a ship?" asked Amelia.

"You know that I won't, Your Grace. And I will have nothing to pay my way back to Dweltford with a merchant's caravan, save my charms."

"You were happy to trade your charms with the prince," Amelia said, feeling a moment's cruel satisfaction, even though the imputation was beneath her.

Dalflitch did not even flinch at the duchess's veiled insult.

"Princes pay better than ostlers and merchants," she replied candidly.

Amelia sighed. The prince had cast the countess out of his favors, so why were they still verbally dueling like this? Dalflitch's usual sardonic demeanor seemed mixed with a new earnestness, but Amelia did not, could not, trust the woman. How could she trust a woman who had been such a bitter rival, even if only for a man she never wanted to marry?

"So, you are poor and becoming desperate, Countess? How will that win you more than my charity? I would think you would be thankful just for that."

"My poverty is only the why, Your Grace. For the how, it would be best if you came with me."

"Go with you?" Amelia's paranoia flared again, and just as she had imagined the earl throwing her body in a dark pool, now she conjured the image of the countess doing something similar. She shook her head.

"I think not."

"You imagine I'm plotting something?"

"No," Amelia lied, but she suspected the shrewd countess could tell the truth.

"By all means, summon a guard if you think it necessary."

"Where do you wish me to go with you?" Amelia demanded warily.

"I cannot say."

"If you cannot say, then I will not go."

It sounded petty in Amelia's ears, speaking so bluntly, but she was tired—tired of feeling threatened, tired of having no one to trust. And now, with Turley dead and Prentice almost certainly lost to her, she was the only one she could trust, unless Earl Derryman was right. Perhaps she *did* have more friends than she knew. And if she needed more friends, could she afford to spurn Countess Dalflitch, no matter how much she might like to? How much was her wounded pride worth in a camp full of courtiers who already disdained her?

"I swear, Your Grace, I would tell you," Dalflitch persisted earnestly, "but it is worth more than my life. There are lurking ears everywhere in this camp, even on just the other side of these curtains."

She cast her eyes about the sides of the tent, and Amelia followed her glance. What did Dalflitch fear that would be a threat to them both? Amelia thought for a moment while Dalflitch's eyes searched hers. Even feeling as paranoid as she did, Amelia recognized that this was not typical of the countess. If this was a ruse, it was far too clumsy for Dalflitch's deft hands. The vixen was too cunning for something like this unless it was true.

"I will call some guards," she said at last, "and you can take me where you wish. But be warned, if this is treachery of some kind, I'll give my men-at-arms express orders, and you'll pay with your life before the sun sets."

Dalflitch's mocking half smile flickered back into place, like a failing fire coming back to flame.

"Something amuses you, Countess?"

"Only the thought of how useful such men prove to be."

"Surely your husband, the count, has such men of his own."

Dalflitch curtseyed. "My husband's men wouldn't snuff a candle to save my life," she said, and though her smile remained in place, there was a sadness in her eyes.

With four houseguards summoned to escort them, Amelia let Dalflitch lead her through the camp to a part of the baggage train, where merchants and servants kept their own places to sleep and eat. It was much busier than the camp proper, and Amelia wondered whether even four men-at-arms would be enough if this crowd were part of some ambush. She was comforted, though, to see that Dalflitch seemed equally ill at ease. Like a hunted animal, the countess's eyes flicked back and forth.

"You seem quite fearful. Do you expect we are being spied upon?" Amelia asked her.

"Until this morning, the prince kept me in his confidences," she replied. "I know how many eyes and ears are keeping watch on his behalf. We would have been less conspicuous if you had not brought four men in coats of mail to announce our presence."

"I would not have come without them."

Dalflitch nodded to acknowledge the wisdom of that statement and then cast one more glance around her before stepping past a campfire tended by two matrons heating washing water. One of the women gave the countess a nod and stood, walking two steps to the back of a wagon that was parked nearby—one of two forming a corner like two sides of a square about the fire. It was the closest thing to privacy that might be created in a busy encampment like this. As if they were conspiring villains in a play, the pair of women, one an elegant countess, the other a threadbare washerwoman, looked about again to see if anyone was watching.

"Tell your men to keep lookout," she told Amelia.

For what? the duchess wanted to ask, but she played along and nodded to her guards who turned to face outward, forming a kind of cordon about the campfire. Dalflitch waved Amelia to the wagon, and as the duchess drew close, she flipped open the flap. Amelia peered inside, having no idea what she would find. What secret could the countess have in the back of a wagon? A bundle of cloth was the first thing her eyes made out in the dimness within, the overcast sky giving little more light than twilight.

A bundle of laundry? Amelia thought. She was about to ask for an explanation when the laundry moved and groaned. Her eyes widened when the other end of the mound of clothes produced a head with a sweat-matted mop of dark hair wrapped in a blood-stained bandage. A canny pair of eyes looked in her direction over a crooked, exhausted, but unmistakably roguish smile.

"Apologies for my recent bad doing of my job, Your Grace," he said. "I've been having a bit of a tough time of it."

Amelia's hand flew to her mouth, and it was all she could to do not to cry.

"Turley! You're alive!"

CHAPTER 32

"Well, giving it my best impression, Your Grace," he joked, but his head fell backward with a groan. Even the effort of looking up at her from the other end of the wagon seemed to have exhausted him. Amelia whirled on Dalflitch.

"You knew he was alive?"

The countess shook her head.

"I thought him dead, as you did, Your Grace. Sir Robant assured the prince he had made an end of him."

"About six of them set on him," the washerwoman said, remembering at the last moment to bow her head, a gesture that devolved into a half-hearted curtsey. The old woman clearly had no idea how to show proper respect to a duchess, but Amelia could not have cared less. "Between clubs and knives, they sure expected him not to live."

Amelia shook her head. As she looked in, she could pick out other parts of Turley's body, disguised by bandages.

"How did he survive?"

"He's strong as he looks," the washerwoman told her. "And he's got more friends around these parts than the pack of mongrels what set on him."

"And your name opened a few hearts as well, Your Grace," Turley muttered from the wagon. With a groaning struggle, he maneuvered himself around so that his head was near the rear opening. With a bandaged hand, he waved at his forelock, a semblance of the proper gesture. Try as he might, he couldn't quite get his fingers to grip his hair as they should. In pity and affection, she took his hand and pressed it down, relieving him of his duty.

"It seemed the canniest thing to keep my head down, back here with the luggage, Your Grace. That's why you ain't seen me. Didn't want them coming back to finish the job."

"That and the poor beggar can't hardly walk," the washerwoman added, picking at her filthy brown teeth with the end of a twig. "He'll be lucky if he ever walks again."

"Pox on that," said Turley, but his words came out breathy and weak, as if even speaking was becoming exhausting for him. "Just need a few days' rest, is all."

"Why didn't you send to me?" Amelia asked, stroking his hair, her concern and relief at finding him alive overcoming her sense of noble dignity.

"I did, Your Grace," he said. "I sent straight away with word. When I didn't hear back, I figured you were being coy to keep safe from Robant. A serving girl said she got close to your fire but never met you before the baron's men seen her off."

"Timid little thing," said the other peasant woman, the one still by the fire. "Didn't fancy waiting around, getting touched up by his men."

Amelia could imagine.

"When I heard that the countess here had fallen out with his highness, I gambled on a woman scorned and sent to her as a way to get word to you."

"Why not through Kirsten?" This was exactly the sort of service a handmaid was supposed to handle—discrete communication on her mistress's behalf.

"Your Grace's maid's been more than a little evasive of late," Turley said. The fatigue in his voice was so great that his words were starting to slur. "Seemed like she was doing it deliberately. I guessed if she knew she was being watched, she might be trying to throw the watchers off the scent. 'Course, if she was being watched, then that would mean Lord Robant knew I was alive, and that don't seem likely."

Amelia had to agree with him. Whatever the details, for the most part, she was simply happy to know he was alive.

"He's a shrewd man, Your Grace," said Dalflitch quietly. There was a tone in her voice that Amelia had never heard there before. "He deciphered the thoughts of my heart, even before I knew them myself. He had a girl find me moments after you left me this morning. I can see why he holds your affections."

Affections? Amelia looked at the countess in shock. "I'm not sleeping with him!" she said before she could stop herself.

"You don't have to fear my judgement, Your Grace," was the noblewoman's response. Amelia glared at her until Dalflitch realized that she was being utterly truthful. It was the countess's turn to be surprised. "Truly? With those eyes and that smile? And those hands?"

The countess's recounting of Turley's attractive features revealed more about her than him, to Amelia's mind. Less than a day ago she'd been the prince's mistress. Did the woman have no notion of fidelity?

"I do not dally with servants."

"Quite right, too," Turley averred sleepily. His eyelids began to droop, but he stirred as a thought occurred to him that he could not let go before sleep claimed him. "There's an apothecary on the march somewhere. She makes unctions and poultices that work miracles, like how she healed Prentice's back after that flogging. Mine too, come to think of it. She weren't cheap, and you'd have to pay again, Your Grace. But if you find her, I'll bet she can set me back to rights quick as grease."

He finished speaking and fell asleep. The effort of moving and speaking looked to have soaked his shirt through with sweat. Amelia's heart twisted for him.

"We've gone looking like he's wanted, m'lady," said the washerwoman, "all up and down the march. T'ain't any woman apothecary in the whole army." She looked at Dalflitch who also shrugged.

"None of which that I've heard."

Amelia held up her hand, shaking her head. "He's talking about Prince Mercad's campaign in the summer. The apothecary was with that army." Amelia remembered the brutality of the flogging that Prentice and Turley had been subjected to under Liam's orders. It had been a miracle that either man had survived, and the apothecary's healing ministrations had been equally wondrous.

"She did good work did she, this woman?" Dalflitch asked.

"Miraculous," Amelia confirmed, not really listening. A new idea was forming in her mind.

"Pity then that she isn't with this march. The way his injuries are, he'll almost certainly not walk right again nor regain the use of that hand. Three of the fingers were severed straight off, they tell me."

Dalflitch looked at the washerwoman, who nodded to confirm the tale.

"There's always a chance, as well, that the wounds will turn septic," the countess went on. "I'm sorry to bring you such fell news, but I knew you would prefer an honest, bitter service, more than keeping secrets from you, however unpleasant the truth."

Amelia nodded, barely listening, but recognizing the truth of Dalflitch's assessment. It was far from a pleasant service she had done Amelia, but it was valuable and worthy. Amelia acknowledged that, at least. Her heart was breaking as she considered Turley's plight. It was true that injuries as severe as his most often led to death as rot and infection claimed the victim. And even if he lived, would he ever be whole enough to be her steward once more? She felt for him, but she also recognized how much she stood to lose as well. It was a cold, selfish line of thought, and she wanted to curse herself for it. She did not. She had a duty to Turley as her servant, but she also had a duty to every man and woman of the Reach, from the least servant under her steward to the highest nobles, like the loyal Earl Derryman.

An idea flashed into Amelia's mind, so completely formed that she had decided to do it before she even realized she was considering it.

"Perhaps I do not need her," she murmured to herself.

"Your Grace?"

"The apothecary. I don't need her."

Amelia explained no more than that as she called her guards to escort her back to her tent. Just before she left, she turned back to her former rival.

"Countess, will you do me the service of watching here with my man for tonight and tomorrow morning?" she asked.

"You have some plan, Your Grace?" asked the surprised Dalflitch.

"I believe I do, though I have no way of knowing what outcome I might receive. Nevertheless, if you will watch over him tonight and see that he is not discovered if someone such as Lord Robant's men come looking for him, I will be in your debt, no matter what other outcome the night has."

Countess Dalflitch obviously had no idea what the duchess was talking about, but she curtseyed, head down politely, and accepted the duty Amelia asked of her.

How did we come to this? Amelia asked herself as she led her house guards back to her tent.

CHAPTER 33

"Your spearheads," said Yentow Sent disdainfully. The wiry Masnian flicked back an oilcloth to reveal a pile of hundreds of polished steel points that glowed vivid orange in the light of the forges. They were long, willow-leafed blades with neat sockets for fitting on the end of a pole. A similar stack next to the spear points was built of halberd heads, blades that were equal parts axe, spear, and pick. It was a truly versatile weapon. The point could be thrust into the seams of an armored man's suit of plates, and the axe blade could hack away the boards of a shield or the flesh of an unarmored man. If those two were ineffective, the back spike would punch through mail comfortably or else could be used to trip an opponent and make him vulnerable from a different angle. And spears and halberds were easier to teach a man to wield, so much more forgiving than the sophisticated artistry needed to master a sword.

But they were not challenging for a smith to make, and Yentow Sent never missed an opportunity to remind Prentice how far beneath him they were as a task.

"These are perfect," said Prentice.

"Of course. If you set me to make you toasting forks, I would allow only the finest to leave my forge. This may only be busy work you've offered me, but my reputation rides on the quality of every edge."

Prentice sighed and shook his head. A craftsman who took such pains in every task should be an advantage to an army, but somehow, Sent managed to make it an absolute annoyance.

"Next break in the rain, I'll start sending men to get their practice poles made into proper weapons," he told the master smith.

"Weapons perhaps," Sent sniffed, "but far from proper."

Prentice turned away. He had no more patience for the conversation. As he walked off however, Yentow Sent followed him.

"Now that these petty tasks are accomplished, is there any chance you might set us to the making of swords, as your duchess warranted us to do?"

"You're like a dog with a bone, aren't you?"

"You call me a dog?"

Now Sent was genuinely offended, and Prentice turned to placate him. "It's a figure of speech, Master Sent. I did not mean to insult you."

"It seems you Kingdom folk are given to many impolite figures of speech."

Prentice could only guess what other figures of speech Sent was referring to. It seemed everyone in the camp had a different story of something to which the Masnian master had taken offense.

"I have no use for longswords, Master Sent. I've made this very clear."

"Not even for yourself? I have seen you practicing with Sir Gant. If you regain your skill, you will need a blade to wield it with."

"Your sword-breaker serves me well enough. But if you want to make swords, then basket hilts on my fangs' blades will be a good next task."

"Bah, you want knives, not swords!"

On one level it fascinated Prentice that Sent could put such a premium on one weapon over all others. By all accounts, the Masnian was a master of all forms of weapon-making, and Prentice wanted him to make swords, but single edged, and that lone difference made one seem like a work of art in Yentow Sent's eyes and the other little more than a glorified farm implement. For his part, Prentice had stood on battlefields with nothing but farm implements with which to defend himself. If it were forged by Yentow Sent or one of his journeymen, Prentice would be willing to face a knight with only a shovel if he had to.

But food was getting short. Everyone was down to only one meal a day, and already the poorly preserved meat they had to eat was starting to turn rancid. That made fatigue and sickness worse, and hunger was breeding paranoia. Between sawdust bread and fantasies of hidden stores of food, the entire camp was only a week or two away from collapse. Prentice was starting to wonder if he should just throw the gate open and give every man and woman a chance to flee for themselves. With a wave of fleeing convicts overwhelming them, the knights wouldn't likely stop everyone. But if he left it too much longer, they'd all be too weak to make a run for it.

"Next break in the rain, I'll send men to bring their poles."

Prentice stepped out from under cover, leaving Sent in the protection of his forge works, and walked into the thin drizzle sweeping across from the west. It was around midwinter, he was fairly sure. No one was really keeping a calendar. Soon, the days would begin to lengthen again, and the rain would pass. They would be dying of starvation, though, if they waited here for the spring. Prentice clasped at his head in the rain and felt the ache there. He hardly slept these days, and his clothes were continually damp. He'd had a bitter chill on his chest back in autumn, and he was sure the combination of hunger, fatigue, cold, and wet would bring it back upon him. Then it really would be the end.

As it was, he was barely in control now. Like the horde of rats in his dream that were hiding in the walls, his men seemed to grow more unruly, sicklier, and more desperate with every day. Fights were a daily occurrence, and at least ten men and two women had been found killed by a secret knife or cudgel-strike in the night. Petty slights were being avenged in the bitterest fashion. His hopes of turning brute convicts into soldiers of discipline and honor were dissolving in the winter rains.

Heading back to the barracks, the overcast sky closed the day in with a heavy twilight that made sight almost impossible. Prentice could barely make out his feet beneath him, and only the thin slivers of firelight that cut through the gaps and flaws in the barrack huts let him know for sure where he was going. Inside, his recruits—convicts he had let off the chain to now starve to death—shivered in misery.

Suddenly he couldn't face them.

He had taken a straw mattress on the floor of one hut, a gesture to show that he shared their miseries. Now, it just made him feel unwelcome. In seeking to make their lives better and serve his duchess in the doing, he'd only succeeded in making their lives even more bitter. Many would swear there was no worse way to live than on a convict chain; Prentice was proving them wrong.

He turned aside from his own hut and sought out a tiny lean-to annex that had been set up against the wall of a different hut. Sacrist Fostermae had set this place for himself when it became clear that he could not sleep in any of the existing huts without accusations of favoritism. His healing skill was continually in demand, and any hut he slept in seemed to feel they had some rights over his treatment. The little lean-to was draftier even than the barracks, and the ground under it perpetually muddy, but Fostermae insisted it allowed him to remain even-handed in his service to every man and woman in camp. Prentice admired the man's ethical commitment. He was sure more than one woman would have offered her mattress to help keep him warm in the night, and any hut would have given the priestly man a place by their oven.

Feeling his way along the hut wall, Prentice found the sacrist's little shelter in the dark. Looking in, he saw Fostermae crouched over a flickering little fire, stirring a tiny iron pot.

"Cooking yourself dinner?" he asked.

Fostermae looked up.

"My last few beef bones boiled with a pot full of grass," he explained. "Not very appetizing but filling at least."

Prentice stood on the threshold and held his hand up to feel the falling rain in the darkness.

"At least we don't want for fresh water yet."

"A mercy from the Almighty."

Prentice nodded without enthusiasm. "May I join you?" he asked. Fostermae offered a spot by the fire. Prentice crouched on his haunches.

"I have a second bowl, if you wanted to share the meal," he offered. "It's not bread to break, but perhaps we can consecrate it to our Lord nonetheless."

"I've already eaten, thank you," Prentice lied. However hungry he felt, Fostermae had looked nearly a skeleton before the siege. Prentice couldn't take food out the man's mouth for any reason. Besides, boiled grass and beef bones hardly made an appetizing meal.

"You're worried," Fostermae said as he stirred his pot. "You think we'll die?"

"It looks that way. Of course, I've just come from the forge. Yentow Sent's made some fine blades. We'll be the best equipped corpses the Reach has ever seen."

"How do his men persevere with their work through the hunger?"

"I made sure they had the best of the food supplies," Prentice explained. "Their work is the most demanding, and they don't take rests to hide from the weather like the rest of us."

"Shivering in a half-built hut," mused the sacrist as he stirred. "Is that taking a rest, is it?"

"Compared to wrestling with fire and steel for hours every day, it is."

Fostermae conceded the point with a nod. He reached under the fire to bring up a burning twig, using its light to look into the pot.

"Done?" asked Prentice.

Fostermae shrugged. "I don't cook grass very often."

"Hopefully, you won't have to for very much longer."

"Do you?"

Prentice didn't understand the question. "Do I what?"

"Have hope?"

Now it was his turn to shrug, but as soon as he did, he followed it with a shake of his head. "No, I don't."

Fostermae said nothing for a moment. He scrabbled behind him, feeling for a clay bowl in the dark. Evening had fully come on, and the only light in the whole space came from the tiny cook fire. Bowl in hand, he scooped stringy, wet lengths of boiled grass out of the pot. Then he took to it with a wooden fork, sucking each mouthful in with loud slurps.

"Well, it tastes disgusting, and probably is no good for my health," he said cheerfully. "But at least it's hot."

Prentice smiled, appreciating the man's effort to maintain his humor. They were all in this bitter predicament together, but in his heart, Prentice knew it was his fault they were. His plan, his duty to the duchess, and his gamble against Baron Liam had played them all into impending starvation. And somewhere amongst them were the traitors who'd set the fires and the stampede.

Perhaps they were the wise ones, Prentice thought, though he would not bring himself say it.

"Starving rats," he said under his breath, not even realizing he was saying it. Watching Fostermae eat and even knowing what it was, he found his stomach churning in misery.

"Do you remember the first time we met?" asked Fostermae suddenly between baleful mouthfuls.

"Of course. It wasn't even half a year ago."

"You asked me about a vision you'd had," the sacrist went on. "A vision of an angel, powerful like a lion. And then you'd been scrambling about through sewers, like a filthy rat. So much so that Coulter's men called themselves ratters when they hunted you."

Prentice had no idea what the sacrist was getting at, and in the chill darkness, he had no way of reading the man's face for clues.

"I remember all this," he said. "It wasn't that long ago." But it felt like years, so harsh had the intervening days become.

"Have you had any other visions since then?" Fostermae pressed. "Recently?"

Prentice shook his head, but then stopped. "A dream," he said. "The night before Liam first arrived with his forces."

"And did you see lions or rats in that vision?"

"Both. And a monstrous serpent, as well as some other creatures, vile and frightening as would befit a nightmare."

By the thin firelight edging his features, Prentice could see the sacrist nodding his head.

"You think it's significant?"

"I don't know," Fostermae conceded. "I studied the scripture diligently to earn my place in the Church, but none of it revealed any gift as a seer or interpreter of visions. But as I think of it, none of your visions or dreams have led you astray, have they?"

Prentice thought about the question. Before he could answer, the sacrist went on.

"There was always a chance you were mad; I think there always will be such a chance. And the Church and its leaders have cause to believe our Lord would never visit himself with men so mean and criminal as convicts such as you were."

"The Lord came to preach freedom to prisoners," Prentice retorted, his old, heretical anger rearing up inside him. Perhaps he was too tired to keep it down.

"I've read that as well. The jubilee of salvation. Of recent years, the Church has said that such freedom comes at the moment of death, but it was not always taught so."

"I've heard as much," Prentice answered warily.

"But if you have had these visions, and now a dream, and you have found freedom in this life, then perhaps that teaching does have a gap in it. Perhaps it is incomplete."

"I was transported over the mountains for this sort of talk, Sacrist," Prentice said coldly, his eyes narrowing in the darkness. "Is that why you were here in the Reach as well, half-starved and serving a poor congregation in Dweltford before you came here to minister to a camp of convicts?"

Prentice wasn't interested in theological conversations, especially not ones that drew this close to heresy. Once perhaps, but not any longer. As far as he was concerned, accusations of heresy were the stick the Church hierarchy used to beat the Grand Kingdom into submission. He'd been beaten with it enough for one lifetime.

"I'm not sure you could say for sure why you were transported, Prentice," said Fostermae, "any more than I could say for sure why I was sent to shepherd my flock in Dweltford, and here. Surely the ecclesiarchs had their reason for convicting you, and perhaps they were just or merely political in their judgement. I couldn't say. But the Almighty may have reasons of his own, ones that even the highest in the Church might never suspect."

Prentice wanted to scoff reflexively, but Fostermae was at least willing to concede that the great men of the Church in the Grand Kingdom were compromised with the politics of the land. That was a rare thing in a sacrist, and Prentice found himself respecting this clergyman for his wisdom and honesty.

Even so, the notion that the sovereign God had a plan for Prentice, one that included the injustice of his conviction and transportation, was more than his pride would bear.

"It's a pretty story, Sacrist, but if the Almighty has a plan for my life, he hasn't seen fit to share it with me."

"Really?" Fostermae asked gently. "How many dreams or visions would you need to change your mind?"

A sharp retort came to Prentice's lips but died there unspoken. The sacrist was right. Since the summer and the arrival of the invaders from the west, he'd had a series of increasingly more powerful religious experiences. They'd pointed the way to his victory over the Horned Man, as well as being freed from the convict chain after so many years. But what did that mean?

"How can I tell if they are real or just some kind of madness?" he asked. "What I think are visions might be signs of a damaged mind."

"A reasonable objection. The word of God warns us that false prophets are known by their fruit, and we are commanded to test the spirits. This angel who appears to you, what is the fruit of his visitations?"

Prentice nodded. He didn't like thinking about such questions. Although he had been devout in his youth, he'd survived all his years on the chain ignoring God and hoping the Almighty would pay him the same courtesy.

"You are a wise man, Sacrist," he said quietly, mulling over the implications of Fostermae's words.

"As are you, Captain. Truthfully, I do not know what the Lord plans for your life. I have little enough sense of his intentions for my own. But if you want, I have faith enough to ask that He reveal His purpose to you, if you'd like."

"Could you ask him to be quick?" Prentice was trying to make a joke, but he suspected he just sounded bitter.

"I can," said Fostermae, not put off. "How soon would you like Him to speak to you?"

"Tonight would be convenient."

"Then I will pray the Lord to reveal His plan to you tonight. Perhaps the angel will come to you in another dream."

"Hmm," Prentice growled, not enthused by that prospect. He stood and brushed off his trousers. Then he bid Fostermae farewell and headed to his bed.

CHAPTER 34

Nearing dusk, as the grey sky was darkening to twilight, Amelia stole through the camp, her cloak pulled tight about her shoulders and her hood up. The fur lining helped to keep the chill wind from her bones, but she was much more concerned with trying to move unnoticed. Both Dalflitch and Turley had insisted that the prince had retainers watching her movements. She picked a path between the lights of the campfires to make it harder to notice her. Whatever the duchess knew about stealth, the prince's watchers knew as well, or even better, since as she looked about, she had no idea who of the camp's denizens might be observing her.

It seemed to Amelia that the camp had a lighter spirit than in recent days. Marching through the wet saltmarsh was at an end now that the causeway west had been found. Also, sometime in the afternoon, Daven Marcus had returned from surveying the other end of the road. A jetty had been found, apparently, but it was guarded by a fortified tower, a stone watch-point surrounded by a curtain wall, defending the end of the causeway. Rumor had it that the prince was delighted. He would get the chance to attack something with his precious cannons. He planned a glorious siege and had been sequestered for hours with his closest courtiers, plotting the assault.

Perhaps now he would finally select a knight commander. At any rate, the thought that the enemy was near had lifted hearts with the prospect of coming victory. She acknowledged to herself that it was also possible that finding Turley alive had also lifted her spirits so that everything around her seemed that little bit happier.

In her hand she carried an oil lantern, lit, but shuttered to conceal its light. In the camp proper, she had little need for light, even with the advancing darkness. The ground all about was already trodden down, and the broad basin was the firmest ground about, save for the top of the causeway. The lantern was for her ultimate goal: the little saltwater woodland. It loomed up in front of her, a mass of shadow in sharp relief against the lesser, overcast dark of the sky. The ground under her feet began to slip, and she felt, as well as heard, the squish of the water's edge. Earl Derryman had told her he found a path into the copse that hadn't required wading through the water directly. It took her some searching, but when she was reasonably certain she'd found it, she unsheathed the lantern's bullseye for a moment to reveal the thin, dry trail into the trees.

Studying the thickly twisted branches in the lamplight, heavy strands and folds of moss hanging from every tree, it seemed again to Amelia as if God had reached into a primeval forest somewhere else in the world and scooped up a handful of deepest wood and then absentmindedly dropped it in the midst of this saltmarsh, forgetting to clean it up.

"With all its darkness and mystery intact," she said to herself, suppressing a shiver. With one quick look about to see if she could see anyone watching, she forced her feet to follow the path into the wood.

She lifted the lantern high and ahead of herself, so that its light showed the way. It made little difference as the path almost immediately disappeared and the tangled branches resisted her. With a little effort, she pushed through the gnarled limbs that seemed to hold onto each other, ducking her head and stepping over tripping roots. Even after those first few paces, she felt a strange difference, like stepping into a closed room. Just beyond that first opposition of branches, the wood seemed immediately less tangled, as if the edge was made to be a barrier, more like a hedge than something grown wild. Yet, the barrier felt real, and even a mere handful of steps into the copse, the sound from the camp was muted, even more than just the quiet of evening.

The lantern light cast long and strange shadows that suddenly danced wildly. Amelia looked about in panic for a moment before she realized that a branch she hadn't noticed had caught on the lantern in her hand and set it swinging. She stopped to steady the motion and her nerves.

"I am not a little girl anymore," she reassured herself, stilling her fears.

This was no dank wood in which she might lose herself. Within earshot in any direction was the army of the Court of Rhales, under the command of the crown prince of the Grand Kingdom. She was in no danger. Even a wild beast, if there were such in this little forest, would be more likely hiding from the noises of the camp than waiting to pounce. At least that was what she told herself.

Nevertheless, looking back the short distance she had already come, she could make out the light of the campfires glowing just outside, but when she looked in any other direction, the trees blocked out all light. It was a strange experience. In spite of the lamp in her hand, the darkness did seem to press against her. She refused to be afraid, not of mere darkness. And Earl Derryman had been in here just this morning, and he'd made no mention of any danger. Feeling for branches with her arm and lifting her feet carefully in case of roots, Amelia made a determined path into the darkness. Then, she stopped short and sniffed the air.

Woodsmoke—a sudden strong gust that filled her nostrils.

In a way, it made perfect sense. The ground to the east was full of campfires. But how had it suddenly become so much stronger here, deep under the trees? A trick of the wind, perhaps.

She paused for a moment, thinking, then pressed on, ducking low under branches that hung from a massive bole, buttressed by roots thicker than her waist. In the darkness, it was hard to tell the details, but the tree was vast—some kind of wild fig—and its trunk was as large around as her tent, if not larger. Lifting her skirts, she clambered over the roots and pressed to the other side to see its whole size. Now the torchlight was all but blocked by the branches and roots so that the light cut into the darkness is strange slices. Yet, as she made her way around, Amelia found she could see more and more until she slipped over another buttress root, and she was in firelight.

At first, she wondered if somehow she'd come back to the camp out the other side of the wood without realizing it, but that wasn't the case. No, there was a fire here in the middle of the copse, and it was in front of a small hut that stooped low at the bottom of the huge fig tree, huddling between two of the vast roots. The hut was wicker-sided, with a peat roof and a small entry covered with a leather curtain, so low that Amelia would have had to crawl to enter. In front burned the little fire that gave the smoke she had smelled, and in front of that was a small pool of water that looked like it gathered from rain that ran down the tree and filled a hole. Even in the light, the ground was almost as dark as the night overhead, a soil that was nothing like the salty sand outside, built of generations of leaf litter so thick that the rich, moist odor of it filled the air, overpowering even the smell of the fire at times. The whole place felt like the deepest part of a forest that must surely cover half the world.

"It did used to be so much larger than this," said a voice, and as if she had simply appeared, Amelia realized that there was a woman sitting on one of the root stems of the tree. She was shrunken and small, wrapped in a patchwork dress sewn from the skins of small animals. Squirrels seemed the most likely to Amelia. The woman pulled a ragged woolen shawl about her shoulders that was greyer than her hair, which was shockingly white, even in the yellow glow of the fire. Of all her appearance, it was the old woman's hair that stood out. She was small and stooped-shouldered, her face heavily lined, and her eyes like pits, deeply receding into her face. But her hair, in spite of its color, was full and lustrous. She wore it in thick plaits that hung in front of and behind her. Other than simple brass rings that bound her plaits in place, the woman wore no jewelry or other adornment.

"That's what you were thinking, isn't it? That this place belongs in a much bigger forest?"

Amelia nodded and then stared, fascinated by the little figure.

"It did used to be, as a matter of fact," the woman continued to explain. "Especially just after the Bright Age. When the brilliant mechanisms broke down, nature sprang afresh in a wondrous rebirth. 'Course, after the mountain was thrown into the midst of the sea and God put his Rampart in the sky, any fresh growth seemed glorious. Then, the forest stretched for ranges in every direction, and this spot was its heart. That was before this little tree."

She patted the root she was sitting on and looked upward, though the light of the Rampart in the sky above them was shut out by the dense leaf canopy.

"At least it was a little tree when I planted it. Well, this one grew from a cutting of the previous one, which was a cutting itself, come to think of it."

"Who are you?" Amelia finally managed to say, confused by every aspect of the woman's presence. Even knowing she was looking for a prophetess, what she was seeing somehow made no sense. "Are you a ghost?"

The woman chuckled.

"Well, I'm old, if that's what you're asking, but a ghost? No, I'm not that, I'm sure. Of course, if a body goes a generation or two without speaking to another soul, then maybe they could die, become a ghost, and never know it, I suppose."

"What are you doing here?"

"I live here," the woman scoffed. She hopped down off the root and poked at the little fire with a long stick. It cracked and spat sparks. "Mind your dress there, dearie. Don't get it scorched."

Amelia pulled her skirts back without thinking.

"You know, when you and your lot arrived from the east," the woman went on, "I was so happy to have some different company, a nice change from hiding from those wicked Redlanders. Not that there's much difference in hiding from them to hiding from you, but it did have the feeling of a nice change..."

Her voice trailed off. Amelia was staring at her, bewildered. This was a prophetess? This little goblinoid grandmother? She was more like the legendary ancient fey from children's tales than a holy woman from Church catechism.

Amelia was roused from her thoughts when she realized the little woman was staring back at her with an equal intensity, and she felt like a student whose teacher was waiting for them to realize an important point. Then it dawned on her.

"Go on," the prophetess urged. "That's the question you most want to ask."

Amelia had in fact come into the wood to ask a miracle of healing for Turley, such as Earl Derryman had received. She could not bear the thought of him broken at the hand of Lord Robant's men. But now that she was faced with this strange little person, there was one question that dominated her thoughts. It was the one question that had ruled her life since the day her river barge had been ambushed by those vile, brightly painted men. Who were the invaders, and why had they come?

"You called them Redlanders? Is that who they are?"

"They don't call themselves that," the crone explained soberly. "They have a number of complicated titles for themselves as a nation and in their individual clans. But they come from a land of iron and blood, a red land. So that's the name their slaves call them, as well as any who come to know of them."

"And where is this red land?"

"You already know that one."

"Across the shallow sea the prince has discovered. In the west?"

The woman nodded. "Far to the west."

"Not from the south?"

The woman snorted derisively and poked at the fire again. Amelia nearly laughed. The prince was wrong; she'd always been convinced, but something about this woman's gentle speech made all doubt impossible.

"You really are a prophetess?" Amelia half asked, half stated. The woman shrugged, as if embarrassed by the question, but then she nodded.

"Or a seer, if you prefer," she said enigmatically. Amelia had no idea what the distinction was. All she cared about were answers, reliable answers—for herself, for the Reach. And healing for her steward, for Turley. As she struggled to order her questions, to find which ones she wanted most to ask, she remembered her vision—the strange image of the prince and his carrion court—and she knew that was what she had to understand.

"What is the serpent?" she half whispered, and the darkness around her seemed suddenly alive with threat. She whirled about, her lantern beam ranging over the branches of the trees. For the first time, she was afraid. Out there in the trees, the serpent was waiting, watching her.

"You're learning now," the woman said, and for the first time, Amelia realized she could not see her eyes for the dark shadows and the faintness of the firelight.

CHAPTER 35

Prentice half stumbled through the darkness, heading to the entrance of his hut. Night was fully upon the camp now, and as much as he was not looking forward to Fostermae's promised dreams, assuming God answered the sacrist's prayer, he needed to sleep. He was cold and hungry, just like the rest of his men and women. It wasn't supposed to be this way.

He slipped as an unseen stone shifted underfoot, and landed painfully on his knee. Swallowing a curse, he leaned against the barrack wall and rubbed at his lower leg. In that crouched position, he felt as much as saw two men creep around the corner, groping in the dark. Prentice could just make them out against the sky, but only just, and it seemed they couldn't see him at all.

"Is it him?" he heard a voice whisper.

"How should I know? It's so bloody dark he could be sitting right on my face, and we wouldn't see him!"

"Well, keep looking!"

"'Course I will."

For a moment, Prentice wondered who they were talking about, but it soon became obvious.

"We have to get him. He's the first. If he gets away, then it won't matter about the knight or the smith or Felix. It's him theys want!"

"I know that," hissed the man closest. Prentice all but held his breath, taking little more than sips of air. He was sure they were no more than an arm's length apart and that if he reached out from where he crouched, he could touch the man.

"He's not here," said the close voice. "Werrin said he'd seen him go off to the smithy, so he should be coming back from the other direction anyway."

"Alright then. Shame about Felix though."

"Fool's own fault. He wants to be sergeant, but he's already forgotten Ranold's first rule; know when the deal's gone bad and when to cut and run. Felix's full of dreams. He ain't cut out to run a mercenary company. Now shut up and keep a lookout. Once we catch this bastard, we can get him stowed and then get out of this damn cold!"

Well, it's definitely me they want, Prentice thought.

Though they're also planning for Felix, Sir Gant, and Yentow Sent. He waited until he was completely sure that the two men had gone back around the corner of the hut before he began to back away as carefully as he could. He'd already slipped once in the dark. Another misstep would bring them back for sure.

As he crept away, eyes scouring the dark for any slight shift in light, any hint they were there, he ran the details he had to work with through his mind. The men were part of Ranold's mercenary company, which meant they were corporals. It made sense that they would plot a mutiny; they had the best hope of going free once they handed him over to Baron Liam. Prentice was sure the baron would put every man jack of them on the chain, but he could understand if they rated themselves a better chance.

He also knew that they didn't count Sir Gant, Yentow Sent, or Corporal Felix amongst their number. Since they were acting by stealth, it was likely their conspiracy didn't stretch to many of the ex-convicts at all. If they had larger numbers, they could do the deed in a rush.

Reaching behind him, his hand touched the opposite corner of the hut wall, and he risked a quick turn in place to see if there was anyone hiding there, ready to run if there were. When he found no second ambush, he paused a moment to draw a deeper breath and plan his next move.

If they intended to take him first, if that was their signal, then he might have some options. If he could capture them before they caught him, make them tell him who the conspirators were, that would be his best possibility. But he had no idea who he could trust for sure, other than the conspirators' intended targets, and to get to them, he'd have to risk being seen and taken. He looked about him in the night. Every shadow was filled with risk, and every refuge harbored potential serpents.

Then he had a thought, and his lips twisted into a sharp grin. There was one refuge they wouldn't have thought of, he was sure of it. He pushed away from the hut wall and stalked as swiftly as he knew how to the women's hut. For a long moment he waited outside, listening for any noise coming from the other side of the heavy curtain that served as the barrack's door. There was quiet conversation between female voices, but nothing that sounded like conspiracy or a waiting ambush. Of course, they might be very cunning. There was nothing he could do but take the risk. He pushed the flap aside and went in, dagger in hand but hidden behind his back.

Inside, the female population of the camp lay in clusters along each wall, close together for extra warmth. There was a handful of guttering tallow candles giving off a dim, dirty light, but after the pitch black of outside, it seemed almost bright to Prentice's eyes. There was no sign of an ambush waiting. The nearest to the entrance were several paces away, cringing from the cold coming in through the opening. At first, they looked at him warily, but soon enough one offered to fetch Righteous. She was the one they sent to whenever they wanted to speak with him.

Righteous came up the middle of the barrack, head down under the low roof. "You want something, Captain?"

Prentice quickly outlined what he thought was going on and how he planned to deal with it. Righteous nodded with a smile, then held up a finger.

"Just one moment," she said. "I got an idea'll go well with your plan. Give us a moment." She retreated back into the dim hut and returned with two women with shawls wrapped around their shoulders. They were thin, but so was everyone else, starving as the entire camp was, but they had bright eyes and an energy that was lacking in most of the rest of the men and women.

"This is Daisy and Flo," Righteous said, introducing them. "They're still doing swift trade with the men in the camp, especially them corporals. They can help us."

The two women were pretty, and they smiled at him sweetly, but Prentice only returned a scowl. He leaned in close to Righteous.

"You know I don't want whoring in the camp," he said in a terse whisper, though he realized that Daisy and Flo could probably still hear him. Righteous was unfazed by his anger.

"I know," she said unrepentantly. "And once there's some actual food to go around, I'm sure they'll think about giving the game away. For now, though, a girl's got to eat, and these two are keeping more than themselves alive, believe it or not."

Prentice wasn't sure what offended him more—the fact that his recruits were so stupid that they would trade sparse food for a roll in the straw, or that these women could do such a brisk trade that they could feed more than themselves by it. As he thought about it, though, he realized he wasn't actually offended at all. Righteous was right. What else could one expect of a starving woman? He wasn't offended; he was ashamed. It was his fault they were driven to this.

"Alright," he said to Righteous and then turned to the two women. "You happy being a distraction?"

Before they could answer, a third woman emerged from shadows. Prentice knew her, but it took him a moment to recall her name. Tressy—the brutalized woman Righteous had avenged. She'd taken to combing her hair over the scar on the side of her head, and she wore a rag tied around her face, covering one eye. She was still as bone thin as she'd been, and she came forward with a poniard, a thin-bladed thrusting dagger, in hand.

"You got a use for me?" she asked, her voice low and angry.

"Tressy?" Prentice asked. He recognized her, but this was not the same cowering mess of a girl he'd met only weeks ago.

"I been showing her how to use a spiker," said Righteous. "She's quick and can make a killing thrust, at least good enough for this night's work."

Prentice chewed the inside of his cheek thoughtfully. Righteous's idea to bring some doxies as a distraction was a good one, but he'd planned to do the night's iron work himself, with Righteous's help. He didn't like the idea of dragging women into a melee. That being said, if Righteous thought Tressy was up to the task, he was willing to accept her recommendation. He nodded to Tressy, and the scarred woman smiled at him.

"What happened to your eye?" he asked her as the little group left the women's hut.

"Infection took it," she said bluntly. "Three nights sweating and shivering after me ear refused to heal and rotted right off." With the last of the light, she pulled her hair back to show the pink scars all along the side of her head where her ear should have been. "Nearly died. Thought for sure I was going to, but Fostermae did his miracle work."

"He's a healer and then some," either Flo or Daisy agreed.

In the dark, Prentice couldn't see which one had spoken. He was surprised when he felt an instinct to offer a prayer of thanks to God for the sacrist's presence in the camp.

The little group made their way back to Prentice's barracks hut. The women seemed surer-footed than he felt, and he wondered how often they came by in the night to trade their favors for food. As they neared the corner, Daisy started giggling and Flo joined her. It took Prentice a moment to realize that they were doing it deliberately, and he smiled at their natural cunning. He held back at the corner with the other two and listened in the darkness. It took only a moment for the two women to trip over one of the waiting ambushers.

"What are you doing out here?" one asked.

"And do you need any company?" the other followed up.

A gruff voice cursed them and told them to be gone. Prentice could hear the pout in their voices as they plied their trade on his behalf.

"Don't be like that."

"We're busy, woman. Get you gone!"

"We can be quick," insisted Flo. Prentice was surprised at how quickly he'd learned to pick their voices apart in the dark. "We don't need to cuddle or anything."

"Get them out of here," insisted another male voice.

Prentice knew there were at least two, but that voice was another. Were there three? Flo and Daisy knew their business.

"How many of you are there? What, four? Well, that's not so bad. We don't mind taking turns, do we, Flo?"

Prentice wanted to curse. Four. That was more than he wanted to deal with. It made a quiet move so much less likely. He frowned in the dark and then shrugged to himself. There was no other choice at this stage.

"Let's go," he whispered to Righteous, who passed the word to Tressy. Prentice led the way, barreling out of the night at the rough point he judged he'd find the first ambusher. His aim was true, and he felt the body go down under his weight. He managed to get his hand around the back of the man's neck while they were falling, and with that guide, his blade found the man's throat, stabbing straight up under the chin and into his skull. The man stopped struggling under him. Prentice wanted to take at least one prisoner, but to make that happen, he needed to know the other enemies were taken care of. This was no time to go softly, even wanting to be stealthy.

There were other sounds of a scuffle in the darkness, interspersed with whispered curses from men who'd expected to ambush one man having the tables turned. One of the ambushers must have had a lit candle hidden under a pot or something similar, ready to see by once they had their victim in hand, because he did the most foolish thing he could have at that point—he uncovered the flame. In the sudden candlelight, he caught sight of Prentice on top of his man with Righteous nearby, her dagger flashing at her target's throat. Tressy was the most terrifying, though, for she had fallen short of her man, but instead of trying to regain her feet, she'd just slashed straight at his legs and groin, hacking the flesh with wild abandon. The man collapsed with a groan of pain, the cudgel he was holding falling from his hand to clatter on the stones.

The man with the light looked about himself in horror, the savage scene unmanning him. He turned to run, but Tressy, being closest, threw herself after him. With one hand she caught his retreating ankle while her dagger hand swung at his calf, slashing the meat there. It was a suicidal move. If the man had held his nerve for even a moment, he'd have been able to fall on her and end her. As it was, he tried to clamber away, and though his scrabbling feet smacked Tressy multiple times in the face, she held him fast and thrust with her blade again, this time catching his foot. He fell backward and she climbed his falling form like a wild animal, steel stabbing all the way up.

"Alive!" Prentice hissed. "We need one alive!"

If she heard, Tressy paid no mind, and soon her fury had torn the fourth man to pieces. She sat back in the fallen candlelight, sprayed with gore and ferociously happy.

"That's my girl," said Righteous proudly.

"I wanted one alive to question," Prentice said through gritted teeth.

"What's this one then, my maiden aunt's mangy cat?"

She slapped the man under her against the side of his head, while keeping her blade to his throat. The man groaned and Prentice realized he was still alive.

"Good girl," he said reflexively. Righteous all but beamed at him, her eyes glittering in the guttering light.

"Tressy's not good enough yet to take one alive," she said, her smile sliding back to its usual wry twist. "'Sides, she's still got a lot of anger to get out. And we've all seen you fight; there's scythes that are more merciful to wheat! So, I figured I better be the one to take a prisoner."

Prentice nodded, then crouched down to whisper to the battered man lying dazed with Righteous sitting on his chest, her blade ready to slash his windpipe open.

"Now, you're going to tell me the whole plan—how many you've got, who's your leader, what you were going to do once you got us all. Every little bit of it. And the faster you tell me, the more fingers you get to keep."

Even in the bare light, the man's terror was obvious.

Good, thought Prentice. *Frightened men didn't lie very well.*

CHAPTER 36

"I saw them when they came this way the first time, these men of the serpent, even before they knew there was a red land for them to settle," the prophetess explained to Amelia. The darkness seemed to flow around the little flame in front of the simple hut, as if blown by the chill wind. Amelia pulled her cloak tight about her and wondered how the prophetess was not shivering with the cold.

"They came fleeing from the east. I didn't need God to show that to me. I watched them—watched while they built their ships, hacking swathes of the forest away for the wood. I heard them squabbling with their fey allies and saw the blood oaths between them break. Then they were gone for a long time, sailing away over the salt water in boats bigger than mansions. That was all I saw or heard for a long time, though the damage they did to the forest never healed, only spread."

"There were fey in this wood?"

"No, not then. The fey of this forest had gone away a long time back, not too long after the Bright Age, not long after I first came here with my husband. They'd turned back to the woods to hide from the judgement, like builders of Babel trying to flee the confusion. It didn't work. No, these were fey from your country, back from before your people had driven them out of all the forests in the east."

Amelia could hardly believe the woman's words. Everyone knew that there were no fey in the Grand Kingdom anymore. They'd been driven out by ancient crusades. The Church had pacified the lands. The forest fey of that era had been bloodthirsty demoniacs, making pacts with devils for sorcerous power, dragging away peasants and children to sacrifice to false gods. How old could this woman be if she'd seen fey from that time? And she said that she was older even than that?

The prophetess went on.

"When the great houses that would become Redlanders refused to settle here in this forest, because back then it was still a whole forest, and so the fey broke off. I think they would have stayed, but those two houses didn't take well to neighbors, if you take my meaning. The fey fled back west and north, into those mountains."

Amelia's head swam as she struggled to keep up with the woman's story. The crusades against the fey in the Grand Kingdom lands were so long ago that they were virtually legends. But even amongst the ancient histories and legends, there was no talk of a people like the Redlanders, with their animalistic powers and painted skin.

"Redlanders are not fey?" she asked to make sure she understood.

The old woman shook her head.

"Not even a little bit, though they coveted their power. But they were mortals like all the men and women of the nations."

"Why did they go west?"

"I can tell you that they were fleeing a treacherous enemy and seeking a refuge after being banished, but more than that is not mine to say."

"Was the Grand Kingdom the enemy they were fleeing?"

"Good guess. You're clever for such a young thing. I'm glad this last meeting was like this." The woman patted Amelia on the arm, and it was such a gentle gesture that it surprised her. There was so much affection in it. Without that surprise,

Amelia would have missed another of the important details the old woman seemed to like to drop in passing. She was so busy trying to absorb the main import of the prophetess's story, that the side points seemed to want to slip past her attention, but she did her best not to let them.

"Last meeting?" she asked, and as she looked up, she realized the crone had moved much closer. Clutched in her withered fingers she had a leather bag, old and cracked. She shook it and something rattled inside. For a moment Amelia was seized with the thought that the rattle might be finger bones or something similar, the kind of thing a witch in a fey tale might gather in a bag.

Greedy children reach into the bag expecting candy, and the witch snatches away their fingers and their souls.

The old woman smiled.

"It's not bones, dearie, don't fear," she said, reading Amelia's thoughts yet again. "And truth to tell, this is not my very last meeting. It's just the last pleasant one afforded to me. Not long now."

She shook the bag again. Whatever rattled inside, there weren't many of the things. The container seemed almost empty.

"When I was a young woman, much, much younger, I was married to a kindly and very upright man, not much different to your husband."

Amelia drew in a shocked breath. "Is there anything you don't know?"

"Oh, certainly yes." Her long-fingered hand patted Amelia comfortingly on the arm again. "I'm a prophetess. I know much and have seen much, but I'm not the one who gives the visions. He's the one that knows everything."

The woman pointed upward, and Amelia realized she meant God in heaven.

"But I have a story to tell, so don't interrupt too much, please. There are things you must hear. Where was I? Oh yes, married to an upright man. A holy man, truth be told, though he was a fine husband to me, never distant or passionless, even when he was fasting. One day, the Creator of all things sent a messenger to us, a beautiful figure who came and took tea with us in our house. I felt so blessed to receive such a glorious visitor, but he came with a message. He took us out of the house, and we walked down by the river.

"I didn't notice it that day, but we walked an awfully long way, far from our home. And then he stopped us by the river and told us to collect stones from the riverbed. We did, and we made a little pile in front of him on the ground. He crouched down and bade us do the same. Then he said that the Creator had called us to a long and difficult purpose, but that in that purpose we would be further blessed and would bless many others. We were a little afraid, but we both accepted the messenger's word, and my husband asked him to say on.

"My husband was chosen to be a prophet, and I to be a prophetess after him. Many would come from lands near and distant to seek his wisdom and then mine. Mostly, we would simply share the wisdom that time and prayer provide, but for a select number, there were specific words to speak. Then, the visitor pulled out this bag and took up the first stone we had found. With it, he pronounced a blessing of long life and many generations of descendants. He told us that when a person came to us and drew out that stone, we must tell them that blessing. Then he picked up each stone in turn and taught us a prophecy for each one. When he had spoken it, he placed the stone into the bag. Once he was finished, the bag was full of stones. He gave it to my husband."

"You said that some people only received prayer and wisdom, so how did you know who to offer the stones to?" Amelia asked. "If it's not too rude to ask."

"You know, we asked that very question ourselves. The messenger just smiled and said that the Creator would give us the knowledge. Then he breathed on us. He told us to build a home near the river and said we would never be hungry or thirsty as long as we lived there. So, we did."

"When did you move here?"

"We never did."

"But there is no river."

Daven Marcus's quest to find a river had ended in a saltmarsh and a shallow sea. Was this woman, this claimed prophetess who knew people's thoughts, was she saying that there really was a river? Or that there had been once, long ago?

"A long, long time ago," the prophetess crone said. "No forest then, some trees but no forest. It was wild for sure, even then, and a long way from any other folk, but I was a happy woman. I had the man I loved and a beautiful world to dwell in, even if it was wild. It was a good life. Time passed, the mountain fell into the sea, and the forest grew up. Pilgrims came, seeking prophecy or wisdom. One at a time, hands reached into the bag, drew forth stones and received the words of God.

"Then my husband died."

She paused for a moment, and Amelia saw the wistfulness in her eyes. She wiped at her eyes with her shawl, even though there were no tears to see.

"He lived a good long time, and we were happy all our years. I'm thankful to have had him. Then I became the prophetess, dispensing the words we had both heard from the messenger by the river. Of course, the river was a stream by that time as the wood took so much more of the water. I became the widow of the wood. That's what they called me, though not in your tongue, of course. Their language was more lyrical. They favored poetry, even over music."

The crone trailed off, and Amelia wondered if she was recalling the poetic language she was speaking of. At last, the old woman shook her head to clear her mind.

"Did you know that speech and peoples are like forests and rivers? They rise and fall, come and go, so slowly that if you live your whole life in one place, you might never know it had once been different and would one day be utterly changed. Unless you lived long enough, of course. And I have almost lived long enough."

She held up the bag and shook it once more.

"Time to make your choice, dearie."

Amelia thought of Turley and his injuries, the reason she had thought to dare the little wood in the first place. "Can I choose for another? Or is it only for me?"

"You're worried about the big fella?" the little woman asked, and this time Amelia wasn't surprised by her mystical insight. She had no doubt now the woman was a prophetess.

"He's a loyal man," Amelia said. "His name is Turley and he's the most loyal man I have. At least close by."

The woman nodded and they shared a look. Amelia's most loyal man was Prentice, and as they stared into each other's eyes, she realized she could ask about him, find out if he was even still alive, and how he went training her a militia. But first, she had to seek healing for Turley. His need was the more urgent.

"Good girl," the prophetess said with a nod, approving Amelia's unspoken choice of priorities. "I'll ask the good Lord to heal him for you. He'll need a day or two more rest, but be assured, he'll heal up fine. When he does, tell him to stop provoking his betters. It's a bad habit."

Amelia nodded and smiled. That was a prophetic message Turley could do with hearing.

"Come now, Duchess, hand in the bag, and let's be hearing the word of the Creator for thee."

This last instruction was spoken with such firm authority that it was almost as if the woman's voice was totally different. Amelia wondered if she could have resisted the command, even if she wanted to. But it didn't really matter because she knew she had to hear the word the widow would speak, no matter what it was. Since becoming the wife of Duke Marne, her life had been nothing like she had expected. At every turn, she was being stretched and pressed and forced to become greater than she had ever imagined herself to be, while men of power and women of ambition hounded her every step. Some sense of guidance in navigating her future, any sense, would be welcome.

She reached her hand into the bag. Inside there were only two stones. She gathered first one and then the other into her fingers, as if by touch she could discern the message each one would convey. But there was nothing to pick between them. They just felt like rocks to her. At last, she grasped one firmly and drew it out. Holding it up to the firelight, she was disappointed to see it was a simple little chip of basalt, barely the length of one of her knuckles. Holding the dark, dull little lump out on the palm of her hand, she showed it to the widow.

The old woman smiled.

"I figured that would be your one," she said. "Time was when it was almost as exciting for me as it was for the pilgrim pulling the stone. Now that they're all gone but a few, it's not hard to guess who hears what. The disappointment of knowing the future, I suppose, even if you only know it in parts.

"Tell me, Duchess of the Reach, are you ready to hear the Ancient Word spoken to you? To know what was written before when the world was still young?"

Amelia nodded.

"Good."

The little woman gathered herself up and her face took on a sober expression, ready to make her pronouncement. Then, she suddenly ducked her head and looked like a kindly old grandmother. She put her hand back on Amelia's arm.

"Don't be worried if you don't understand it at first. Most folk don't. Some never understand it in their lifetime, and that's alright. Maybe they had to hear the prophecy in order to pass it down to the folks who would understand it. Just do your best."

Amelia opened her mouth to ask for a better explanation, but the widow had resumed her oratorical stance. She began to pronounce.

"Amelia of Dweltford, widow of Marne, first Duke of the Western Reach." Even after all the little signs of the widow's powers, Amelia was still surprised to hear the woman speak her name as if they had known each other for years.

"Planted in the east, your branches spread in the west.
Though you sit a throne, and will sit a greater one yet,
   you will never wear a crown.
Your line will rule after you, but the child of your
   love can never be among them;
You will be called the mother of the pride, and lions will
guard you, ahead and behind, all throughout your days.
Where you walk there is no road before you, but behind
   you come settled generations.
Only have courage, and do not fear,
   it is all given into your hand,
until the west and south and east bow their knee to you."

The widow's shoulders slumped, and she sighed happily. "That was a good one."

Amelia blinked.

What was that? What was she to make of it? While she was puzzling, the little crone began to totter toward her hut.

"Wait!" Amelia cried. "I don't understand."

"I warned you about that. Don't worry about it."

"But I want to understand. Can you explain it to me?"

"To some are given the gift of prophecy, to others the gift of interpretation. My husband, he had the gift of interpretation. Such a wise man. Myself, not as much. Now I need a rest."

"You can't just leave it at that."

"Yes, I can, dearie."

"Can I come back again?"

"Not to speak to me."

"Then I order you to stay here and answer my questions."

The little woman chuckled, a low sound that seemed to make her whole frail body shake.

"There's great authority in your command, girl, and in years to come there'll be a good deal more. But you'll never have the power to command this from me."

The woman was at the curtain in her doorway, and Amelia felt desperate.

"Please, I need to know what to do. I need advice."

"You have advisors. Listen to the ones you know you can trust and stop pestering a tired old woman with too few good nights' sleep ahead of her."

Amelia was going to keep pleading, even as the woman went inside, but suddenly she realized she wasn't there. Even the little hut was gone. Looking about her, Amelia realized she was standing on the eastern edge of the copse, exactly as if she had been turned around in the dark. The lantern in her hand was flickering, its oil running out. Looking out from under the branches, she could see the overcast winter sky lightening on the horizon. It was nearing dawn. She'd spent the whole night in the wood.

She stepped out, following the same little dry path through the salty water. Around her, the camp was waking up. She slipped out and was making her way back to her tent when a small force of men on horseback, their jingling armor marking them out as knights, rode into the camp from the west. Amelia stepped back into the shadows of a tent and watched them approach. When the leader came into view, she had to put her hand to her mouth to keep from gasping out loud. When they had ridden past, she rushed back to her tent, trying to think how to prepare for the day ahead.

CHAPTER 37

"I need men who count themselves loyal," Prentice told the men in his hut as they looked at him in the little light they had to spare. "There are traitors amongst us who think to sell you and me out to the baron. They'll get their freedom and you'll be back on the chain." There was a resentful growl that flowed from dozens of throats at that suggestion. Prentice smiled at that.

"Of course," he went on, "that won't affect me because, one way or another, I'll be long dead. Either the baron will have me torn apart by his horses, or flayed, or God knows what he'll dream up, but that'll only be if they can take me alive. I'll fight to my last breath before I let someone put me on a chain again."

At one level, Prentice knew he wasn't being truthful with them as he gave this speech. Not about fighting to his last breath, he meant that. No, he wasn't being honest about the conspirators' plan. The traitors were thinking to negotiate for everyone's freedom. It was just that Prentice knew Liam. There was no way he would allow even one of the convicts to go free, though he might be persuaded for the mercenaries, and according to their prisoner, at least half the conspiracy was made up of mercenary corporals.

It had taken their prisoner little time to reveal everything he knew of the conspiracy against Prentice. There were eleven of them still left, poised around the camp, waiting for word that their first ambush had been successful and Prentice was caught. The plan was to capture him, then Sir Gant, then Felix, and finally to go in force to the smithy and seize Yentow Sent and the best weapons and armor they could get their hands on. Then, at dawn, they'd open the gates and lead the prisoners out to hand them over to Baron Liam.

They'd set four men each for Prentice, Gant and Felix, to make sure of their task, and left three men watching at the smithy since that was where they had originally planned to take Prentice, but he'd accidentally slipped them there, heading to speak with Sacrist Fostermae rather than going straight back to his hut to sleep. Turning the traitor's ambush back on themselves had worked well enough this first time, but Prentice doubted they could do it again. So, he was going to have to trust himself to these men, ex-convicts, who might well just seize him for themselves and try their own version of the conspiracy. It would be an ironic turnabout for the men lying in ambush in the cold night, but Prentice would be no less in the hands of Baron Liam.

"How long until dawn, do you think?" he asked Righteous, who was standing beside him.

"A few hours yet," she confirmed.

"Right, let's get this done."

He turned to the men gathered about, waiting to hear his orders.

"I need about fifty volunteers. There'll be rewards for this night's work, but I only need fifty."

Not all of them seemed willing, but Prentice was surprised by the number that clasped their fists and gave the salute he'd taught them. He stood by the doorway and counted the first fifty, telling the rest to remain behind. He'd gone out into the dark a short way before the sound from behind told him that the rest had ignored his orders. He wanted to order them back, but he knew there was no point. His plan needed speed, since fifty men were no use for stealth anyway. As the fifty made their way to the smithy first, he ordered rushlights to be lit, and soon he was leading a torch-lit procession over the ruined ground of Fallenhill.

Prentice sent Righteous and Tressy ahead, still stained with blood from their fight, to catch the three ambushers who were lurking by the keep wall near the smithy. With the sudden large crowd in the night, the three men had decided to keep their heads down and wait. When the two women found them, they called for help, and ten men with poles came over to take the three prisoner. It took next to no time at all to have them tied up, wrists behind their back and seated on the ground, but even in that short moment, Yentow Sent and several of his journeymen were awakened and emerged from their workshop.

"What is this madness?" Sent demanded.

Prentice outlined what he knew.

"Good that you came to protect the workshop first," said the Masnian. Prentice didn't know if he meant from a practical standpoint, or if Sent simply valued himself and his men as the most important in Fallenhill.

"How many blades have you got ready?" he asked Sent.

The smith frowned. "Just over two dozen," he said. "Surely you do not mean to arm this rabble in the night."

"I do, but only for tonight."

Yentow Sent sighed and then said something to his men in the lyrical Masnian tongue.

"And bring me that longsword you made for me," Prentice added.

Sent froze momentarily, like a thief caught in the act, then cocked an eyebrow.

"You did not want me to make you such a blade," he said, sniffing dismissively.

"But you made one anyway, didn't you? In case I changed my mind."

Sent folded his arms and his eyes narrowed for a moment. Then he called again over his shoulder. Soon enough, the lesser weaponsmiths were returning with swords—practical, tool-like weapons, with single-edged blades and simple basket-hilts to protect the wielder's hand. There were buckler shields as well, and halberds, the spiky axe blades already fitted to poles, making weapons nearly seven foot in length. As these live, steel-bladed weapons were being handed out, another was brought, wrapped in oilcloth. It was handed to Yentow Sent, who pulled back the cloth to reveal a cruciform longsword with an engraved brass cross guard. The blade was pattern-welded, with a double fuller and a perfect taper. As Sent offered the hilt to Prentice, he took it and hefted it in his hand.

"It's a masterwork," he said, feeling the weight. The Masnian nodded to accept the compliment, then his usual disdain reasserted itself.

"Of course, it is," he said huffily.

With his new blade in hand and a core of properly armed men behind, Prentice led the way toward Felix's barracks. Ideally, he would have moved to rescue Sir Gant first, but Felix was closer, and he had better faith that Gant would be able to protect himself, even against four men if they tried to take him when they realized things were going against them. The three they'd already taken prisoner were gagged and left behind for the smiths to watch over.

By the time he and his torch-lit army reached the next barracks hut, the whole camp had begun to stir. The four ambushers waiting for Felix simply sat where they were, perhaps thinking to front it out and pretend they were just men taking air in the night, away from the close atmosphere inside the hut. All four of them were captured that way, though one tried to make a run for it and shouted a warning to his fellows as he did so. Men emerged from the hut and were quickly told about Prentice's version of the conspiracy.

When he was sure that Felix was safe, Prentice led his force to the last hut. By this time, the conspirators had realized their plan had failed, and they had rushed in, taking Sir Gant hostage on his mattress before the knight was fully awake. Prentice arrived to hear them telling the men around them they had a way out of the siege, and that they could still prevail if they just held their nerve and used Gant as a bargaining chip.

"They put a lot of stock in your friendship with Sir Gant," Felix observed, having caught up to Prentice now and helping to keep order. He had one of Yentow Sent's swords in one hand and a buckler on the other. "Smith does good work," he said admiringly when he took the blade in hand. Then, the light shifted and he got a better look at Prentice's blade. "*Good* bloody work."

At the door of the hut, Prentice took stock. There was a mass of convicts between the door and the conspirators at the back. Further behind them was a figure in the dim light that Prentice took as Sir Gant.

Prentice loudly sent for lamp oil. There was little such fuel left in the camp, and it was all kept in the smithy.

"We're going to fire this hut," he shouted in the door. "Any man still in there when the oil arrives will die as a traitor. Come out now or die in the fire. Your choice."

"Bollocks," an angry voice shot back. "We've got his best mate in here! He'll never light us up with him prisoner."

"Knights swear to give their lives for the honor of their lords," Prentice called into the dimness. "Sir Gant would rather die than be a hostage for dogs like you."

"Here, here!" shouted Gant from the back of the hut, but then his voice was cut off with a gurgle that sounded like he'd been struck in the belly.

"They're bluffing!" declared the same angry voice.

Prentice wasn't really bluffing, but he did hope the men would give up before he had to put fire to the roof. He would do what he said, but if it came to that, he would rush the hut by himself, if necessary, to try rescuing Sir Gant. Knight's honor or not, he couldn't leave the man to die in a fire.

Men returned from the smithy, pottery jugs in hand.

"Last chance," Prentice called, and two men suddenly burst out into the night.

"Don't burn us!" one of them shouted.

Prentice tackled the first one out and threw him at some of his nearby men. They grabbed that one and the other man as well before he could get past.

"Are they part of this?" he asked Righteous, who'd been at his shoulder through the whole night's enterprise except for when she and Tressy had caught the three by the smithy.

"They ain't in on it," she said, looking at their faces in the torchlight.

Prentice turned to Felix.

"Form the men into a cordon around the entrance," he ordered. "As they rush out, check each man. Make sure none of the traitors get away."

Soon enough, the men with swords were on either side of the door. Every man leaving the hut would run a gauntlet with torches in their faces.

"Put the oil down that end," Prentice ordered. In the dead of winter, there was a good chance the peat would be too damp to catch alight, but Prentice hoped the oil would give it the needed push.

"They're pouring the oil," a different, panicked voice shouted inside the hut. "I can hear it running down."

The conspirators were defiant.

"The minute I smell peat smoke, we'll cut the knight's throat! We'll do it."

"Either Sir Gant emerges unharmed, or you go to the judgement day with burn scars. Your choice."

Prentice stepped away to look to the men standing near where the oil had been thrown on the roof.

"Torch it!" he ordered.

Three men standing by with rushlights hesitated a moment, perhaps wondering if it was a bluff on Prentice's part or if he was genuine. Then, one after the other they threw their brands on the roof and the oil quickly caught.

"They actually done it!" someone inside shouted, and there began a rush toward the one doorway.

Prentice stood aside and let the gauntlet receive the rush of bodies. Men were roughly handled but quickly passed down the line until they were identified or at least confirmed as not part of the traitor's cabal. There was a pause, and Prentice was sure the last men still inside were either traitors or had thrown their lot in. Almost certainly they were trying to plan something quickly, such as escaping in a rush. He turned to his closest men who only had their blunt-ended drill staves as weapons.

"Bring them down on everyone who comes out," he told them. "I'll get Sir Gant out of your way, don't fear."

There was a shuffling noise in the back of the hut, but what small light there was to see by was becoming obscured by thick, black smoke from the burning peat. If they stayed in there too much longer, the smoke would kill them before the flames ever could.

There was another sound of movement and as he expected, the last conspirators rushed out, pushing Gant ahead of themselves as a human shield. No sooner had the knight's greying head emerged from the doorway than Prentice leapt forward, tackling him and driving him sideways, out of the path. Whatever the man who'd had Gant in his grasp thought, it didn't matter. There was no way of stopping the rush as the last clutch of conspirators tumbled forward into a hail of staff blows that rained down on them like drumbeats. In moments, any weapons they had were knocked from their grasps, and they clutched at their heads, begging for mercy. The rebellion was over.

Prentice rolled over on the ground, glad for a moment just to let some of the tension ebb away. Next to him Sir Gant hawked and spat, trying to get the taste of the smoke out of his mouth. Prentice ducked his head when they made eye contact.

"Sorry about that," he said.

Sir Gant only shrugged.

"What else were you going to do?" he said emotionlessly. "Pay my ransom and grant them parole to quit the field? I think not!"

Gant's wry assessment of his short time as a hostage made Prentice smile, but it also raised another question.

What was he going to do with these men?

CHAPTER 38

"Must they be killed?"

Righteous rolled her eyes in disgust at Fostermae's question, and Prentice couldn't blame her. The entire camp was gathered in a crowd, shivering in the growing predawn light. In the open ground in the middle, the twelve surviving conspirators were lined up on their knees, arms tied to poles behind their backs. They were a mixed bunch but exactly the sort of men Prentice would expect to try this kind of plan. The ex-convicts among them had brawler's marks and other judicial scars that showed they'd been convicted and transported for crimes of violence. More than half the cabal, though, were mercenaries. As Prentice looked them over, Corporal Felix leaned in close to whisper.

"That's Donnen," he said, indicating a bull-shouldered man with dark eyes and close-cropped hair. "He'll have been the ringleader."

"You're sure?"

"He never wanted this contract from the start, and he doesn't favor me as Ranold's successor."

"Favors himself, does he?"

Felix shrugged and Prentice nodded.

He turned back to his other advisors standing by where Fostermae and Righteous were in a heated, if whispered, conversation. The entire camp was waiting to see what they would decide. This nattering looked like weakness, and Prentice knew it.

"You want me to show mercy, Sacrist?" he asked, cutting across the hushed debate.

"What does God want?" Fostermae replied enigmatically.

"You tell me!" Prentice hissed, struggling to keep his voice down and his temper under control. "You ask God for a sign for me, and this is what I get?"

"You spared that man on the wall," Fostermae argued quietly. "Can you not show mercy again?"

"No."

"Because once is your limit?"

Prentice surged forward and almost slapped the sacrist, holding his hand back only by a furious exertion of will. He changed his open hand to a pointing finger, using it to emphasize the elements of his argument.

"Because we're all in here starving to death. The two who tried to push me off the wall were the first, and now there's this dozen. For a while yet, the rest of this mob might see them as traitors, but as the hunger spreads, that will change. A week from now, maybe two, and there'll be ten times this number making a try like this. And any of these I leave alive will be leading the charge."

Fostermae shrank from Prentice's anger but didn't look away. Prentice gave him credit for that. He forced the anger inside himself back down, lowering his hand as he did so. Finally, he looked away, his eyes running across the twelve prisoners. Some hung their heads while others looked away, refusing his gaze. One or two met his look, their eyes reflecting the fury he was sure was in his own face. From them, he looked over the hungry, shivering mass of men and women, standing around and waiting for justice, whatever that was supposed to look like. Prentice looked down at his own feet and shook his head wearily. He was tired, cold, and hungry, running on nerve alone. He knew that if this day went on much longer, he'd be nearing collapse.

"Rats I understand," he muttered, not sure if he was merely talking to himself, or perhaps praying. Of late it seemed he only prayed if he was miserable or angry. Or tired. "And lions I understand."

That much was true in his mind. Convicts were like rats—dirty, savage and continually desperate, living in the dark corners of the world. He understood that life; he'd lived it. And were knights and nobles lions? He shook his head, remembering his dream. No, they were dogs, wild packs of dogs, falling upon the weak and clambering over each other to rend the carcass. That insight brought him up short, and he raised his head, looking at the crowd around him again but not really seeing them this time. He had tried to rise above his birth, to become what should have been—a lion—but instead he had found only wild dogs, and the pack of them had driven him away.

How could he teach these men to rise to become lions when he hadn't been able to do it for himself?

"Turn rats into lions? Why not send me some water to turn into wine while you're at it?"

Prentice sighed and looked back at Fostermae and the others. The sacrist wanted him to show mercy, and Righteous and Tressy couldn't understand why the twelve men weren't dead yet. In each other man's face, he read some combination of these two extremes. Baron Liam and his knights outside the walls would not show mercy, not to traitors like this. They would be beaten and flayed, pulled apart by horses and vivisected by butchers. All manner of hateful executions would be devised for them.

Like a pack of dogs, tearing its victims apart.

He looked at the sword sheathed at his side—a longsword, a knight's weapon. He'd all but sworn to Yentow Sent that he wanted none for his men, but the moment the conflict had erupted, he'd gone straight to the smith to demand one. He tried to tell himself it was just because his sword-breaker, his usual weapon, was in his hut, but that was a lie and he knew it. He still wanted to be a knight, to complete the plan for his life that had been disrupted by treachery, conviction, and transportation.

He sighed again.

Reaching down, he unbuckled the sword belt he'd put on to carry Yentow Sent's masterwork blade. He wrapped the belt around the sheath and carried the blade to Sir Gant, offering it to the knight with two hands.

"I'm sorry I had to risk your life like that," he said, looking over to where the lighted hut still smoldered and smoked. They would have to pull the peat roof apart completely, or the fuel would burn for days.

"You did what you had to, and I survived," Gant replied with a stoic shrug. He looked down at the sword Prentice was offering him, cocking a quizzical eyebrow.

"I'm no knight," Prentice said to him. "You served loyally, even in the face of death. You deserve a reward."

Gant accepted the sword with surprise, but before he could ask any questions, Prentice had already turned away. He walked over to one of the men standing by with a practice stave, a seven-foot length of hardwood that would one day have a steel-bladed head attached to it. For the moment it served as a functional quarterstaff. Prentice took it and, aware that everyone was watching him, walked the line of kneeling men until he was standing over Donnen.

"So, what happens now?" he asked the brutish rebel.

Donnen sneered back at him.

"Now? Now you make some silly speech and let us go," he answered, his voice dripping with contempt. "We go back to starving while you play pretend lord."

Prentice smiled wryly to himself. It was exactly as he'd feared; he'd shown mercy to Markas on the wall, and Donnen and his fellows had taken it as a sign of weakness.

"Did you stampede the herd?" Prentice asked him. Donnen's dark eyes narrowed, and from his expression, Prentice knew it was him, and probably not alone.

"We're all starving, thanks to you."

Donnen looked away dismissively. Prentice slapped his face, not angrily, but with the same disdain. Donnen looked back with a furious scowl.

Prentice pointed at Righteous and Tressy.

"They want to cut your throat and be done with you."

"Of course, they do," Donnen sneered again. "They're the ones with the stones. All the stories that get told about you, how you killed monsters and fought battles, but you get old men and girls to do your killing. You needed that strawberry scarecrow to save your arse on the back wall. Those two did the iron work this night as well. You aren't going to do anything. You don't have the stones!"

Prentice nodded to himself. He reached his hand into the pouch on his belt, the pouch that held the duchess's signet ring, the symbol of her authority she had entrusted to him. He drew it out and thrust it on his finger.

"See this? You know what this is?"

Donnen made a show of not answering the question.

"Of course. You're so sure you're right, aren't you?"

This man was a lion. Prentice could see it in every element of his behavior. Even faced with death, Donnen's recourse was to his heart and his strength. That was how a lion led the pride, and that was how Prentice should be leading. Of course, belligerence like Donnen's needed to be tempered with wisdom. This fool was ready to die on his knees because he couldn't imagine being defeated by a weaker man. Donnen the lion just could not imagine being taken down by the dogs outside the walls. Prentice had the wisdom to avoid a fight he didn't need, but there were moments, like this one, where the lion had to fight for control of his pride.

Prentice nodded and turned away from Donnen toward Sir Gant, Felix, and the others. He waved them over.

"It's time to make a judgement," he told them. "Let's get the prisoners over in front of the gate."

"What's your plan?" asked Sir Gant.

"You'll see. And when you do, I don't want to hear a word, not a word."

Gant was puzzled but accepted Prentice's command with a nod.

"Oh, and I need to borrow that sword again, if you don't mind."

Gant handed it to him, belt and scabbard. Felix began giving orders, and the twelve prisoners were hoisted to their feet and frog-marched toward the main gate, the crowd of recruits following. Prentice sent two men ahead to open the gates as they drew close. He had the crowd stop some distance back from the gate house, leaving an open space. Walking into that gap, Prentice turned to face the crowd, the conspirators held by their bonds at the front.

"Through that gate, we are all wanted men and women, escaped convicts under a sentence of death. We've all seen what the baron and his knights do to escaped convicts," he shouted, and the words echoed off the walls. Virtually the entire camp was here, listening to these words. The only guards with the strength to stand watch on the walls were standing over the gate. Yentow Sent's men were likely still at the smithy, but they were not who Prentice needed to see and hear what he was about to do.

"Inside these walls, we are all free," he went on. "But free to do what? To cower from the cold and starve? What freedom is that?"

Every eye was on him, but as far as Prentice was concerned, he might as well be only talking to Donnen and his crew. He lifted his hand to show the signet ring on his finger.

"This is the duchess' signet. By it, and by her authority, I have the right of life and death over every one of you. She chose me, right or wrong. These twelve see it differently. They think I'm a lapdog who doesn't deserve to command. Too weak and too cowardly, they say. They think we're all in here because the baron only wants my blood, and I'm cowering behind these walls. Offer me up and he'll let the rest of you traipse away free as birds, they say.

"They're all bloody fools."

There were angry mutterings in the crowd, and many hands reached forward to slap the traitors on their heads or shoulders. Prentice drew the longsword from its sheath and cast the scabbard away. He laid the blade flat on the ground and stepped back several paces, well out of reach of his own staff. He looked to Donnen, then to the men holding him up, and then back again.

"You want out? You want to make your own way against the knights outside? The gate's already open. You could have tried sneaking away in the night, a rope over the wall, but you didn't only want to be freed, did you? You wanted to be rewarded, paid a bounty for my head. Well, I'm the only one between you and your plan's success now. Take up that sword, take my head if you can, and offer it up to the baron. See what reward he offers you. I promise you won't like it."

Prentice nodded to the men holding Donnen back.

"Release him.

There was a moment's hesitation, but then they did as he ordered, untying Donnen's wrists. The lead traitor snatched his hands away from them once he was free and rubbed at them to restore the circulation.

"I'm no fool," he spat at Prentice. "I try to strike you and your people come get me. I know how this works."

Prentice looked over the crowd and raised the signet ring again.

"In the name of the duchess and the Western Reach," he shouted like a crier making a pronouncement, "if I am defeated, Donnen may march free through that gate. That is my command."

Prentice heard the murmur of voices, and he didn't dare look at his closest advisors. He knew what Gant or Righteous would think of this plan. But there was nothing else to do. Donnen was a rival, challenging for control of the pride. The time for wisdom had passed. Now was a time for might. From the corner of his eye, he caught sight of Fostermae, head down, apparently in prayer. He wondered if the sacrist would approve of this tactic.

"Well, Donnen?" he called. "Take up the blade and fight for your freedom, or else let us all see you for a coward."

"And what are you going to fight with? That stick?"

"I've faced worse than you with less than this."

Donnen stalked forward with hesitant steps, expecting a trap to be sprung at any moment. He stopped twice before finally covering the distance to the longsword and snatching it up. He hefted its weight, and Prentice took a fighting hold on his staff. There was a pause, and then Donnen turned to the crowd.

"Come on, you lot," he shouted. "If we rush him, he's ours and we can be out that gate. No one'll stop us!"

Not a single person moved. Prentice remembered the day he'd first met Liam, when the knight had tried to motivate a group of weary and beaten-down convicts to defend the Duchess Amelia. He'd had the same success Donnen was having now. It made Prentice smile.

"It's just you and me, Donnen," he said. "You want to leave, I'm the only obstacle in your path."

Donnen turned back to face Prentice and spat on the ground.

"I'm going to gut you like a pig," he hissed, taking up a stance and aiming the sword point at Prentice's chest.

"Best of luck," Prentice replied and set himself, feet apart, weight slightly forward.

Donnen came on calmly, occasionally waving the sword in half-hearted forays, feeling Prentice out. Prentice only moved once, disengaging the staff's end in a flicking motion when the longsword almost struck it. Otherwise, he projected utter calm, and it was not for show. This was where Prentice always preferred to be, in this simple moment, when the only thing to worry about was the opponent.

The longsword swiped again, and when Prentice disengaged his staff, Donnen pressed in, following with a smooth combination of strikes. Prentice was finally forced to step aside to his right to keep his opponent at distance. Donnen had experience and no small amount of skill, but watching him use the longsword, Prentice could see he was as unfamiliar with the knight's signature as Prentice himself was. If Donnen were to face a true knight, like Sir Gant, he would fare no better than Prentice did. In the chaos of battle, such a small difference in skill probably wouldn't tell, but in a duel like this, it could easily be fatal.

You should have asked for a pole like mine, Prentice thought as he watched his opponent.

Donnen made another foray, again pushing Prentice to his right. It was so deliberate this time that, seeing it coming, Prentice was able to thrust his staff straight at Donnen. The blow thumped into the man's shoulder—a painful strike but not telling. Donnen pressed Prentice away to his right a third time and Prentice finally realized what he was doing.

Donnen didn't want to fight, he wanted to run.

The pair had circled around each other so far that Donnen now had no one between him and the open gate. Prentice watched and waited, recognizing what was coming. In a sudden turnabout, Donnen ran for the gate, choosing freedom over honor. But Prentice was ready for him. As soon as Donnen's sprint began, Prentice leaped forward, the quarterstaff striking at the back of his opponent's legs. The blow caused Donnen to stumble, and in that moment, Prentice was on him. To his credit, Donnen managed to keep his feet and almost raised the longsword to a reasonable guard, but Prentice gave him no space to fully recover. The whole gathered company needed to see a fair fight, to know Prentice had the strength and courage of a lion, the strength to lead the pride, but when Donnen had chosen to flee, that became irrelevant. They'd seen him break and run. He wasn't a lion; he was a dog or a rat, bold in his pack, but unable to stand alone.

A quarterstaff was a length of solid hardwood with hardly any bend in it at all. Nevertheless, in the hands of a skilled practitioner, a staff could be made to flex and flicker with such speed that it resembled the dance of a striking snake. And Prentice was a very skilled practitioner. The longsword was the knight's weapon he had never mastered, but staves and spears had been in his hands since before he was ten. He rained blows on Donnen with such force that the traitor lost his grip on the sword and fell insensible in the wet dirt, bleeding from a cut to his scalp and bruised all over.

Prentice turned back to face the watching crowd.

"Next," he said calmly. His body ached with the exhaustion of hunger and lack of sleep, but the ferocious joy of victory gave him a strength he'd not felt in months. No one moved. Overhead, the wind drove fresh clouds over the sky so that the rising sun would soon be lost in rain again.

No one stepped forward. None of the other eleven conspirators made any move to take their chance. The whole body of men and women were frozen in place, impressed with the ease of his victory. It was time to move forward.

"Donnen was right about one thing," he told them all. "If we stay here any longer, we'll starve. Someone, tie this lot up somewhere we can leave them." He pointed to the prisoners, and they were quickly dragged off, Felix assigning one of the loyal corporals to the task and then going along himself to make sure.

"The rest of you, those with a sword or a pole, a knife, or even a chunk of rock if that will do you, come with me and let's put an end to this damnable siege."

That caught everyone by surprise. Sir Gant openly blinked in disbelief. Righteous smiled her predatory smile and punched the air. Many in the crowd hefted weapons, while others looked about for exactly what Prentice had said, a heavy rock to throw or swing. A number seemed uncertain but most had caught the scent of victory, and Prentice was not going to let it go to waste.

Sir Gant stepped up to him while he bent down to recover the fallen longsword. He handed it the knight.

"Thank you for that."

Gant could not have cared less for the blade.

"Is this what you want to do?" he asked earnestly. "You've always said you don't want to throw untrained men at knights in armor. You don't want rogues, you want soldiers."

"If we starve, there'll be no soldiers or rogues," Prentice answered him. "Either we break the siege, or we die. We'll soon be too weak from hunger even to make that choice."

Sir Gant shook his head, uncomfortable with the logic of that assertion.

"So, you stir up a rabble and hope the weight of numbers sweeps the baron away?"

"This is the sign. Either we are lions, and we live and die like lions, fighting to the end, or we are rats, and we die cowering in the walls."

Gant still didn't look like he understood, but it was too late. Prentice led the way out of the gate, and the mass of his company followed with him.

CHAPTER 39

They poured out of the gate and around the tumbled wagon that had kept Baron Liam from ever bringing a ram against their defenses. At first, they were only a trickle, but like a breaking flood, they pressed against the wagon until it was forced upright and began to roll out of the way, the press of bodies flowing around it in all directions. In moments, hundreds had emerged, and the crowd still grew.

Baron Liam's knights had a number of small patrols ready to capture escapees, holding haphazard siege fortifications, so there were about fifty men at arms waiting outside the gate in little clutches. Some had crossbows to bring to bear. Knighted retainers didn't lower themselves to mere sentry duty, but a few had been awake in the early hours, or their squires were. Drawn by the sounds of conflict inside the walls, they had clad themselves in armor and ridden up the short slope to see what the commotion might lead to. None of the baron's men were ready for the sheer mass that flowed down the hill toward them.

Prentice was in front of his company, little more than an armed rabble as they were. When he came around the cart, he barely paused to assess the situation before he broke into a run. He felt no fear, just the exultation of his purpose. Something flashed across his vision from his left, and it took him a moment to realize that it was a crossbow bolt, fired by a besieger. He ignored it and ran on. A knight on horseback, clad in plate and mail, started charging up the slope towards him. The hoofs beat upon the earth, but Prentice refused to let up, still running forward. The knight drew his side sword, planning a passing stroke, but as he closed the gap and leaned in the saddle, Prentice jammed the butt of his staff into the ground. The other end he aimed at the knight's chest. His aim was off, but the grounded pole still hammered into the charging man's pauldron. The blow to the shoulder threw his sword arm wild, and Prentice heard him curse inside his helmet as he overran his target.

The knight wheeled his mount to make another pass at Prentice, but by the time he was turned about, he was swamped by the other former convicts following their leader's mad rush. The knight swung about himself with his sword, and his horse kicked and bit as it was trained. More than one convict went down, but the human wave still rolled over mount and rider, dragging them down under a hail of blows that rang off polished steel armor like the ringing of a tuneless gong. Other knights charged the crowd, to similar effect, while men-at-arms fired single shots from their crossbows before fleeing. Prentice was nearly two hundred paces from the open gate when the first alarm was properly sounded as someone thought to blow a hunting horn. The low-pitched blast echoed across the vale in front of Fallenhill, reflecting from the stones of the wall before being cut savagely short. The horn-blower had been overrun by the convict wave as well.

At the bottom of the slope, about five hundred paces from the wall, the baron's camp was buzzing with panic. Squires and pages rushed about, rousing sleeping knights and trying to arm them too late for the battle that was sweeping down upon them. Whatever they expected after half a winter of siege, it didn't include a dawn assault by every convict in Fallenhill. The truth was, Prentice had never expected this either. He wasn't planning or leading, just riding the wave of repressed rage as it broke its dam and poured down the hill.

"Liam! Where is Baron Liam?" Prentice shouted as he leaped the guy-lines of the camp's first tent. A squire came around the corner carrying a boar spear, with a look of terror on his face. Prentice didn't break stride, and his staff cracked the young man across the face, felling him with a single blow. Prentice threw the staff back to one of the convicts following him and took up the spear.

"Liam?" he called again. "Find the baron."

Now that they were in the camp, Prentice's rational side, the cold logic that came upon him in battle, was reasserting itself. Up to this point, his people had had the advantage, but if the baron rallied his forces and managed to get a knot of fifty to a hundred of them into a strong defensive cordon, this spontaneous move would spend itself like a wave breaking on the shore. They would have no choice but to retreat. They were not ready to face knights or other disciplined men-at-arms in close formation.

A man in an arming doublet, with gauntlets on his hands and a salet helmet, suddenly lurched out of the space between two tents, swinging a poleaxe wildly. Prentice stepped back and tried to check the axe with his spear, but the man pressed on, and the steel axe bit the air in front of Prentice's face. Then the axe-man's foot caught on something and there was a break in his swing. Prentice's boar spear had a long willow leaf blade and, beneath that, a pair of short side bars called quillons, or sometimes wings, that were designed to stop an impaled boar from riding up the spear, and with its dying energy, killing the wielder of the weapon. Those wings were also useful in combat against a man, and Prentice used them now like a hook to catch the poleaxe and pull it out of line. Then, before his opponent could recover, Prentice corkscrewed the spear into a thrust that took the man in the throat. He died without making a sound.

Prentice stepped into the gap the man had emerged from to find a page cowering inside a small tent while two convicts squatted by a cookfire to raid the porridge cooking there. He slapped the spear into the fire and scattered the ashes to get their attention.

"We'll eat later when we loot the whole place," he growled at them. "For now, we fight 'til every knight is dead or throws down his arms!"

It surprised him when they instantly jumped up, grabbing purloined weapons of their own. One of them even thumped his fist to his chest in salute. Then they were off, back into the chaos. Prentice looked at the terrified lad whose master he had probably just killed.

"Look to yourself," he told the boy. "If you see a gap, run, and come back later."

He didn't wait to see if the boy accepted his advice.

At every turn, Baron Liam's camp was dissolving, torn apart by the fury of hungry men and women, yet the baron himself was nowhere to be seen. Prentice was certain the cunning nobleman was gathering up as many as he could, preparing a counterattack. Even now, the urgency was ebbing away from the convict assault, and the melees around him were less savage. More and more of his people were stopping to grab mouthfuls of bread or cheese, or to swill watered wine from skins. Prentice knew how they felt. The emotion that had driven him out through the gate was fading inside as well, leaving the all-too-familiar ache of hunger and fatigue to reassert itself. He pushed himself onward. He had to find Liam before it was too late.

Then suddenly, he came through to the other side of the camp. The knights' tents just stopped, and there was a set of rails to which the horses were tied, with stacks of hay and grains going green in the rain under ineffective tarps. Beyond the horses was a small winter stream, barely worthy of the name, and beyond that another camp of much less proud and much less expensive shelters. Prentice rushed forward between the horses and stepped over the little flow of water. As he rushed toward this second encampment, a small crowd came forth to meet him, dressed in homespun and rude leathers. They were farmers and peasants, one and all. Perhaps there was one or two craftsmen amongst them.

"Baron Liam!" Prentice bellowed as he rushed at them. They flinched away fearfully, but one man, with a long black-and-grey-streaked beard, stepped forward. Others crouched behind him.

"Where is Baron Liam?" Prentice demanded. It took all his force of will just to raise his voice now.

"Gone," said the bearded man. "Gone two weeks now. They won't tell us where."

Gone? Prentice's mind could barely process the news, but the man's sincerity was unmistakable. There was no deception in this crowd of confused peasants. Baron Liam was gone. The ogre besieging his walls, haunting his every waking hour, wasn't even here and hadn't been for two weeks.

"Who are you?"

"Settlers mainly," the man explained. "Mountain folk and the like. We weren't touched much by the wild men out of the west, and so when harvest was done and them riders came up into the high country to tell us it was safe, we come down here to trade. Then the baron told us we had to stay and serve his army for the siege. Most of us ain't seen our homes since winter set in. Please don't hurt us."

The riders in the hills were Prentice's men, he was sure of it—the ones he'd sent into the high country himself. And all the folk they'd gathered had been pressed into service with Liam. Prentice's eyes ranged over the cowering peasants and their modest second camp, and then he looked over his shoulder at the rage spending itself on the baron's camp. Once his people realized there was more food and more booty to be had here, these folk would be doomed for sure.

"Return to your places," he told them breathlessly. "And be ready to defend them if you have to. I'll see no man is judged harshly for defending his hearth and his own."

Prentice wondered what they thought of being given orders from a man he was sure they thought was an escaped convict, a bloodthirsty rebel, but he had no time to persuade them to listen to him. He jogged back toward the horses, forcing his exhausted legs to run as fast as he could, which wasn't much. Even before he reached them, the first few curious convicts were circling the gap between the two camps and looking at the peasant settlement. He was elated when he saw Felix emerge from between two tied mounts, carrying a halberd and looking curiously at the second camp.

"What's that?" he asked as Prentice ran up.

"Peasant camp," Prentice told him. "Forced to supply Liam's men-at-arms."

"Oh God," Felix swore, and the look in his eyes told Prentice that the corporal understood. It was one thing to see rage vented on those knights and their retainers, but peasants didn't deserve to be pillaged for Liam's crimes.

"We've got to turn them back on that camp," he told Felix. "Tell them to start the looting and promise them twenty silver guilders apiece for every captured prisoner."

"That'll only stop some."

"I know. As they come across, grab the best men you know and promise them my gratitude; then form a cordon. None of ours cross this stream, or I'll put them to the sword myself."

After his run-in with Donnen this morning, Prentice hoped everyone would believe that threat. Felix surprised him by chuckling.

"What?" he asked.

"Just wondering what these knights'll think about being held for a ransom of twenty guilders," the corporal observed wryly. "I'll bet none of them's had his life held so cheap, ever."

"It's not a ransom; it's a bounty," Prentice assured him. He had no idea what he'd do with prisoners, but he had to head off any chance of a mass killing. Otherwise, once the bloodlust was given full flight, he'd have no hope of stopping it flowing over onto these innocent free folk. He and Felix began redirecting convicts back into the knights' camp, prompting them with promises of loot and food. And in the back of Prentice's mind was the one question he had never thought to have to answer.

Where was Baron Liam?

CHAPTER 40

The afternoon was dark and cold, the sky close and cloud-locked. The smell in the air was of threatening rain, and somewhere in the camp Baron Liam lurked.

When she had seen him ride in that morning, Duchess Amelia rushed back to her tent, half to avoid meeting him out and about, and half to be ready if he called on her. She'd spent the night scrabbling through the close wood, and she knew her appearance showed it. The last thing she wanted was to have to receive the hateful nobleman without at least the shield of the dignity of her station.

Reaching her tent, she'd been surprised and annoyed to find Kirsten was not there yet again, nor had she been seen that morning. The girl's absences were becoming troublesome, and Amelia worried for a moment that her maid had fallen victim to some secret assault, as Turley had. Amelia tried to dismiss that thought as mere paranoia and settled quickly to brushing her own hair and changing her clothes. Leaves and twigs fell to the floor as she untangled the knots thoughtfully, reviewing in her mind the news and events of recent days.

Turley lived, and she gave thanks for that. Countess Dalflitch had been dismissed by the prince. Strangely, now that they had no rivalry, the countess was both more amenable and less useful to Amelia than ever.

And now Baron Liam had arrived in camp.

The prince had sent for him before the crusade left the hunting lodge, but between the baron's injuries, the cold of winter, and the fact that he had to find the "missing" convicts before he could bring them to the prince, Amelia hadn't expected to see the baron before spring. As she readied herself to give him audience, she brooded over what his arrival might mean.

Had he brought the convicts? Was Prentice with them if he had? Or was he dead? She sent a steward's man to see if any large group of convicts had arrived with Liam. If they had, she expected they were shivering to death in the marshes surrounding the camp. The steward's man had not returned when she received a summons to attend the prince. With no ladies' maid to help her prepare and no suitable escort, Amelia arrived at the prince's tent shortly after, alone, with her hair hidden beneath a simple hood, wearing Reach blue over a simple, undyed woolen underdress. The floor of the tent was laid with bundles of fresh rushes cut from the marsh, but she decided to keep her waxed leather covers on over her slippers.

Even though it was only early afternoon, the darkened sky meant that there were lit lanterns throughout the tent, and in the main chamber, two large braziers burned amidst a gathering of a hundred or more highborn nobles of the Reach and Rhales. Most were gathered in cliques, speaking quietly and watching closely where Daven Marcus and his entourage had gathered at the table at the back of the chamber. There, the prince and a handful of his very closest nobles were sitting, eating the last of a noonday meal. Next to his gilded plate and goblet, the prince had papers and parchments spread under a lit candle, and between bites and sips from his cup, he read and discussed the documents with two men behind him. In the dimness, it was hard to make them out, but one was a scribe of some sort, dressed in a guildsman's robes, and the other Amelia finally recognized as the prince's chief gunner, the captain of his Royal Dragons.

Amelia let her eyes adjust to the dimness and looked about to see if she could spot Liam. She was sure he was here somewhere, as close to the prince as he could get. As she studied the room, she was surprised to see her maid, Kirsten, standing amongst a group of worthies a short distance off to one side of the prince's table. Beside Kirsten was Lord Robant, dressed in a black velvet doublet with matching hose. He stood proudly, and as she approached, Amelia noticed he had his hand on Kirsten's arm. She realized that the baron was the reason her handmaid had been missing for so long, and it made sense to her. Robant had engineered the ambush that attacked Turley, and no doubt the prince had set the baron to remove her other supports, like Kirsten.

You better not have hurt her, Amelia thought as she drew close. She was almost by Kirsten's side when a part of her mind noticed that her maid was wearing an unfamiliar dress, something of red velvet, finely made, and she had a jeweled chain about her neck. Amelia had been too eager to reassure herself that Kirsten was alright to recognize the potential import of the girl's new clothes.

"Kirsten, I had not thought to find you here," said Amelia. "I trust you are well?" She looked past Kirsten to Robant, whose eyes were fixed on the prince's table.

"Quite well," Kirsten answered. She was watching the prince's table closely as well—so closely, in fact, that she seemed to be all but ignoring Amelia.

"Baron Robant hasn't harmed you at all, has he?"

Kirsten's lips turned up in a harsh smile.

"Why would you think that?"

Amelia felt as if there was a secret being shared, and she was the only one who didn't know what it was. Worse than that, her maid was being rude. Kirsten could be headstrong, but she was normally impeccably polite. Amelia looked past her to Robant, wondering if he was somehow causing Kirsten's unusual behavior. As she looked closely, she realized that

Robant was not holding Kirsten in place, like a guard, as she had first thought. His hand was not on her arm as it had seemed from a distance. The pair was holding hands,. Amelia looked up at the baron, and even though he never looked at her, she knew he could tell she was looking, because his mouth took on the same cruel smile that Kirsten had flashed her.

"What is happening here?" she demanded in a cold whisper.

Robant and Kirsten assiduously refused to meet her eyes, clearly enjoying this chance to politely disdain her.

"I would have ended up an old maid, waiting for you," Kirsten said, and Amelia couldn't tell if she wanted to laugh or cry.

"You...are...?"

"Betrothed, finally? Yes, Duchess, I am." Kirsten finally turned to face her mistress, and the contempt in the girl's expression was unmistakable. "At last, I can be envied instead of whispered about. You might enjoy sour loneliness, a dried-up widow before you even have a full year of marriage to your name, but I won't have to follow you into your exile from love."

"What on earth are you talking about?"

"Duchess Amelia," Robant sniffed, "if you would keep from distracting my betrothed, this is an important council of war we are witnessing."

Amelia's eyes went wide, and it was all she could do to keep her voice down and not lose her decorum.

"I am speaking with my handmaid, Lord Robant," she hissed furiously. "She will only be your betrothed when, and if, I give my permission. In the meantime, I'll thank you to keep your rebukes to yourself."

"The matter of betrothal has been resolved above you," Robant said, and Amelia knew that meant the prince had given his blessing, taking the matter out of her hands.

"Not everything is about you," Kirsten added with such prideful venom that it was like a slap in the face. "Such a plain thing, you should be grateful your dowry bought you the attention it has instead of playing the princess in the tower, beautiful and lonely. You'll get to be a princess in truth. Be thankful. I had to acquire my love's pledge by my beauty and sweetness of temper, something you are utterly unsuited to."

Amelia could feel her teeth grinding, and to keep from shouting at her rebellious maid, she looked down at her feet for a moment. As she did so, she noticed that the dress Kirsten was wearing was pooled at her feet. It was too long for the girl and needed tailoring. In a flash, Amelia realized where it had come from. It was one of Countess Dalflitch's gowns. Kirsten was betrothed to Robant and Dalflitch was dismissed, all in one night?

"You told the prince I asked you to draw close to the countess, didn't you?"

Kirsten smiled.

"I told my liege everything about your petty machinations as a loyal and true servant of the Grand Kingdom. As a reward, he offered me his ex-mistress' wardrobe. He prefers women without excess ambition in his court."

"You have a mountain more ambition than I gave you credit for."

"A product of your own stupidity."

"Wear all the new dresses you want," Amelia said, feeling her voice rising but unable to stop herself. "Marry this murderous cur tonight and sire his heir by morning, if you can. You will still be beneath me! As you always have been."

"Bitch!" Kirsten retorted, but Lord Robant pulled her close.

"You are disturbing, My Lady," he chastised the duchess. "I insist you stop at once."

"You forget yourself, Baron. You don't insist on anything from me. I am the peer and you a raised noble. I insist to you!"

"Not in this company, Duchess," Robant said, and before Amelia could argue any further, he raised his eyes and called to the prince's table. "Highness, the one you wanted to see has arrived."

"Ah, the traitor wench graces us with her presence, does she?"

The prince's voice stilled every quiet conversation around the tent chamber, and the hush fell to a silence so profound that even the crackle of the flames in the braziers seemed muted.

CHAPTER 41

T raitor?

The word hung in the air like a death knell. Daven Marcus's contempt was nothing new, and his attempts to humiliate Amelia had become so commonplace she hardly even noticed. But to call her traitor was not the same thing. That alleged a high crime against the throne itself, and it came with a death penalty, as well as excommunication from the bosom of the Mother Church. A traitor to the crown was killed and their soul sent to hell. Even the scent of treason was enough to destroy nobles politically.

Treason was not something about which anyone made jests, not even a brat like Daven Marcus.

"I am here, Highness, answering your summons," Amelia said politely, detaching herself from her conversation with Robant and Kirsten to curtsey to the prince. She bowed her head and waited for him to acknowledge her. Her mind raced, readying herself for the details that would follow his accusation. Liam would be at the center of it, she was sure, but what was he going to tell? That she had given the convicts into Prentice's charge? That was already so close to the story she had already told the prince that she was sure she could argue her innocence from it, especially if Daven Marcus tried to bring her to account publicly.

"Oh, raise your head, damnable sow," the prince commanded her, and she stood straight. "No one here is fooled by your shows of false devotion."

"My obedience to you has been absolute, Highness, truly. What word of yours have I defied?"

Daven Marcus's teeth clenched. He threw a half-chewed bone across the table in her direction, a gesture of contempt.

"You have been favored with the attentions of the greatest of men. Every woman adores me. Many would kill to have what you have disdained! Yet what sweet words do you honor me with? What praise do I receive from your lips?"

Kirsten made a small, approving noise and when she heard it, it infuriated Amelia. She felt her indignance rising, and it defied her control.

"I am a widow. My husband is not dead a year," she vented, glad to speak bluntly to the prince for once, even though a part of her protested in her mind that it was a mistake. "You boast that you have come to rescue the Reach from its weakness and sloth, to conquer more than your great uncle, yet so far you have done nothing except led a dismal, wet parade through grass and marsh! Winter is almost passed and not one dead Redlander have we seen. Their fortress is at the other end of that causeway. Go, take their tower from them and I will be the first to praise your triumph!"

The entire Rhales court drew in a shocked breath as one, as if a great animal had suddenly sighed in disbelief. The prince's eyes narrowed in unreserved fury but also dark cunning.

"How do you know that name?" he asked.

"Highness?" she asked, recognizing that she had given something away but not sure what it was.

"Baron Liam, how does she know?"

From somewhere in the shadows of the tent, Liam emerged, his face grim and ugly. He stared at the Amelia with unrestrained hatred.

"I cannot say, Highness, though I am not surprised to hear that she does."

Daven Marcus had not looked away from Amelia. His dark eyes scoured her face.

"When my uncle, Prince Mercad, questioned prisoners he captured at Fallenhill, they told him of the name these Veckander fools had taken to try to disguise their origin. They called themselves red landers." The prince separated the name into its base words, "red" and "land," pronouncing each individually.

Amelia's mind was racing again, working to integrate this revelation. The "prisoners" he was referring to had to be the one Prentice had captured.

"I was told nothing of this," she said truthfully.

"No indeed," the prince agreed. "My great uncle, dotard though he was, was wise enough to forbid the sharing of the name. Only his interrogator and his knight commander heard that name with him, and I learned it only by Ironworth's report. So how do you know it?"

"How does Baron Liam know it?"

"The baron enjoys my trust."

Liar, Amelia thought, though that didn't mean the prince hadn't shared the name at a time when he did trust Liam. Daven Marcus's trust was a fickle thing.

"I learned the name only this last night passed," Amelia said. "From a local."

"A local? What local?" asked Lord Robant, injecting himself suddenly into the conversation. His tone showed how ridiculous he found the notion.

"From a...," Amelia hesitated to use the word prophetess, as that would invoke a further religious element into the conflict that she didn't want to deal with. "An old hermit woman. She lives in the wooded copse and has done for many, many years. She says they come from across that shallow sea you discovered."

"Liar!" the prince shouted suddenly, thrusting himself upright, scattering his goblet and nearly tipping the lit candle over onto the papers. Only the swift intervention of the scholar standing close by prevented disaster. Daven Marcus did not even notice.

"Lying whore!" he went on. "You are a traitor, selling out my Reach to the Veckanders, mongrel princes that they are! That's where my silver has gone, to pay for this causeway that they plan to invade with and the fortified tower to protect their pier, to land their ships. There is nothing on the other side of that salt *lake!*" He emphasized the word lake so vehemently that spittle flew from his mouth.

"Sir Duggan embezzled the silver," Amelia protested, picking one of the prince's crazed accusations at random to refute. "You were present when he confessed, and by his own mouth, I had nothing to do with it!"

"Lies! Shut your lying mouth, bitch, or I will shut it for you. You think I do not see through your ruses? Journeys to the Vec? Red landers? Missing silver? And now the baron you could not woo with your wiles returns to tell me that you have sent all my convicts north. You have them holed up, ready no doubt to raid the Reach as bandits in the coming summer."

Finally, the prince had returned to the issue Amelia had expected, and mention of the missing convicts brought her also to a moment of pause; it helped her gather her thoughts and regain her calm. Daven Marcus was in a rage, but so far all he had done was make far-fetched accusations. He'd not actually touched on anything she'd done. Now, if she could get her own emotions under control, it should be possible to refute the claim of treason. She was reasonably sure she could do it.

"Of course, the convicts are at Fallenhill, Highness," she admitted, adopting a gentler tone for a moment. "The town was butchered and burned—man, woman and child. It must be cleared and rebuilt for the defense of the north."

"Rebuilt?" Daven Marcus repeated and then looked at Liam, who sneered, the expression making his deformed face even uglier.

"Her pet has the ducal seal," he said, obviously referring to Prentice. "And he has set himself up as a bandit lord, freeing the convicts and holding the town against the crown."

"Of course, he has my seal," Amelia argued, emphasizing the point that the seal was hers to give or not. "How else will folk know that he has my authority to rebuild the town?" She watched Liam blink at the question. It was a reasonable one, and even through his disdain, he could see that.

"He is in rebellion, in your name," he persisted.

"Rebellion against whom?"

"Against the prince."

"Truly? How is that, Baron?"

"He refused my command to relinquish control of the convict chains to me that I might bring them here, according to the prince's command—a command with the full backing of King's Law. It does not matter what you claim to have said, he is in rebellion against the crown and thus the throne."

"Did you show him the letter?" Amelia asked, and Liam's face again revealed his surprise. He was an ambitious man, but he was not mentally suited to these courtier's games.

"I need not have shown him the prince's letter," he insisted, and Daven Marcus added his own sneer.

"You want a baron of your realm to treat with a convict? God almighty woman, you're not just a traitor but a fool into the bargain."

"A patrician of my capital," Amelia dared to correct the prince. "An ex-convict perhaps, but a free man in my service now, patrician by rank, and carrying my signet. But that is not the letter I meant, Highness. I sent a letter of my own to the castle in Dweltford. Baron Liam has an unpleasant history with my man, Prentice Ash, whom I gave command of the convicts. Indeed, Prentice was the one who saved me lately in the autumn when the baron here struck me to the ground. A crime for which you pardoned him, Highness."

That revelation caused a ripple of consternation around the watching courtiers. The Reachermen would never respect a knight who had struck his own liege lady, no matter who pardoned him, but it seemed to Amelia that many of the Rhales court were also shocked at the revelation. To strike a liege was an unmistakable act of treason, and if Daven Marcus had pardoned Liam of that crime, then his indignation at Amelia's supposed conspiracy would ring false, at least. Just the fact that Liam had been pardoned was a minor scandal in its own right.

Amelia pressed on. "When you told me, Highness, that you had sent Baron Liam to fetch your convicts, I sent a letter to Dweltford castle, to the baron, for him to show my man Prentice. I knew, because of their past hostility, it would be hard for them to trust each other, so I sent instructions for the baron to show him to smooth the way."

"Is that true?" Daven Marcus asked. It looked like his fury might be beginning to melt into bored annoyance. Amelia had counted on this. The prince liked to lord his power over her, not to have to defend it in the face of legitimate objections.

Baron Liam swallowed visibly, but the hate never left his eyes.

"No, Your Highness."

"You call me a liar to my face?" Amelia said, raising herself up. The prince could command her deference. Liam was her inferior. Let him question her in public at his own peril, especially now that his reputation was publicly tarnished by the revelation that he had attacked her in a fit of rage.

"I never saw any such letter," he insisted, and for a moment Amelia felt the tiniest flicker of pity. He had not seen the letter because she'd never written one. She was lying, but just as no one could question Daven Marcus, Prince of Rhales to his face, so Liam could not challenge the Duchess of the Western Reach to hers. He was her bondsman, and his word was worth that much less than hers. Besides, if the letter became an issue, she would make sure that one was found amongst papers somewhere in Dweltford. It would be simple enough to write one quickly if needed.

Then Amelia remembered Kirsten standing beside her, and there was the fearful recognition that her handmaid had the power to prove her wrong. She quickly turned her head back to the prince, but it was too late, he had seen her moment of panic. He looked to Kirsten.

"Tell me, Baron Robant," he said. "Does your betrothed confirm the duchess' nonsensical tale?"

Robant looked at Kirsten and bade the girl tell the prince. Obviously thrilled at being given a chance to speak publicly to the crown prince of the realm, she curtseyed perfectly, even managing her over-long dress with aplomb.

"She's always reading, and writes many things, often, Your Highness," Kirsten reported. "And she sends them everywhere, it seems, or she did when her steward was still alive. I don't know exactly what she wrote because my mother always said that reading was not a fit pastime for a maiden."

Amelia wanted to shake her head with pity. Kirsten was smart enough to err on the side of honesty, but not cunning enough to learn from Liam's mistake, or Dalflitch's, for that matter. Daven Marcus didn't want the truth. He wanted a simple report that he could use to condemn her. If Kirsten could remember letters being written but not say what they contained, there was no way to refute Amelia's claim.

Now boredom truly did seem to be claiming the prince.

Amelia watched his face as he cast a sneering glance around the entire court, feeling a growing confidence. She'd always known she would have to face this moment when Daven Marcus discovered exactly where she had redirected the convicts at the beginning of the march west. It was beginning to look like she would survive the storm relatively safely. The confrontation had been miserable, and had cost her Kirsten's service, though after the maid's treacherous behavior, Amelia counted that no great loss. Let Kirsten find out for herself what it was like for a woman of court to be beholden to men who had no loyalty to her. The girl should have listened more closely to Countess Dalflitch's gossip instead of being entranced by her clothes and jewelry.

Amelia was angry about her own losses of temper though, and she chided herself in her thoughts. Rudeness was never a useful tactic, to her mind, although she had seen men like Prentice and Turley use provocation effectively at certain moments. She was so relieved at the anticipated outcome, that she barely noticed as the prince sat back down and a courtier beside him provided him with his gold coronet. Daven Marcus received it and placed it on his head while looking straight at her. The duchess had a fraction of a moment to wonder about the symbolism of the gesture before the prince opened his mouth and shattered her calm.

"Duchess Amelia," he intoned like a sacrist at prayer, "I have judged the evidence against you and find you guilty of treason against the throne. You have conspired with your own knights and foreigners from the Vec princedoms to sell the Western Reach to those same Vec princes."

Amelia felt as if the world had been tipped sideways. Dizziness threatened to take her. Up until now, she had been sure she knew the outcome of all these games of power with the prince. He was supposed to win, that was inevitable, buy she hadn't been playing for victory, only to secure her best position before entering the miserable fate of being the royal monster's wife. A conviction for treason and a sentence of death was something she had never imagined.

"You have suborned banditry and undermined the saving role of the Mother Church," the prince continued. The candle flickering beside him on the table gave his face a haunting, wraithlike cast. As he spoke, he stared at her with such furious hate that it frightened her even further. He always showed her contempt, but now there was no amusement in his demeanor.

He had no motive in this moment except to see her destroyed. "You are guilty of theft of the king's taxes and betrayal of your duty of fealty to your own nobles. I name you traitor and condemn you to death by dismemberment, this day before God and men. Hell awaits your soul."

Amelia began to tremble, and she barely noticed as two royal house guards stepped up to take her by the arms. Like a cornered animal she looked left and right, though in her mind she was trying to think of some answer, some response to her situation. Nothing would come, only the roar of panic in her ears. As she looked about, she caught Kirsten's eye for a moment and the maid at least had the decency to show some pity for her. The guards pulled Amelia back to face the prince, who had not finished his pronouncement, it seemed.

"As you are condemned and have no legal progeny or heirs, I will accede to the duchy of the Western Reach by right of birth and honor. Your demesne will become royal territory for the protection and wellbeing of the Grand Kingdom. There will be no need to transfer your short-lived peerage."

That statement caused an unexpected murmur from the back of the tent chamber where the Reacher nobles were gathered. They didn't like that. Daven Marcus was using her supposed treason as an excuse to seize the Reach for himself without having to marry her first. The Reachermen would be bitter over it, but there was little they could do. From her reading of law and tradition, once the prince took her peerage away from the Reach, they would have no one to stand against his ambition in the King's Court.

Then she realized that Daven Marcus was overreaching himself, either through ignorance or in the hope no one knew to question him.

"King's Law," she muttered, but no one seemed to hear her. The prince continued with his legal-sounding pronouncement that Amelia realized from her reading had no soundness in law.

"King's Law," she shouted this time, and heard her voice crack with the emotions inside her. Even so, she kept shouting. "King's Law. King's Law!"

Daven Marcus had stopped speaking, perhaps just because he was not used to being shouted over, but his hateful look had again taken on a mocking, amused cast. He must have thought Amelia's mind had broken with fear and seemed to enjoy letting her descend into madness in a public setting. Amelia was not mad, though, and now that the prince was silent and every eye was on her, she made her final play.

"You have charged me with treason against the throne, in the sight of witnesses, but you cannot judge me. I demand my right to be tried before the throne in Denay!"

"You have no rights..." Baron Liam started to say, but Amelia cut him off. The duchess had no fear of speaking over her own retainer.

"I am Duchess of the Western Reach and a peer of the Realm."

"You are a milk maid again, silly sow," the prince spat. "I have stripped you of your peerage."

"For the crime of treason, which you cannot have proved, as only the king may judge me for it. You cannot take my peerage for the crime without the trial. So. I. Demand. My. Right."

There was another murmur behind her. Were they supportive, or had she gone too far? She couldn't tell, and at this moment she did not care.

Amelia straightened herself in the men-at-arm's grip and looked straight at Daven Marcus. She offered him no sign of deference. He wanted to strip her of everything her beloved husband had left to her, rape her lands to feed his indulgence, and have her killed for good measure. She was done being respectful with him. He was her enemy, and the enemy of the Western Reach.

"You talk of law, but your woman's mind cannot stretch high enough to even reach such matters, let alone encompass them," the prince said. He was going to dismiss her claim, she could see it. "You have no such right, and your girlish dream to twist the law to protect you from your deserved punishment is meaningless. You are guilty and I senten..."

The prince was interrupted as the scholar behind him leaned in to whisper in his ear. Amelia looked at the man and suddenly realized that he must be a guildsman at law, a legal advisor and advocate. Some of the documents on the table before the prince must have been the sentencing decrees, which this man would have prepared for Daven Marcus. While the prince had been pronouncing, he had been reading from a paper in front of him.

"Don't tell me that!" Daven Marcus swore at the black-coated man, shoving him away violently. The man was forced backward but managed to keep his feet. He bowed to the prince apologetically and said something quietly, which Amelia could not hear. She noticed several of the nobles nearby looking shocked by the words, though, and that made Amelia want to smile. If the man was a guildsman at law, then he was sworn by oaths to God and king to always speak the truth about the laws of the land in any official circumstance, such as this one. Watching the interaction, the duchess was sure the counselor had just informed the prince that she was right. Everyone in the room had seen it happen.

Daven Marcus fixed her with his hateful glare again, and Amelia could see he was weighing his options. If he had suddenly drawn his dagger, vaulted the table, and rushed to stab her at that moment, she would not have been the least bit surprised. He wanted her dead and her lands in his grip for good. He'd expected to do that today, but now his own legal advisor was interfering. If he wanted to, he could likely force the issue, have her killed on his order, and defy any Reachermen to oppose him. He'd have his Rhales nobles to back him, but it could still lead to insurrection. He was a self-absorbed popinjay, but Amelia was sure he would recognize the risk he was contemplating.

"You want a trial before my father?" he asked rhetorically, his voice dripping contempt like acid. "So be it. The whole of Denay can watch your execution when he finds you guilty." He looked to the guards holding her arms. "Put her in irons and let her be kept with my horses. She is my prisoner until she is put on trial. I will govern the Reach in her stead. As. Is. My. Right."

Before she could say another word, the two guards lifted Amelia by the arms and marched her from the tent, her feet dangling under her so that her toes rarely touched the damp ground. They carried her past the Rhales courtiers and then the Reacher nobles, and she hung her head, tired and ashamed. She had preserved her life only at the price of her dignity. She still held the title, but in all other ways she was no longer duchess.

Now she was just a prisoner, no better than a convict.

CHAPTER 42

"There was nothing we could do about it," Aiden, the leader of the riders who were supposed to be under Prentice's command said, shrugging his shoulders. "We come back in to find the baron's men sieging you and they just started giving us orders. There weren't nothing we could say."

Prentice nodded, accepting the man's explanation. He had hoped the riders had gone west to the prince's march to report to the duchess. Prentice was sure that if Duchess Amelia had learned they were besieged, she would have done something to help. Instead, the riders who were supposed to be messengers between himself and his liege lady had been dragooned by Baron Liam to search the nearby hills and bring any peasants or refugees they found into the little village he forced to support his siege.

"We did some good, I'd wager," the lanky rider went on. "Lots of folks had seen Fallenhill burn, or at least the smoke, and had gone to ground, fearful. They welcomed us when we said we came from a baron who offered protection. 'Course he ground 'em under his heel to feed his knights, but that's not out of the ordinary for low-born folk, even here in the Reach. And subject to your own lords is still better than being slaughtered by your enemies."

Prentice couldn't argue with that.

"The duchess thanks you," he said formally, showing the signet on his finger.

Aiden nodded acceptance.

"How are your men?" Prentice went on. "Are they needing payment?" After nearly a whole season of deprivation, the one thing he had to offer folk was silver. It seemed like even that would not last long, though, not after Liam's heavy-handed government of the lands around Fallenhill.

"My men an' me, we live off the land, mostly," Aiden said, shaking his head. "We can wait to the end of the season for our pay."

After gathering all the free settlers around that he could, Liam had promised them silver for their food and other services, but he had none of his own to pay with. He'd planned to pay with Prentice's coin once he took the town, it seemed. So, every peasant and trader in the siege camp had a debt of guilders already owed to them. They were reluctant to offer up their goods and services until that was paid, since Liam had incurred the debt in the duchess's name. If Prentice wanted to govern by the same name, the debt fell to him. It was going to drain his little coffer, and swiftly. Aiden said he had an answer for that problem, which was why he was leading Prentice off to a small tent and wagon sitting apart from the rest of the peasant settlement.

It was dark, the second night since the convicts had conquered the knights in an assault that every reputable military manual would have described as suicidal. In the past two days Prentice had slept no more than an hour a night, administering a vast number of tasks. Knights and men-at-arms taken prisoner were stripped of their weapons and armor, and others were detailed to collect any spare arms. It was surer to pay a bounty rather than opt for straight confiscation, so he found himself spending his silver hand over fist.

The positive consequence of that was that virtually every convict had coin to buy from the freemen and traders. He'd had only one incidence of theft he'd had to deal with. Transported convicts were officially already under suspended death sentences, so Prentice had no choice but to hang two men who'd been caught robbing a farmwife. The two had danced from the Fallenhill walls, reminding him of the bodies that had hung there in the summer after the invaders had burned the city. Nonetheless, he was astonished at how accepted his actions were. The rest of the convicts looked at the bodies with a sense of stoic acceptance.

"Why steal when you don't have to?" seemed to be the question most posed to explain the thieves' fate. "Some fools are too stupid to live."

The harsh discipline also helped with the freemen, who were consoled that criminality would not be tolerated, and they became even happier to trade with Fallenhill's no longer besieged populace. The captured knights were imprisoned within the walls, and the weather was still cold and wet so there was little to fear of convicts escaping, especially as they were still weak from prolonged hunger. Inside and outside, the walls were merging into one reasonably peaceful settlement.

Nonetheless, Prentice still carried his purloined spear with him and was watchful for further treachery. The resentment that had prompted Donnen's rebellion might be asleep, but he was sure it wasn't dead, not yet. So, he was fully alert and watchful as Aiden led him aside from the rest of the settlement in the dark of night.

"These are mining guild folk," Aiden told him as they rounded the single wagon and came upon a small campfire and a lone tent. "Silvermen mostly, but some iron-breakers as well."

Seated around the fire were about a half dozen men, all broad-shouldered, with corded, muscular limbs. They wore sleeveless leather tunics to a man, as if it were a uniform. Their fire barely lit their faces so that their eyes were shadowed, and in his watchful state, Prentice hesitated to get too close to them. If they turned out to be hostile, he wanted to be free to run. Alone, there was no chance he could fight them off if they wanted to take him.

"You the leader?" one of the men asked when Aiden introduced them. Prentice nodded, but that wasn't enough. "You got the proof?"

Prentice held the duchess's signet out for them to see. The one who questioned him leaned in and seized his hand. The man's grip felt rough as uncut stone. He studied the signet in the firelight.

"That's the seal alright," he said to his fellows, which made Prentice think he must have worked for some time in the ducal mint, making silver guilder coins. That was where he would have seen the seal so closely that he could confirm it.

"We asked the baron to show us and got a beating for our troubles," the man went on as he released Prentice's hand.

"Weren't fit of him to do that," another man complained. "We're mining guildsmen. We got the right to ask."

"Never mind that," said the first. He looked back to Prentice. "You got her authority?"

"I do."

"Then we need to show you this."

The rough-handed silverman led Prentice to the back of the wagon and pulled back a sheet of oilcloth.

"This is the summer's haul, due for Fallenhill to mint the coins. We figured it weren't right to surrender it, not 'til we heard for sure who was who. There's Rumors the mint was robbed, and it was a renegade knight what did it."

Prentice barely paid the man a moment's attention, instead looking down at a stack of small bricks laid in a false bottom in the bed of the wagon. The wooden lid was pulled back, but it could easily be slid into place to hide the secret compartment. Even in the sparse light, the little blocks glittered, and they were cold to his touch. His fingertips stroked their surface, and he felt rather than saw the seal etched into their surfaces, the mirrors of the seal carved into the ring on his finger, the seal of the Western

Reach, the rampant lion. They were trade bars, silver ingots, mined and smelted in the hills north of Fallenhill. They were the duchess's by right, and thus were Prentice's to disperse as he saw fit once he held the royal tax back. He couldn't help but smile. The compartment in the back of the wagon contained more than double the value of silver he already had from the duchess. He'd be able to pay and feed and train every one of his men, plus the mercenaries, the riders, and every farmer and tradesman still owed anything in the growing settlement.

"Do you have iron ore? Or bars?" he asked the miners.

They nodded.

"Some," they said. "No ore, but bars."

"Close this up and stack the iron bars on top," Prentice told them. "Then we'll get this wagon inside the walls straight away. Up to the ruins of the keep."

"Straight into the mint?" asked the silverman.

"Is that where it was? It's burned out now, but we've set our smithy there, and it's the most secure space we have. If we bring in a wagon of iron bars, it will look like we're just delivering more for making weapons. No one will suspect otherwise."

"A goodly plan."

Half an hour later, nearing midnight, Prentice escorted the wagon through the gates of Fallenhill. The guards on the gate greeted him and assured him everything was quiet inside. After weeks of near starvation, and suddenly with money to hand and folk to buy from, his men had indulged themselves heartily. Most of his convicts and other charges were either sick or passed out from drink. The only ready movement in the whole encampment was a swift run from the huts to the slit trenches, and at any moment there were a dozen or more making that journey, hands clutched to painful stomachs. In spite of the weather, the continuing cold, most were at peace, and if not comfortable, at least more relaxed than they had been since Liam's men had arrived at the end of autumn. Prentice knew that this was the exact time that an enterprising convict would seize to make his escape, but he couldn't find the strength in himself to be too concerned about it. Come the morning, he'd send Aiden and his men out again to hunt any escapees.

Right now, he needed to sleep.

After guiding the wagon to the smithy, he woke Yentow Sent and quietly explained the reason he was disturbing the master smith's precious sleep. Sent was proud and difficult, but Prentice was confident that the man's honesty was scrupulous, at least as much as the guild miners who'd brought the bullion. All had too much pride to lose to crass greed for silver, at least as far as Prentice could tell. It made him smile. The highborn imagined they were the only ones in all the Grand Kingdom with honor to lose or gain, but they were wrong. Honor, dignity, and reputation had different forms to men and women of different birth, but everyone experienced them.

Prentice shuffled his exhausted way back to his hut, barely able to keep his feet under him. He was nearly there when he was accosted by someone waiting for him in the shadows. Fatigue dimmed his thoughts, as well as every survival reflex, so that by the time he realized it might be a threat, he could see it was only Righteous, waiting to speak with him. She had a lit candle that she'd been hiding with a blanket that she'd wrapped around her shoulders against the cold.

"Hi there, old man," she said with her usual flippancy, but in the dim light there was something uncertain in her expression. Prentice prayed inwardly that she hadn't brought him another problem to deal with because he could not do it, not without some sleep first.

"Cold night to be out," he said, hoping she might take the hint.

"I needed to talk to you."

"Alright, follow me."

"No," she said, shaking her head. "Out here. I need to do it out here."

That made him more watchful, birthing a tension in his tired mind. He looked about to see if there was anyone he could call for help if he needed to. Under other circumstances, he would trust his own skill and power, even against Righteous's considerable expertise, but feeling as he did, he didn't exactly favor his chances one on one, even with his spear to hand.

"What do you want to talk about?" he asked, hand twisting around the long wooden haft in the darkness. Righteous stared at him for a moment and then looked away. It was so hard to read her expression in the candlelight.

"I hate you sometimes, you know?" she said.

"Only sometimes?" he joked, hoping to lighten the mood. It did not seem to work.

"I was happy enough to go out hunting with you when you came to the women's hut," she explained. "It was sweet bringing the ambushes back on their own heads. That was real fine. But then..."

She paused and drew in a breath. Prentice tried to understand what could be troubling her, but his thoughts were dragging like footsteps through deep mud.

"Why do you do fool things like you do?"

"What are you talking about?"

"Challenging Donnen? Fighting him with a daft stick?"

"I had a quarterstaff," Prentice began to protest, but she cut him off.

"That's just a daft long stick! You gave him a bloody sword—one of Yentow Sent's special master blades. Damn thing's probably sharp enough to shave a baby with, and you just handed it to him. He could have had your head off with a single stroke."

"I didn't hand it to him, I left it on the ground..."

"Stop arguing, old man!"

Prentice blinked. He was fairly certain now that Righteous meant him no harm, but he still didn't understand any point she was trying to make. Whatever it was, it was important to her, but his mind could not puzzle it out.

"Look, Righteous, I'm tired. I imagine you are as well. Whatever this is, why not leave it for the morning. I swear, I will listen to you then."

She shook her head, looking half resolute and half panicked.

"No, I have to do this now. If I don't, then I might not...I mean, like as not..."

Prentice could feel his features twisting into a frown, and his patience was running truly dry. He needed to sleep. He was about to dismiss her when she suddenly threw aside the candle and surged forward, crossing the distance between them, and wrapping her arms around his neck. He flinched, fearful that it was an attack after all.

And then she kissed him.

Right on his mouth.

It was that kind of desperate, all-or-nothing kiss born of passion or hope. She held herself to him for a long moment while he tried to puzzle out what was happening. A delayed instinct in his mind told him to hold her in return, but before he could, she broke the kiss as suddenly as she had begun it and stepped back. The stub candle had guttered as it fell on the wet ground, and now he couldn't see her face at all. Before he could say anything, she turned and fled into the night.

"What the hell was that?" Prentice muttered to himself, though even as the words left his mouth, another thought rose in his mind to surprise him. "Not unwelcome, though. Huh!"

He considered going after her, but the ache of his weary limbs said no. Even as he shook his head in disbelief at what he'd just experienced, his skull throbbed with an insistent fatigue headache.

In the morning, he told himself. Assuming I remember. And assuming this wasn't just another odd dream. If this was prophetic, then God or his angel lion had a questionable sense of humor. He staggered around to the entrance to his barracks and pushed through the leather curtain into the relative warmth inside. When he awoke in the morning, he had no memory how he had made it from the door to his mattress. He was sure he'd just collapsed as soon as the curtain flapped down behind him.

CHAPTER 43

Amelia shivered as she sat upon straw on the ground. The improvised prison to which the prince had constrained her was little more than a rude shed, hammered together from rough-cut boards and used to shelter Daven Marcus's horses. The prince's guards dragged her here where a blacksmith was waiting with a set of fetters and manacles to place on her wrists and ankles. Then, they chained her to one of the corner posts of the building.

That had been days ago—how many, she wasn't sure she remembered correctly but at least five. There were no windows, and even though the little shed let light in through its many cracks, not to mention every winter wind that blew, the overcast days were frequently so dark that it was hard to tell when the sun rose or set.

At times, the duchess remembered how miserable she had thought living in a tent had been, and that made her smile grimly. That woman, the woman she had been only a week previously, had not begun to imagine misery. She realized that now. Hugging her legs to her in the straw, dreaming of nothing so much as a little fire to warm herself by, Amelia wondered at Prentice and Turley and all the years they had survived winters like this. They'd had it even worse, though, because her clothes were at least in good order. Convicts dwelt in rags.

"I will endure," she told herself, and her teeth chattered as she did.

The first night she had managed to reach out and unhook a horse blanket from where it hung on the wall and wrapped herself in that. Every morning she was brought a bowl of oat gruel and a cup of water by a man she took for a steward. He never spoke a word to her, but he wore a doublet in royal red. On the third morning, he had come with Lord Robant. The vile nobleman had observed her disinterestedly and then instructed the steward to take the blanket from her. Then the next morning, no food had come, and Amelia began to lose track of the days.

She slept fitfully because of the cold, even burrowing into the noisome straw, but with nothing else to do, boredom quickly became her worst torment. A book, that was what she longed for, though it made her chuckle to herself that if she had one, she'd much rather burn it for warmth than read it for a distraction.

Lying half asleep in a cold darkness she was sure was probably still nighttime, there came an unexpected sound of activity beyond the wooden walls. There were guards on the outside, she knew. She could see their shadows moving, hear their feet shuffling. Whoever they were, they were disciplined men under strict orders. They never once answered any of her questions or requests, and they never spoke with each other in her hearing. This time, though, someone was speaking to them from a distance, insisting upon something. Amelia tried to listen, but whoever it was spoke quietly, and she found it too hard to concentrate.

Then the door to the shed opened and lamplight poured in. Amelia blinked and lifted her head, trying to see who carried the lamp. Whoever they were, their breath misted in the chill air, and that sight reminded her of how cold she was. Two figures rushed forward, and as her eyes adjusted to the new light, the duchess realized that one of them was Earl Derryman, who now crouched in front of her, his features full of compassion. He was dressed in a heavy, woolen coat with a fur trim, and as she watched, he pulled it from his body and threw it around her shoulders. The material was so thick that the weight of it actually made her groan a moment.

"Good God," Derryman muttered. "She's a block of ice. The wine man, pour her a cup, and ready a bowl for that soup."

There was a sound of liquid pouring, and Amelia felt a brass goblet pressed between her fingers. She was urged to drink, while nearby the second man, obscured behind Lord Derryman, took the lid from a second container and a steaming, savory aroma filled the shed, mixing with the smell of rotting straw and old dung. Despite the foul concoction of stench and flavor, Amelia found her stomach growling with hunger. She sipped at the wine and felt it burn down her throat.

"I had it spiked with brandy," the earl said, as if reading her thoughts about the heady drink. "Sip it."

Amelia did as she was bid, holding the cup to her lips. From behind Derryman, the second man emerged, holding a clay bowl of something steaming hot. The sight of warm food cheered her, but nothing like the sight of the man bringing it to her—Turley, upright and hale, exactly as the prophetess had promised. She smiled with chattering teeth that rang painfully against the goblet between her lips, which caused her to pull back from the discomfort like a wounded animal.

"Maybe best if you let me do this for you, Your Grace," Turley said to her, and he fetched out a spoonful of the soup, feeding it to her like he would feed a child. Too weak to be shamed, Amelia let him, enjoying each spoonful as it slid into her stomach. Her strength slowly returned as she ate, and soon, as the two men fussed over her like a sickly niece, her thoughts became stronger and more active. She noticed Turley's scars, especially on the hand that fed her. As he drew the spoon back after a mouthful, she reached up and touched that hand. Half of the thumb was missing.

"Oh that?" said Turley, almost apologetic. "Damnedest thing. They broke my finger up but good when they set on me. The bruises turned black and the chirurgeon, he said for sure the rot was in them. They stank like rotten meat. Then, one morning I woke up and they were all good. The black and the smell was gone. They unwound my bandages and three little lumps dropped out. Top of my thumb on this one and the tips of two fingers on the other.

"And that was that. By noonday I was up and about, right as rain. I tell you, Your Grace, Bellam didn't heal up half this fast, and he was no ways as bad as I was."

"By God, man," Earl Derryman muttered, though he didn't sound too angry. "You are too familiar."

Turley tugged his forelock in deference.

"A miracle," Amelia said.

"With respect, Your Grace, you'd be best not saying so in the hearing of any sacrists," Turley counseled. "They don't like the thought of the Almighty bestowing miracles on men of low cunning like myself."

The duchess smiled and, feeling much revived, she took the bowl and spoon for herself and finished it off. When she was done, she looked to them in the lamplight.

"Why am I still here?" she asked.

Earl Derryman looked truly embarrassed by the question.

"It has taken this long for the prince to accept our petition, even just to bring you these tiny comforts."

"You both petitioned the prince?" she asked, astonished at the idea that Turley might have been given an audience with Daven Marcus.

"Not we two," Derryman responded, looking at Turley with the same surprise the duchess felt. "We, the Reach, Your Grace."

"The Reach?"

"Every Reacher noble on the march," the earl explained. "All have written, or signed by seal, letters to the prince. And many have sought audience with him; some have demanded it even."

Amelia stopped eating to think about the earl's words. She was in chains awaiting trial for treason, and the Reach was petitioning the prince for her comfort. How could that be?

"We adore you, Your Grace," Derryman went on, perhaps seeing her confusion. "You are Marne's widow, and his strength is in you. We can all see it. He was my best friend in all this life. Only my wives were dearer to me. A moment in your company and I would know you had been his wife."

"But no one came to me," Amelia protested. "They were all so distant."

"We thought you had turned your back on us. Forgive me, Your Grace, but we watched you chase the prince and his wooing, such as it was. And you had us all held at bay."

"What do you mean? I never..."

"Your ladies, your handmaid, and your companion. None of us knew how to approach the countess, since she was so obviously dallying with the prince. But whenever we went to your maid, she disdained us so thoroughly that we thought you had ordered her to it."

"My maid?" Amelia could scarcely believe what she was hearing. Kirsten had been approached by Reach nobles seeking audience and she'd refused to pass their messages to her. For how long? Even as she thought about it, Amelia knew it was true. Kirsten wanted to go to Rhales. She wanted her mistress to take a place among the highest nobility and forsake the Reach, disdaining it as a frontier backwater. She wanted her mistress to rule in absentia, so the prince's attentions must have thrilled Kirsten to the core, even with their brutal cruelty. The thought that she would be handmaid to a princess was irresistible. That was a pathway to high nobility in itself.

The duchess shook her head.

"I have been outwitted by people I took for granted."

The earl ducked his head to avoid her eyes and spare her shame. Turley only shrugged his shoulders and grinned at her.

"I never knew, Your Grace," he said. "I'd 'a been swift to tell you if I did, I swear."

"I know."

"He is your loyal man, Your Grace," Derryman added. "The rumors spread about you and him put us all aback, but in recent days I have seen his righteous devotion. He's nothing like the rogue we feared, for all that he is forgetful of his station."

"You are too kind, My Lord," said Turley and he half turned to tug his forelock for the earl. Derryman sighed with exasperated affection, much like the emotion Amelia herself felt for him, and she wondered at just how much goodwill Turley had engendered so swiftly. Was he really that charming? Perhaps she should have sent him to woo the Countess. He might actually have done it. That thought made her smile a moment, but then her thoughts returned to the earl's story.

"If the Reach thought I was turned from them and the rumors about me were so base, what changed them, My Lord?"

"You did, Your Grace. When you offered that feast and announced you had executed the men who'd poisoned the duke, in that moment we loved you. You acted for us, as one of us. Then the prince arrived, wearing that..." Derryman's voice trailed off in disgust. He surprised Amelia by suddenly hawking and spitting into the straw.

"That insulting livery?" he continued. "To call us cowards. We who have fashioned the Reach by sheer will and the sweat of our brows. And we had just driven the invaders, the Redlanders, away. Late to the fight and he called us cowards to our faces. Many wondered at that. They thought that was your true reason for holding the feast, that moment. They thought you agreed with the prince."

"I never..." she protested.

"But you never objected," Derryman returned, his passion for his story overpowering his usual deference for her station.

How could I object? Amelia thought. Daven Marcus was the prince. Didn't they see she'd been doing what she could to stop him?

"Then Wolden was slain for your honor, and the prince wouldn't let us wait a day for his funeral. His blood makes him prince, but he is a cur by his deeds."

Amelia nodded slowly. Earl Derryman was a man of honor and dignity. He respected rank at every turn, as every Grand Kingdom noble was expected to. For him to insult the prince, even in private, reflected the depth of his indignation.

"You still have not said why the Reachermen have rallied for me, Earl."

"It is as I said. And you drew us to you when the prince charged you with treason."

Amelia shook her head in disbelief. How could being called a traitor win her loyalty? Earl Derryman smiled.

"Daven Marcus is crown prince, a prince of the blood, but Reachermen, no matter their status, judge by more than blood. We judge by deeds. That is why we allowed for Marne to marry you without too much fear, and we were vindicated when he was taken from us. Whatever your blood, Your Grace, you have lived every day as our duchess. We could have asked for no better. Even when you put convicts off the chain, some wondered at that, but your judgement is sound. This one..." Derryman slapped Turley on the shoulder. "I wish I'd ever had a hunting hound with his mix of cunning and loyalty."

If Turley objected to being compared to a dog, it didn't show.

"And your man Prentice? I know the true story of the Battle of the Brook. I only thank God there was a man like him there. If a prince has to fall, then let flowers like the Ash rise, watered by his blood."

Even Turley looked surprised by that assertion.

"You don't believe Baron Liam was the hero of the Brook?" Derryman scoffed.

"He's got knights from Rhales fooled and Daven Marcus as well. But Reachermen keep their own counsel, and we know who brought back the Horned Man's head. Even if we had doubts of that, Liam showed his true colors when he struck you, and Daven Marcus showed his by pardoning him. But your man Prentice, he broke the baron's jaw, standing over your body. We count him a Reacherman, true despite his meanness."

That wasn't quite how it happened, but Amelia was pleased the essential facts of Liam and Prentice's confrontation were being put about, despite the baron's lies.

Derryman was coming to the conclusion of his story. "But to the point, Your Grace, when you finally stood up to the prince, your maid, and Baron Liam, all at once, and with such passion, we saw that we hadn't lost you after all. Daven Marcus has us wandering the west in winter. The cold weakens our bones, and the distance empties our purses. Even the halest of men are taking chills, living in a tent in winter. A fool's errand. And Daven Marcus fusses over his godforsaken cannons, whining all the time that he needs convicts to help push them—a campaign held up by devices without honor and the want of men of the same cloth to drag them into place.

"And Liam? Like a whining dog, always at Daven Marcus' heels, begging more men be sent back to capture Prentice. Everyone can see the siege he speaks of is just an excuse for his revenge. Your man shamed him, and his face will never heal because of it. He doesn't care one whit about the Reach.

"The prince has us wander in the west, sickening and weakening while he plays at crusade. Liam plots revenge with selfish obsession, and your own handmaid betrays you, and us, for the hand of Lord Robant. But you, Your Grace—you have never betrayed us. You marched north with Mercad in Duke Marne's name for the honor of his memory. You returned to Dweltford and had the traitor Duggan executed for his crimes. Then you set your man to hunt out the duke's murderers to make an end of them. And at the last, you sent him north with every hand of labor you could to rebuild Fallenhill and to heal your wounded land.

"You are our duchess, and we love you."

Tears rolled down Amelia's dirt-smeared cheeks. All her efforts had not been in vain. She had been noticed, had been seen. They understood what she was doing, finally. Her eyes met the earl's, and they shared a moment of unguarded affection, with none of the barriers of duty and station between them. Then Derryman remembered himself and he coughed, looking away. As he did, the full impact of Amelia's current condition reasserted itself.

"And to see you chained in this hovel? It is an indignity too far!"

He pushed himself to his feet and stepped away into the shadows, perhaps to get control of his feelings again. Amelia looked to Turley in his absence and found his expression as full of affection, though mixed with the usual roguish gleam in his eye.

"Why am I still here?" she whispered to him.

"You demanded to be tried by the king, they say, Your Grace," Turley explained.

"But that was days ago. Why does the prince still wait here?"

"He's not leaving until he takes the tower and the pier in the sea."

"He hasn't done that yet?" Amelia could scarcely believe it. "I thought it was a simple tower with a single wall?"

She knew she was no expert on military matters, but the war manuals she had forced herself to read described actions against such fortifications. It should have been a simple matter for the army the prince had at his disposal. Sheer numbers should have told the tale.

Why did he delay?

"He wants to bring every cannon to bear," said Derryman from the shadows.

Amelia shook her head; she didn't understand his point.

"The causeway can take the weight of the bronze dragons, but it's too narrow for more than one to be positioned to fire at a time. That's not enough for the boy playing at soldiers. He has ordered a new extension built to the causeway across the marsh to place his cannon in a neat row. He wants all of them to fire, so that the supposed Veckander sneak thieves will be 'terrified by the might of the power he wields.'"

Contempt dripped from Earl Derryman's words. It seemed he was not persuaded by the prince's claim that the Redlanders were secretly from the Vec either, which likely meant few of the Reach nobles believed it.

"Building a length of road in a salt marsh? That's work for convicts, but they are all in Fallenhill. The prince won't send for them again because that will mean waiting and, if Baron Liam's story is true, would require sending a portion of his troops back to force the siege, which would result in the death of many, if not most, of the convicts in the first place. Which defeats the purpose."

"Moreover, who amongst us, after being called to a supposed holy crusade by the crown prince, wants to stoop himself to corralling convicts?"

Earl Derryman paused and sighed dramatically.

"So now, instead, every man of the rank of knight or below has been set to the construction. Men who've never held a shovel or an axe in their lives now labor, bare chested, beside ostlers and stewards. And no matter how fast we dig and chop and carry, he insists we work faster."

Amelia looked at Turley, who flashed her a smile.

"I served my turns hauling," he confirmed. "It's not too bad. If it was being done by convicts, there'd be overseers' whips to contend with. Men of birth will labor but won't suffer to do it under threat of a lash."

He winked, but Derryman scowled.

"I should think not. There are limits to even a prince's authority."

"Of course, Lord Derryman," Amelia said, sharing Turley's amusement inwardly but recognizing the affront to the earl's dignity. Quite unexpectedly, she yawned and realized that she was bitterly tired. The food and drink had relaxed her tormented body, and now it wanted to rest. She tried to cover the gesture with her hand, since she would have felt churlish to complain of fatigue while men were being worked to exhaustion to build the prince's folly, but both men noticed, and their eyes were filled with concern.

"The assault must come soon, Your Grace," Derryman consoled her. "Then we will press the prince to return you by road to Denay. I will petition for the right to be your escort as the Reach's next ranking noble. I have undertakings from all the other senior Reacher nobles as well, in case one of them distinguishes themselves in the prince's attack and wins the right to claim a prize. If any of us wins honors in the assault, we will claim the right to be your escort. Then we will get you out of this hovel and bestow you as your dignity deserves. And every man of us will testify at your trial before the king, I swear it to you. You will be home in Dweltford as quickly as can be."

"Assuming the king acquits me."

"He will, Duchess Amelia, have no doubt. His son might be a vain fool, but King Chrostmer is a righteous man and wise."

Amelia was not as confident as the earl, but she was encouraged by everything else she was hearing. Her plan had succeeded after all. She just hoped it would not be too late.

"Will you be able to come again?" she asked. "Perhaps with water and some soap to wash?"

"Of course, Your Grace. I will come every day, unless the prince forbids me, and your man here will be free to serve you now as well."

Amelia smiled in acceptance, but a thought caused her to shake her head suddenly.

"No, Turley, don't come yourself again."

"Your Grace?" Turley's expression made it clear he did not like that order. Derryman did not appreciate it either.

"Lord Robant imagines you dead," she explained. "If you come back and forth, he will quickly learn that you live and are hale and healed. If that happened, he would set his men on you again, I'm sure of it. Better you keep out of sight. Send a maid to me. Any kitchen girl will do."

Since my handmaid is now betrothed to my enemy's henchman.

"That is wise, Your Grace," said Derryman.

The two men made to go, Turley leaving the soup and wine. He gathered up the lamp, which made Amelia think the prince had probably forbidden them to let her keep it. Perhaps he thought she would try to use it to escape, engineering a fire to burn the shed. As the two men turned away, taking the light with them, Amelia called after them.

"My Lord, your coat," she said, beginning to shrug out of the heavy, warm garment. Derryman held up a protesting hand.

"It would be my express honor if you were to keep it, Your Grace."

"You are very kind."

The earl bowed his head, and the two men were almost out of the shed, leaving her in pitch darkness, when she made one last request.

"Perhaps you could send one of my books with the maid, Turley. There's sometimes enough light in the day to read by."

He tugged his forelock before ducking out the door. "I'll see to it, Your Grace."

Finishing the wine and soup in the dark, Amelia was so strangely relieved by the little gesture and mild news that she fell into the deepest, most restful sleep she'd had since the crusade began.

CHAPTER 44

"Can you imagine he would ask for that?"
It seemed Sir Gant clearly couldn't believe the story he was being forced to tell.

"He says he needs it to make the powder," Corporal Felix explained.

Prentice could not help but smile. Every day, new problems demanded new solutions, but the makeshift village Baron Liam had forced into existence provided him with a ready market for many of the goods he needed, and he had silver, more than enough to pay. The weeks since the siege had broken had been mild, at least for rain. No one would starve, and it seemed like most of the folk dragged down from the mountains were happy to stay at least until full spring.

This new problem seemed like it would be simple enough to solve, but having to deal with it was beyond Sir Gant's sensibilities. As a hedge knight, he was already primed to endure many indignities that would make a landed nobleman think twice, but Yentow Sent's latest plan was a step too far, even for him.

"You've dug a slit trench before, surely?" Prentice asked him. "And as a squire you must have shoveled your share of dung."

"Master Sent wants more than just a shovelful of horse droppings," Gant retorted, rolling his eyes. "The man is a catalog of demands. Every day a new problem—oft times many for each day. He insists on a new crucible and men to build it. His current ones are little better than blooms—his words. He says we need to make our own black powder for the serpentines and that we need charcoal burners for that, as well as leavings, so he says."

"Did he tell you how many serpentines he has already forged?" Prentice had given oversight of Yentow Sent's weapon-smithy to Corporal Felix, whom he told to report to Sir Gant. Ostensibly the hierarchy was to enable Prentice to focus on training his cohorts in the field, which was true, but it was also because Yentow Sent was a difficult man to manage, and Prentice had had enough. He wanted someone else to field the Masnian master's insistent demands for a time, especially now that the camp was finally settling into a rhythm.

"He says he'll have forty by the end of the week and a hundred by spring."

That was slower than Prentice wanted. He wanted to train his lions to roar, and that required weapons to practice with, not to mention the powder to fire, which brought them around to Sir Gant's objection.

"I've set charcoal burners from the village to start doing us mounds," Prentice said. "Two are alight already. He'll have the first load in a few days. And then he'll need the saltpeter."

"And you know what that is?" Gant pressed.

"I do." Prentice had learned the making of black powder, at least in principle, during his studies in Ashfield.

"And do you know where it comes from?"

"The royal cannoneers import their powder from the Vec. I know the Vec princes all make theirs in caves in the mountains and the Launcens in the south, where bats live."

"They make it from the droppings," Gant exclaimed in disgust. Felix and Prentice both smiled at the man's discomfort. "And when they can't get that, they make it from other animals' leavings, or men's."

"Well, that should be easy enough. No lack of that here."

Sir Gant's lips twisted further under his moustache. "But do you know the process? What it will take? He wants to farm the damn stuff, fermenting it, it sounds like. And he wants to lay claim to every man and woman's leavings in the whole camp and the village. He wants me to make it a punishable offence to not do one's business in his specific place. He's already marked out some flat ground that he likes for the task."

Prentice smiled at Sir Gant's discomfort. While it seemed odd to make rules about how a man or woman might relieve themselves, if the waste itself could be used, it made sense to do it. And if he wanted to field the number of serpentines he was planning, then he would need all the black powder Yentow Sent could make. That meant all the charcoal they could produce, as well as all the dung, mortal and animal they could gather and extract the saltpeter from.

He put his hand on Gant's shoulder. "It'll be a disgusting business, but I seem to remember a short constitutional you and I took through the sewers of Dweltford. What was it you said? You weren't unfamiliar with the taste of ditchwater?"

"That was different," Gant protested, but with less vehemence. Then he laughed and the other two men laughed with him. "I'm a knight sworn and blooded. How do I let you keep making a gong farmer out of me?"

Prentice shook his head and turned back toward the two cohorts nearby, each of fifty men, as they drilled, forming themselves first into two separate squares, six men by eight, then merging quickly into one square of a hundred, ten men by ten. The drumbeat shifted and the formation changed again to a rectangle, twenty by five.

"It's coming along," said Felix, watching with him.

"It's still too slow, and they get tangled in each other's weapons too often."

"We'll keep them practicing. They'll get it. If the rains hold off like this until spring, you'll see." The corporal gave a salute and stepped away to supervise the maneuver practice as the drums sounded a reset.

"Come on you lot!" he bellowed. "That's 'beat to ranks' they're playing. You've only heard it a thousand times by now! Get back to first station right quick or you'll go without supper tonight!"

Prentice nodded and smiled as men stepped quicker under Felix's tongue lashing. Despite his impatience, the progress was actually quite sound.

"What about the sword work?" he asked, turning to Gant again. As the most skilled swordsman Prentice had, Sir Gant had the duty of training the fangs—the soldiers chosen to wield the sword and buckler combination for the closest fighting. Dividing the men up for each duty had proved to be one of Prentice's easiest tasks. The pikes that Yentow Sent made were twelve feet in length, long enough that when the front rank was fighting, two more ranks behind them could engage the enemy by thrusting over their shoulders. But that was heavy work, reaching the long wooden polearms out to their full length. So, the pikes went to the tallest and the strongest men.

The halberds were only seven to eight feet, but they were heavier and still fought at reach, so they needed strong men for those as well. That left the smallest to wield the sword and buckler, but that had its advantages, too. The fangs would have to fight close, with all the pikes and halberds thrusting around them. That meant small would be an advantage. Nevertheless, they still needed to be taught to fight close, which was another challenge Sir Gant did not enjoy.

"I've cut techniques from the different repertoires my masters taught me, sewing them together in a motley that seems to work," he said to Prentice. A repertoire was a group of moves for a weapon, a set for drilling techniques alone. All knights knew a variety for each of their weapons. Good knights became familiar with the moves that suited them best, then drilled to correct their other deficiencies. The best knights combined other men's repertoires into their own synthesis, expanding the art and correcting old teachers' errors. In a sense, that was what Prentice was asking Gant to do, but not for a knight's weapon—for a blade made like a tool, functional not artful.

"Righteous has some at training right now," Gant went on. "Why not come and see the progress?"

Prentice accepted the invitation but felt a reluctance inside himself. It was over a week since Righteous had kissed him in the dark and he'd barely seen her since. He was sure she was avoiding him, and he was so busy he had no time to do anything about it. And the truth was, he wasn't sure what he wanted to do about it. He wasn't accustomed to being offered unexpected kisses, but whenever a few quiet moments came during the day, he found his thoughts drifting back to the memory of her lips on his.

Gant led the way back inside the walls. The guards on the gate saluted them both and they returned it. Seamstresses had been set under Sent's armorers to start sewing buff coats for the soldiers—heavy, quilted jackets that could absorb lesser cuts and thrusts. It was the cheapest form of armor, but it was effective, and Prentice had ordered that every footman of the militia should at least enjoy that protection, along with his own helmet if it could be arranged. The men on the gate already had their own buff coats, and the uniformity was encouraging. Men in armor felt braver in a fight.

"How are they going, taking instruction from a woman?" Prentice asked as they approached the drill square where men were shuffling back and forth, practice blades clashing on shields as they sparred and learned their craft.

"They liked it about as well as taking instruction from a hedge knight," explained Gant. Prentice could imagine. His trainees were former convicts, men who'd already shown some level of disrespect for the established order. "At first. Then when she got them in front of her with a blade in hand, it only took about half an hour for them to see why you made her a corporal."

"She didn't have to kill any, did she?"

"No, but it took some thick skulls a few good whacks to learn the lesson. And one fool got his cheek opened up. He'll have the scar for the rest of his life to remind him."

They wended their way around the training ground to the other side where Righteous was supervising the sparring. Prentice was surprised to see she was wearing new armor as well. Instead of a buff coat, she had a proper arming doublet, dyed Reach blue, with a rampant white lion on the chest. It wasn't quite the duchess's heraldry, but it was so close it didn't matter. Over the doublet, Righteous wore a steel gorget piece that protected her throat, and attached to it were two spaulders that protected her shoulders and upper arms. The pieces were fitted to each other and her shape perfectly, and the steel was blued so dark it looked almost black.

"Yentow Sent made her the armor himself," Sir Gant said quietly. "It's a fitted panoply, and she paid him extra for the best fixtures. He offered her a breastplate or a brigandine as well, but apparently but she refused. I think she likes to move more freely, doesn't like the weight—too many years fighting half naked in pits."

"Is that what she said?" Prentice asked.

Gant shook his head. "Her exact words were, 'any bastard gets close enough through her guard to make a shot for her heart deserves the best chance', before she guts him."

Prentice smiled. Back when they'd met her, she was hiding as a boy and seemed brash and arrogant, making these wild challenges and daring life to prove her wrong. Now that she was living as a woman, she could be herself, and she was still a wild, defiant creature. It surprised Prentice how much he liked it, now that he didn't have starvation staring him in the face every moment.

"Too slow! Too slow!" Righteous shouted suddenly at one of the sparring pair. "You're not dancing with him! You're trying to cut him. Save flirting for maidens in the harvest festival. Get in there!"

"Problems, Corporal Righteous?" Prentice shouted suddenly, and every eye on the field turned to look at him.

CHAPTER 45

Righteous looked up at Prentice, and even with the ten or so paces separating them, her expression looked uncertain, perhaps even worried. She met his eyes for a long moment, and then her mask of belligerent defiance fell back into place and she all but sneered at him.

"Of course, I've got problems," she shot back. "These big bears are always trying to finish everything with one swipe. I keep trying to tell them that they won't have the time or space for that, that the knight there's fancy repertoire is for learning, not for fighting, but they don't listen. They can't seem to get it through their thick heads."

She slapped the shoulder of the trainee standing next to her.

"This one keeps holding back, waiting for his opening, like he's taking a flag in a tourney duel. They need to learn to make the opening for themselves. This is going to be close, the kind of fighting you want them to do, and slow and strong isn't going to cut it!"

"There won't be a lot of space to dance about, once they've got pikes and halberd behind and beside them," Prentice countered, schooling his face to a stern expression, even though inside he felt strangely happy. It was an emotion similar to the cold calm he felt in the midst of a fight for his life, but warmer, lighter, more enjoyable.

"All the more reason to be quick" Righteous protested, refuting his argument. "No space to play or wait. Straight in, straight out. That's the way."

"I don't think I see it," Prentice continued to argue. "Perhaps you should show me."

He reached out a hand to a nearby trainee, and the man passed him his practice sword and buckler, taking off his leather gauntlets and handing them over as well.

"You know she's right," Sir Gant whispered, leaning in as Prentice forced his hands into the gloves. "What are you doing?"

Prentice looked at him, his back to Righteous.

"Having fun," he said, flashing a quick smile.

Gant blinked in surprise. Prentice wondered if the knight was more astonished by the idea of his captain having fun or that fencing with Righteous would be his chosen form of recreation.

"You know she scars men for life just to make a point?" Gant said quietly.

Prentice nodded and winked. Why did he find the prospect so enticing? "I've got plenty of scars," he told his lieutenant. "One more won't hurt me."

Then Prentice schooled his face again, took up his blade and shield and turned to face Righteous.

"You want a demonstration?" she demanded as he approached. "Is that it?"

"Please."

By this point, all training on the field had stopped, and every man was watching the captain and his corporal as they took up stance facing each other, weapons on point.

"How do you want to do this?" Righteous asked, her eyes slitted in suspicion.

"Treat me like one of your students," he replied lightly. "Teach me your lesson."

She stared at him for a long moment, as if judging for herself whether he was being truthful with her. Then she moved forward, a deft set of steps that pushed her into striking distance, and she opened up a set of attacks. Prentice shuffled back with small steps, deflecting each technique in turn with his sword and little shield. At the last lunge there was a pause as Righteous realized he'd absorbed her full combination and drawn her out of position, making her vulnerable to a counterattack; it never came. She drew back to reset her stance.

"Right," said Prentice. "That's the slow attack you don't want them using. Show us fast, like you want them to do."

Prentice saw his words sting her pride, and a mocking half smile flashed across his lips. She, in turn, saw his expression, and the next attack came with blistering swiftness. Swords were not her weapon of choice, even the slightly thinner, faster blade these men were learning, but Righteous had been a pit fighter for years before being transported west, and that professional experience showed. Prentice felt himself driven back so much harder this time, his own blade flashing and his buckler catching blow after blow. She pressed him so hard that when the point of her blade leaped at his face, it was more by good luck than good technique that he managed to keep both his eyes. As it was, his desperate defense left him open in another quarter, and Righteous rammed her buckler rim-first into his belly. It drove the breath from him, and he doubled over for a moment.

"That's what I mean by fast," she said disdainfully as she turned away.

"Excellent," Prentice gasped as he sucked in air. He pushed himself up from his knees and winced before putting his smile back on. "Again."

Righteous blinked at him. With an angry sneer, she nodded and set herself again. Prentice was barely back in stance when the attacks came on a third time, and this time he counterattacked more reflexively, if only to give himself space.

"See how the captain keeps his buckler out in front of himself," Sir Gant said loudly. "Watch him. Like I've always told you, a buckler's too small to hide behind. It's not a knight's shield. You need to put it out in front, force your opponent to deal with it, not just aim around it!"

At least someone's trying to make a lesson of this, Prentice thought. As far as he was concerned, this sparring was the most fun he'd had since the siege started, and Righteous's face looked about as prideful and indignant as it always did when she was angry. He found it almost irresistibly endearing. The woman trying to all but kill him was the one who'd kissed him not a week before. It was...delightful.

For several more passes, the two of them sparred with an intensity not typical for a mock fight. As Righteous kept up the pressure, Prentice found himself responding with less and less restraint, and his blows were the quicker and surer for it. He even managed to strike her with a thrust directly in the gorget, the practice sword's blunt end ringing on the blued steel. Without that piece of armor, he would have collapsed her windpipe, blunt end or not. With a live blade, it would have been a killing blow straight through the throat.

She responded by catching him on the inner thigh of his lead leg with a stinging slap that a sharp edge would have made into a potentially fatal slash.

"The inside of the thigh is linked straight to the heart," Sir Gant said, continuing his instruction as the fight went on. "Cut a man there and he could bleed out before he even hits the ground. And it's a difficult place to protect with armor. Watch out for it to protect yourselves in battle, and look for the opening whenever you can."

After two dozen passes, Righteous and Prentice had both worked up a light sheen of sweat, even in the chill air. At last, he raised his hand for a pause, his breathing somewhat labored.

"Enough, Corporal," he said. "I see what you mean and think you have taught a goodly lesson, with Sir Gant's excellent tuition, of course."

Prentice looked to the hedge knight to give him a respectful nod, and as he did, he realized that every man standing around was staring, fascinated, at both of them. He looked back to Righteous, and though her face was still cold with anger, she was also breathing hard, and her limbs looked heavier with fatigue. He saluted her with the sword still in his hand, holding the hilt to his heart. It took her a moment, as if she didn't want to return the respect, but at last she put up her salute, and the flat of her blade clanged on the metal of her spaulder. Around them, every man saluted them both, even Sir Gant. Then Prentice dropped his hand and turned away to return his borrowed equipment to its owner. There was a long moment of quiet that Sir Gant ultimately broke with another bellow.

"Alright, you lot. You've seen how it's done, now get to learning it."

Men all around hesitated only a moment before returning to their drills. Righteous stalked between the sparring pairs.

"Oh, for God's sake," she swore, still huffing a little, getting her breath back. "You heard what the knight said. Keep your bloody shield out in front of you."

She pushed one man's hands roughly into the right position and then bade him try again. Prentice watched for a moment more. He gestured to Sir Gant, telling him to stay and help with the training, and then headed off. Even walking away, he glanced over his shoulder at Righteous behind him more than once. She never seemed to be looking his way, but he found himself hoping she would.

He wondered at that and the pleasure he felt at fighting with her. Through every pass and strike, he felt the memory of her kiss on his lips. What did that mean? Prentice had not known many women like her, and certainly none were skilled at fighting in the way she was. The Duchess Amelia had some of the same character Righteous showed under her cloak of bravado, the same steel in her will, but there was a savagery in Righteous, born of the harshness of her young life, no doubt. In his mind she was almost not a woman at all, not a mere woman at least. No, she was like a force of nature, or like divine fury in feminine form. Prentice wasn't sure what all the implications of that were, especially in the context of that late-night kiss, but he found he liked thinking about it.

He had other distractions to focus on for the rest of the day, but every now and then, especially when he felt the bruises Righteous had left on him, all these notions returned to his mind, and he smiled to himself.

CHAPTER 46

Amelia's requested book arrived the next morning in the hands of a serving girl she didn't recognize, along with the promised water, some more clothing, and a small, rough piece of launderer's soap. The girl bobbed and ducked her head apologetically at the sight of the soap.

"There's almost nothing else left," she explained. "Any fine soaps are long used up. Merchants aren't selling none now, not even rough bits like that one. Master Turley says the fine ladies are probably keeping a little back for themselves, or some oils or perfume, but he ain't been able to scare none up. He says to say sorry."

"Thank you," said Amelia. "Tell him he need not waste his time."

The girl nodded. She looked at the duchess's filthy gown under the earl's coat.

"Do you...I mean, My Lady Your Grace, do you need me to help you dress and wash? Steward Turley said I was to offer. I don't have no experience with dressing in a fine lady's manner, but he said to offer, My Lady Your Grace."

The girl was clearly frightened to be with this strange, high-ranking woman in this painfully mean condition. Amelia smiled comfortingly at her and nodded.

"I have two arms and two legs, just like you," she said. "And I wear my skirt and my bodice much the same way you do. I'm sure you'll have no trouble helping, thank you."

The duchess shrugged off her borrowed coat and peeled away the filthy garments underneath. She shivered in the cold air.

"We warmed the water on the fire 'fore I come," the maid explained. "But we'd best hurry 'else you'll catch a chill."

We might already be too late for that, Amelia thought but didn't say it. She had no doubt that night after night sleeping in the straw was doing her health no favors.

Amelia bathed herself, using a rag from the bucket and the coarse soap, while the girl kept her eyes averted, arranging the fresh clothes she'd brought with her.

"What's your name?" the duchess asked.

"Lene's what I'm called, My Lady Your Grace. It's short for Raelene."

"Lene. Raelene. It is a sweet name."

Amelia scrubbed at her fingers, trying to wash the dirt from beneath her nails, and she wondered at Lene's awkward form of address. Turley had no doubt coached the girl to refer to her as "Your Grace," but she hadn't properly understood. Lene had likely never even stood in the presence of someone of Amelia's rank, let alone had to speak with them. When she thought about it, Amelia marveled that there were all these people around her who depended upon her and upon whom she depended, and yet they would never speak to her, would not even know how to do it. The notion fascinated her.

Once she was done washing, Lene helped her dry herself quickly and pull on fresh clothes. They were all simple wool garments without embroidery or too many layers, but they were warm, and she welcomed them.

"Leave the covers," she told Lene, pointing at her leather overshoes as the girl gathered up the discarded garments. "They keep my feet a bit warmer at night."

Lene nodded and bobbed again.

"There's a piece of rye bread there," Lene said just before she left, "wrapped in the same cloth as the book master Turley sent. We tried scaring up some cheese, but it's like hen's teeth these days. I'll come back to bring you some pottage before noonday."

When Lene was gone, Amelia sat down on the rotten straw in the corner of the shed and leaned against the wooden wall to read by the shafts of light that shone in through the gaps. The book Turley had sent was a collection of tales and poems written centuries before. She would much rather have had a book of laws to prepare herself for her trial, but since Turley didn't read, how would he know to pick one from another? The book was distraction enough, and she went back and forth between its verses and her dismal thoughts, waiting for more word from the earl.

She passed four more days that way.

At dawn on the fifth day, her breakfast wasn't brought by Lene but by a lady in fine clothes that were in need of laundering, the unmistakable sign of someone of high birth, fallen in their estate.

"Countess Dalflitch?" Amelia asked, recognizing the woman even before she removed her hood. Early morning light filtered in through the open door behind the countess, and their breaths still misted slightly in the chill. Amelia sneezed suddenly, and with no handkerchief to hand, rubbed her sniffling nose on the cuff of her sleeve. It was a humiliating breach of etiquette in front of the countess, but she was almost past caring.

A few more days of this, Amelia thought, and Daven Marcus won't have to send me to trial. I'll sicken and die right here. Perversely, the thought amused her. If she was to die, she would rather do it denying the prince his final condescension of a trial.

"Have you come to gloat?" she asked Dalflitch quietly, her thoughts of Daven Marcus blurring in her wearied mind with her opinions of the prince's ex-mistress.

"Do not take this amiss," said Dalflitch, placing a steaming pot on the ground between them. "But I am here against my will."

"Truly?"

Amelia took up the wooden spoon from the pot and began to eat the pottage inside, potato and wild grain with a little bit of carrot and turnip for sweetness. It was bland but hot and filling. Seemingly, a few days imprisonment had blunted her tastes to such simple considerations. She consoled herself with the memory that Prentice and Turley had endured years living in conditions far worse than this—nearly two decades worth when you added their time together.

I am the Duchess of the Western Reach, she told herself. *I will endure.*

"Against your will?" she asked between mouthfuls. "On someone's orders?"

"The prince's," Dalflitch confirmed.

"Truly? Are you back in his favors then?"

Dalflitch shook her head sharply.

"It's the sort of thing Daven Marcus thinks is funny. This is his idea of a joke."

Amelia nodded. That made sense. Set his ex-mistress to serve his incalcitrant betrothed. She blinked with fatigue. Were they still betrothed?

"He's too busy with his little siege, I take it?" she asked when her head cleared once more.

"Preparations continue."

"Still? How long until he finally orders the assault? Even the Rhales court must be champing at the bit by now."

Dalflitch gave the duchess a wicked, secret smile.

"His construction works do not proceed smoothly. There's not enough local rock to make the new causeway solid. Engineers from the royal dragons tried to warn him, but he ordered one of his cannons wheeled out before the ground was ready. It slid down the side as the construction collapsed and ended up half buried in the water and soft sand. They have not been able to get it out."

"A lost toy?" Amelia joked, sharing Dalflitch's smile. "The little boy won't like that."

"Tantrums were thrown, Your Grace," the countess nodded. "Or so I hear. I am no longer welcome at court, as you know."

The two women shared the pleasure of Daven Marcus's unhappiness for a moment, but then the countess's expression soured, and she looked away.

"Then there's the business with the old crone," she said, almost under her breath.

"Crone?" Even as she asked, Amelia realized who they were talking about, and a sense of dark foreboding shadowed her already clouded mind.

"They took the old woman from the wood, the one you met with. She was not treated kindly."

"Why?" Amelia asked.

"It's not a pleasant tale, Your Grace."

"Then the longer you take telling it, the worse you'll make it!" Amelia didn't mean to sound so irritable, but her fatigue was working against her. If Dalflitch was offended by the rebuke, she did not show it.

"Men have been cutting the trees to use in making the new causeway," she began. "One morning a day or two ago, the widow was discovered amongst the trees. It's said she looked like a little goblin creature and that she just appeared under the trees."

The duchess nodded. That had been her experience of the little widow.

Dalflitch went on. "The men she appeared to were eager for the prince's approval, and they marched her straight to him. Daven Marcus was not in a good mood to receive her, it seemed. He accused her of being a spy for the Veckanders. She laughed at him, apparently. You and I both know how unwise that would have been."

In her mind, Amelia imagined the little old woman with her otherworldly aspect being presented to the self-important prince. The thought made her smile for a moment, although it also gave her a stronger, darker premonition of what happened. She agreed with Dalflitch; Daven Marcus would not enjoy being laughed at.

"They say that he stood there dumbfounded for a moment. Just to see him at a loss for words, that would have been something," said the countess. "Before he could vent his inevitable rage, it seems she offered him a gift, from a leather bag, of all things."

"A stone, a single pebble," Amelia whispered and Dalflitch nodded.

"Apparently some thought it a trick or a trap, but Daven Marcus showed no fear. He reached straight in and pulled it forth, a rough piece of sandstone, they say. Then the little woman spoke. They say her voice became like thunder and the light was sucked from the room, as if blown forth by a terrible storm."

"She prophesied."

"Indeed. Everyone who heard it trembles to recall the words, but I have asked about from highest born courtier who is still willing to speak with me to the meanest pot boy, who happened to be clearing away plates and cups with a steward, quietly in the back corner. Everyone who was present remembers the same words, and perfectly."

"What did she say?"

Dalflitch swallowed and then looked Amelia straight in the eye.

"That Daven Marcus is the last of his line. That men will flock to him for ancient glory, and he will feed them death and rot. He will be called a king-slayer and a pestilence that lays waste from the ocean to the mountains. With stolen righteousness, he will lay claim to every throne, and he will be cast down by a throne he has claimed but never known. There are other words, but those were the ones that offended the prince most sorely. He crushed the sandstone pebble between his fingers and then they say he stared at the woman, seemingly for an age. Then he fell on her and beat her with his fists.

"It was an horrific assault, it is said. Even his closest entourage speak of being sickened by it. Yet when he was spent, with his hands swollen and his face spattered by her blood, she still lived. She was little more than a bundle of red-streaked rags, so they say, but in the completion of his rage, Daven Marcus ordered her executed as a witch and false prophetess. They tied her to a stake and burned her alive."

Amelia shuddered at the news. She didn't want to, but she found her mind conjured a vivid image of the old widow tied to a post and writhing in the flames.

"So, she is dead."

"But not without one last warning."

"Which was?"

"As she was dying," Dalflitch said, "with the flames already licking her feet, she cried out that the enemy was coming from the west, across the water."

"The Redlanders," said Amelia, nodding.

"That was the name she gave them. She said they would come in ships out of the west in five days' time. And then the war we have feared will have its last prelude. One more winter and the pregnant storm will give birth to the deluge."

"She was quite lucid for a woman dying in fire," Amelia said bitterly. It seemed a heartless thing to say, once she'd spoken, but the countess did not take it amiss.

"If she was only a madwoman playing at being a mystic, then she played the role perfectly through to the last agonized breath."

The two fell to silence then, and Dalflitch knelt before the duchess while Amelia sat eating her pottage. Their mood was grim and dark, suited to the shed and its dim filthiness.

"Did they find her hutch?" Amelia asked as she scraped the last of her meal out of the bowl.

"Hutch, Your Grace?"

"Where the old woman lived. It was a humble little dwelling, nestled in the roots of an ancient fig." Amelia was fascinated to think what a woman who was old when the Grand Kingdom had been born might have collected in her home across the ages of her life.

"I don't think they found any such thing, Your Grace," said Dalflitch, uncertainly. "I could ask about for you, if you wish."

"Perhaps someone could go into the wood to look for it."

"The wood is gone, Your Grace, every tree sacrificed to the prince's siege."

Amelia nodded to herself. It was the perfect metaphor for Daven Marcus's ambitions. He would lay the world waste in pursuit of his desires.

"With your permission, I should go, Your Grace. The prince will have me being watched. I was only set to bring you your food. If I stay too long or give too much comfort, he will take it amiss and I will be punished, I'm certain of it."

"You have my leave then, Countess, and I thank you for your visit," said Amelia. She was surprised to realize that she was not merely being polite. While she could not trust the countess not to turn on her again should the advantage be offered, at this moment, when they both enjoyed the prince's disdain, it was nice to have someone with whom she could speak openly. This was the handmaid friendship she had longed for. What a pity she'd had to sink to this point to find it.

The countess recovered her feet and was brushing bits of straw from her skirt when an unexpected thought occurred to Amelia.

"Five days?" she muttered.

"Your Grace?"

"The widow said five days as she was dying. When was that?"

"The day before last, Your Grace."

"Then dawn, two days from now is the day she prophesied."

"Indeed, it is, Your Grace."

"I wonder what will happen, if anything?"

Dalflitch nodded soberly.

"I think the whole court wonders that, Your Grace," she said as she left. "Only Daven Marcus has no fear, I would hazard a guess."

CHAPTER 47

"This is them," said Yentow Sent.

The Masnian handed Prentice a pair of short steel bars, like chisels, but far more precious. On one end the bars were worn and splayed by repeated hammer strikes, but on the other end they were cut in complex patterns. One had a crown on the end, the other tool had a man's head and the name of King Chrostmer. These were coin stamps of the royal mint. Little discs of silver would be hammered by each stamp, once on each side, to be turned into guilders, the official currency of the Grand Kingdom.

"Where did you find them?" Prentice asked.

"Exactly where the silver miners said they would be, in that part of the keep, buried under the ash and fallen wood from the floors above. We found four full pairs and one crown stamp by itself. Its partner is lost to the fire."

Prentice nodded. When the miners mentioned the old mint had been contained in a corner of the fallen keep, he had ordered Yentow Sent to have the area searched. There were only two mints in the Grand Kingdom, both located near sources of silver, and these stamps could only be possessed by those with the royal warrant. For a peasant to be caught even holding them was a death sentence, and any attempt to steal them or use them illegally would lead to the perpetrator's entire family being condemned and convicted, all their wealth and possessions forfeited to the crown. Whatever else happened, Prentice could not leave these lying around to be found. And now that he had them, he could begin minting his own coin under the duchess's authority.

"Do you wish to have my men searched?" asked Sent. When Prentice gave him a puzzled look, the smith shrugged and explained. "Perhaps one of them became greedy and stole the missing stamp for himself?"

"One stamp wouldn't do him much good."

"Any of my journeymen could easily use the one as a model to make its partner. Even if not, greed alone makes fools of men. I would not have any suspicions hanging over my workshop."

Prentice thought about the offer. Even if he did as Sent proposed, there would be no point. If they were trying to thieve the last stamp, they could have it hidden anywhere by now.

"You have always been scrupulously honest in all your doings, master smith," he told Yentow Sent. "I will not repay that virtue with insults now."

The compliment seemed to meet Sent's need, and he bowed.

"So, how much longer until we have all our swords and serpentines forged?"

Sent sniffed indignantly.

"I could have my men throw pig iron at you all day, if you are in a rush. Quality weapons take time, I have told you this."

"We need to teach men how to use the serpentines," Prentice objected. "And the fangs need to learn to care for live blades. A little corrosion isn't the end of a practice steel, but a live blade, a quality blade, needs care. You know this."

Prentice hoped the Masnian didn't realize the extent to which he was trying to play to his pride.

"I appreciate your concerns, Captain, but they are not mine. My concern is to ensure that only worthy steel leaves my workshop. That will always remain paramount."

Prentice sighed and nodded. He handed the stamps back to Sent.

"See these bestowed with the rest of the silver bars. I know you can't spare any journeymen to act as coin minters, but maybe some of the new workers might be right for the duty."

"If you can trust them."

Since the lifting of the siege, Prentice and the remaining mercenaries, those who'd not joined in Donnen's mutiny, had finally had a chance to march and drill all the male convicts. From the nearly two thousand he'd had initially, after deaths and winter's sickness, only about fifteen hundred had been suitable for military duty. The rest—some crippled, some too old or too weak—Prentice sent to work about the various chores and tasks that normally fell to convicts. They weren't put back on chains, but pains were taken to make it clear that if they ran, if they fled their service, or if they were even found somewhere they didn't belong, their lives were forfeit.

"There will be a standing bounty of fifty silvers to any Reacherman who takes the head of an escaped convict," he'd told them. That made them unwilling to take too many risks with their time.

Now they labored to improve the huts, when the weather allowed, as well as continuing to clear away the debris of Fallenhill. A hundred or so had been given over to Yentow Sent, and they toiled for him, doing every menial chore he could devise, so that even his apprentices did almost nothing but work the forge. Fetching and carrying, digging the saltpeter pits, building roofs to keep the rain off them, breaking down the existing crucibles and rebuilding them better—all these tasks fell to the convicts. The workshop area was an anthill of activity as the Masnian master's limitless energy plotted new developments in his little empire. Sent was already sorting among his laborers, looking for some that might make possible apprentices.

"You want me to supply your army indefinitely, I assume?" he'd said. "That will need new apprentices and new journeymen. I'm sure I can find one or two nuggets among you northerners. You can't all be dross."

That made Prentice smile when he remembered it.

"Maybe you can set one of your nuggets to learning to mint coins."

"And lose a possible apprentice? Coin minting only needs a hammer and a simple mind that does not get bored."

"Well, you surely have a couple of them."

"More than enough."

Prentice cocked his eyebrow, and after a moment's resistance, Sent took the hint.

"Very well," he said with another sigh. "I will choose a meathead with an honest streak and ask one of your silvermen to explain the minting of coin to him. I am sure they will be able to teach one of them to swing a hammer and press a stamp into a silver, especially for coins as ugly and simple as your northern fish scales."

"Good man."

Prentice clapped the smith on the shoulder and ignored his sour frown. Leaving the workshop, he kept an eye on the men digging the saltpeter pits. One pit was already completed, with a multi-layered wooden roof that did a very effective job keeping the rain off. Yentow Sent insisted it would be yielding saltpeter as soon as spring, and gong farmers had been appointed to manage the pits. Prentice pitied them the smell they had to work with. It wasn't as foul as the sewers under Dweltford had been, but with the entire camp under instruction to do their business here, it was still a disgusting duty. Prentice had given orders that these men were to have their own baths and priority at every meal. If they had to suffer, he would make it worth their while.

Past the pits, he walked the now well-worn path back to the huts. As he crossed a grassed hummock that had once been someone's backyard wall, he saw Righteous sitting down behind the women's hut. Her strawberry blonde hair was growing longer, and she was attacking it with a bone comb with the same ruthless efficiency she showed every time she pulled a dagger on someone.

"Now you look more like a girl," Prentice said, and she started, wincing as she did. Not wearing her steel gorget, she reached up and rubbed her neck.

"Dammit, old man!" she pouted. "I'm still sore from that hit you gave me. It fair whipped my head right back."

"Would have killed you without your armor."

Instead of acknowledging the truth of Prentice's words, Righteous sneered and looked away, flipping her hair over the side of her face to obscure her eyes from his as she continued combing.

"Is there something you wanted?" she asked.

"I wanted to speak with you about something."

"Oh?"

"About Tressy, in fact."

"Oh," she said, apparently trying to sound disinterested, but there was an unmistakable hint of disappointment in her voice. Prentice didn't need to see her expression to hear it. "What did you want to say? And why not say it to her?"

Prentice ignored her questions, though he heard the sullenness in her tone. Clearly Tressy was not the subject she wanted to talk about. He went on, regardless.

"I was thinking that I'd not thanked her for her help with Donnen's crew," he explained. "You've taught her well enough, and while I'd rather your steel beside me than hers, her assistance was invaluable."

If Righteous heard his compliment for her in his words, she didn't show it.

"When I started showing her short knife cuts, she just practiced them every hour of the day," she said, "like she was afraid every man around her was going to be the next rapist coming for her in the night. Then she stopped being afraid and became angry. Sometimes when I drill with her at night, she puts me on my heels now. A proper pit fight, she'd get taken apart by a technique fighter, but you seen her when she's got them by surprise. She's a right little mongrel's bitch." Righteous turned to look at him. "You want to tell her thank you," she went on. "You don't need me for that."

"Does she sew?"

Righteous was surprised. Prentice had something particular in mind.

"You mean embroider and what not?" she asked, shaking her head. "I guess, but I ain't really seen. She grew up in her uncle's house, she says. He was a carder, so she sure learned to spin wool and weave. Maybe she sews as well."

"Perfect," said Prentice, and Righteous cocked her eyebrow. "She asked me to give her a new name, remember?"

"I remember."

"Well, she earned one that night, for sure. Tell her Spindle."

"Spindle?"

"That's right, Spindle." Prentice nodded and smiled. "Happy at home, something any goodwife would know, but sharp enough to kill if needs be. Tell her that to me she will always be Spindle Tress."

Righteous's expression softened for a moment. "She'll like that," she said softly. Then her eyes narrowed again. "Why don't you tell her?"

"Because you are the one who trained her. It is your right."

Righteous nodded and looked away again. A taut silence stretched between them. From the wall, a call between two guard points echoed through the air, and a breeze made a low, whisper as it ran through the grass and weeds. Prentice looked down at Righteous, and she kept looking away. A group of women rounded the corner, chatting, and the sudden disturbance made Righteous jump again. Prentice watched the women go and then looked back at her.

"Was there something else you wanted to say?" she demanded.

"Yes, actually," he said, and he sat down next to her.

She pulled back slightly, as if she were a skittish animal. Her face was hard as stone, and she sucked her teeth and sneered at her own words. "I understand, you know! I'm not a complete fool."

"How's that?" he asked, taken by surprise.

"I see what you're doing here. I see what we're about. I'm not a little girl!" she insisted vehemently. "You've been keeping the things cold between us, and it's that kiss. I'm not a fool! You don't want a doxy, some dimwit slut who lifts her skirts for you every time you come back to camp. You want me to train this lot to fight and..."

Prentice leaned forward suddenly and caught her face in his hands. He kissed her, passionately, as she had in the night, and for a long moment it was returned. Then she pushed back from him, and her poniard flicked up to be held at his throat. He felt the razor edge through his unkempt beard.

"I ain't no man's whore!" she all but shouted. "I was wrong to try it on with you, and you don't get to make free with me because of it! I ain't sitting around waiting to be tumbled just when you get the urge." Her eyes were full of fury.

Despite her threat, and the blade, Prentice did not back off. He looked at her scowling expression and smiled. He felt like he was dropping a heavy weight. For days now he had been planning this moment, virtually unable to keep it out of his thoughts. To finally speak it out was a vast relief. "Marry me."

"What?!"

"You heard," he said. He felt strangely but happily foolish, especially when he recognized that they were out in the open where they would definitely be seen. He had no clear plan, just an impulse he no longer wanted to control. It was a wild, disconcerting feeling that he found he was enjoying, like the furor of a battlefield. No more manoeuvring, no more thinking. Just action.

Her eyes glittered wetly. She sniffed. "Why?"

"I need a wife."

"Just like that?"

Prentice thought about it. "No," he conceded. "I don't just need a wife. I need you."

"No, you don't," she said, and the tears came fully into her eyes. "I'm a widow who's so ugly she can pass for a boy. I killed my own husband. I got scars up my body you can't imagine, and I ain't bled right since they raped me. There ain't no babes in my future, I'm sure of it. What kind of wife is that?"

"Any fool that told you, you were ugly was blind," Prentice said.

"Is that right?"

"Yes."

For a long moment he stared into her eyes. She refused to withdraw her dagger.

"I could kill you right now."

"I know."

"Why?" she demanded again, and her voice had faded to a whisper. "Why?"

"Because you make me smile. Because you aren't afraid of me or my scars. I lived ten years on a chain; I am a monstrous, wild thing and full of fury. The only time I feel calm is when I'm fighting for my life. How many women could stand such a man? But with you I am calm, and you make me smile." He paused and watched his words sink into her mind. She was beginning to relax when a wicked temptation seized him. He looked her up and down. "And besides, your bum looks sweet in those pants."

Her eyes went wide in shock. She flicked her blade, cutting him ever so slightly, and broke out of his grip, jumping to her feet. He was too surprised to stop her. His hand went to the cut, and he knew immediately it was superficial. She was playing with him. As he had that realization, his eyes met hers and she knew that he knew. Her lips split into an impish grin.

"You're a brute," she said, pouting. "I could never marry someone so crass, so base."

He stood up and stepped close to her, grabbing her by the arms and spinning her around, pinning her against the hut wall. She made no effort to resist him.

"I want poetry," she whispered as he leaned in close.

"Poetry?"

"Poetry. I want poetry, and flowers, and a ring, and a dress—linen bleached white, with embroidered flowers and lace on the bodice."

"You want all that?"

She nodded and smiled mischievously. He drew in a deep breath and realized his heart was beating heavily, but still he felt calm like in battle. And it *was* a battle for both of them, a battle against themselves. That was why she could turn so swiftly from belligerent to sad to playful. All those emotions were in her, just like in him.

"Alright," he said. Her eyes stared into his, and he knew she was joking, but he was happy to play along. "I know some love poems, and I'm sure I can find some flowers around abouts."

"Don't you dare!" she said, slapping him on the chest with her free hand. "As if I want a lovesick dandy chasing after me. Get a sacrist to say the words over us and pledge to me. That's what I want."

"Is that all?"

"Do that and I'll lie happy next to you in a pile of rags under the open sky every night until the end of time."

"I'll ask Fostermae today."

He kissed her lightly, one more time, then released her. He felt happier than he had been since before they had arrived at Fallenhill.

Foolishly happy, he thought and shook his head. He hadn't felt this happy since he'd been transported over the Azure Mountains. It was possible he'd never been this happy.

"And a ring!" she called after him as he headed off, and when he looked, she smiled and cocked her head. "I don't want to make it easy for you! Get me a pretty wedding ring. Something precious, like them fine ladies you know get to wear."

"Oh, you don't want to make it easy for me?" Prentice laughed at that, and his hand went involuntarily to the fresh cut on his neck. He turned away, leaving her smiling to herself, her loose hair blowing wild in the breeze, and wondered how Yentow Sent would respond if he was asked to make a wedding ring.

That thought made him laugh again.

CHAPTER 48

Countess Dalflitch came to Amelia the next morning, and had water and soap brought again, along with fresh clothes. Amelia bathed and changed and felt almost hale. She could not be sure, but it seemed as if the previous nights were not as bitter as earlier in her imprisonment. She wasn't certain, and there was always a chance that it was simply a mild patch of weather in the midst of winter, a break in the clouds, but she hoped it heralded the approach of spring.

Would that be early? She hadn't kept count of the days since they had begun the march west. Daven Marcus's machinations had taken up too much of her thoughts. And they were not finished yet.

"The prince has called you to audience again," Dalflitch told her.

"Tomorrow is the day of the widow's prediction," Amelia said, thinking aloud. "He will order the assault then, if the cannons can be in place."

Dalflitch was impressed by the duchess's insight.

"That is exactly what has been announced," she said. "The last of the devices was wheeled down the causeway this afternoon. Every Reacherman has labored hard for the prince's strategy, and I think some begged a day's rest to recover before the assault."

"And the prince refused, of course."

"Of course, Your Grace."

Amelia could not help but snort in disgust. Daven Marcus's pettiness was nothing if not predictable.

"So, am I summoned to a forfeits council?" she asked. Such councils were an ancient tradition on the eve of battle where knights and nobles boasted about what they would achieve in the next day's conflict and offered promised forfeits if they did not achieve to match their boasts. The previous prince, Mercad, had held a forfeits council while on the campaign in summer, but it had not gone as he hoped. Amelia would have been surprised to hear Daven Marcus was repeating that mistake.

"There is no word of such a thing," Dalflitch confirmed. "But perhaps."

"Perhaps he has appointed a knight commander at last."

"I've not heard that either, Your Grace."

The countess helped her into a clean underdress of white linen, and when it was laced, held a velvet overdress of Reach blue. When it was in place, Amelia felt warmer than she had in days. The dress did not fit perfectly but was nonetheless soft and pleasant to wear.

"Where is this from?" she asked. "It's not one of mine. Is it yours?"

Dalflitch shook her head.

"Even if I still retained the main of my wardrobe, Your Grace, I doubt much that what I wear would fit you, if you'll forgive me."

Amelia could see that was true. Dalflitch had a more pronounced waist and broader hips, not to mention a bosom that seemed far too generous for a woman who had no children—at least none about which Amelia knew.

"So where does it come from?"

"The earl had it made," she said. "From a cloak of his, apparently."

"Well one of the earl's cloaks would surely render enough cloth for my spare frame."

"For both our frames I would hazard, Your Grace."

Amelia cast a sidelong glance at the countess, and as she caught her eye, she saw a mocking gleam there. Of course, Earl Derryman really was an enormous man, tall and stout. If Kirsten had made such a joke, Amelia would have rebuked her without hesitation. But as she thought about it, she realized that Kirsten would never have made a joke like that, or any joke for that matter. She found herself sharing a sly smile with the countess.

"We will not show such disrespect when it comes time to thank the earl for his gift," she said, only barely able to keep from laughing.

"Heaven forfend, Your Grace," said Dalflitch, hand clutched to her heart, but the laughter never left the woman's eyes. In a sudden rush, Amelia realized what the prince must have found attractive about the countess and what a fool he'd been not to show her more respect. It was a strange set of notions that reminded the duchess of the infidelity and treachery that had been at the heart of this strange triune relationship. Her mood soured and she frowned. Dalflitch's expression matched hers immediately.

"I am sorry, Your Grace."

How can I trust you? Amelia thought, and that was the thought that dominated her mind as they finished dressing her and then stepped out into the darkening twilight. Lit rushlights flickered in the wind, and a pair of guards waited to escort them.

"Baron Robant no longer takes personal interest in my imprisonment?" Amelia observed.

"The baron is never far from the prince's side these days," said Dalflitch quietly. The woman was adroit at whispering in the presence of such as their escorts while still seeming polite. "I suspect he is not sure how to react since his betrothal has become more complicated."

"What do you mean?"

"Your former handmaid seeks to supplant us both, it seems, Your Grace."

"Kirsten?" Amelia could hardly believe what she was hearing. "With the prince? Oh, the poor, young fool."

"It's not clear which of our two roles she occupies, though I have no word that she has found her way to the prince's sheets."

"How do you hear all this?"

Dalflitch shrugged. "There are ways, Your Grace. In fact, since Daven Marcus has put me aside, all sorts of tongues are willing to wag in my hearing. It's somewhat ironic."

Once more they were ushered into the prince's presence, the audience chamber seeming more sparsely populated than usual. Even in the poor light, it took Amelia only a moment's glance to see that almost no Reachermen were present.

Just the vultures from Rhales, she thought coldly. She had no allies here. Perhaps Dalflitch might be one, but fully trusting the countess was beyond her, although she enjoyed the woman's company much more than she ever would have expected. After Earl Derryman's pledge of loyalty, Amelia knew she wasn't alone on the march, but in this company, she still played the game by herself.

"Welcome, Duchess," the prince said flatly. He was seated on a throne placed on a wooden dais and draped with a gold tasseled carpet. His usual table had been removed. "I trust you find your accommodations suitably unpleasant."

"Do you care, Highness?" Amelia replied in an equally emotionless tone. He had charged her with treason against the crown; she was done with kissing his ring.

"In truth, I do not care. This time tomorrow you will be gone, and I will be plagued by you no more."

"Until the trial."

He smiled then, and several of his courtiers chuckled. The prince waved to his right.

"Lord Robant, show the duchess what you have there. I'm told she likes to read."

The baron stepped up from where he stood by the prince's dais. As he did, Amelia caught sight of Kirsten standing in the shadows behind the dais. She was wearing another fine dress and new jewelry, no doubt purloined from Countess Dalflitch's lost wardrobe. She had a nervous look on her face that made Amelia think perhaps she was already beginning to regret having won the prince's favor. There was little enough difference between Daven Marcus's favor and his wrath, but she found she had little pity for the treacherous girl.

"Your confession," Robant said as he stepped up to her and offered her a sheet of paper.

"Confession? I have confessed to nothing."

"You will."

Amelia looked from the baron to the prince, then down to the document in her hands. The dim light made it difficult to read, but she forced herself. Her name and title were at the top of the page, and what followed was a written tale of how she had married Duke Marne as part of a plot, then traveled south with his money to bribe Vec princes to send soldiers up the as yet undiscovered river and the salt lake. Just that first paragraph contained many lies. The money was hers, not Marne's. It had been her dowry. And she'd gone south to the Vec to pay off her husband's debts. Most ridiculous of all was not only the prince's insistence that the Redlanders had come from the Vec but that she was somehow in league with them.

"How can I be in league with them? They attacked us on the river as we returned," she demanded, looking up from the document. The prince had obviously anticipated the question.

"We have your own retainer's testimony."

He looked to the crowd at his other side, and Amelia noticed Baron Liam among them. He must have been standing at the back again when she entered.

"Baron Liam," she said to him, indignant that he would put his name to such a lie, even taking his ambition into account. "You know this is not true! You were there, my escort through the entirety of my journey to the Vec. I met with bankers, not princes."

"I know you went south and met with men in the Vec," Liam responded icily. "You paid them money. Who they were, I cannot say for certain!"

"You lie! And what of Sir Dav? Did your former captain conspire with me, too? He met with the Golden Heron as well as I, chaperoning me every step. Do you accuse him? Will you defame the name of your mentor, first by suggesting he conspired to hire the invaders and then by the thought he was fool enough to be killed by them? You were at the village when we all barely survived. Is that part of your testimony?"

Liam had shown Amelia disdain many times in the short time they had known each other, but he had never seemed fuller of hate for her than he did at this moment.

"I do not know what you conspired with Sir Dav about," he growled, the words emerging as if spoken through a mouthful of broken glass. "I know you paid men in the Vec and then the invaders came. You lived, and your pet survived too. Perhaps Sir Dav was not supposed to die. Or perhaps he was bewitched."

"That's enough of that fool talk, Baron," the prince cut him off and he stepped back into the shadows of the tent. "Read on, Duchess. There's better yet for you there."

Amelia read on, not bothering to hide her disgust as rumor was heaped upon lie. She scoffed openly and twice looked up at the prince to roll her eyes in disdain. Some part of her thought to wonder why the prince thought she would sign this nonsensical document, or why he would let her read it publicly like this where she could reject it so openly. Whatever his reasons, she soon came to the end. She looked up at the young man on his throne and gave a barked laugh.

"You read it all?" asked Daven Marcus, mildly. "That last part, especially?"

She looked again. It was just the prince's name at the bottom as the supposed witness of this "confession."

"What of it? I will not sign it."

The prince didn't answer but looked to the courtiers gathered around.

"You all saw her read it?"

Every man nodded. Amelia noticed that Kirsten did not, but then the girl's assent was probably irrelevant to the prince. Daven Marcus gave a gesture to Robant, and the baron snatched the paper back from her fingers. He smiled triumphantly, and it was a reflection of the prince's own predatory visage.

"It's over, little sow!" Daven Marcus hissed suddenly. "Your conspiracy has come to an end."

"I'm sure everyone here is accustomed to your odd pronouncements, Highness, but you'll have to make actual sense if you wish me to understand what is going on." Just the relief of speaking directly to this man who had so long tormented her exhilarated Amelia.

"Oh, then let me explain, you worthless piece of pig turd. Tomorrow, I will give the order, and we will crush this petty tower that has been a thorn in the Western Reach's side. But first, you and I will marry, and I will accede legally to the dukedom."

"I'll never sign that, and I will never marry you!"

How are we back to this? Amelia thought. She was charged with treason. No man could marry her under that, surely, prince or commoner.

"You'll do as I command," shouted the prince, standing from his throne and coming down one step. "You'll marry me as you should have all along. I'll consummate right there, and then you'll confess your treason to me. As your husband, I'll affix my seal to your confession and surrender you to the full legal penalty for the good of my own soul!"

Amelia sucked in her breath as he stood back to glare down at her. It was such a ridiculous plan she could hardly believe it. Looking around her, she suddenly realized why there were no

Reachermen present, other than Liam, because no single one of them would accept this legal circus act as valid.

"You'll have a rebellion before sundown," she said, scarcely able to believe that any man in this room thought this could go ahead. "The Reach will never stand for this."

"The Reach will do as it is commanded as it always should have, especially once your treason is affirmed by confession and I send for inquisitors to root out your confederates."

"Inquisitors?" That left Amelia breathless. The Inquisition of the Church mostly concerned itself with heresy against true doctrine, but since the rulership of the Grand Kingdom had been ordained by God, under the Church's auspice, the Inquisition was sometimes willing to lend its investigative services to the throne. They were not known to be gentle, and because they acted outside the ordinary structure of King's Law, they had powers that frightened even the highest-ranking nobles.

"You had foreign invaders from Vec, commissioned by you, and a duke slain by poison, doubtless on your order," Daven Marcus was saying. "Knights and merchants conspire to loot the royal treasury, and you have escaped convicts rising as bandits in your own lands. All of it leads back to you, Duchess. Of course, you have confederates, other conspirators to root out. And once they are, their lands will be given to loyal men of the Grand Kingdom, men of Rhales who can be trusted to cut all this treachery out of the Western Reach, root and branch."

So that was why they were going along with the prince's nonsense.

"Put her away under guard," the prince said almost dismissively as he sat down again. "And see that no one speaks with her on pain of death."

Guards seized Amelia by her arms, and before she could call out, one clapped his hand over her mouth, no doubt already instructed by the prince to do so. As they turned to carry her away, she looked at Dalflitch in desperation, trying to communicate all her need by her eyes alone. The countess looked truly terrified, and that fear was justified, for the prince turned his attention on her directly.

"Grab that bitch of a new maid of hers," he spat cruelly, not even deigning to look at Dalflitch directly. "She talks entirely too much already."

More guards seized the countess, and the two women were gagged and bound, then dragged from the prince's tent and returned to the horse shed. In the dark Amelia could hear sobbing and thought the countess must have finally broken down under the prince's abuses. Then she realized there were two women's voices crying in the shed, and she noticed that her own cheeks were wet. When she realized that, she wiped her eyes on her shoulder as best she could and steeled herself to die like a duchess.

It was a long night.

CHAPTER 49

"A fine day for a long march," said Sir Gant, standing next to Prentice, Felix, and Righteous all in a row.

Winter's darkest clouds were gone, blown away to reveal a watery sunshine that grew warmer with each passing day. The promise of spring was in the air. Prentice watched five hundred men march from through the gates of Fallenhill and turn westward over the dale. Drummers at their head and behind kept the practiced rhythm as a column of forty-five ranks, five men across, kept perfect time in lockstep over the easy ground—nine cohorts in what Prentice had taken to calling militia order. Behind them came a tenth cohort, pulling handcarts and leading pack animals that carried tents and cook gear, enough for the entire company to make camp.

"You'll be fine staying behind," Prentice replied to Sir Gant's unspoken complaint. "I promise the next march will be yours to command."

This was the culmination of the long winter's training, and in Prentice's mind, the final test of all their hard work. The troops had been drilled hard every day until they would just as soon march and maneuver as walk. Their weapons were extensions of their arms, and wielding them was the skill of their trade. And this five hundred were the best. When he had imagined a march as the final test, Prentice had put it about that this was an honor to be highly sought. Men in years to come would boast that they were the first Lions of the Western Reach. He'd set the cohorts to compete for the honor, and they had risen to the task. Fed, trained, rested and equipped, Prentice had a true militia at his command. All he needed to do now was to see if he had their complete loyalty; hence, the march to an open camp two days from the walls. If there were men who still held to hopes of fleeing, this would be the time.

"How many do you figure will try to run off?" Felix asked quietly as the column filed past them.

"Ideally, none," Prentice replied, feeling an unexpected rush of pride.

"You ain't that naïve, old man," said Righteous. "And where's my ring?"

"Not now," he said sternly, trying to ignore the smirks from the two men standing with them. Without having discussed it with anyone, Prentice found that news of his betrothal had passed through the entire camp. Righteous, of course, protested that she had not breathed a word to a soul, but now that it was known, she saw no point in trying to keep it secret.

"Besides," he went on, "I've been busy."

"Too busy to honor a promise to your betrothed?"

"I am a man with duties to fulfil. You knew that when you said yes."

Righteous kicked at a tuft of grass. "Should have asked for more than a ring," she muttered.

"Be glad you got the pledge at all," said Felix. "Most soldiers in the Vec'll tumble a girl, get her a fat belly, and then bother to think about what to do about it afterward."

"I'm sorry, when did you become my uncle that you get to speak into my marriage affairs?" Righteous stood with fists on her hips and the three men chuckled at her indignation. With a scowl, she turned away from them.

"I need to get back," said Sir Gant. He turned to Prentice and saluted. "Be careful."

"You as well."

Aiden and one of his rovers rode up and saluted.

"I've set men ahead of the line and riders out down each side. Anything amiss, we'll spot it."

Prentice returned the salute and they rode away again. Ostensibly, the rovers were scouts, to watch for anything unexpected, especially invaders from the west. But every man on the march, reformed convict or not, knew that they were also there to track deserters, as they had always been meant to be. Of Aiden's little company, two had been sent west to find Prince Daven Marcus's camp and deliver long-delayed messages to the duchess. The rest would be riding on the fringes of this march. Prentice hoped to find loyalty amongst his men, but Righteous was right, and he was not going to be naïve about it.

The column snaked westward through the abandoned farmland and increasingly wild frontier terrain, a long, cream-and-blue-colored parade. Of the men back in Fallenhill, fewer than a quarter had armor, but every man on this march was issued with at least a buff coat—long jackets made from quilted layers of bleached cloth. It was significantly weaker than a knight's plated steel, but it was easily the equal of the invader's armor, and unbleached cloth was so close to ducal cream in color that it suited the Reach Militia perfectly.

But not everyone was dressed so.

The front ranks and the fangs, who would be forced to fight the closest to the enemy, had been issued with steel sallets and brigandines—quilted doublets with metal plates riveted between the layers. This was another way to honor the men who trained the hardest and served the best. More expensive and better protection, Prentice ultimately wanted every one of the militia wearing brigandine, but time and cost meant that barely one man in five on this march had the stronger armor, and none of the helmets had visors. Yentow Sent had fairly whipped his men to try and fill Prentice's orders, complaining every step of the way. As it was, the captain knew the Masnian had driven his workshop to produce a near miracle just by providing this much equipment. Rumor had it that half the goodwives in the little village outside the walls had been mobilized by Sent to weave and quilt enough cloth for the task. Prentice would have the weavers' and carders' guilds down on his head soon enough, demanding to represent so many dedicated workers in a town.

Let them try, he thought to himself.

As they marched, Righteous kept close to Prentice, and though she didn't speak much, he enjoyed her presence. She was wearing her arming doublet, which was thinner than a buff coat or brigandine, dyed its dark Reach blue. Prentice had decided that would be the model for his officers. Corporals and above would wear the full blue, a further honor to mark them apart on the battlefield. Knights wore their own house colors; his lions would wear Reach colors.

Setting camp went smoothly the first night, and they broke again at dawn the next morning without problem. A different cohort was passed the duty of hauling the tents and supplies, and the march resumed. When they made camp that next night, Aiden reported that no deserters had been seen, and Prentice went to sleep tired and happy. In the small hours, he got up to relieve himself, and as he made his way back to his bedroll, he heard whispered voices. Suspecting another attempted coup, he drew his poniard and listened closely in the night.

Didn't ambushers know better than to chatter like washerwomen? What he heard though, surprised him.

"Don't be a bloody fool," hissed one voice in a deep, gravelly tone.

"Bugger that!" came another, with a bitter edge, angry.

"Where are you going to go?"

"Who cares? Anywhere away from here."

"And what about them wild men from the west? Or the rovers? You'll get caught and killed."

"I won't get killed 'cause I don't plan on getting caught, not by wild men and not by them rovers."

"Oh, not like the others who *did* plan to get caught?"

There was a moment's quiet, and then a third voice chimed in.

"Look, we're on a good thing here. There's meat and cheese most days. You and me ain't never et so good in our whole lives."

"Sure, and we have to march around and take orders and salute for it. And fight one day, too!"

"How's that any different to anywhere else?" asked gravel voice. "You know some place where there are no bastard nobles? Is there some heavenly country where no man's ever gonna rule over you again? Tell me where that is, and I'll go there with you."

"Don't be stupid," angry hissed back.

"Right. You seen what that baron did in the siege. So why not stay here then? There's food, like he said, and shelter. And hells, if the captain likes you, you can actually rise. And there's even land going if you stick it out for your seven years. Your own bloody land! Where else in the world do you or I have a chance like that?"

"You're only saying that because he made you a first."

"Damn straight, and as your first, I'm telling you, you're not going anywhere."

"The hell with you!"

There was a sound of a scuffle, and Prentice decided it was time to speak up.

"Who goes there," he challenged, as if he had just heard them. Three men drew closer out of the shadows so that he could just discern them by banked firelight. Two of them were carrying a third man between them, who seemed dazed, and Prentice was sure they'd given him a few solid whacks.

"Sorry, Captain," said the larger of the two men, one whom Prentice recognized as one of the cohort firsts, gravel voice. "Our friend here went for the call o' nature and lost his way. Took a bit of a tumble. We were just bringing him back to the fold."

Prentice nodded, forcing himself not to smile. "Have a care. You wouldn't want to be mistaken for invaders...or deserters."

"No indeed, Captain! Wouldn't want that."

The two men awkwardly saluted and carried their semi-conscious comrade away with them in the dark.

Prentice returned to his blanket and lay back down, happy and proud. They were ready. The next morning, he told Aiden to scout out an open field, flat as they could find. It was time to put the capstone on the duchess's militia.

CHAPTER 50

R oyal men-at-arms were sent to escort the duchess and countess at dawn, and although the sky was almost half clear of clouds, a thunderclap from the west shook the air. A flock of seagulls feeding on the camp's midden pit took flight in raucous discomfort, heading east and then south to flee the terrible noise. A second and third crack split the morning quiet, and Amelia realized that the prince's prize toys had finally begun firing on the tower and its wall. The two women were marched a short distance to their carriage and bundled in.

So that no Reachermen will notice us carted to the prince, Amelia realized. She would have said so, as well, but their guards had not deigned to remove either woman's gag. With hands bound and mouths stopped with rags, the two noblewomen were driven unseen through the camp and up onto the causeway. Trying to ignore the discomfort of her wrists and cheeks, Amelia did her best to prepare herself to die with dignity.

I will not beg him, she told herself, and that was the promise she most wanted to keep. If Daven Marcus gave her a chance to speak, she hoped to say something worthy, something epic, like a betrayed maiden in a fable, but even if she wept and wailed, as she knew execution victims often did, she resolved not to beg for mercy. Not from the brat prince.

The journey to the end of the causeway was both longer and shorter than Amelia expected, which she knew was a trick of her mind. When the carriage rolled to a stop, the door opened and a man-at-arms clambered in awkwardly. Neither introducing himself nor saying anything else, the burly man pulled a tool, and with practiced swiftness, removed their manacles and fetters. Then he used a dirk to cut away their gags. He was about to step down out of the carriage again when he paused and turned back to face them.

"The prince has made his command clear," he told them. "If he gives the signal—just a nod, mind—we're to cut you ladies down. No questions. Whatever you do, don't give him cause to make us." There was a strained mix of emotions in his words, half command, half entreaty.

Then they were invited out of the carriage with all the politeness due a duchess's rank. It was such a sudden change in their circumstances that Amelia almost laughed at the bitter irony of it—to be freed from your chains and politely invited to your own execution. She stepped down and blinked in the surprising light.

"It's almost spring," Dalflitch observed quietly as she stepped down behind her.

Amelia nodded but did not say anything because the main of her attention was drawn to their surroundings. They were stopped on the causeway, just short of a branching intersection. One path continued on to the tower they had come to conquer, a narrow finger of built stones, barely ten or fifteen paces across and thrice as tall. It was pale, made from native Reach sandstone—like the walls of Dweltford so many leagues away—and nestled behind a curtain wall of the same material. The tower was still a goodly distance, and in the space between, hundreds of men on horseback were tightly packed together in a waiting column. They were arrayed in full panoply, polished and gilded plates, and mail glittering in the watery, late-winter sunshine. Pennants hung from lances and bright colors danced in the morning light. Amelia couldn't recognize any of the heraldry of the massed knights; she hardly even knew the colors and livery of the Reacher nobles by sight, let alone those of the Rhales court. But she knew there wasn't a single Reacherman out there on his horse. The prince was intent on humiliating the Reach as he took control of it. He would not give them the chance to win any glory in the assault. In all likelihood, there wasn't a single Reacherman anywhere nearby, save for Baron Liam, of course.

He would be here somewhere.

The other branch of the causeway was the newly created part, neither as broad nor as high, and clearly built more of sand than anything else. The new path ran parallel with the defensive wall, with a gap of salty shallows in between. The tower was built on an island, barely more than a rocky outcrop, but it and the causeway were the only solid ground amidst the marsh in every direction. The rest was flooded sand and coastal grasses, picked over by gulls and long-legged waterbirds.

Along the newly built branch of causeway, three of the royal dragon bombards were lined up, their huge maws facing the walls. In the water at the front of the slope, Amelia could make out some parts of the fourth gun that had survived the marshes to this point, only to be lost in the shallows in front of their goal. Her view of the guns was obscured though, by a silk pavilion of wine red edged in gold. Under its shade, Prince Daven Marcus sat on a throne in full panoply, every fluted armor piece embossed with gold and interlocking, so that it moved with him naturally like a mere suit of clothes, glittering wherever any light shone upon it. His fair hair was pulled back under a circlet of gold, and on a table next to him was a helmet crested with a red-dyed cockade. When the time came for battle, his squires would help him fit the helmet to his plate bevor, and he would then be encased in steel from head to toe.

Around him were his entourage, all similarly attired for battle. Scanning the faces, Amelia recognized them as the regular favorites, men who had never bothered to even introduce themselves to her. And then there was Baron Liam, sneering at her with the open contempt he seemed to always have for her nowadays.

"At last. Leave it to women to make us wait for the business of men," the prince said airily, and his entourage laughed or smiled. Liam gave a wolf's grin, his eyes full of cruelty. Amelia didn't curtsey, and Dalflitch followed her example. Looking about, she realized that they were the only women on the causeway. She saw Lord Robant amongst the prince's entourage as well and realized that she had half expected Kirsten to be here, but perhaps her maid had already served her purpose. Seducing her from her mistress's service might have been enough humiliation for the prince's intentions.

"You have waited?" Amelia asked, hoping her voice sounded as light as Daven Marcus's, though she feared it trembled with every word. "You seemed to be taking so long to ready yourself for the attack, I was afraid I would be rushing you." She was pleased to see him scowl at that. *You've already told me you plan to rape and murder me today, she thought. What cause do I have for meekness now?*

"Everything is ready for us, Duchess." The prince gestured to a steward behind him, and a curtain of the pavilion was pulled away to reveal a bed made with fine linens and strewn with dried rose petals. A marriage bed.

Amelia could scarcely believe the prince was continuing with this farce. Did he plan to consummate his false marriage while still in his armor?

"I thought I heard the dragons already," she said, looking past to the cannons.

"Mere ranging shots, readying for the assault. The first volley will fire to announce the ceremony, then they will trumpet our marriage by hammering this little fort of yours into dust. They have orders to leave the gate unmolested. I intend to line the heads of all your friends from the Vec over top of it, and your head will be the crown—capstone to an arch of heads. Then the Vec will know that the Reach finally has a true defender."

She nodded but didn't speak. What could she say to that?

"Captain, begin firing the bombards. Show me some cracks in that wall."

"With pleasure, Your Highness," said the captain of the cannoneers, standing by and dressed in a brigandine coat of plates, also in royal red and gold. He dashed away, shouting orders to his crews. Cylindrical-shaped sacks were shoved down the cannon's throats and rammed home with mace-like staves so heavy they took four men to wield. Behind the guns were more such sacks, stacked like barrels. Then a cantilevered crane that had been set up next to each gun helped them lift and maneuver the heavy iron cannonballs into the barrels. The iron rolling down the bronze tube gave off a metallic screeching like a distorted eagle's cry, a sound twisted to something dark and evil. Amelia cringed from the noise as it set her teeth on edge. Then the guns were ready, and hot wire was brought from a lit brazier and inserted into the touch hole at the back of the nearest cannon. This crew had the honor of firing the first shot, and their beast erupted with a fury that beat the air with a hot wind. Fire and smoke belched at the fort, and for an instant, Amelia thought something had gone wrong because she couldn't see the cannonball. But the iron sphere struck home on the fort wall in an explosion of dust and stone for which she had no words. Blocks of stone that looked like they could endure any natural fury shattered into pieces like glass. A shower of pebbles fell into the water of the marsh, which was barely a handspan deep, though the night's tide not yet turned to ebb. The assaulted wall was not beaten down, but the front of it had been broken, and pieces that had not been blown clear slid slowly down into the water.

Around her, the gathered knights and nobles applauded the shot, and Amelia thought she could hear a cry of pain carrying over the water. That sound was obliterated as the next bombard fired and struck a section further down the wall's face, where it too demolished a chunk of masonry. The third dragon loosed its fury, and after one full volley of shots, the fort wall already resembled a crumbling rockface.

"It seems we'll need our horses sooner than I thought," said a man on the other side of the prince from Amelia. Many around him chuckled, and even the prince smiled. Watching this simple display of power, Amelia finally understood the faith the prince had placed in his favorite weapons. They were more than mere toys, even if commanded by a man-child. Surely no fortification could stand long against such monsters. After firing, water was sluiced over the cannons to cool the metal, and men used rags on sticks to clean the inside of the barrels. Then they began the laborious process of reloading. In the quiet of waiting for the next volley, screams of pain could more clearly be heard. The invaders had men on those walls, there could be no doubt, and some were wounded.

Good, Amelia thought. She loathed Daven Marcus and his love for cruelty, but she still wanted the invaders to suffer so they would learn to leave her people alone.

"Time for our vows, I think."

From near one corner of the pavilion, a man of the cloth was brought—a sacrist and likely the prince's chaplain, though Amelia could not remember ever seeing the man before. He was short but well-built, and his tonsure was neatly shaved. His dark robes were finely embroidered, and he wore rings of gold and silver and had a cross of gold hanging from a chain. Nonetheless, there was a haunted look in his eyes, and Amelia felt sure she could detect a bruise on his face. Was he reluctant to oversee her forced wedding? Daven Marcus would not have been kind if the cleric had raised an objection.

The chaplain stepped forward and, holding a prayer book in front of him, began to intone the marriage blessing. His voice trembled slightly, and he had barely begun when his words were swallowed by the next roar of the cannon. He stopped a moment and was about to recommence when the next cannon was fired. The prince was absorbed in the firing, but when he noticed the sacrist had stopped his ritual, he struck the man on the shoulder with a gauntleted hand.

"What are you doing? Get on with it!"

"But the noise, Highness. No one will hear the words."

"No one cares!" the prince said dismissively. "Just say them."

The chaplain nodded in resignation, and he gave Amelia an apologetic look before starting his ritual once more. Every time a cannon fired, he cringed from the sound, but no longer stopped speaking for the blasts. Finally, he folded his prayer book closed and looked at her.

"Are you going to ask if I consent?" she asked him. He only hung his head in shame. Amelia felt suddenly enraged. "I do not consent! I will never consent! Add that to your empty prayers!"

CHAPTER 51

Daven Marcus was focused on the cannons' shots against the stone wall, but he turned to look at Amelia when he heard her vehement rejection of the marriage vow.

"Oh, for God's sake, shut up, you mewling bitch!"

He looked at the chaplain.

"Finished, are you?" he asked. The sacrist nodded, keeping his head down. "Good. Finally."

The prince looked to his entourage, some of whom were still distracted by the cannons' performances. Most, though, were alert to their master's whims, ready to fulfil any little duty he set for them, like dogs chewing bones from their master's table.

"You will be witnesses," the prince told them, and Amelia felt a shiver run through her. Like Absalom with his father David's concubines, Daven Marcus planned to rape her in the sight of his followers. The thought made her sick to her stomach.

"Bring her," he ordered the guards behind her, and she was seized by the arms.

Amelia wanted to fight, to struggle, but the pointlessness of the action filled her with despair. Behind her, she heard a sound like horses' hooves, but she barely noticed as she was lifted bodily onto the prepared bed. Her eyes were fixed on the prince, with Robant near to his shoulder, both men wearing expressions of cruel triumph.

There were shouts and a commotion from around the carriage that preceded the blast of a horn. The cannons fired again, drowning out all other sound and making Amelia's ears ring. A courtier nearby put his mailed glove to his mouth in shock, and then shouted in disbelief.

"Sails! By God, so many sails!"

Daven Marcus turned away in surprised annoyance, and as his gaze broke from Amelia's, she risked sitting up on the silly bed. Her eyes searched first to the tower and then to the water. There, on the other side of the knights waiting on the causeway, was a flock of sails visible above the couched lances and pennants. She counted five sails in a column, and then many more, smaller in the distance behind them. Each flapping cloth was colored in strange patterns, and she blinked in terror as she recognized the shapes. They were the same as the foreign emblems' colors that the Redlanders used to paint their own bodies—the colors of the men who had ambushed her on the river in the summer not even a year ago. Here they were, come to kill and mutilate once more.

"The prophecy!" one of the nearby courtiers gasped, echoing Amelia's other thought. The widow in the wood had not lied. What she had predicted was coming to pass. Daven Marcus wanted none of it. Stepping away from his false marriage bed, his gauntlet crashed into the courtier's jaw, sending the man sprawling.

"There is no prophecy!" he shouted. The entourage all stepped back, shocked by the sudden violence, but Amelia sneered at them for once.

You made yourself subjects to a mongrel dog, she thought. *You can't be surprised he bit one of you.*

But her contempt was short lived as she saw the sails passing behind the tower and dozens of little colored dots out to the horizon that were growing into sails as she watched—dozens and dozens of ships, a fleet larger than any she had ever imagined. It was happening faster than seemed possible, faster than natural winds should allow. Men on the causeway were breaking formation to get a better view of the approaching ships, and even the commotion at the carriage seemed to grow still for a moment.

The five closest ships passed behind the tower's island and then swung east, heading into the shallows and aiming straight at the new arm of the causeway. They had high prows, carved and painted, and their sails were pulled taut and full in spite of the bare morning breeze. Three had cloth the color of deep forest green, and the other two were slashed with blue. The ships had sailed south with a strong wind driving them, and now they had turned eastward, seeming to benefit from the same wind, while there was hardly enough breeze to scatter the smoke of the guns on the causeway.

That was magic; it had to be.

And if they had such magic, Amelia realized what else these ships would bring. Looking at the five advancing vessels, she could make out some of the crew now. They were skipping over the low tidal water between the fort and the cannons, barely two hundred paces away. The shallow water was no impediment to the draft of these ships. The decks were full of men, armed and weapons drawn, skins brightly colored. But in amongst them were dark shapes, and these were the ones that sharpened the duchess's terror to its fullest. The invaders had skinchangers among them—men who could turn into wild beasts as powerful as the strongest wolves and bears, and there they were, waiting on the decks of those ships.

"You wanted to defend the Reach, Daven Marcus," she said, and her voice sounded like ice in her mouth. "Here is your chance."

The prince heard her and looked about to strike her as well when the horn sounded again.

"They have forty or fifty men on each vessel," said another courtier, ignoring the horn. Events were rushing forward, moving so swiftly that as the chaos rose, Amelia could barely follow what was happening. The cannons roared again, and she watched in fascinated horror as one of the clouds of flame billowed over an oncoming boat, setting the vessel aback. It stopped dead in the water, and the sail was set ablaze. Whatever sorcery empowered the colorful cloth, it didn't protect it from destruction. Some of the invading sailors tried to save their vessel from the flames, but most simply dropped over the sides to sink to their thighs in the water and then began wading forward to the causeway. Among them, three dark shapes, man-like, but covered in fur and too large to call mere men, scrambled for the water's edge. The beastmen were coming ashore.

Around Amelia, the prince's closest entourage looked at each other and then at him, and it was clear they were waiting for him to give an order. Daven Marcus seemed as confused as Amelia felt, but with no appointed knight commander, no man was ready to take charge when the prince was overwhelmed. Every man-at-arms was paralyzed, awaiting an order. Some began to move of their own initiative, but in all their toadying and pandering, no clear order had been established. Each man led a banner force of his own, according to his noble rank and wealth, but they had no idea how to coordinate themselves if the prince didn't do it for them. A number rushed immediately toward the cannons, just eager to be part of the affray, while others headed north to summon their own bannermen from the ranks waiting on the main causeway. And Daven Marcus still stared, confused.

"Protect my dragons!" he ordered at last, as Redlanders began to clamber up the causeway to attack the cannons. He stepped away from the bed a moment, drawn to the conflict. As he did so, there was a cry cut short from the opposite direction. Amelia looked to see one of the guards standing by Countess Dalflitch collapsing to the ground. The other guard stepped back as a huge man rushed at him, a flanged mace raised high.

Turley? Amelia felt a swell of hope as her sworn man knocked the second guard aside with a single swipe. Then he leaped from Dalflitch toward the bed. In the confusion, with his entourage rushing about in every direction, shouting and shoving, and the cannons under threat, Daven Marcus had no sense of what was happening only paces behind him.

"Back off or you'll get the same!" Turley told the two men who'd carried Amelia to this damnable bed. They put their hands to their side swords, planning to make a fight of it. Behind Turley, Earl Derryman erupted from the madness, wearing helmet and a coat of mail, and with longsword drawn, accompanied by knights of his own banner. He charged on toward the prince.

"Unworthy cur!" he shouted. He lunged for the prince, his blade scraping across the fine steel of Daven Marcus's breastplate. Around them, men came to their senses as they recognized the threat to their liege lord.

"The prince!" Amelia heard Baron Liam shout in his slurring voice. "Defend the prince!"

The fight around the bed was now in earnest.

One of Earl Derryman's bannermen helped Turley drive off Amelia's two guards, and the steward had just reached out his hand to help her when Lord Robant emerged from the melee to thrust that man-at-arms through the eye with the point of his sword. The prince's loyal hound then turned to face the duchess's second rescuer and stopped still in shock.

"You?" he hissed in disbelief tinged with fear. "You're dead! We left you in a bog."

"Guess again," Turley growled, and he used the hand he was reaching out with to seize the edge of one of the bed's sheets, throwing it over the baron like a net. Robant reflexively slashed the cloth away, but Turley wasn't finished. He used the momentary distraction to hammer the baron with his mace. Striking from his shoulder, the flanged head rang again and again on armor, driving Robant backward in desperate defense.

"Go, Your Grace," Turley shouted over his shoulder. "The earl's sent men. We'll get you to safety."

Amelia hesitated, trying to sort the confusion around her. She watched Earl Derryman fighting for his life as the prince's entourage, finally shocked out of confusion by a treasonous assault on the royal person, crowded in against him. Soon enough, even with some loyal men beside him, it was clear that he was overmatched. But he never backed a step away, and Amelia remembered the words of the widow's prophecy to the earl—he would die defending the Reach. She never imagined it would be against the crown prince of the realm, but it was clear that Derryman had accepted that fate.

Turley had knocked Robant off his feet, tangling him under the slashed sheet, and rushed back to Amelia's side.

"We must go now!" he shouted in her ear, and it was an order. He was not asking permission.

The horn sounded yet again, and as she was dragged toward the main causeway and the path back to the shore, Amelia saw a fleet of sails all rushing south, though some turned aside to skip through the shallows toward land and the camp further east. The Grand Kingdom forces were dissolving into chaos as the raiders from the ships swarmed over the cannons and their crews and up into the massed knights, now fighting defensively in a packed formation, not ready for the melee. Turley dragged his duchess by the hand, mace held ready to defend her. As they broke away from the chaos, she saw two others ahead, making straight for camp, and was pleased to realize one was the countess. Yet even as they approached the shore, there was the sound of screams. The first raiders from the ships were bursting into the unsuspecting camp.

The Redlanders had returned in force, just as the prophetess had foretold, and far from punishing them, Prince Daven Marcus's crusade into the west was about to be consumed by them. The Western Reach would be at their mercy.

CHAPTER 52

Turley and Amelia snuck back into the camp while the invaders rushed in from the marshlands, slaughtering as they went. Stewards and servants fled in terror, ignoring the demands of court ladies who screamed orders to be defended. Fires were kicked over in the panic, setting tents alight, while horses and other stock, startled and unnerved by the chaos, broke their traces and stampeded about. Everywhere was madness, and while all knew to fear the painted Redlanders and their savagery, no one cared to look at the duchess or the countess and the two men guarding them.

A clutch of men-at-arms formed a tight knot around a brown-and-white-striped tent and were holding out against invaders while they could. They waved at Turley and Amelia to come to them, but he shook his head. Still pulling the duchess by her arm, he led the way to a space between two other tents, and the four hid there as a dozen men with skin the color of the reddest roses fell upon the men-at-arms' line with long hafted axes and picks. The fighting was brutal, men shouting, arms and armor clashing in desperation.

Amelia felt herself trembling and clenched her fists and teeth, trying to make it stop.

"Is there anything can't be replaced in your tent?"

"What?"

She turned to Turley, and he repeated the question.

"In your tent, Your Grace?" Turley hissed. "Is there anything there you can't replace."

She thought about it. There was jewelry and clothing, some of it unique or sentimental, but none of those things mattered at a time like this. She shook her head.

"Then now's the time to go!"

"Go where?"

"East."

"Flee? What of the defense? What of the Reach?"

"He's right, Your Grace," Dalflitch said, leaning in. "Your earl raised his blade against the prince in your defense. That's actual treason. And Daven Marcus already has you marked for death for the same crime. If you stay, no matter who wins this fight, you will die."

Amelia swallowed but was thankful for the countess's directness. It cut through her confusion.

"We saw how many ships they had coming," Turley added. "Derryman knows he is to die today; he's embraced it. But he made me swear to have you to safety. The Reach will need to be defended. Hope is that Prentice has his militia ready when they come. Otherwise, the Dwelt's the only thing between them and the whole of the West. This isn't the Horned Man's little bandit clan, Your Grace. With that many ships, they mean to stay. We need to find horses and make a run straight east."

"Meadow Dancer," she said, grabbing his arm. "I must save Meadow Dancer."

"Trust me."

Turley led the way to the nearest stores of food, with the two women following and Derryman's man bringing up the rear. They crawled through smoke and under fallen tents and furniture, scrambling through mud and dirt one moment and then holding deathly still as Redlanders stalked past the next. Amelia's mouth was dry, and the acrid smells of battle and death made her eyes water, but she stayed close to her escort at every step, and she and the countess never deviated from their instruction. Turley left them for a moment behind a horse trough as he went into a tent and looted waterskins and food. Hiding there, Amelia pressed herself down on the ground, trying to be as small as she could make herself, when her palm rubbed against something hard in the mud. She turned her hand over and there was a stone, a small basalt pebble, and she marveled. It was the widow's stone, but it couldn't be. Surely that stone, if it was anywhere, was in her tent, or in the horse shed where she'd been prisoner these last days.

Unbidden, her mind traced a path of possibility—of a horse treading on the stone near the shed and getting it caught under its hoof, and of its master discovering the thing lodged, and seeing a risk that his mount could be lamed. That rider had taken a blade and dug the stone out to cast it away behind this water trough. It was such an improbable story, she wanted to reject it outright, but somehow, she knew it was the truth, every word. This was her stone. She dipped it in the water of the trough quietly to wash away the mud and placed it in her sleeve. Turley returned with two water skins slung over his shoulder and half a wheel of moldy cheese clutched to his chest. He waved them after him.

"There was a ham there, but it was already turning slimy, so I left it."

So far from home, with so little wildlife to hunt, no matter which way this battle went, the prince's army and court would soon be overwhelmed with hunger.

Soon, they reached a spot on the other side of the camp where Meadow Dancer was saddled, along with several other horses, all held by two rail-thin riders dressed in buckskins, two of Prentice's rovers.

"They're Reachermen, Your Grace," Turley explained.

"We been sent by Captain Prentice, Lady," said one of them roughly, though both readily tugged their forelocks.

Captain Prentice? Amelia's mind could barely make sense of that.

The two riders had even-tempered mounts, but none of the other creatures were war blooded, so they were all skittish and unnerved from the sounds and smells around them—the smoke, the blood, and the screams. Then came a clap of thunder, a hammer blow in the air louder than all the cannon shots so far. Amelia wondered if this was some new magic of the invaders. Or had a Royal Dragon made that sound? She hugged her beloved Meadow Dancer's neck, stroking the mare's roan coat and calming her with her presence. Then Turley was pushing Amelia up into the saddle.

"We have to go, Your Grace," he said as he tied the cheese to the saddle of another mount while Derryman's man-at-arms cursed at a horse of his own that refused to be settled, wheeling about in growing panic. There was no horse for Countess Dalflitch. Apparently, from this point, she was expected to make her own way in the world. When she saw this, she threw herself at Amelia's stirrup.

"I beg you, Your Grace. Do not leave me to them."

Amelia looked down into the woman's face, not knowing whether she meant the Redlanders or the prince and his flunkies. It didn't matter. The duchess never hesitated for a moment. "We need a horse for the countess."

Turley turned to look about immediately, but the earl's man was no longer willing to help.

"Bugger that," he said and spurred his mount away, riding south around the outskirts of the camp.

"We don't have long," warned one of the rovers. At that moment, a man emerged from the camp behind them, arming sword in hand.

Lord Robant.

The prince's loyal henchman was in a wild fury. His perfect hair was matted with blood, and his face was streaked with sweat and dust. There were dents in his armor, likely from Turley's mace assault. One eye was bloodshot, and he bellowed in rage, pointing his blade straight at Turley.

"I'll skin you for a blanket for my horse! And I'll gut your bitches too!"

"No time for another horse," said Turley, suddenly reaching down and hauling the countess bodily into the air with one hand and all but throwing her behind him on his saddle. She cried out in fright but clung to him as he spurred his mount. Amelia geed Meadow Dancer as well while one of the rovers wheeled about and put himself and his horse between them and the onrushing baron. It was a futile gesture as the skillful Robant showed again why he was the prince's chosen champion. He slipped the rover's attempt to batter him away with the weight of his mount and then surged up with a single slash that cut the man from belly to collar bone in a spray of gore.

"Ride, Your Grace!" Turley shouted. "We're right behind you!"

Amelia touched her heels to her horse's sides again, and Meadow Dancer leaped forward. She looked back once to see Turley and the countess coming on more slowly, their mount struggling under the extra weight. Robant was a filthy, rabid beast at their heels, and though their horse was slowly outpacing him, his sword wheeled in one more blood-dripped arc before they left him behind. They let their mounts run east a long space until the rover finally reined his own beast in and signaled that they should do the same. Amelia looked over her shoulder and realized that Turley's horse was no longer behind them.

"Where are they?" she asked, but the rover only shrugged.

With their horses' chests heaving and their coats sweat-soaked, they let them walk for a long space, and as Amelia watched the west, a dark column of smoke rose in the distance. It took an hour by her estimate, but at last a single horse appeared from amongst the rise and fall of the grassed dunes. It carried two riders—a dark-haired man and a woman in a filthy dress. Amelia's relief nearly overwhelmed her, and she called the rover to an even slower walk until Turley and Dalflitch caught up with her.

As they approached, she noticed a dark mark on the horse's side, and once they drew near, she saw it was a long spray of blood. At first, she though it was the mount that was wounded, but she realized at last that it was Turley. The blood was dripping from a wound on his arm.

"You're hurt?" she asked, worried at how bad it might be.

"I'm sorry, Your Grace," Turley said with a forced smile. His face was pale, and he was as wet with sweat as their horses. "After you fetched me a miracle healing, I've gone and let that bastard Robant wound me all over again."

He gasped in pain as he bounced in the saddle. Born a commoner in the main of the Grand Kingdom, Turley was no horseman. The cheese that was tied to the saddle and bouncing as they rode sat better than her steward.

"The blow was meant for me," the countess said fearfully. "He deflected it."

"I know nothing about treating wounds," Amelia said weakly, looking at Turley's limply hanging hand.

"All we can do now is bind it and hope he don't sicken," said the rover. Turley nodded, his eyes half closed with pain and fatigue. "And best get the lady off the back of his mount. Thing's exhausted as it is. She can ride with me."

"I'll take her," Amelia commanded, nodding at Dalflitch. The man smiled at her, but she dismissed his condescension. "Two women are a lighter burden for a mount than a man and woman, surely."

"Alright," the rover conceded. He hopped down and helped Dalflitch off Turley's horse. Turley groaned involuntarily as the change caused the horse to shy. When she was out of the way, the man pulled a bodkin and began to cut a length from the horse's blanket. "Let's make you a bandage, big fella," he said and set about binding Turley's wound.

The countess made to climb up behind Amelia on Meadow Dancer but slumped down in exhaustion, leaning her head on the saddle for a long moment. Amelia could not blame her. When she looked up, the two women exchanged a moment of shared suffering.

"Thank you for this mercy, Your Grace," said Dalflitch, her eyes wet with tears.

Amelia could think of nothing to say in return, so she nodded and waited quietly until Dalflitch had mounted at last.

CHAPTER 53

B y sundown, Daven Marcus stood in the ruins of the sea
fort. Of the three of his beloved bronze dragons, two were
completely destroyed, and the last had lost its wheels and slid
down the front of the embankment to land in the salty shallows
not far from its comrade. All but two of the cannoneers were
dead. During the fighting around the cannon, while the prince
had been fending off Earl Derryman's assault and trying to
organize a hunt for the escaping duchess, the lit brazier that
heated the firing wires was knocked over and the coals scattered
toward the bags of black powder. The resulting explosion blew
knights, Redlander warriors, and beastmen in all directions, and
set fire to the other ships. The force tore down the prince's
pavilion, sweeping away his throne and the marriage bed. His
chaplain was found many paces away, face down in the marsh,
drowned. Later in the day, one of the surviving cannoneers had
been heard to remark that they had been lucky, for the powder
reserve had been running low and runners were about to be sent
for another load of bags. If the same disaster had occurred at the
beginning of the day, no one on either causeway would likely
have survived. While no one doubted the man's assertion, no
courtier who heard it made any effort to repeat it in the Daven
Marcus's hearing.

The prince himself recovered his wits swiftly after the
explosion, but by the time he had, the sea fort's contingent

of warriors was pouring out of the gate, the painted men whooping and obviously hoping to take advantage of the explosion. Daven Marcus rallied the remaining nobles who could still fight around himself and rushed to take command of the forces on the causeway. The fight that followed was a grim affair, with two crowds of men pressing each other on the narrow front. The clashing lines of both sides were often crushed in the press of bodies or else tumbled off the side into the water. Those who were injured were often crushed underfoot. In the end, the Kingdom's superior armor and numbers told the tale, and when the last few Redlanders broke and retreated into the fort, the prince drove his men in after them, not stopping until every invader was dead and he had soaked his own blade with blood. He stood on the pier at the fort's far side and watched the vast fleet—hundreds of ships sailing from the north and past the fort, heading south.

It was then that word of a bitter defense in the camp came to them, along with a call for aid. The Reachermen who'd been left behind in the camp were formed into a cordon to protect women and servants, though many men of low birth had taken arms and were joining in the defense. They had fought the Redlanders to a standstill and only needed some fresh soldiers from the siege to swing the battle decisively. The prince refused to send a single man, and the battle went on for another hour before the remaining raiders finally retreated to their ships. In the late afternoon, the mystical sails brought them back out through the shallows of the marsh and into the sea to join the last of the south-sailing invasion fleet.

The prince's throne was recovered, damaged but usable, and he sat in the gate of the assaulted tower, his bloody longsword across his lap, to oversee the execution of every painted man they found alive. Some shouted curses in a foreign language as they were dragged before him, but none spoke the Kingdom tongue and none begged for mercy. By sundown, the ground in front of the prince was a puddle of blood, and every man who stood nearby was splattered in it. Still, Daven Marcus's rage was not sated. Baron Liam pushed his way through the crowd, accompanied by Baron Robant. Both men were filthy from the battle, their armor scored and bloodied, but neither was seriously injured. They bowed.

"The camp is secure, Highness," Liam reported. There was a level of anger to his tone that bordered on insolence. Perhaps he did not like that the prince had sent no help to the defenders there. After all his boasts and speeches, when the time came, Daven Marcus had left the Western Reach to its own devices. Did that offend the baron? Daven Marcus did not care.

"And where is the bitch?" he demanded.

"Fled," said Robant, his anger as savage as Liam's and the prince's but clearly directed at the duchess.

"You let her go?"

"I laid a blade on three of her men at least," Robant countered. "It's more than all these others did."

There was an angry murmur among the gathered nobles and men-at-arms, but Robant only stared at them defiantly. If they didn't like his words, they were free to challenge him over it. The prince turned his eyes back on Liam.

"What say you, Reacherman? Your province is in rebellion, conspirators under every rock. Why shouldn't I put the whole damned land to the torch?"

"Do what you will," Liam responded with no deference at all. "The slut is riding back to her convict mongrel to get his litter and breed yet more rebellion. The Reachermen are still here, mostly. I see a convict uprising, not a province in rebellion."

Daven Marcus launched himself from his throne, longsword in hand, and splashed through the puddle of blood to seize Liam by the shoulder, holding the blade's edge at his throat.

"That's what you see, is it? What else do you see? Hmm? Do you see death coming for you? Do you see the gates of hell opening before you?"

A single slash would end the baron's life right there, but Liam didn't flinch. His twisted jaw clenched in fury, and he answered the prince through gritted teeth.

"I saw you marry her," he said, eyes meeting Daven Marcus's. "I saw you take her to your marriage bed. That makes you liege of the Western Reach. I'll swear it before God and men. She's a wayward wife and yours to do with as you will, as is the Reach."

Daven Marcus's eyes narrowed with cruel cunning.

"You think the Reachermen will believe you?"

"Enough will."

"Enough?" The prince released his grip and half turned from Liam, thinking for a moment. "Five hundred knights? That's what you wanted wasn't it?"

Liam nodded.

"You think you can find that many?"

"I know I can."

The two men regarded each other in the torchlight for a long moment, and everyone standing by could see each man's hatred reflected in the eyes of the other.

"Go then, in the name of the Prince of Rhales and the new Duke of the Reach. Dig this tick of a convict rebellion out of the flesh of my Reach and I'll give you Dweltford for your own. But make sure you do it. Make Fallenhill a charnel house again. No one lives, not a single, filthy soul. And send me her head, along with her man's. What was his name?"

"Prentice, Highness."

"Make sure I get this Prentice's head as well."

"Send me, too," Robant requested suddenly, as if feeling left out of the murderous plot. The prince shook his head without even looking at the other baron.

"No, Lord Robant, I'm not done hunting down these Veckanders yet. We will march south from here until we find where this piss puddle of a marsh meets the Vec. Then we will lay waste to every village, town, and castle we find until it's all ours again."

Liam accepted the prince's dismissal and rushed away into the night to gather up every knight he could, Reach or Rhales, to ride after the fleeing duchess. She had many hours head start, and it would take him more hours yet to gather them all, but there was nowhere for her to go. His bannermen had Fallenhill besieged. He would pin her between that force and his pursuing knights, capture her, and take the town.

The walled camp full of convict rebels with purloined silver would be in his hands before spring. The duchess and Prentice he would torture, making sure to keep their heads for the prince. Every other man he would burn alive. It was becoming a tradition for the ill-fated town. The prince had ordered the slaughter, and Liam would oblige.

The silver he would keep for himself.

CHAPTER 54

Four days hard march southwest of Fallenhill, Aiden's riders found a field of long grass, beaten down by winter's rain, almost perfectly flat amidst the rise and fall of the grasslands. Prentice ordered camp be set in the mid-afternoon. The sky turned wintery grey again in the afternoon, and late-winter winds stirred the grass into waves all the way west to the horizon. The company beat the grass down fully and cleared a space for their tents and campfires. Rovers found a waterhole nearby, and the company used it to refill their own supply. The camp was fully set for the night and the meal was soon to be prepared when Prentice ordered the drummers to beat to arms.

Every man knew the sound intuitively now, and the entire camp rushed to their ranks as corporals and firsts saw them into their right order. The whole movement was disciplined and swift. There was a pride to the company's movements, and Prentice had to smile as he saw it. He stood with the drummers himself in the middle of the cleared grass space. Even while the ranks were forming, he gave the drummers another order and they beat maneuver. Smoothly, the ranks of men adjusted their direction, and formations split and merged as each new order came. No pike staffs clattered, and no steel clashed. Every man knew his place, and he kept it in time to the beat. At last, they were arranged in a square, a single line on each side, with Prentice and his drummers right in the center. Firsts reported to corporals that every man was present and in order, weapons ready. Corporals ran to the captain and reported readiness.

Then, everywhere was quiet. A single shouted order was issued, and five hundred men saluted as one. Prentice returned the salute, and then nodded to a young man he had waiting with the drummers for this purpose. He gave a signal, and the youth hoisted a pikestaff into the air. Unlike all the other pikes held upright around the square, this one had a crossbar near its point, and from that bar fell a banner, a field of midnight blue edged in cream thread with the ducal lion rampant.

"This is your standard!" Prentice shouted, his voice rolling out over the grasses to be swept away in the wind at last. "These are your colors! That's not just the duchess' lion; it's yours, too. Look to it on the field. When you hear the drums, you form around this standard. Knights fight for their colors, and so do we, but we are not knights, so we don't get our own colors. We all have to share.

"We were convicted men and swords for hire. We had no honor. Nothing more than rats, we have all spent our time hiding in walls from the master of the house. Well, no longer! Today you are lions, the Lions of the Western Reach. We march for the Reach; we fight for the Reach. And when the duchess requires it, we die for the Reach.

"What say you?"

Corporals and firsts, having been briefed on this moment, began to beat the butts of their pikes and halberds on the ground or the pommels of their swords on their bucklers. Soon enough, the rhythm was taken up by every other militiaman. The lions were roaring, and at his final arranged signal, forty serpentines were raised to shoulders, and as one, the black powder weapons were fired, powder only, into the air. The suddenness of it caused a pause in the thumping, but when the company realized what had happened, a cheer went up and the beating continued. After a long, proud moment, Prentice gave the signal and almost as one, the noise ceased. The unity of it was intoxicating.

"Felix," Prentice shouted, "front and center."

Wearing a new brigandine and carrying a halberd, Felix trotted out to stand in front of Prentice. He came to attention and saluted.

"Your company of mercenaries has taught us well," Prentice shouted at the sergeant so that everyone could hear him. "But at great cost. Ranold is remembered by our company with honor. The time has come, and after this march, any man who wants will be dismissed with pay. Do you accept this?"

Felix nodded. He was the only mercenary on this march. The rest were back in Fallenhill. They weren't necessary anymore.

"Do you wish to be dismissed?" Prentice asked.

"I do not!" Felix shouted back. "Let them that want to leave go, and they can take my contract with them, every guilder owed shared between them. I will stay and serve the duchess."

He saluted again and there was another cheer.

"Then I name you Master Sergeant Felix, first under me and master of the colors."

Prentice leaned down to a waxed cloth bundle and drew out some armor pieces. One was a blued steel gorget, similar to the one Righteous wore but with only a right-hand pauldron attached. Prentice stepped forward and fitted the armor piece into place, buckling it to Felix's brigandine. He reached down again and lifted a second piece, this one polished to a near silver sheen.

"Front rank, firsts, and corporals wear the blue," Prentice said as he held the armor piece aloft. It was a left-hand pauldron, and in the fading light it was not as bright as he'd hoped, but every man would see it, he was sure. "But only sergeants will be marked by the white steel."

He fitted the pauldron to Felix's other shoulder. Not only was it brightly polished, but it was embossed with an engraved emblem, a lion's pawprint with the claws out. Felix was a sergeant of the claws, a pike- or halberd-wielder. Sergeants of the fangs would have their white steel embossed with a roaring lion's mouth with fully bared teeth. The serpentine sergeant's shoulder would show a lion in profile, roaring at the moon in the night. Their weapon was the lion's roar.

"Now that you are master sergeant of the colors, your corporal under you will be promoted, which means your corporal will now take your place in the ranks as a sergeant. And a first will need to rise to his rank. Who will that be?"

"Franken," Felix answered.

"Franken, front and center!"

Franken, the burly man with a gravelly voice Prentice had seen in the night, detached himself from his place in the rank and trotted over to stand at attention next to Felix.

"First Franken," Prentice addressed him in the same bellowing voice, "you are now corporal of your cohort."

Franken blinked his eyes in surprise, then remembered to salute. Prentice nodded to him, and as he returned the nod, said something quietly that only he and Felix could hear.

"You were right when you said I would raise men in my service," he said, enjoying the further surprise on Franken's face. "But not because I like them. I will reward loyalty, every time. Keep up your right service and there will surely be a parcel of land for you at the end. I swear it."

He lifted his head to address the company.

"Franken, a corporal of the White Lions."

That drew another cheer.

"Sergeant Felix, we need a man to bear the standard. A man of courage and bold action is called for such a duty. Do you know of such a man?"

"I do, Captain. Markas, front and center!"

When Prentice had first asked for Felix's suggestion, he was amazed to hear Markas's name. Only weeks before, he had tried to kill his captain. He walked through every day with the noose still hanging around his neck, the rope fraying and filthy, but

Felix had been adamant. Since his pardon, Markas was a man transformed. Felix called him the most diligent soldier he'd ever known, and when he'd trained with the fangs, Righteous named him as one of her best students.

"He goes straight at it," she reported. "Courage and cunning, he's got 'em both in full measure. How he ever missed you on that wall? You must be dead lucky."

"Perhaps I'm just that much better," Prentice had told her.

"Pah! Lucky's more likely," was her scoffed response, but her laughing eyes said she didn't mean it.

When Markas was in front of him, wearing his sword and buckler, Prentice waited for the man to salute, eyes on the weapons.

This is your chance, he thought, looking at the man. *If you harbor any resentment, if your diligence is just a ruse, then now's the time you'll strike.*

He watched, and Markas watched him in return, his eyes wary but his lips wanting to smile. Pulling his dagger, Prentice stepped forward.

"The duchess's standard-bearer can't entrust her honor to a man wearing a noose."

Markas hopeful smile fell flat. As Prentice reached him, he flinched, but before he could get away, the captain had caught the end of his noose and lifted it up. With a wrenching cut, the dagger severed the noose, and Prentice threw it away. Turning to Felix, he received a different loop that he pulled over Markas head, tied out of white linen into a knot similar to a noose but far more dignified and not the same symbol of death.

"Let this lanyard be the marker of the standard-bearer of the Lions, a part of his uniform forever. You have worked to clear your name and wash your honor clean. All debts are forgiven. Our honor is yours now."

Markas let Prentice slip the knot until it was fitted close around his neck and then saluted again, his smile beaming.

"I will never stand against you again. Until death, I am your man."

Prentice pointed at the banner.

"Take up your duty."

Markas took the banner eagerly, holding it up in the final light of day and receiving another cheer.

"Everything is done," Prentice cried out one last time. "The Lions of the Western Reach are ready."

"Not yet, Captain!" cried Righteous's voice from outside the square. Prentice hadn't realized she was not in the formation somewhere. He had offered her the position of sergeant of the fangs quietly, but she'd turned him down. She was sure that too many would whisper she'd received the rank between her legs, and she wasn't going to have it.

"The first time I heard someone even hint at it, I'd put my steel right through 'em, you know I would! Then where's all your precious discipline going to be?"

Prentice watched bewildered as Righteous led a squad of four men, each in brigandines, into the square. Each one carried a lit torch and a bundle under their arms.

"What's this?" he asked Felix.

The newly promoted master sergeant only shrugged and gave him a knowing smile in response. Righteous's little honor guard marched directly to him, and he noted that they all wore smiles like Felix's. Looking past them at the gathered ranks, it seemed like most of the soldiers were also smiling. Was this something everyone knew was coming but him?

"You've set out the ranks and the orders," Righteous shouted, her voice sounding shrill in the chilling air. "You've set the weapons, the armor, and the training. And you've given every one of us a place in it. But what place have you taken for yourself?"

"I am the captain," Prentice answered loudly, frowning, feeling put upon and surprisingly annoyed. He had intended this makeshift ritual to set the tone for the future of the Lions, a tale the militia could tell new recruits, to inspire them from the company's very founding. He didn't want it undermined by a joke.

"That's right, you are captain," Righteous went on. "And you should bloody well look the part, at least." She waved to the first of the four men behind her, and he stepped forward. He pulled a sheet of cloth back to reveal a brigandine, newly made and finely trimmed.

"I've got one of those," Prentice objected, slapping the brigandine he was wearing.

"Not like this one," Felix assured him.

"Come on, old man," Righteous said more quietly. "Get that plain thing off and this one on. Yentow Sent claims he's done his best work here. Don't disdain it."

Prentice nodded reluctantly and allowed Righteous to help him untie and unbuckle the steel-and-leather-armored jack on his body.

"If I were a knight, I'd have a squire and pages to help me do this," he whispered to her, feeling odd to have someone help him like this while others watched.

"You ever let anyone else but me help you like this," she whispered back, "man, woman, or child, I swear I'll take their fingers! You're mine now, and I don't share!"

That made him want to laugh, but as the brigandine came free, and the evening breeze hit his chest with only his shirt on, he shivered suddenly. Then they were fitting the new armor onto him, and immediately he could feel the difference. There was an extra underlayer of linen, that was soft against him. The quilting of the cloth was slightly thicker, and the seams were roll-stitched. The outer layer was doeskin, dyed ducal blue, and every one of the rivets that held the plates under the cloth were of blued steel. As a piece of armor, it was a masterwork, almost too fine to wear into battle. Even as he was admiring it, Righteous lifted a gorget into place and buckled it around his neck. Blued like the others, he noticed she attached a fangs pauldron to it for his left shoulder.

"I'm to wield a sword and buckler, am I?" he asked, but she held up her finger.

"Shush," she said.

Turning back to her honor guard, she took another polished pauldron, this one for the claws, and fitted it on his right shoulder.

"I don't understand."

"We all know you're fast with blade and buckler," she explained. "And we saw you take that spear off a knight the day we broke the siege. So, the captain can be both. Or he can carry one of them damn firesticks if he likes, instead. But tonight, you get these."

Another of the men stepped beside her and she received a sword and baldric from him and a buckler. She buckled the baldric over Prentice's shoulder, slipping the belt under the gorget.

"Should've put this one on first," she whispered to him, then arranging the scabbard so that it hung correctly on his left hip. The buckler she clipped to the scabbard by a special hook. When she stepped back, he looked down at them. The fang's roaring mouth was embossed on the steel of the buckler and the sword's basket guard was carved as two lions leaping on the prey. As he studied it in the firelight, Righteous leaned in once more.

"It's a male and his she lion," she said. "I made sure there was one of both."

Prentice could see it was true, the female on one side, the male on the other, springing together toward the same prey. The male's mane streamed behind it so that the hairs formed the rest of the basket to protect the wielder's hand. It was all in polished steel, so fine that he knew he didn't need to draw the blade. The edge of that weapon would be like a razor and the steel as well made as any he had ever held. Conscious that everyone was looking at him, Prentice tried to look past his corporal betrothed, but she had one more set of gifts for him. The final man of her escort handed them to him.

The first was a polearm, different from every other man's present. Not as long as a pike but longer than the halberd, it was a spear with a long, double-edged blade, but at the heel, where a spear would simply round back to the haft, the blade flared to form two small wings, like the quillons on the boar-spear he had captured but also lesser blades in their own right. Bound under the blade was a tassel of white hair, probably horsehair, but in the firelight, it reminded him of the lion's mane in his visions and dreams.

"Sent says it's called a partisan," Righteous explained to him. "Like that boar-spitter you been carrying but longer, so you don't have to be front rank to wield it. I don't want you any nearer the danger than you have to be!"

"I'll go where I choose to go," he rebuked her but without any anger.

She nodded. "I know that."

Finally, they gave him a fine steel sallet. Righteous placed it on his head, and though he'd never been measured for it, it fit him perfectly. Yentow Sent and his journeymen knew their craft.

Righteous turned to face them all.

"The captain is ready to lead us!" she shouted, and the drummers suddenly struck up a thunderous beat that echoed out into the coming night, copied and redoubled by the beat of every staff butt and sword pommel. Then there came a cheer that repeated and repeated.

Prentice watched them and marveled in himself. Where were the half-starved rats who had cowered behind the walls of Fallenhill half a winter ago? Of course, many back at the settlement were still sickly and not fully recovered, not to mention the handful of knights and Donnen's rebels who were still chained as prisoners in a damp pit. But these five hundred? They were lions. As the chant went on, Prentice looked at himself. Years ago, he had trained to be a knight of the church, only to be convicted of heresy and banished west to labor on the chain. Now he was free and garbed as finely as any but the richest knights could hope to be. He would never master the longsword, the mark of the knight's rank, but his partisan would be a match for any weapon of rank, and the sword at his waist, whose maker disdained it as a 'peasant's tool,' was finer than he would ever have imagined wielding. He was not a knight and never would be; he was something better, harder forged and more loyal. He was a Lion of the Reach.

Captain of the Lions.

At last, the chanting and the beating died away, and every pair of eyes was fixed on him. He smiled at them, looking around the square at each line in turn. Then he let his smile drop and resumed his place as the stern, demanding commander of the duchess's militia.

"Right, you lot! Back to your fires and get dinner cooked. We march again in the morning. You all need to eat and rest."

Corporals turned to their cohorts and firsts to their lines. The whole company fell out and went back to their duties. Markas took the banner and accepted instruction from Felix on how to roll it up and carry it when it was not on the march. Eventually, only Prentice and Righteous were left standing together in the dark. By the light of the distant fires, he could see she was smiling, and he reached out to take her hand. She let him pull her close, but as he leaned in to kiss her, their gorgets clashed unexpectedly. They both laughed, and he reached up to pull his own gorget aside slightly so they could manage the kiss.

"You know, if we'd said our vows, we could have shared a blanket on this cold night," she told him.

"Soon," he replied, and she nodded.

CHAPTER 55

A melia woke to find her hair wet from the dew. Her head was leaning against her saddle, and she was curled up under Meadow Dancer's blanket. Not far from her, the mare was cropping the grass in the dawn light. The air was cold, and the sky had cleared so much that even as the dawn sun rose, the Rampart that arced across the northern sky was clearly visible. It was a sign that spring would break soon upon the world. Staring up at that ribbon of light, beautiful and bright, Amelia thought about the widow's words. Some said the Rampart was a defense placed there by God to hold back the flood when the mountain was thrown into the sea, as prophesied in the Revelation. She knew it also touched on the Second Flood heresy, which Daven Marcus had accused Earl Derryman of thinking when they found the salt sea. The Church ecclesiarchs taught that the Rampart was like unto the rainbow, a sign of God's love for His people, and any more inquiry than that was discouraged. Of course, Lord Derryman was certainly dead now and perhaps the prince as well. And still, the Rampart shone in the sky.

As she rose, Amelia decided to be glad that its visibility heralded warming weather. Her body ached from another night's sleep in a cold camp and too many hard days' ride. To her left, Turley and Dalflitch curled together under their own mount's blanket. Amelia was glad they at least were getting some rest. Turley's injury pained him continually, and the countess was forced to take the reins more and more as they rode.

Leaving them to sleep, Amelia stepped quietly away to find their rover guide staring at the dawning sky. For days he had led them east, back toward the safety of the river Dwelt. She approached quietly to see him lift his hand to the horizon.

"Morning, Duchess," he said, using the wrong form of address but meaning no disrespect. When they were safe, she would see to the niceties like titles and introductions. In truth, after days of riding, the only thing she knew of this man was that Prentice had sent him and his name, Dray.

"What are you doing?" she asked.

"Finding my bearings," he explained. "Stand facing the rising sun and point your hand at the spot on the horizon where the Rampart hits the earth. Then, hand out in front one, two, three handspans, and that should aim us right at Dweltford."

Amelia was impressed. To her, the grasslands looked the same in every direction. Without the sun or that ribbon, she'd have no idea of north from south or any other compass point.

Dray offered her some lengths of green herb freshly picked. "Not much to break a fast," he apologized, "but it'll keep the hunger out of your belly for most of the morning, at least."

Amelia smiled thanks and crumpled the bitter leaf into her mouth to chew. She looked east.

"Are we far?"

"Hard to say. They keep running us about, but mostly north and east. Maybe two days, or three." He looked over his shoulder at their mounts. "Horses are losing their strength. We run 'em like this too many more days and we'll have to put 'em down at the end."

"I'm not killing Meadow Dancer," Amelia protested.

"It'll be the kindest thing to do."

She refused to accept that thought and turned away from the man. At the same moment, she and the rover spotted a lone rider cresting a hillock in the grass to the south less than an hour's ride away.

"Down!" he ordered, pushing her by the shoulder to crouch in the grass. They watched the lone rider through the long grass as he paused on the crest in the distance. There was no doubt he was a scout for the force that pursued them. They'd seen individual riders the first time during the second day after they fled the prince's camp. That hadn't concerned Dray too much, but two days later the pursuing force had drawn close enough to be seen en masse, and when Amelia had seen the leader's red and blue banner, she knew they were no friends.

Since then, they'd ridden through the nights when they could, never lighting a fire in camp, and riding their poor horses to near exhaustion. Dray was right; their mounts would not last too many more days' hard ride. Then again, neither would they.

"Has he seen us?" Amelia whispered, even though the distance between them was too vast to be heard even if she'd screamed at full volume. Her question was answered when the man put a hunting horn to his lips and blew a full blast. A scream wouldn't carry very far over the grass, but that horn would. Keeping low, the duchess and the rover crept back to the horses to find that Dalflitch was already awake and helping Turley to his feet.

"We heard the horn," she said. Turley nodded with her, but his eyes were unfocussed, and his face was red. He looked like he was sickening. His wound needed cleaning, but there was no time for that.

"We must saddle the horses and ride now," said Amelia. Dray shook his head.

"He's too close. He'll see us ride out and track us the whole way for the knights behind him. It's a hunt now, and the dog's got the scent."

The rover looked south and then to the sky. He was weighing his options, Amelia could see that, and it took all her will not to panic, waiting for him to say something hopeful. He sighed and hefted her saddle from the ground, taking it to Meadow Dancer and putting it in place.

"You all get saddled, but wait for a moment," he said. "We'll try to split the hounds, give 'em two trails to follow."

"Two trails?"

"My gelding's got the most heart left. I'd offer him to you, but I'll need that heart if I'm going to lure them away."

"Can you do that?" asked Dalflitch.

"I'll try. I'll ride out high in the saddle, head back west and north a bit. You start walking east, keeping below the crests and rises like I showed you before. When you hear him sound his horn, then you mount up and go like the clappers. If it works, I'll lead them away from you and maybe you'll make it all the way to the river Dwelt. That's the only thing you can stop for now, even through the night. Thrash your mounts; run 'em to death if you have to. It's the only way now."

He left Meadow Dancer for Amelia to cinch by herself and went to his own mount, which he must have saddled himself as soon as he woke in the morning. As he put his foot to the stirrup, Amelia asked one last question.

"How will you get away?"

He stopped, one hand on the saddle horn, then stepped back down and turned to look at her.

"I was there in the market at Dweltford," he said to her, recalling the duchess's meeting with the rovers back at the beginning of autumn. "I heard that speech you gave, and I thought, this one, she understands. She's a Reacherman, duchess or no. I decided then I'd ride for you."

Amelia blinked back tears, touched by this unexpected expression of fealty.

"You find your bearing every morning, just like I showed you, and you'll be making for Dweltford. Ride hard, Duchess Amelia, for yourself and for the Reach. We need you."

He threw himself into the saddle without another word and rode west, sitting high in the saddle as he crested the rise. With tired limbs, the two noblewomen and their wounded steward managed to get their saddles back in place, but even as they did, the hunting horn sounded again to the south. They mounted and fled. Perhaps Dray would be able to lead the hounds away, but none of them looked back to see, not even once.

CHAPTER 56

The angel came to Prentice again in a dream.

He was standing in the grass, facing east. In the distance he could see the lights on the walls of Fallenhill. The sky overhead was clear of clouds, and the Rampart glowed in the north. He was wearing his new armor, with his sword at his hip and his partisan in hand. Though the night was cold, he felt only comfortable and happy. When the moonlit lion emerged from the long grass, its pony-sized mass still gentle as the whisper of a breeze through the grass, Prentice greeted it with a salute.

The creature's eyes searched him up and down, and then he shivered under that sovereign gaze. For a moment, he felt a thrill of fear. This irresistibly magnificent creature was only a servant. What power must the god that commanded it wield?

"You must go west," it said.

"But we're headed home," Prentice objected and pointed to the distant lights of Fallenhill to the east.

"Look west."

The angel cast its eyes in the other direction to a point in the grass behind them. Prentice turned to look, and through the darkness, he saw three lions—two females and a male—running toward the pack. Their skins clung to their bones and their tongues hung from their mouths as they panted for breath. Behind them, pursuing through the grass, a pack of red-eyed hounds bayed and harried them, slavering from open jaws. Over it all, like a shadow against the stars, a giant eagle flew, but it was no magnificent creature like an eagle should be. It was sickly and covered in sores, and it had a moth-eaten lion's skin draped over its shoulders like a cloak. Its feathers were patchy and fell behind it in the air as it flew. It dove down upon the fleeing trio of lions as the patchy skin fell from its shoulders.

"That fallen skin must be recovered," said the angel mildly.

Prentice had no idea what that meant. Suddenly he was surrounded by the lions of the pride, and they roared over the baying of the hounds. The fleeing trio turned towards the pride, and the hounds turned with them. Pack and pride fell upon each other, and Prentice found himself in the midst of two animal cohorts, rending each other in murderous fury. Prentice couldn't imagine how any of the creatures could survive such violence, but the conflict was short-lived, and when it ended, the eagle overhead cried once—a hideous, hateful sound that echoed through the air as it flew away to the south.

"This is the signpost in the road," the angel told him. "Do you understand this vision?"

"No," Prentice answered honestly.

"You will," said the angel. "Now close your eyes."

Prentice did as he was commanded, and when he opened his eyes again, his head was on his pillow. It was just before dawn. He got up and looked about at his encamped five hundred. Already, many of the men were moving about, beginning their morning. Prentice went to Felix's bedroll to find the master sergeant already dressed and eating a pot of boiled oats.

"Strike the camp," he ordered him. "I want everyone ready to move as soon as possible. We're heading west again."

"West?" asked Felix. "I thought we were headed home."

"Not yet."

Prentice left him to rouse the drummers and send out the orders to strike camp and ready the march. He also sought out Aiden to send him and his rovers west, looking for three lions. Well, looking for something. For all the loyalty and devotion the company had shown him, he still didn't feel he could give orders based on a dream.

————◆◯◆————

Sunrise came over the horizon, and it took a moment for Amelia to realize that they were no longer heading east, but north. They must have gotten turned in the night again. She lifted her hand to the horizon as Dray, the rover, had taught her, but the rise and fall of her horse made it impossible for her tired arms to line up like they were supposed to. Looking over her shoulder, she checked to see Dalflitch and Turley behind her. The countess was in front, and he was slumped over her shoulder. Amelia had no way of knowing if he was sleeping, unconscious, or worse. The countess's eyes were marred by dark circles that sunk into her face, staring seemingly into nothingness. There was no time to stop, though, for even as the light grew, they could hear the sound of the hunting horn behind them. The pursuers weren't far behind now. Soon, she would be captured and dragged back to the prince and her execution. She pulled an empty waterskin to her parched lips, hoping to draw out even a drop, but there was nothing. They had finished the last of the water yesterday. Or was it the day before?

She couldn't remember.

Underneath her, the duchess could feel Meadow Dancer's gait fumbling and failing. The poor mount had been ridden to exhaustion, exactly as Dray had warned, and if she was not yet lamed, she soon would be. Amelia's heart broke for her faithful horse. It had served her so well and even now would not give up. And as the sound of knights in harness began to jingle through the morning air behind them, she knew that it had all been for nothing. Within the hour, Baron Liam's knights would be upon them; the hounds had the scent and were baying for blood.

From out of the shoulder-high grass, three horsemen appeared, clad in buckskins and riding fast from the east. They approached and leaped from their mounts. One seized Meadow Dancer's reins from Amelia's hands, and in her fatigue, she just let it go. These were rovers; Dray had made it. He'd found his fellows and sent help. Her mind was cheered for a moment until the horn sounded again, closer and more menacing still.

"Their mounts are spent," said one of the men. "We'll have to carry one each."

"Easy for you to say," answered another. "You won't get the brute."

"I'll take him. You two get a woman each, and kindly. One of them's the duchess, so he says."

"How'd Captain Prentice know they were out here?"

"Never mind that now. Those knights are too close for comfort."

Amelia felt strong hands lifting her down from her horse. She tried to object.

"I won't leave her," she protested, but the wiry man's arms brooked no compromise. He took her and threw her over the front of his mount like a sack, and she found she had no strength to resist.

"It has to be this way," he said in a hard but strangely kind tone. "She has nothing left to give you." He drew a long knife from a sheathe at his belt and went back to her horse. Amelia knew what he was doing, but only heard a soft whicker and the sound of her beloved pony falling to its knees. Meadow Dancer's journey was over, and hanging over the rover's saddle, Amelia wept.

"Is he still alive?" the rider asked as he took his saddle behind her on the pony.

"Just," came the answer. "He might lose his hand though, and if the rot's in his blood, it'd be kinder to finish him with their horses."

"That's not for us."

Suddenly there was a cry of huzzah from somewhere in the grass to the south, and the hunting horn rang out a third time.

"We fly," cried the rider. "Straight run back to the captain and the company."

"Those are knights behind us," answered one other, "and the captain's only got men afoot. Can he really beat them off?"

"Captain Prentice knows his business," asserted the man who'd taken charge of Turley.

The rovers kicked their heels to their mounts, and the beasts surged away. Amelia could scarcely believe it when she heard Prentice's name, but even as the hopeful relief began to dawn in her mind, the horse beneath her rose to a gallop, and the pain in her exhausted body was too great. She passed out.

CHAPTER 57

The three rovers slapped their mounts' sides with the reins as they bolted through the grass, forcing them to hold to a gallop despite the weight of two riders each. The two women were laid across the front of saddles, but the burly man with the wounded hand was riding behind. His rider had tied his arms around his own waist, but the sickly man's dead weight nearly drove the skilled rider out of his saddle. It was a desperate wrestle for the entire ride. They rode pell-mell over a rise, and there, arrayed in good order, were the Lions of the Reach. The banner was unfurled in their center, flapping in the breeze, and the ranks ran to either side, forming a disciplined oblong of bristling, glittering pike and halberd. The serpentines were in two short lines of twenty at the corners, the slow matches of their locks already lit and sending up tiny curlicues of smoke.

Prentice stood at the center of the line in the second rank, watching his outriders coming in carrying heavy burdens that he prayed were living people. And behind them, not two furlongs back, was an array of Grand Kingdom knights, hundreds of them, thundering on at full pace.

Even weighed down, the rovers proved fast enough, and they maintained their lead over the final distance. Prentice shouted an order for the ranks to open enough to bring the rovers, their mounts, and their burdens into the safety of the company. The riders jumped down and lowered the three people they carried

with them to the ground. Prentice pushed back through his
men to see the Duchess Amelia, his best friend Turley, and a
third woman he could not name. The ladies' dresses were filthy
and torn, their hair was a wild tangle, and they looked barely
alive. Turley was groaning and sweating with pain, and his left
arm was wrapped in a disgusting rag masquerading as a bandage.
Seeing them like this—the liege to whom he was sworn and his
best friend in the world—Prentice felt a bitter fury rise inside
him that burned like bile in the back of his throat. He had
labored through a brutal winter to make a professional militia to
protect this woman and her lands, and here she was, all but alone
in the wilderness, unconscious and hunted to her last breaths.
As he looked, the duchess came awake and looked him straight
in the eyes from where she lay on the ground.

"Prentice," she said in a broken whisper. "How are you here?"

"We are here for you, Your Grace," he answered.

She smiled wanly. "Of course, you are." She closed her eyes
again.

Prentice had only enough time to wonder if she was dying
when he heard the sound of horses approaching. He stood and
looked west to a cadre of knights riding forward. He looked
from them to the hounded three at his feet. It was then that he
noticed Righteous standing next to him. He pointed Righteous
at the unconscious duchess.

"Until your last breath!" he ordered his betrothed and she
nodded, understanding implicitly. Then he shouldered his way
back to his place in rank, looking at the approaching knights.

Baron Liam rode up in the center of his personal honor
guard, every man in polished steel plate and mail but a little
flushed and harried from the hard ride of the morning's final
pursuit. Their horses breathed heavily, their breaths misting a
little in the cold air.

"Welcome, Baron," Prentice called as the knights reined in a
few steps beyond the furthest pike points. "Rebelling against
your liege lady has become your pastime, has it?"

Baron Liam looked down at Prentice with burning contempt, but also a sense of confusion.

"What are you doing here, worthless mongrel?" he demanded.

"Guarding the duchess from you," Prentice retorted. He made it sound like a jest, but his face was set like flint.

"I left you cowering in Fallenhill's ruins. How are you here?" The baron's voice almost cracked with rage.

"The siege? Oh, we broke that before mid-winter. We've had the run of the north for weeks on end, and we've done a better job of bringing order than your petty force ever did. By the way, did you want to ransom them? We've got more than a few noblemen looking very peaky in chains."

All along the ranks, the lions began to laugh, mocking Liam and his comrades. The baron nearly erupted with indignant fury.

"Silence, you scum! You turds! How dare you laugh in the presence of your betters!"

Prentice let him rage on for a moment, then gave the nearest drummer a silent signal. The young man beat a single stroke on the skin of his drum, and as one, every lion became silent. It was an admirable display of discipline, and it made Prentice proud. Although the sound also silenced Liam's rant, the other knights were not impressed. Several of them looked at each other in surprise that became amused disbelief and finally disdainful scoffing.

"You weren't lying, Baron," one said loudly. "Bandit rebels in service of a rebellious bitch! This one's her pack-leading cur, I take it?"

"The prettiest convict rogues I ever saw," said another, looking over the company as a whole. "Only a fool woman would dress mutts up like this."

Prentice wanted to laugh back at them. They faced five hundred men in armor, with new weapons, and arrayed in disciplined ranks, but their arrogance only allowed them to see worthless, degraded convicts. His eyes narrowed in contempt, and he was about to speak, but Liam raised his hand for his comrade's silence and spoke first.

"You are escaped convicts, bandits and thieves," he said, his barely healed jaw slurring his words. "You have stolen royal silver and rebelled against your righteous liege, the crown prince, Daven Marcus, Prince of Rhales. In your midst is a woman under the prince's sentence of death. I carry the warrant and will execute it. Surrender! Lay down on your bellies, beg for mercy, and perhaps we will spare you; if we are kind, you can live out the rest of your days on a chain, purging your souls before God. It is more mercy than you deserve. If any of you stands, even one of you, all of you will die with that bitch today. Make your choice."

Prentice was certain the baron was lying. He'd been humiliated too many times. If Daven Marcus had given him a warrant for the duchess's execution, Liam was going to spill as much convict blood as he could as he did it. Of that, Prentice was sure.

The baron looked up and down the lines to see if any took him at his word and lay down their arms. Prentice kept his eyes on Liam, not bothering to look. He knew not one of his men would take the offer.

"This is not all your renegades, is it?" Liam asked Prentice, finally. He didn't seem much disappointed that no one had asked for mercy. "I want you to know that when I'm done here, when we've split that bitch in twain from crotch to gorge, I'm going to hunt every last one of them. They'll all die cursing your name and hers!"

"You keep telling fae tales about your exploits, Baron," Prentice said, putting a mocking emphasis on Liam's title. "Boasting about things you've never done and never will—enemies you never faced, trophies you've never won—it's a bad habit."

Both men knew that Liam had risen to his rank by claiming responsibility for a victory that Prentice had won, but Prentice had had enough of this trading pointless insults. There had to be a battle; this could end no other way. Might as well get down to it.

Many of the knights were insulted on Liam's behalf by the very notion that a former convict would dare insult a man of rank, but Liam only wheeled his horse around and led them back to the rest of his force waiting about a furlong distance, perhaps a hundred paces—an excellent distance for a lance charge, for destriers to reach maximum momentum. The militiamen stood their ground, watching quietly as the knights arranged themselves for the charge in ranks of a hundred at a time. The Lion's Roar ran across the company's front rank, taking position to shoot.

The knights formed up in tight ranks, every horse so close to the next that each man's knees touched to the man next to him. Each steel-clad professional had his lance ready, and visors were pulled into place. In practiced order, they spurred forward, beginning at a walk and pushing swiftly upward through a trot and canter until they were galloping forward at a breakneck speed. The ground shook under the thunder of their hoofs, and the waiting militiamen could feel it resonate up through their bones, beating in their chests. There was no hesitation in the entire knightly line. This was warfare the way it had been fought in the Grand Kingdom for centuries, practiced and perfected. When they had crossed half the distance, they lowered their lances as one and began to pick their targets—the first men they would run through as they struck the company of upstart convicts. A knight on horseback was an engine of destruction, and a hundred of them at the charge were invincible. The slaughter was only moments away.

When the lances were lowered, Prentice's drummer beat out as he bellowed his orders.

"Claws out!"

Pikes and halberds were grounded and lowered to receive the charge. Ranks behind held their own pikes forward, too. This was the moment. Everything they had been through—hunger, cold and pain—it all came down to this. The pack of dogs was falling upon them. Either they were lions and would be triumphant, or they were mere rats, and they would die. Prentice felt his jaw clenching, and it took an act of will to force his mouth open for the second command.

"Roar!"

The second-order drum beat the air over the hammering of charging hoofs.

As one, the gunners pulled their triggers, and the burning long-matches fell into the waiting pans of black powder. Forty guns fired, flames and smoke launching forty iron balls into the charging line. The gunners then dashed straight backward into the mass of men behind them and the protection of the claws. There would be no chance to reload for a second volley before the charge struck home. The smoke had not begun to clear before the knights burst through and onto the readied polearms, but at nothing like the pace or force they had before the shot. It was hard to tell in the sudden rush, but Prentice guessed the knight's line had lost about fifteen horses and men to one volley of shot. Several mounts were riderless, the well-trained beasts keeping their place in the line, not fouling the charge. In other places, there were open gaps in the line, so some horses had been killed as well. Worst of all for the knights, the fire and smoke had spooked many of their chargers, and although they kept them pushing forward, the whole line had lost easily half its momentum.

Then they were upon the pikes, and here, at last, half the mounts shied outright, refusing to complete the charge. Some even turned in place, risking injury to their own legs and spoiling others near them as they turned from the deadly steel points. Prentice had trained his pikemen to aim at the horses' faces to spook the animals. Only the wildest or most disciplined animals would run headlong into a blade it could see. The few knights who managed to force their mounts past that first threat were met with halberds, which also struck at the horses. The lions' claws were doing their jobs and blunting the charge. Several knights stood their mounts and thrust with their lances, leaning forward in the stirrups, but with the force of momentum drained out of the charge, these were just hopeful pokes with over-heavy spears. And every man who leaned forward like that took more hits to his armor from the pikes thrusting over the front ranks' shoulders. Steel squealed on steel and men cried out as they were taken down.

The lance charge was the prime battlefield weapon of the Grand Kingdom knight, and faced with it being stalled, the survivors did what they were trained to do; they turned about and withdrew to reform and let the next rank take its turn to charge. The ones who had been unhorsed scrambled out of the reach of the polearms and then turned their backs and stomped off in their armor. Prentice knew they were going to fetch their change mounts from squires hiding at the back of the battle, or perhaps to take up some weapon more suited to fighting on foot, even though most had longswords or sideswords hanging from their belts. Prentice couldn't believe their arrogance, simply strutting away as if they owned the field.

"Roar!" he ordered again, and the serpentines who had now reloaded rushed out again and fired their weapons. The next charge was blunted, just as the first had been, and this one faltered on the pike and halberd as well. When they expended themselves, they too withdrew, diminished by casualties, and a third rank was summoned to charge. And so it went, for nearly an hour, the three lines taking their turns and then withdrawing to reform. But with each reformation, the lines were smaller and the glorious, gilded war men more desperate in the attack. Twice in that hour some knights stood their ground, and Prentice signaled his third order.

"Fangs out!"

Swordsmen trained to fight in the narrow space between the hafts of pike and halberd leaped forward and thrust at knights hampered and harassed on every side. With their simpler armor and basic steel caps, not to mention their more limited experience, these men would be no match for a knight one on one, or even two on one. But with so many threats to face, the reckless noblemen were swiftly overwhelmed. If they focused on the pike or halberd, then the swordsmen struck freely, thrusting points into whatever weak spots they could find. If the knights gave the swordsmen their full attention, then the halberds hooked behind their legs to trip them or else just fell like axes to hack them down. The fangs withdrew again once the knights too brave to withdraw were dead, and on it went.

At last, a final charge reformed only about seventy paces away, with many squires pressed into the rank, easily distinguished by their lesser armor or weapons. Liam still lived, and Prentice could see him right in the middle of the line. The baron put a horn to his lips and blew a long blast that trailed away mournfully. Around him, Prentice heard his men draw in their breaths to ready themselves once more. They were weary, but they had a place, and every man had seen now that they were safer standing together than they could possibly be if they tried to run.

The destriers started again, so much more slowly than at the beginning. If Prentice's men were fatigued, Liam's men and horses were exhausted. They came on so much less eagerly, warily even, but that only gave the serpentines time to ready and fire more than one volley. Knights and horses fell, still dozens of paces distance, and as the charge broke apart, the serpentines stayed in place and reloaded in the open. The second volley fired, and the final charge simply stopped. As the smoke blew away, Prentice could see it was time for the pride to hunt.

"Arms at the ready!"

Pikes and halberd were lifted to a different position, and drummers began to beat the advance. The entire company began to stalk forward as one, marching the short distance to the broken and confused remnant of the baron's force. Knights on the ground who could not retreat in time were struck down, and if they were alive when the ranks reached them, the fangs fell upon them. The men still ahorse were forced back, having no notion what to do when infantry pressed the attack. They were Grand Kingdom knights, all but born in the saddle. They were noble men of steel and honor, too high to fall to mere rogues afoot. They were invincible, were they not?

This was beyond their comprehension.

Some turned their horses to face the oncoming steel and fell, unable to stop the advance. Two or three fled into the grass.

And the battle was over.

The drummers beat relief, and a cheer went up. Prentice gave orders to look for survivors and to have the duchess, the countess, and Turley immediately taken to be washed and fed, and their injuries treated. He could only pray their ordeal wouldn't kill them after the fact. He ordered prisoners to be taken, if any knights were still alive and willing to surrender, and he set Felix to see that there was no looting.

"Every living man keeps his clothes," he ordered. "Armor and weapons are to be collected. Yentow Sent will want the steel. And round up the horses. We'll need them to transport the spoils and the wounded back to Fallenhill. Every man in the ranks gets his share of that spoil. Any who stood the field and lives gets a share. Otherwise, it goes to his widow or his child."

Prentice knew there'd still be looting. Too many of these men were thieves, after all; they hadn't been convicted and transported over the mountains just for rude behavior. But he wanted to give them as little reason to steal as he could. It was difficult enough for a man to repent his old life without forcing him into hardship.

And the fallen had to be buried. Victory was sweet, but battle was ever a bitter business.

When the orders were given and he had a moment to draw breath, a wave of exhaustion washed over Prentice. He wanted nothing more than to sit, or even lie down and sleep. He knew better, though, and to keep from thinking about it, he walked the field, letting his men see him and sharing their victory. Success had restored their energies, and men saluted when they saw him before returning to their duties.

That was how Prentice found Baron Liam. Thrown when his horse died, and before he had a chance to fully regain his feet, a second horse had knocked the baron down again and fallen across him, breaking his arm. When militiamen came upon him, he waited for them to get him clear from under the horse carcass before trying to kill them with his dirk for their trouble. The pain made him far too slow, however, and they dodged away easily as he swung his dagger back and forth to fend them off. So, there he was, leaning on the dead horse and spitting threats at the soldiers around him, refusing to be taken prisoner.

When Prentice saw the baron, he tried to remember his hate, to take pleasure in his enemy's total defeat, but it just wasn't there. The Lions were the victors. They had stood the field as a pride united and broken the invincibility of the slavering pack of hounds that tormented them—tormented all the Western Reach. Knights would never rule a battlefield in the Reach unchallenged again because of him and the militia he had raised.

Liam's defeat seemed a trivial thing in that light.

"Put it down, Liam," Prentice ordered, no longer bothering with the man's rank. "It's over."

"Dog! Cur! You're not fit to wipe my arse!"

Prentice shook his head. Liam swung the dagger again, even though there was no one within a half dozen paces, then cursed as the pain of the movement wrenched through his broken arm.

"You're finished. Drop your weapon and we can bind your arm."

"Go to hell!"

Prentice shrugged. The baron would never surrender to convicts. He turned to walk away, and Liam called after him.

"Face me, you worthless coward. Give me a sword and we can finish this!"

Prentice looked around at the ruin of the battlefield, the horses fallen, and the men slain, then back at the baron.

"Why?"

Liam stared at him for a moment in sheer disbelief.

Prentice nodded to his men and turned his back. Liam screamed in inarticulate rage as pike and halberd advanced on him and hacked him down with the same mercilessness villagers would show to a wolf that had been stealing their livestock and children.

Then the screaming stopped.

Righteous found Prentice soon after. "Want to know how many we lost?

"Not really."

"Seventeen," she said happily. "Just seventeen, and only four of them's actually dead. The rest is bad but might live, though they won't fight again. One's lost his eye, but he swears he'll be fine."

"Cheap enough."

"Is that all you have to say?"

Prentice shrugged. "What else do you want me to say?"

"Well, if this is how you're going to greet good news when we're married, maybe I'll have to reconsider my betrothal. I don't want some miserable bastard for a husband."

He turned to face her, and she stood with her arms folded, pouting.

"Do you mean that?" he asked.

She frowned and cocked her head as if thinking.

"Nah," she said at last, grinning her impish grin. "I know I can make you smile, and you ain't even had me in a bed yet." She danced forward and planted a kiss on his cheek, holding her neck armor out of the way to do it. That did make him smile.

"Just make sure you get me a ring and take me to church. And soon. A girl can't wait forever, not even a scarred old widow like this one!"

He laughed quietly as she walked away, giving orders as naturally as any other corporal. He couldn't explain it to her; he barely understood it himself, but this was why he wanted to marry her. There was a deep bitterness inside him; men like Liam had put it there. It was a well of pain filled with iced water, black and terrifying like the ocean at night. But she made him laugh. She wasn't afraid of that black water, and she made him laugh.

CHAPTER 58

"I hope this will be comfortable enough, Your Grace."
Prentice looked inside the wagon where cushions and blankets had been arrayed for the duchess to rest in comfort. Even before the Lions had reached Fallenhill, Prentice had sent messengers to Dweltford to have transport brought up for Amelia. The spring weather was starting to warm, but mornings were still cool, and while the encampment at Fallenhill was so much less rudimentary than it had been when the convicts arrived, it was no place for Her Grace to convalesce. At Prentice's request, Fostermae had negotiated with the merchant Caius Welburn to send this wagon loaded with cushions and fine cloths for the duchess to travel to her castle in relative comfort. Along with the wagon, Prentice was sending an escort of a hundred men.

"I am most comfortable, thank you, Captain," Amelia said, though her voice was still nowhere near its full strength. She had taken to calling him Captain Ash as a matter of course. "When will you be joining me in Dweltford?"

"There are some matters I want set in order before I leave, Your Grace. I am sending Sir Gant to command your guards on the way back," he said. "I will have to be here for some while yet; not all the men are correctly outfitted. That will take the rest of the spring, or so Master Sent tells me."

Amelia was not worried. Her new militia already had over a thousand fully armed footmen, but if Daven Marcus marched the remnant of his army back to Dweltford, she would need every one of them. There was no sign yet of the crusade's return, but she was sure it must come soon.

"I should devise an appropriate reward for that smith," she mused. "He has done my land a great service."

"Just don't offer him coin. He'd likely only take offence and throw it back in your face."

"Such odd pride for a craftsman," she said.

Prentice didn't disagree.

"Speaking of silver, I will send to the miner's guild to reopen the mines and the mint. You will provide guards for them?"

"To guard your holdings in the Reach is the duty of your Lions," he said and gave her the militia's salute, bowing his head as he did so.

Amelia lay back on the cushions and sighed. After a year of fear and uncertainty, to hear Prentice's loyalty and to see the powerful army he had created for her was a comfort she could hardly express. When she had awakened and heard of Liam's thorough defeat and the baron's own death, she'd felt a rush of relief. One day, she might feel compassion for the man's passing, since hate was such a low emotion, but for now all she felt was satisfaction.

"One last thing, Captain Ash."

"Yes, Your Grace?"

"I had a visit from one of your corporals last night."

"Yes?"

"A most forward creature who I would have sworn resembled one of your rats, a youth named Cutter. She insisted she was, in fact, named Righteous."

"I'm sorry, Your Grace," Prentice began to apologize, but the duchess raised her hand and smiled.

"This Corporal Righteous all but commanded me to send the sacrist Fostermae back from Dweltford as soon as I arrived. She claimed she was done with waiting while you dragged your feet."

"Did she, Your Grace?" he said with a scowl.

Amelia couldn't help smiling. It was rare to see Prentice embarrassed, and she enjoyed the novelty.

"You plan to marry?"

"Yes, Your Grace." He paused, and she could see an unexpected thought cross his mind. "Do I need your permission?"

It was common practice for courtiers and servants to obtain their liege's permission to marry, but Amelia never had cause yet to give or withhold it. Even with everything she'd been through, she'd not been a duchess for even two whole years.

"You certainly have it," she said. "I think I have no choice but to give it. Your betrothed warned me that if I didn't send this sacrist for the ceremony immediately, she was going to, in her words, 'end up ripping off your britches and making a doxy of herself.' She's quite set on you, I think."

"Yes, Your Grace." For a moment he was still embarrassed, but then he chuckled to himself.

She was glad to see it. "I will go now," she said and lay back on the cushions, ready to sleep the whole journey back to Dweltford if she could. Prentice gave the order, and the wagon began to rumble away. The second half of her escort fell in behind her, marching in two columns and looking like they were ready for anything.

EPILOGUE

T he nobility of the Western Court, the flower of Rhales society, was wilting. Nearly half of the men of rank had been slain in the prince's siege of the tower in the marsh or died under the claws and fangs of the Lions of the Reach. Many of them were firstborn sons and heirs to great houses. A wretched number of the court ladies had been butchered when the Redlanders attacked the army's camp. As supplies dwindled and nobles perished, the ladies who remained came, first in ones and twos but ultimately en masse, to beg leave to depart the crusade and travel back to Dweltford and then across the mountains to Rhales.

The prince refused every request at first, and even had several of the woman beaten with canes to make them stop asking, but still they begged. Any mention of Dweltford or of the Western Reach drew his ire. He ranted and cursed the province, its renegade duchess and nobles. When word came of Liam's death and Amelia's survival, writs were issued claiming the dukedom for the prince, denouncing Duchess Amelia as his lawful wife and an avowed traitor, and offering a bounty on her head. That only split the army as many Reachermen simply quit the camp.

Despite the fleet witnessed by all coming from the north, Daven Marcus continued to insist that the invaders were from the Vec, using the colors on their skin to disguise their origin. He accused the Reachermen of being in league with the

Veckanders. As supplies dwindled, he ordered the remains of the army to march southeast and return to Reach lands south of Dweltford. They would resupply there, the prince assured his surviving entourage. To that end, he released all men of knightly rank and higher to take from the land whatever they needed and to kill any man, woman, or child who objected. When they were replenished, he assured them he would turn north for a swift spring campaign to take Dweltford out of the hands of his condemned spouse, then back south again to finally punish the Vec Princes.

Within days, the army began to diminish. In small numbers but a steady trickle, nobles left the crusade. No one asked the prince's leave, and no permissions were given. The court just awoke each morning and more were gone. Soon, the crusade was nothing but a threadbare party of diminished men-at-arms and their few harried servants, with dwindling supplies and little heart, driven only by the cruel determination of their liege lord. Twenty-three days after the siege at the sea fort, messengers in royal livery arrived at the camp. They carried a letter for the prince.

"How did you find us?" asked one courtier, hopeful that these men heralded the arrival of reinforcements and merchants who would accept notes of credit.

Daven Marcus looked up contemptuously from the letter at the question but didn't say anything. He went back to reading.

"We have been ranging up the Dwelt, hoping for news of his Highness," the messenger replied, obviously as unsure about the courtier's earnestness as he was about the smallness of the company with the prince. "Some knights of the Western Reach met us and told us that the prince has been chasing enemies down the coast of an unknown sea here in the west. We scarce believed their tale, but they persuaded us. Thank God they did."

The prince coughed gruffly and looked up again from the letter.

"This says the king summons me for the business of an invasion. Is that correct?"

"It is, Your Highness," the rider confirmed.

Daven Marcus smiled his first full smile in days. "At last, my father has seen sense and invaded the Vec. Of course, we will join him!"

"Forgive me, Your Highness," the messenger said, clearly embarrassed to have to correct the prince publicly. "The Kingdom has not invaded the Vec. The Vec princedoms have been invaded from the far southwest. Unfamiliar ships carrying a vast army have sailed up the Murr from some unknown land. Vec armies have met them in at least one battle and been thrown back. Now King Chrostmer has mustered an army on the north bank to stop them raiding Kingdom land from their boats on the river. He summons you to the defense."

Daven Marcus slumped down into his throne. He had been wrong. Everything he insisted was happening in the west was untrue, and everything he'd expected to find was a mirage. For a long moment, he stared at the curtained wall of the tent he had taken as his new audience chamber since his pavilion had burned in the Redlander assault. A hesitant courtier edged forward, thinking to ask his commands, but Daven Marcus just shouted for them all to leave him.

Outside the commandeered tent, nobles waited to hear what their liege's orders would be. After a short time, the messengers were summoned back inside, but that was all that was heard. It was late in the evening before someone finally found the courage to enter the prince's tent unbidden to discover that Daven Marcus, Prince of Rhales, had already ridden away, abandoning the remains of his army with no orders and no leadership.

The crusade into the west was over. The Western Reach was safe, but not by Daven Marcus's hand.

And the Grand Kingdom was in more danger than ever.

GLOSSARY

The Grand Kingdom's social structure is broken into three basic levels which are then subdivided into separate ranks: the nobility, the free folk, and the low born.

The Nobility
King/Queen – There is one King, and one Queen, his wife. The king is always the head of the royal family and rules from the Denay Court, in the capital city of Denay.

Prince/Princess – Any direct children of the king and queen.

Prince of Rhales – This title signifies the prince who is next in line of succession. This prince maintains a separate, secondary court of lesser nobles in the western capital or Rhales.

Duke/Duchess – Hereditary nobles with close ties by blood or marriage to the royal family, either Denay or Rhales.

Earl; Count/Countess; Viscount; Baron/Baroness – These are the other hereditary ranks of the two courts, in order of rank. One is born into this rank, as son or daughter of an existing noble of the same rank, or else created a noble by the king.

Baronet – This is the lowest of the hereditary ranks and does not require a landed domain to be attached.

Knight/Lady – The lowest rank of the nobility and almost always attached to military service to the Grand Kingdom as a man-at-arms. Ladies obtain their title through marriage.

Knights are signified by their right to carry the longsword, as a signature weapon.

Squire – This is, for all intents and purposes, an apprentice knight. He must be the son of another knight (or higher noble) who is currently training, or a student of the academy.

The Free Folk

Patrician – A man or woman who has a family name and owns property inside a major town or city. Patricians always fill the ranks of any administration of the town in which they live, such as aldermen, guild conclave members, militia captains etc.

Guildsmen/townsfolk – Those who dwell in large towns as free craftsmen and women tend to be members of guilds who act to protect their members' livelihoods and also to run much of the city, day to day.

Yeoman – The yeomanry are free farmers that possess their own farms.

The Low Born

Peasants – These are serfs who owe feudal duty to their liege lord. They do not own the land they farm and must obtain permission to move home or leave their land.

Convicts – Criminals who are found guilty of crimes not deserving of the death penalty.

Military Order

Knight Captain, Knight Commander & Knight Marshall – Every peer (King, Prince or Duke) has a right to raise an army and command his lesser nobles to provide men-at-arms. They then appoint a second-in-command, often the most experienced or skilled soldier under them. A duke his Knight Captain; a prince his Knight Commander; and the King his Knight Marshal.

Knights – These are the professional soldiers of the Grand Kingdom. All nobles are expected to join these ranks when their lands are at war, and they universally fight from horseback.

Men-at-Arms –A catch all term for any man with professional training who has some right or reason to be in this group, including squires and second and third sons of nobles.

Bannermen – This is a special form of man-at-arms. These are soldiers who are sworn directly to a ranking noble.

Free Militia – The free towns of the Grand Kingdom have an obligation to raise free militias in defence of the realm.

Rogues Foot – A rogue is a low born or criminal man and so when convicts are pressed into military service, they are the rogues afoot (or "on foot") which is shortened to rogues foot.

Other Titles and Terms

Apothecary – A trader and manufacturer of herbs, medical treatments and potions of various sorts.

Chirurgeon – A medical practitioner, akin to a doctor or surgeon, especially related to injuries (as opposed to sickness, which is handled by an apothecary).

Estate – A person's estate can be their actual lands, but can also include their social position, their current condition (physical, social or financial), or any combination of these things.

Fiefed – A noble who is fiefed possesses a parcel of land over which they have total legal authority, the right to levy taxes and draft rogues or militia.

King's Law – This is the overarching, national law, set for the Grand Kingdom by the king, but does not always apply in the Western Reach.

Magistrate – Civil legal matters of the Free Folk and Peasantry are typically handled by magistrates, who render judgements according to the local laws.

Marshals/Wardens – Appointed men who manage the movement of large groups, especially of nobles and noble courts when in motion. They appoint the order of the march and resolve disputes.

Physick – A term for a person trained in the treatment of medical conditions, but without strict definition.

Proselytize– Attempt to convert someone from one religion, belief, or opinion to another.

Republicanists – Rare political radicals, outlawed in the Grand Kingdom and the Vec who seek to create elected forms of government, curtailing or overturning monarchical rule.

Seneschal – The administrative head of any large household or organisation, especially a noble house of a baron or higher.

Surcoat – The outer garment worn by a man-at-arms over their armor. Typically dyed in the knight's colours (or their liege lord's colours in the case of a bannerman) and embroidered with their heraldry.

Te tree – A tree, known for its medicinal properties.

The Rampart – A celestial phenomenon that glows in the night across the sky from east to west in the northern half of the sky.

About Author

Matt Barron grew up loving to read and to watch movies. He always knew he enjoyed science fiction and fantasy, but in 1979 his uncle took him to see a new movie called Star Wars and he was hooked for life. Then Dungeons and Dragons came along and there was no looking back. He went to university hoping to find a girlfriend. Instead, the Lord found him, and he spent most of his time from then on in the coffee shop, witnessing and serving his God. Along the way, he managed to acquire a Doctorate in History and met the love of his life, Rachel. Now married to Rachel for more than twenty years, Matt has two adult children and a burning desire to combine the genre he loves with the faith that saved him.

Learn more at:

mattbarronauthor.com

Also By Matt Barron

Rage of Lions

Prentice Ash

Rats of Dweltford
Lions of the Reach
Eagles of the Grand Kingdom
Book 5 Coming Soon

More from Publisher

Be sure to check out our other great science fiction and fantasy stories at:

bladeoftruthpublishing.com/books